Guilty till Proven Innocent

Richard Pelc

PublishAmerica
Baltimore

First printing

ISBN: 1-4137-6757-5
PUBLISHED BY PUBLISHAMERICA, LLLP
www.publishamerica.com
Baltimore

Printed in the United States of America

Acknowledgments

I'd like to thank Leah Kochanowitz, my very good friend and co-author of *Lol-love Online*, for her encouragement and help as I continue to pursue my dream.

Thanks to Chief Fred Corbett of the Corry Police Department for information on police procedures while conducting a criminal investigation.

Also, I'd like to offer my thanks to Robert Saxton, retired district justice, for his help on proper procedures for a preliminary hearing.

Finally, my gratitude goes to my wife, Linda, for her ever-present love and devotion, my sons, Charlie and Matt, who have added so much to my life, and to my family and friends who are so supportive in my endeavors.

Chapter 1

"God, he's soooo hottt!" Sheila squealed to her best friend as they stood in the school bathroom in front of the mirror, freshening their makeup. "Being in his class is gonna be cool. This is one class I'm not gonna mind going to! Imagine me being interested in history. I'm more interested in *his* story! I think I'm in love."

"How did you get so lucky?" Cindy asked. "Absolutely everyone tries to get into one of Peterson's American history or sociology classes. I tried to get into his history class too, but I got stuck with that old cow, Mrs. Kovach."

"I've got the guidance counselor wrapped around my little finger," Sheila boasted. "That old coot, Mr. Klingensmith is such a dog. I went in to talk to him the other day, all sweet and innocent. I was wearing a short skirt and a low cut sweater, and I kept leaning forward to give him a good view. He was practically drooling! I told him that if I didn't get into Mr. Peterson's class my life would be ruined, and I was almost crying when I begged him to transfer me. I even told him that I'm planning to major in history."

"I can't believe he bought that. He obviously doesn't know you. He's so gullible. I'm always envious at the way you manipulate people to get what you want, Sheila." A dreamy smile came over her face as she remembered other times Sheila had manipulated people to get her way. "Remember when you got Jimmy Clark to put our names on the absentee list, so we could cut school and go meet Tim and Randy? We partied with them in the woods all day."

"You really had a ball that day, Cindy; actually, I seem to recall, you had two!"

Sheila giggled at her pun. "Wasn't that the day you gave it up to Tim?" Sheila snickered. "I don't recall your complaining about my scheming then."

Cindy smiled and blushed just a little as she remembered that day. "Did I remember to thank you for that?" And returning to the topic at hand, she whined, "I just wish I could have conned my way into Mr. Peterson's class too. I don't suppose you'd charm Klingensmith for me too?"

"Sorry, Cindy. I've gotta play it cool with him; you never know when I might need him again." Changing the subject back to her excitement about getting into the history class, Sheila declared, "I'm gonna get Mr. Peterson to notice me."

"Do you think he will?"

"In a few more days, I'm gonna give it my best shot," Sheila declared confidently. When she finished applying a coat of shiny red lipstick, she puckered her lips and blew a kiss to herself in the mirror. Winking at Cindy, Sheila posed seductively and assured her friend, with an air of self-confidence, "He's a man! He'll be putty in my hands. I want to get much more out of him than an A."

* * *

Wednesday was the mid semester in-service day, and Chad Peterson sat alone in his classroom looking over the new class lists he'd been assigned for the second semester of the school year at Emerson Central High. It was eight and a half years ago that Chad had returned to his hometown where he took a job teaching at the same high school he had attended, in what seemed to have been a lifetime ago.

Although, initially, he'd been uncertain about teaching in his hometown, Chad enjoyed his job at Emerson. He had wondered if too much familiarity might tempt the students (and the administration) to take advantage of him, but his fears proved unfounded as his dynamic teaching style and sense of humor easily won over his first groups of students, who then provided very good PR for the kids who came later. Chad tried to make himself available, when possible, to help kids who were having problems—not only in history and sociology—and had gained a reputation among the kids as being fair and easy to talk to. The fact that the high school girls thought he was "a hunk" only enhanced his popularity. That Chad had been hired to replace the now retired Mr. Karns, who had a reputation for constant lectures, pop quizzes, and a penchant for sending students to detention, hadn't hurt either.

He was also popular among his colleagues who appreciated his dry wit and camaraderie. Sounds of laughter often resounded from the teachers' room when

Chad was around. That Ms. Hargrove, the principal, consistently gave him good reviews and positive feedback following her semi-annual classroom observations, added to his feelings of accomplishment.

Reviewing the names on the list, Chad found many that were familiar. There were a few who were children of people he'd known growing up in the area, and some were siblings of students he'd taught in previous years. He was pleased to see that he'd be averaging twenty-five kids in each of his four classes; not bad considering that in past years he'd had over thirty in each class.

Although some of the teachers were getting together now in the faculty room to compare notes on the kids (getting the rundown on the troublemakers and the problem kids), Chad preferred to judge for himself and give them all an equal chance. A few of his colleagues had passed by and invited him to join them, but Chad begged off, explaining that he had to finish entering the grades before this semester ended.

He had one more set of grades to enter when Belinda Landis came into his room. Belinda, one of the high school's art teachers, was also popular among the kids and staff. She and Chad had started their teaching careers at Emerson the same year and had become instant friends. Her sense of humor mirrored Chad's, and they shared many common interests. They were both young, single and good looking and, after close to eight years of being pals, they were finally starting to explore a deeper relationship.

Over the years, Chad and Belinda had purposely avoided a personal romantic relationship, fearing the awkwardness they'd face in school if it didn't work out. They'd convinced themselves that it wasn't worth possibly ruining a good friendship and had settled for that. They'd often double-dated and occasionally even fixed each other up with friends, inevitably spending time consoling each other when their respective attempts at relationships failed.

It was just a few weeks earlier when they'd joined a group of friends from school for an evening of dancing and dining, that somehow Chad and Belinda had become the focus of the conversation. Everyone was discussing how strange it was that they hadn't gotten together, even though it was obvious to them all just how suited Chad and Belinda were to each other. Chad recalled that Charlene Simpson, a history teacher and frequent matchmaker in school, had issued a challenge to both of them to "give it a shot," almost daring them to go out on a date. Neither Chad nor Belinda had even considered it at the time, but a bit later, they were returning to the table after sharing a dance, and they overheard the others, still immersed in a discussion about the two of them. They were actually placing bets whether or not Chad and Belinda would have the guts to try.

It made them stop and think. Rather than confront their friends, Chad led Belinda back to the dance floor. Taking her into his arms once again, they began to move in sync. They'd danced together many times before and were comfortable with each other. This time though, while they moved automatically, they had a frank discussion about their feelings.

"I'm beginning to realize, Belinda, that maybe our friends were right after all. We've pretended to be just friends, but I admit I like the way you feel in my arms." Looking into Belinda's eyes, he could see that she felt the same way. Pulling her in closer as they swayed together, Chad leaned in and gently touched her lips with his. The sparks that passed between them during that one gentle kiss surprised them both so much that they stopped dancing and just stood there, staring into each other's eyes. Neither knew how long they stood there before realizing that the music had stopped and they were the only ones still on the dance floor. Chad took Belinda's hand as they left the dance floor.

"We should talk about this, Chad. Alone!"

By mutual, unspoken consent, they took their coats and left, without even saying goodbye to their friends.

Still holding hands, they walked silently to a nearby coffee shop, and didn't speak until they'd been seated. Then they sat in a quiet corner and talked—really talked—for a long time, exploring their feelings.

"We've shared a lot of fun times over the years, Belinda. We bowled together on the faculty team for the past three years. That was fun."

"Yeah, especially the celebrations at the tavern afterwards. We partied till late in the night."

"Even more fun were the gags we often played on each other. Do you remember how we tricked Ron into going to Lawson's market to pick up his 'free' turkey for Thanksgiving? We were all in stitches the next day when he came to school. He laughed along with us, though, when he found out it was a tradition played on all new teachers."

"The next week he got you back when he told the manager at the bowling alley that all the drinks and snacks were on you."

Chad laughed. "He made sure the rest of the team left before I did. It cost me thirty bucks. I seem to recall you were in on that one too."

"I asked you for a ride home and made sure to take my time, pretending that my bowling shoes were knotted. I even feigned having to go to the bathroom to stall for more time."

Chad chuckled again.

"What?" Belinda questioned.

"Remember that time when Matt and I kept sending you those e-mails at school? You kept running up to the administrators asking what they wanted."

Belinda smiled. "They thought I was going nuts. It wasn't till the fourth time that I realized you guys were playing a prank on me."

As their reminiscences came to a close, Chad added, "You know that I care about you, Belinda. I was afraid of hurting you if we got involved, so I avoided demonstrating any affection. We've been good friends for so long."

"I realize it's wrong for us to deny our feelings. So, what do we do?"

"I think we should keep things professional at school so as not to start any unwarranted gossip, but I'd like to move our relationship beyond friendship."

"I'd like that too, Chad. We'll just move slowly at first and see how things go."

"I promise you that if our feelings change someday, we'll still remain friends."

They sealed their bargain with a kiss. Chad took Belinda home and, when they stepped inside, he pulled her into his arms. It was a concerted effort for him to kiss her goodnight and leave, despite his every instinct which told him to stay, but since they had decided to take it slowly, that's just what he did.

Despite their efforts at work to be discreet about the new direction their relationship had taken, Belinda and Chad didn't seem to mind very much when their friends took special delight in being proven right, and they joined in the laughter when hearing, "I told you so," with increasing frequency.

Even before this change in their relationship, Chad and Belinda had made a habit of spending a few minutes together every morning in school before classes started. Since he'd become more aware of his feelings for her, he could feel his heart skip a beat whenever he saw her approaching, just as it did now when she walked into the room.

"Hey, Chad. 'Sup?" she said, sitting down on the corner of his desk.

Chad laughed out loud. It was a little game that they played, imitating the kids' lingo. As he stood up, he checked to see that they had some privacy so he could give her a proper greeting.

"Nuttin', 'sup wit ya?" he replied in kind, and when he saw that they were indeed alone, he took her into his arms and they shared a kiss.

"Would you like to come over to my place tonight? I'll make dinner," she offered. Belinda didn't often offer to cook, and Chad looked at her questioningly.

"Special occasion?" he asked.

"No big deal! I just thought it'd be nice to relax and stay in for a change. I can throw some burgers together, maybe a salad and some chips. Like I said, nothing special."

"When I'm with you, then it's always special, Belinda," Chad said with a wink.

"Ooooh, good one, Chad!" Belinda squeezed his hand and smiled, appreciating his corny, yet charmingly romantic quip.

"Sounds good to me! I'll pick up some ice cream for dessert, okay? Should I pick up a movie? What time do you want me?"

Not to be outdone by Chad's charm, Belinda quickly responded, "I want you all the time, honey!" and they laughed together. "Ice cream sounds great, and you can pick up a movie if you'd like. I have to get to the market and make a few other stops on the way home, so how does six sound?"

"Six is good." Hearing the sounds of people in the hallway, Chad gave her another quick kiss before moving to sit back at his desk. Changing the subject momentarily, Chad asked. "So, how do your classes look for the new semester?"

"I have two introductory art classes, a sculpture class, and a photography class. I'm really looking forward to teaching that one. Pictures are a passion of mine."

"Yeah, I can see how it would be exciting. Something always develops!" Chad always had what Belinda called a "smartass answer." She grimaced, but laughed anyway.

"Play your cards right, Mr. Peterson, and maybe I'll let you join me in my darkroom!" Belinda giggled, pleased that she could hold her own with the quips.

"Let's forget the movie! I wanna hear more about your darkroom," he teased. Although their relationship hadn't yet reached a level where they spent a lot of time in dark rooms, it was definitely headed that way.

Belinda stood up and winked seductively. "You don't have to bring the ice cream either, honey," she whispered. "I'll take care of the dessert and we'll see what comes up," she added before she blew him a kiss and exited the room with a wave.

Chad left school at 3:00 and headed to the mall to run a few of his own errands. After a quick stop at the dry cleaners, he stopped to get a new battery for his watch. He went into the ice cream shop and took a few minutes to choose a couple of pints of ice cream. Although he preferred chocolate, Belinda always liked to try exotic flavors, so he chose some kiwi-mango flavored sherbet for her. On his way back to the car, he walked into the florist's shop and chose a colorful bouquet of carnations—Belinda's favorites.

When Chad walked out of the mall, he encountered a group of kids from school, gathered around his car. The yellow Ford Mustang convertible was easily recognized around town. It was Chad's pride and joy, and every day after school he'd find a bunch of kids in the parking lot standing by the car in the hopes that he'd weaken and offer them a ride. So far he'd managed to come up with some very creative excuses to avoid it, without actually saying no. It had become something of a ritual, and the fact that Chad played along with them was just one more reason that the kids liked him so much. As he approached the car, he tried to think of an excuse to make a quick getaway without seeming too abrupt.

"Hey, Mr. P., cool car!" one boy yelled as he approached. "Whatcha got under the hood?"

"It's a 4.6 supercharged V8 with 390 horsepower. Not so great on gas mileage, but it's a honey."

"That rocks. You ever really wind it out?"

"Nah! Not totally. I just like the sleek lines and the sporty feel. Listen guys, I'd love to stand and chat, but I'm in a hurry."

"I bet you don't have trouble attracting girls with a great car like this," a girl unfamiliar to him said in a snickering tone.

Something in her tone grated on his nerves, and he responded to her in an admonitory tone. "I didn't buy the car to attract anyone; I just like sports cars." Chad hung up the dry cleaning in the back of the car and put the flowers on the rear seat. Waving to the other kids, he got into the driver's seat.

The kids, sensing his annoyance, didn't want to alienate him, so they waved back and moved away from the car. As he drove away, Sheila McMasters muttered under her breath, "Geez, how rude!"

* * *

When Chad got home, he dropped the flowers on the table and, still holding his dry cleaning in one hand, he used the other hand to put the ice cream in the freezer. With the freezer door still open, he grabbed a few ice cubes and dropped them into a glass which sat on the countertop. He took a bottle of Coke out of the fridge and filled the glass, taking a long drink before refilling it. Leaving it on the countertop, he went to the other room to hang up his dry cleaning. Checking his now-working watch, he saw that he had plenty of time to do a load of laundry before it would be time to leave for Belinda's. He grabbed the pile of laundry from the hamper in the bathroom and, after putting the load in the washer, he picked up the glass and sat down with the newspaper.

He tried to read the paper while the machine was running, but found it difficult to concentrate. Chad was looking forward to the evening ahead and wondered if perhaps he should pack a few things in case Belinda invited him to stay overnight. He was certain of his feelings for her. Although they had been sticking to their bargain to take things slowly, he thought that they were both ready to move ahead to the next level. Deciding not to make it seem so premeditated, he decided not to pack a bag, but he checked and was relieved to see that the condoms he'd put in his wallet the week before were still intact—just in case.

Once he'd moved the clothes into the dryer, he went to take a shower. During those few minutes, he again reflected upon some of the fun times he'd shared with Belinda. He chuckled when he recalled their rides on the roller coasters last summer at an amusement park. Each time, Belinda feigned panic and Chad acted as her protector. His thoughts then turned to the end-of-the-year faculty parties. Even though they weren't dating then, they often arrived together and did silly things that entertained their friends. Suddenly Chad broke out into an impromptu rendition of "Cel-e-bra-tion Time" as he remembered the karaoke version that he and Belinda performed to mark the end of the last school year.

Afterwards, he dressed comfortably in a lightweight pullover sweater and some jeans. He had just enough time to fold the clean clothes before it was time to leave.

When he arrived, promptly at six, Belinda greeted him with a big smile and hug. "Hi, Chad. C'mon in."

He held up the bag with the ice cream and asked, "How does kiwi-mango sound?"

"Mmmmmmmm, sounds great!"

She reached to take the bag from him, but before she could, he pulled the flowers from behind his back and presented them to her. "These are for you," he said gallantly.

"Ooooooooh, they're beautiful!" She pressed a kiss to his lips before she accepted the flowers from him and took a deep whiff of the fresh fragrance. "I love them. Thank you, Chad. If you'll put the ice cream in the freezer, I'll put these into some water." She led the way to the kitchen. "Are you hungry now? I can put the burgers on whenever you're ready."

"Starved," he said as he reached for her. He wrapped his arms around her and devoured her lips, giving her the clear message that it wasn't only burgers for which he had an appetite. Chad offered her a chance to set the pace for the evening. "I guess, if you insist, we can start with the burgers…" he began suggestively and then, not wanting to pressure her, asked, "Is there something I can do to help?"

"Yes, definitely burgers first or we might not get to them at all," Belinda responded, clearly indicating that they were on the same wavelength. "I've got things pretty much under control. Thanks. I still have to set the table and make a salad. Can you help with either of those?"

"Sure, I can make the salad."

"I already took out some tomatoes and cucumbers and put them over there on the counter. There's also some lettuce and I think a couple of peppers in the fridge. If there's anything else you especially like, just ask."

Chad's wit immediately kicked in. "Ummm! I'll definitely remember your offer! I know what I especially like," he laughed seductively, "but I'll save that for dessert."

"I meant for the salad, silly," she chuckled, knowing full well what his innuendo suggested, and said, "but now I'm looking forward to dessert!"

Chad winked and suggested that they start eating now in order to get to dessert more quickly.

"Then I'll put these on to cook." Belinda blew him a kiss and took the burgers she'd prepared and put them into the broiler. Chad took the knife and began dicing a tomato. They talked while they worked, catching up on the news of each other's day.

Belinda suddenly remembered something she'd heard before Chad arrived. "Hey, did you hear that Matt Stairs was in an accident on the way home today?"

"No, what happened?" Matt was the girls' volleyball coach at school, and he and his wife Maggie were good friends of Chad and Belinda.

"I first heard about the accident on the local news at five and didn't really pay that much attention, but about twenty minutes ago Brian called and told me that Matt was hurt in what was apparently a three-car accident. I tried to call Maggie, but she was at the hospital and had her cell phone off. I called the house and spoke with Maggie's mom who was sitting with the kids."

"Oh, no! Is Matt okay?"

Maggie's mom said he was very lucky. He has a damaged disk in his back and a badly sprained neck, but he's expected to recover completely. It looks like it'll be several weeks, though, before he can return to work."

Chad was relieved that it wasn't anything more serious. "Thank God he'll be fine. What an awful break! Do you know how long he'll be in the hospital? Maybe we can stop by."

"I don't know. We can try Maggie's cell phone again later," Belinda suggested.

"Yeah, I don't imagine they'll let her stay at the hospital after the visiting hours, so we can try calling her in maybe an hour or so. Remind me tomorrow to talk to Samantha about sending him a fruit and activity basket from the staff's Sunshine Fund."

"Good idea." Belinda made a mental note to remind Chad about that. "I wonder what the girls will do for a volleyball coach if he's going to be out for awhile," added Belinda. "Matt was bragging that we have a dynamite team this year. Hey, you played volleyball in college, didn't you? Maybe you could fill in for him."

"Yeah, I played, but playing's a lot different from coaching. If they're in a bind, I guess I'd consider it. After all, it'll be temporary. I've gone to most of the matches for the past couple of years. It might be fun to get back into it, if Matt'll give me some tips and fill me in on the girls' strengths."

They discussed Matt's condition and the possibility of Chad covering for him with the volleyball team as they finished preparing the food. When everything was ready, and Belinda began putting it on the table, Chad offered to put on some music.

"Sure, that's a great idea. You can turn on the radio, or if you prefer," she said, indicating the cabinet that held her music collection, "look through the CDs in there and choose a few. The stereo can take up to five disks at a time, so you can program a bunch of them at once."

"Let's see what we've got here," Chad said as he looked through the pile of CDs. Even though it was supposed to be a casual dinner, Belinda had lit a couple of candles which, together with the flowers that she'd arranged on the table, had created a romantic ambience. Chad carefully chose music that suited the mood. As they heard the first strains of music from the Phil Collins CD he'd chosen, Belinda nodded her approval.

The romance in the air was palpable and, as they ate, Chad found himself looking often into Belinda's eyes. Once, when she caught him just staring, she asked, "What's the matter?"

"Nothing at all," he replied, reaching across the table. He took her hand and entwined his fingers with hers. Staring into her eyes, he told her, "Did I ever tell you that you have beautiful eyes? I love looking at them."

Belinda blushed. "Flattery will get you everywhere," she said with a smile and squeezed his hand.

The food on the table was forgotten and they just sat looking into each other's eyes, Belinda's hand still clasped in his. When Celine Dion's voice penetrated their consciousness, singing a beautiful love song, Chad stood and, still holding her hand, gently pulled Belinda to her feet, taking her into his arms. "Sweetheart, I've been waiting to do this for a long time," he said before he leaned forward and pressed his lips to hers. Her lips parted and their tongues met as one of his hands moved behind her head and his fingers threaded through her hair. Belinda's arms encircled him. They gently swayed to the music and let passion take over. They were locked in a loving embrace when, at last, reluctantly, the kiss ended. Still moving to the music, their foreheads rested against each other's, their breaths coming quickly and heavily.

When he was finally able to speak, Chad lifted Belinda's chin, ever so slightly, just enough so that they could see into each other's eyes. Feeling that he could see into her soul, he felt his own respond. He spoke more surely than he could ever remember when he said, "Belinda, I'm falling in love with you."

"I feel the same, Chad!" she responded and felt her heart soar with his. Belinda reached up to his cheeks and pulled his face back to hers as they shared another passion-filled kiss.

Brad's hands caressed up and down Belinda's arms. His touch caused her to shiver with excitement. He ended the kiss just long enough to tell her, "I want to make love with you; I want you so much."

"I want that too." Her breaths now came in short bursts and her body longed for his touch.

He returned his lips to hers and the kisses they shared set them both on fire. Belinda slowly lowered her hand from his cheek and moved it down the length of his arm to hold his hand. She led him to the bedroom and, as their desire grew, she moved his hand to her breast. She pressed kisses across his cheek until she reached his ear. She traced the shape of his ear with her tongue and moved to nibble at his earlobe as he slowly outlined the circle of her breast through her blouse. He felt her body tremble with excitement which only inflamed him more.

Belinda helped remove his sweater and he crushed his body against hers. His hands moved over her back and he held her tightly to him.

Still standing, they began to explore each other's bodies. Chad whispered words of love and desire for her as his hands and mouth continued to roam over her. His touch sent jolts of pleasure raging through her, and under his hands, he could feel her nipples grow hard. Her excitement increased as his lips traced a path along the outer edges of her breast and then over each nipple.

They were so in tune to each other, and he could tell the exact second that her knees began to buckle. He didn't let her fall, but lifted her in his arms and carried her the short distance to the bed. Belinda's arms entwined around his neck and she rained kisses over his face as he placed her gently onto the bed and then lowered himself beside her.

"Your body is so warm and soft, Belinda. I love how close I feel to you right now." He massaged her back, her shoulders, and the nape of her neck as they continued to touch and kiss.

Although they were both still half dressed, Belinda could feel the heat of his body merge with hers. She snuggled even closer to him, feeling her breasts crush against his chest. She could feel Chad's hardness pressing against her and her body responded. Belinda hoped this moment would last forever while she also longed for more.

Eventually their bodies took control. Chad knelt between Belinda's legs and watched as she arched her hips to help him remove her jeans and panties. She sat up, and he guided her hands to him, so she could unzip his jeans and help him out of them and his boxers just as he'd helped her. He tossed his clothes to the floor. Her passion was so strong that her body felt as if it were on fire. Chad reached over the side of the bed for his pants, took a condom from the pocket, and placed it on the nightstand.

Their pleasure was mutual and unending. Very slowly Chad brought her to the heights of ecstasy. Every nerve within her felt as if it would explode. He explored her thighs and then moved his hands up to her stomach. She felt his hardess press against her and she desperately wanted to feel more of him. She reached to touch him. She could feel the ripple of his muscles under her hands and watched the look on his face as she reached lower. Hearing him moan as she stroked his hard length thrilled her. He reached over for the condom and Belinda helped him put it on before he moved above her and slowly lowered himself, giving them both pleasure as he filled her. They abandoned themselves to a whirlwind of pleasure and rode together toward fulfillment. Simultaneously, they echoed "I love you" and shared a kiss as they reached the climax of their pleasure.

Chad lay on Belinda, his head nuzzled onto her chest, their arms and legs wrapped around each other, both completely satisfied. Their growing love had developed into an intimacy that they knew could only grow deeper and more enriching.

They dozed in each other's arms, rousing occasionally to share some more loving.

At 10:30, Belinda tried calling Maggie Stairs to get an update on Matt's condition. "Hi, Maggie, it's Belinda. Chad and I heard about Matt's accident, and we wanted to know how he's doing and if there's something we can do to help."

"Thanks for calling. I just finished settling the kids, and it's just hitting me now how lucky we are. Matt'll be laid up for a while. He'll be in the hospital for a few days while they continue to monitor things. He may have suffered a slight concussion, but the doctors assure me that, with time, he'll be fine."

"Thank God! That's good news. Hang on a second, Chad also wants to talk to you. Please let me know if there's something I can do to help." She passed the phone to Chad.

"Hi, Maggie. I'm sorry to hear about the accident. As Belinda said, if there's anything either of us can do for Matt or for you, be sure to let us know."

"Thanks, Chad. I appreciate the offer."

"Do you know what happened, Maggie?"

"Matt said that he was going through the intersection at Fourth and Maple Streets when a small car ran the red light. Matt was already in the intersection and was broadsided. The car behind him couldn't stop and hit him from the rear. Thank God nobody was seriously hurt."

"Had the guy been drinking?"

"Not as far as I know. He apparently was coherent enough to tell the police at the scene that the sun was in his eyes, and he didn't even see the light there. He's not from this area."

"Well, we're thankful it wasn't more serious. Belinda told me that he's in the hospital. Is he allowed to have visitors?"

"Yes. He'll likely be there at least three or four days, Chad. I'm sure he'd be glad to see you. It looks like he could be out of school for several weeks. We just don't know yet."

"Belinda and I will stop by tomorrow afternoon. Take care now, and again, if you need anything, let us know."

"Thanks, Chad. I'll do that. Bye."

Having worked up their appetites, they went back to the table to see if there was anything worth salvaging from the dinner they'd abandoned earlier. Belinda put the burgers into the microwave for a few minutes. Once they were ready, they sat down and, in between holding hands and exchanging kisses, they discussed plans to stop at the hospital after work the following day.

Sorry now that he hadn't packed a bag, it was almost midnight when Chad finally left for home. Deciding that the work he had planned to review wasn't critical for the next day's classes, he prepared for bed and crawled under the covers. He offered a small prayer of thanks for the direction his relationship with Belinda had taken and he knew it would just get better.

Chapter 2

"Sheila, you're going to be late for school again," yelled Mrs. McMasters from the bottom of the stairwell. "I'm not going to make excuses for you if you're late again."

"Yeah, Mom, I heard you. Get off my case!"

Sheila rolled over and put the pillow over her head. She was definitely not an early morning person. Twenty minutes later her mom stood beside her bed, yanking the covers from her daughter.

"I said get up now! I have to leave for work in thirty minutes, and I don't have time to coddle you. You're old enough now to act responsibly. GET UP!"

Sheila rolled one leg out of bed very slowly and said sharply to her mother, "Just quit nagging me! I hate when you do that!"

Mrs. McMasters sighed in exasperation and slammed the door on her way out of Sheila's room. She was in no mood to get into another argument with Sheila. It seemed to her that more and more often they battled about every little thing. Sometimes it was about her lack of help at home. Other times it was about her endless time on the telephone. Worst of all were the arguments that they had about boys coming over to the house at all hours of the day or night. She felt as though she had lost control of her daughter. "Did all parents face these conflicts with their teenagers?" she wondered.

Sheila wandered into the bathroom. "I feel like shit," she thought. "I shouldn't have stayed up till two a.m. talking with Donnie in that chatroom. Maybe a hot shower will fix me up."

After ten minutes and another yell from her mother about being too long in the shower, she wrapped herself in a towel and stood in front of her closet, trying to pick out something to wear. "I gotta find something really hot for school today. This is my first day in Mr. Peterson's class and I want to make an impression." She chose a top that revealed just enough cleavage to make any boy, or man, notice and a skirt that covered her to mid thigh. "Yeah, this'll do," she said aloud as she surveyed her appearance in the mirror.

When she finally came downstairs, the battle began anew. "Why do you have to dress like that for school," asked Mrs. McMasters. "When you sit, you'll look like a slut with your skirt up around your ass. And with those thong panties you wear, you'll give quite a show."

"It's not like you walked around in a big sack when you were my age. This is what's in style. Check out any of the fashion magazines. You're so out of it. I'm not doing anything wrong and nobody's gonna *see* anything."

"Why don't you wear jeans like a lot of other girls?"

"Because jeans are boring. And I don't want to be like the 'other' girls. I'm a woman and I want to look and feel like a woman, even if it's just at school." Her thoughts went to Mr. Peterson and his reaction, but she'd never reveal thoughts like that to her mother. She deftly changed the subject. "Mom, Cindy asked if I could stay over at her place tonight. She got this DVD movie that's hilarious." Suddenly sweet and contrite, Sheila asked, "Can I go, please?"

"Absolutely not! You know how I feel about your staying out on a school night. Why can't you watch the movie over the weekend?"

"It's a rental movie and it has to be returned by tomorrow. C'mon, Mom. A lot of the girls are gonna be there. I can handle it and be good for school the next day. I'm not a kid anymore. Quit treating me like one."

"I suppose you'll con your brother into doing your chores too. It's not fair to take advantage of him the way you do."

"I'm gonna go ask dad."

"Sheila don't…" but before Mrs. McMasters could finish the admonition, Sheila was out of the room. She found her father in the bathroom, shaving. He let out a whistle when he saw Sheila's attire.

"My little girl's growing up too fast," he commented. "What are you all dolled up for?"

"I'm glad somebody approves of my appearance. Thanks, Daddy." She walked closer and gave him a hug, carefully avoiding the shaving cream still on his chin. "Daddy, I wanna stay over at Cindy's tonight. A lot of my friends are gonna be there for a sleepover. It's ok with you, right?"

"What'd your mother say about it?"

"Oh, she's so old fashioned. You know her. She screeched at me, 'You can't stay out on a school night!' Please, Daddy. We have a fun night planned together."

"I guess it's alright. I'll speak with your mother." He added as an afterthought, "Make sure it doesn't affect your school work."

"Thanks, Daddy. You're the best!" She gave him another bear hug and skipped out of the bathroom with a smirk on her face. A few minutes later her mother came into her room as Sheila packed an overnight case.

"I just went in to say goodbye to your dad before I leave for work. I see you got your way with him again."

"G'bye, mom. Have a nice day at work," Sheila said without even turning to face her mother.

Mrs. McMasters, defeated again, left without another word.

Sheila immediately went to the phone and called Cindy. "It's ok. I can stay tonight. Mom put up her usual fuss, but I got Dad to say it's ok. He usually gets his way with Mom; she'll do almost anything to avoid a confrontation with him."

"Cool! Everything's falling into place. My parents'll be gone all night at that convention. I think we have at least ten others who'll be here too, including Tim and Randy. I've got plans for Tim. I even bought some packs of condoms, just in case!"

"Good planning, Cindy. Maybe I'll borrow one of them from you. I gotta get going now. I'll see you at school. We'll work out the plans then. Bye."

"Okay, bye."

Sheila finished packing her bag and ran downstairs. She gulped down a glass of orange juice and kissed her dad. "Bye, Daddy. Love ya!" she yelled as she ran out the door to catch the bus.

When she arrived at school, Sheila immediately headed for her locker. She was gathering her things before homeroom, when Rod Lawson, a senior and captain of the school's football team, approached her.

"Hey, Sheila. I hear there's a party at Cindy Bennett's house tonight. Can you wrangle me an invitation?"

"Are you kidding?" Sheila chuckled. "Consider yourself invited." Sheila fluffed her hair and, using the pretence of taking something out of her backpack, she leaned forward and let Rod have a long look at her cleavage. "I'm going early to help Cindy, but you can meet me there." She watched, smiling, noting that he couldn't tear his eyes from the front of her shirt. "Come any time you like," she added with a snicker at the intended innuendo.

Rod quickly picked up on her intonation. "You gonna be with a date?"

"Nobody's bringing a date. It's just a bunch of guys and girls hanging out. I'm sure a few will pair up at the party. We'll have all the usual stuff that makes a party rock."

"Cool, then I'll see you there. Thanks." He gave her a quick peck on the cheek.

With just five minutes before the beginning of homeroom period, Cindy spotted Sheila and ran up to her. "Everything's set. Jimmy Clark got someone to buy some beer for us and some others are bringing pretzels and chips. I talked some of the girls into bringing their latest CDs, and get this. Frank's gonna sneak a couple of his dad's porn movies."

"Rod just asked if he can come tonight. This is gonna be one fantastic night, Cindy."

The bell rang and both girls raced to their respective homerooms. Sheila made it just as Mr. Swanson began to close the door. "Just in time, Sheila," he remarked. "Remember, one more tardy and it's detention for you."

Nothing out of the ordinary occurred during her morning classes. Since Sheila's English class continued all year, students worked in groups preparing for a debate. In math class, she pretended to give full attention to Mr. Sweet's geometry explanations, but she daydreamed of other things.

She sat during lunch with a number of friends and finalized last minute details with Cindy. She made plans to meet Cindy and Tara Litz right after school. They'd ride to Cindy's place with Tara, who said she had a friend who could score some grass for the party.

Sheila left her friends a few minutes before the lunch period was over so she could stop in the restroom to check and fix her makeup. She was applying fresh lipstick as she said to herself, "First impressions are important, and I've got big plans for Chad Peterson, so I've got to make this impression count."

Her first class after lunch was the one she'd been waiting for, American history. This was one class where she didn't want to be late. She made a dramatic entrance, being sure to greet Mr. Peterson with a big smile and hello as she took a front seat right in front of his desk. She positioned herself in a manner that would afford him an ample view of her legs, but not in a revealing manner. It was intended as a tease but, much to her dismay, Chad didn't seem to notice. She hoped that he wouldn't assign them seats and was thrilled when he announced that students could keep their chosen seats as long as they behaved.

"No problem, I'm gonna be very, very good. I promise," Sheila muttered under her breath.

Chad passed out a course syllabus, described some of the projects that would be required during the semester, and then proceeded to ask the students to tell something about themselves that might distinguish them from the others. When he came to Sheila, she stood up and faced Chad when she said, "I'm a history buff." Then she added suggestively, "And I'm so looking forward to your class, Mr. Peterson.'

The kids in the class laughed at that and some murmured under their breaths, "since when is Sheila interested in anything besides Sheila?"

Sure that she'd made an impression on her prey, Sheila sat quietly for the rest of that class, but didn't take her eyes off Mr. Peterson. If asked, she couldn't have repeated a word he'd said. As she left the room, she made a point of addressing Chad. "Goodbye, Mr. Peterson. I enjoyed your class very much. Have a *very* good day. I'll see you tomorrow."

Chad just nodded and gave a half hearted wave goodbye. To him, Sheila was just another student who wanted attention and looked for ways to get it. Having the last period free, he gathered his things and walked to the faculty room. He found Jenn Downing and Barbie Green, two middle school English teachers, and Andy Brickman, a senior high English teacher, sitting together. Their laughter indicated that one had obviously shared some kind of amusing story.

"Hey there, is this a private gathering of the English department?" Chad inquired in a joking manner.

"Nah! C'mon in Chad. Barbie was just telling us about what happened in her second block class today. Tell him, Barbie."

Again, they all broke into immediate laughter as Barbie tried to relate the story. "I had just entered the classroom and the bell rang. The group of kids were rather noisy and I politely asked them to settle down. The room got instantly quiet and, just as I was about to begin, one of the boys in the back of the room, Robbie Jones, left this loud fart. Well, you know how immature middle school kids are. Farting is *funny*! The poor kid slunk down low in his seat while everyone cracked up. I tried to alleviate his embarrassment but one of the smart alecks in the class chimed in by saying that next time I needed to get their attention, I should use him. That only made everyone laugh even more. Then another boy said if I ever needed to clear the room fast, Robbie could manage to help. It took me ten minutes of class to get order restored."

"It's a good way to get a teacher to learn your name fast, huh?" joked Andy.

Chad sat down with them and related his story. "I'm not sure if that's worse than having a flirt stand up in front of everyone and show off for the rest of the class."

"Who's that?" asked Jenn.

"Sheila McMasters."

The others quickly reacted. Simultaneously they uttered a long "Ahhhh!"

"Everyone knows Sheila," Andy added. "Her reputation precedes her. The junior and senior boys follow her like a bloodhound sniffing a trail. But it's not their tails that go up when she's nearby," he quipped.

All four staff members broke into riotous laughter.

"Well, it certainly got me to learn who she is right away. I think I briefly met her in the parking lot of the mall the other day. She's not someone you can easily forget."

The conversation among the four continued until the bell signaled the end of the school day and they returned to their respective classrooms.

* * *

As soon as she heard the bell, Sheila practically ran down the hall to find Cindy and Tara. She didn't even stop to talk with several boys who greeted her, but instead, gave a quick wave and a cheery hi. The girls were waiting for her as she grabbed her coat from her locker and made her way to their designated meeting place near the gym.

"Hi," she spoke breathlessly. "Sorry to keep you waiting."

As they walked to the car, questions were fired at Sheila in rapid fire succession.

"So, how was Mr. Peterson's class today? Did you make a good first impression? asked Cindy.

"He pretended not to notice me and played it cool, but after the show I put on, I'm sure he already knows my name."

"What'd you do, flash him some skin?" laughed Tara.

"I wasn't that obvious. I just told him I was a history buff."

"You don't really think he's gonna fool around with a teenager, do you, Sheila? Anyway, I heard a rumor that he and Ms. Landis are an item."

"I'm just out to get a good grade, for now. But you never know, I certainly wouldn't turn him down if he were interested in something else." She winked at both of her friends and gave a deep guttural laugh.

On the way to Cindy's house, Tara stopped briefly and asked the girls to wait in the car while she went to an upstairs apartment. "I'll be back in about ten minutes, ok? I have to pick up something for the party." Both girls knew instantly what she meant. She arrived back at the car right on time and handed two small packets to Cindy. "Stash these in the glove compartment for now."

"Oh my God!" cried Sheila. "How much did you have to pay for them?"

"I didn't pay money, if that's what you mean," said Tara. "I have this arrangement with this guy whenever I need something. I get what I want and he gets what he wants," she added with a sly grin. "There's no telltale sign, is there?" she laughed as she glanced into the car's mirror.

When they got to Cindy's house, they cranked up the stereo and began moving furniture so that there would be room for dancing. Cindy brought the strobe light from her bedroom and then said, "Let's find something to eat now. It's a good idea to have something in our stomachs before we drink anything or smoke some grass. I don't want to get too much out of control, anyway. I have to be sure that nobody gets so trashed that they damage anything in the house. After we eat, we'll move anything breakable into my mom's room."

The kids began arriving at six-thirty. Although everyone brought something to add to the festivities, they were especially glad to see Andy Stewart when he showed up with four large pizzas. With a piece of pizza in one hand and a beer in the other, they were ready to have a good time.

For the first couple of hours, the music set the mood for the fun. Some of the fourteen teenagers danced in an animated fashion, strutting and swaying to the beat. Cindy draped her arms around Tim's neck and his hands seemed glued to her butt as they danced. A few sat around the perimeter of the room, already feeling the effects of the liquor and drugs.

Around ten, when she noticed that groups were beginning to pair up, Cindy shouted, "Hey guys, Frank brought a couple of porn movies. Anybody interested?"

Immediately the guys saw that as an opportunity to score and quickly voiced their approval. None of the girls objected. Tara said, "I always wondered what those were like? Yeah, let's watch."

"Whatcha got, Frank?" one shouted.

Cindy walked over to the DVD player and picked up two DVDs and read the titles. "This one is called *Too Hot to Handle*." She picked up the second title. "Hmmmm, *Teenage Cheerleaders*," she murmured as she read the title.

The boys unanimously voted for the second one, and Cindy popped the cassette into the player and turned on the big screen TV. A couple of the more shy kids moved into the kitchen but the rest gathered in front of the TV. After only a few minutes, some oooohs and ahhhhhs could be heard in the room and one girl cried, "Oh my God!"

Sheila and Cindy cornered Rod and Tim before any of the other girls could make a move on them. They took a seat on the floor about ten feet from the TV and behind most of the others. As the movie played, the influence of the alcohol and the suggestive nature of the video caused a few couples to begin groping each other. Rod was making out with Sheila without regard to onlookers. His hand went inside her sweater and up to her breast. She didn't resist.

"Wanna find a place where we can be alone?" Rod asked.

Sheila got up, took his hand, and led him into the family room. They sat on the sofa and began making out. As he fondled her breasts, she surrendered completely to his touch. Her hands went to his thigh and moved upward and things heated up quickly.

It was well after midnight when the knock came at the front door. Instantly Cindy turned down the volume on the stereo and the group grew quiet. With her clothes still in some disarray and with apparent hesitation, Cindy approached the door. Her fears were realized when Officer David Howell entered.

"We've had a report of a party going on here tonight," he said. Looking around the room at all of the underage kids, he again addressed Cindy. "If your parents are home now, I'd like to speak with them."

Cindy, in almost a panicky voice, answered him. "They're away on a trip, Officer. I'm just having a few friends over tonight."

"It's very late. Are there any adults providing supervision?" Spotting what appeared to be empty bottles, he began to survey the room more closely. When he spotted the beer and recognized the smell of pot, he instructed all of the teenagers there to line up along one wall. "I want all of you to give my partner your name and address." Turning once more to Cindy, he said, "You know that you're in a lot of trouble. I'm sure you have a phone number where your parents can be reached. I want it, now."

Sheila came forward and tried using her charm to persuade the officer. With her biggest smile and a very polite tone, she said, "Officer Howell, please let us go. You can take any of the beer that's left from us. There's nothing else. We were just having a little fun. We haven't harmed anyone."

"What's your name, young lady?"

"I'm Sheila McMasters. My dad works at the post office. You probably know him."

"Yes, I know him quite well. I'm sure he won't be happy about this little party tonight."

"No, he won't but we don't *have* to tell him, right?"

"I think I detect the smell of pot too. That and the underage drinking are serious offenses."

In her most persuasive tone, Sheila continued. "There's no pot here. Look around." She was confident that they wouldn't find proof, because as soon as there was a knock at the door, she had signaled and helped Tara to grab every joint and the remaining grass. They flushed it down the toilet.

Undeterred, Officer Howell finished his statement. "We're going to notify all of your parents. You'll be taken home and events here will be reported to them. This party is over!"

At 1:30 a.m., the sound of their front doorbell awakened Steve and Laura McMasters. Steve quickly threw on a pair of pants, and his wife covered herself with a bathrobe. Steve was surprised to see his daughter standing beside Officer Howell. "David, what's going on?" he asked.

"May we come in, please. Your daughter's in a bit of trouble."

Mrs. McMasters came down from the stairs as both Officer Howell and Sheila stepped into the room. "My God, Sheila, what've you done?"

"Don't blow a gasket, Mom. I'm fine."

"There was a party at the Nelson's house. Your daughter was there and we had to break it up. There was alcohol and suspected use of drugs. We're making sure the kids get home safely to the custody of their parents. There may be some charges filed when our investigation is completed."

"Thanks for bringing her home, Dave. I promise we'll deal with this too."

"We just don't want to see anyone get hurt. Goodnight, folks." Officer Howell tipped his hat and left.

Sheila was quick to jumpstart the conversation. "I didn't drink any alcohol, nor did I do any drugs," she lied.

"You told me that you were just going over to Cindy's to watch a movie and spend the night," yelled Laura McMasters. "You said some girls would be there. Were boys there too?"

"We *did* watch a movie," she answered truthfully, neglecting to mention what kind of movie they watched. "And yes, there were a couple of guys there. It was no big deal. It's not like we had an orgy or something. There was just some music, snacks, and dancing."

"And booze!" Mrs. McMasters retorted.

"I didn't know that someone was bringing alcohol. I admit that part got a little out of hand," she added with her sweet, innocent tone. She turned to her dad. "Daddy, you believe me, don't you? It was supposed to be just a few friends getting together. It got bigger when some of the invited kids asked others to come too. I really didn't do anything wrong."

"I want to believe you, Sheila, but you must promise me that if anything like this happens again, you'll phone us and we'll come get you. I don't want you any place where illegal activities are going on, even if you aren't participating."

"I promise, Daddy. Thanks for believing me." She gave him a hug and kiss.

"Now, go to your room and get some sleep if you can. You still have school tomorrow and you're not skipping it."

She quickly dashed past her mother and ran up the stairs to her room. As she undressed and crawled under the covers of her bed, Sheila breathed a huge sigh of relief that she had weathered the storm.

As they closed the door to their bedroom, Laura McMasters voiced her complaint. "So you're just gonna let this pass and not punish her? Steve, she lied to us about going to Cindy's place. She *had* to know about the party. She's likely lying to us about drinking too."

"We don't know that for sure, Laura. I prefer to give her the benefit of the doubt unless we hear otherwise. She knows being there was wrong. She's just a girl feeling her oats. I wasn't too much different at her age."

"I think she should be grounded for a few weeks. We shouldn't just overlook this. You're too lenient with her, and she plays on your sympathies."

"Let's sleep on it, and we'll talk more about it in the morning. I'm tired now and not in the mood for a debate."

Laura McMasters knew that once again Sheila would win. She said goodnight, turned her back to her husband, and went to sleep.

In her room, Sheila lay awake with a smile on her face. She'd gotten what she wanted out of the party. Getting it on with Rod and getting high were both good, but getting away with it made it even better. Tomorrow she'd talk to Cindy and find out if her friend had managed to get away with it too.

Chapter 3

On Thursday morning, Sheila bolted past her mother and blew a quick kiss toward her dad.

"Can't take time for breakfast now. Don't wanna be late. I'll be home right after cheerleading practice at the end of school. Bye."

She ran the entire four blocks to school, glancing both ways before dashing across the streets. "I have to talk with Cindy before school starts and see what happened to her." She wasn't disappointed when she spotted Cindy near the water fountain on the second floor of the school.

"Hey, Cin. What's the news? Your parents freak out?"

"Oh, hi, Sheila," she responded in a downcast tone. "Not too good, I'm afraid. My mom and dad came right home when the police called them. One of the cops stayed at my place until they arrived. I wanted to crawl into a hole and hide."

"So what's the verdict?" Sheila persisted.

"Well, I'm grounded for a month, which means I have to quit the cheerleading squad, because I can't make practices. I tried to explain but my dad was so pissed. He didn't want to hear anything I said. I might also be charged with providing alcohol to people under the age of twenty-one. I'll have a juvenile record. Since it was our house, I'm responsible."

"I'm sorry, Cindy."

"I knew the risks. It was just stupid. Word was bound to leak out in a small town like this. So, what did your parents say?"

"My mom, of course, hit the roof. I convinced my dad that I wasn't drinking or, heaven forbid, smoking. I told him that I just watched a movie and danced with a couple of the boys. He didn't punish me and this morning I didn't give them time to say much. I dashed out of the house."

"Girl, you're a master escape artist!"

"Hahaha! Just call me Lucky McMasters!"

Cindy let out a small chuckle, but the humor did little to change her mood.

"We'll still be able to talk on the phone, right?" asked Sheila.

"I'm not sure about that. Like I said, my dad is clamping down hard. I have to come home right after school each day. I'll probably be lucky if I can come down from my room to watch television. Maybe you shouldn't try to call for a few days. Things might cool down by then, okay?"

"Sure. I'm really sorry that things worked out the way they did, but it was fun while it lasted."

"Yeah, I think Tim wanted to start dating, but now that I'm grounded, I don't know if he'll just wait around for me. I'll just have to wait and see. I gotta run now. I'll see you at lunch."

"Okay, later."

* * *

Chad met Belinda in the faculty lounge that morning for a few minutes before classes began. She complimented him on a colorful tie that she had never seen him wear. Looking around and seeing nobody nearby, he gently kissed her and whispered an "I love you" in her ear. "Last night was incredible, baby," he added.

"I assure you it was totally mutual. I love you too."

Smiling at her apparent contentment, he joked, "Be careful that the kids don't ask about that smirk on your face."

Belinda grinned. "It's *that* obvious, huh?" She attempted a few serious faces, but had trouble keeping the smile off her face.

He hugged her before they left to begin the day. "Oh, I already took care of the business about the Sunshine Fund gift for Matt. It'll be delivered sometime later today. Do you still want to go with me after school to visit him at the hospital?"

"That's my plan. He'll be happy to see us together, since he was one of those who was betting on us. I'll see ya later."

"Have a good day."

"You too." Belinda gave him a wink as she walked toward her classroom.

* * *

Having a few extra minutes before homeroom began, Sheila talked with a few other friends until she spotted Rod. Then she grabbed his arm. "Hey, big guy! I was looking for you. I really had fun with you last night." Still holding his arm, she asked, "Wanna walk me to my classroom?"

"Sure." They talked as he led her along the hallway. "Did you get into any trouble when we got busted? If that had happened during football season, I'd have been kicked off the team. Coach doesn't tolerate even the suspicion of drinking or smoking. Then again, I probably wouldn't have come if the season was still going on."

"My parents were pissed, but I don't think anything's going to happen. Cindy has to quit cheerleading, but I don't think Mrs. Hargrove can do much since we weren't on school property or school time. I can still keep cheerleading."

When they got to her homeroom door, she stretched to give Rod a peck on the cheek, knowing full well that Mr. Swanson would admonish her. As she waved goodbye, Rod dashed toward his homeroom.

Later that day, when it was time for American history, Chad stood near the doorway as his students filed into the room. He greeted each one with a casual hello. Wearing her cheerleading outfit, Sheila pranced by him like a little pixie.

"Hi, Mr. Peterson," she crooned. "What interesting things are we gonna do today?" She didn't wait for a response but was pleased with what she thought was a flattering question.

In class, Chad gave each student an individual assignment. Then he distributed information packets and gave them the balance of the period to read the information and begin preparing a report. When he explained that the resulting report would be given orally, beginning on the following Monday, a crescendo of yuks and boos ensued. Students always hated getting in front of the class to speak, but Chad knew that was an important aspect of education. Some complained that this would involve homework over the weekend too.

Everyone showed discontent except Sheila, who chimed in with a suggestive response. "I'm very good at oral things, Mr. Peterson," she said.

When it drew the usual class guffaws, she quickly added in a less than innocent tone, "I'm a cheerleader. We have to be very vocal."

Chad tried his best to downplay her remark. He directed them to various other resources and assisted them as needed. The kids in the class did not miss the many times that Sheila approached him during the period to ask for his help or to seek his approval for what she had accomplished.

* * *

After school, Chad quickly gathered his things and walked to Belinda's classroom.

"Hello, Ms. Landis. Do you have time to help a poor man in distress?"

"That depends upon who the man is and what kind of distress he's in," she said straight faced."

"Well, if he looked a lot like me and was in desperate need of a kiss, might you oblige?"

Belinda came over to him, kissed him lightly on the lips and uttered, "I never could resist a handsome man in distress. Does that help?"

"Ummm, that's perfect. And I won't forget to use your response against you when I have other needs," he laughed. Changing the subject, he added, "Are you ready to go?"

Belinda gave him a little pat on the butt and then grabbed her coat. "Let's go cheer up a good friend."

A few minutes later they entered Matt's hospital room. Chad and Belinda both gave Maggie a hug and then turned toward Matt.

Chad set the tone with his humor. "This is a pretty weird way to get a few days off from school, Matt. I know the kids can get to us occasionally but..."

Picking up on the teasing, Matt cut him off in mid sentence. "It's not the kids this time, Chad. Maggie snores so much that I needed a good night's rest, so I figured this was the quietest place to come for sleep."

Maggie gave him a playful slap on the arm and she joined in the fun too. "You wait until these nurses get a peek at that body of yours. They won't let you sleep either."

Belinda commented innocently, "Yeah, I hear they've been looking for a pincushion."

Everyone laughed.

"I'm glad to see the accident hasn't affected your sense of humor, Matt. How are you feeling?" Belinda asked.

"To be frank, my back hurts like hell, but the doctors say the accident may have knocked some sense into me."

"If you now think you're Frank, you're more messed up than we thought," Chad quipped.

After a few more minutes of joking, the conversation took on a more serious tone. Matt revealed that he would likely be unable to return to work for five to eight weeks. "I'm sure someone can easily cover my classes," he said, "but as you know, I have a terrific bunch of girls on the volleyball team. We have a very good chance to win the district championship this year. I don't want to let them down."

"Can Harvey move up and take over?" Chad asked.

"Harvey's a good JV coach, but he prefers working with the younger kids. Honestly, I think the pressure of taking over a potential championship team might be too much for him. And the fact that he's a first year teacher adds other demands to his time."

"Matt, I don't know how you'd feel about this. When Belinda and I heard of your accident, we discussed my helping Harvey on a temporary basis until you return. If you think I could do the job, I'd like to apply."

"I have a better suggestion, Chad. As a matter of fact, I told Maggie that you'd be my first choice. The girls know and like you. They'll work hard for you."

"You want me to take over as head coach? As much as I love the game, I have no coaching experience. Do you think I can handle that?"

"I'm confident you can. I'll fill you in on all of the girls' strengths and weaknesses. You'll do great. If you agree, I'll call Mrs. Hargrove at her home and recommend you. I'm sure the board'll approve."

"Well, if I can count on you for a lot of input and advice, I'd be willing to try."

Leaving Chad and Matt alone to discuss volleyball, Belinda took Maggie down to the cafeteria where they had some coffee and a chance to talk. Maggie admitted that it would be difficult to watch over her husband and work at the same time, but she was determined to make things work.

Around dinner time, Matt and Chad shook hands. Maggie thanked them for spending time with them. On the way back to school to pick up Belinda's car, they stopped at McDonalds.

"Belinda, I see one disadvantage to my taking over for Matt. Have you taken into consideration that this will cut into some of our time together?" He raised his eyebrows suggestively, hinting at what they'd be missing.

"Don't be silly, Chad. This is something you'll enjoy, and it's not like we won't see each other. I'll come to the games and root for you and the girls."

"The games are only part of the problem. It's all of the practice time."

"If our love can't stand a little separation, we're not meant to be together," she professed in a very articulate manner. "I love you and if you want to do this, then I think you should go for it."

Chad reached across the table and clutched her hand. "Thanks for being so supportive."

* * *

On Friday, just before school let out, Chad received a note asking him to stop in to see Mrs. Hargrove before he left for the weekend. She explained to him that, on Matt's recommendation, the administration had approved Chad as the temporary volleyball coach. He would begin with practice on Monday after school.

The weekend passed too quickly as Chad prepared lessons for the upcoming week and studied a few books on volleyball strategies that Matt had asked Maggie to drop off for Chad. Even though he knew the game, he wanted to be well prepared. He made frequent phone calls to Belinda since they didn't get together that weekend. She reassured him that everything was fine and reminded him that this was a temporary situation; they'd find a way to make up for lost time.

Somehow he managed to make it through his regular classes on Monday, but his nervousness manifested itself as he chewed on his fingernails all day.

He was uncharacteristically nervous by the time he met with the girls at volleyball practice. It took only a few moments for the uneasy feeling to pass. All of the girls rushed him and greeted him enthusiastically. When Samantha Grinder said, "Don't worry, Coach P., we're gonna win the championship for you," he felt the excitement build.

"I'm happy that you're all okay with my taking over for now. Yes, we *are* going to win, but let's win this one for Coach Stairs. Now, get on the court and show me what you've got."

Practice went well, and Chad waited until all of the girls departed the locker room before leaving. He was pleased when each girl stopped into the coach's office and slapped his hand and told him that he'd done a nice job.

It was 9 p.m. when he walked out of the locker room and bumped into Sheila McMasters. "Hello, Sheila. What are you doing here this late?"

"I'm waiting for my dad to pick me up after practice. It looks like he's late, as usual."

Not seeing anyone else around, Chad said, "Maybe I better wait around with you until he arrives."

"I'd like that, Mr. Peterson. Thank you," she said. "I saw you coaching volleyball. You're replacing Coach Stairs, huh?"

"Yeah, probably for this season. It doesn't look as if he'll be able to return for a few weeks."

"I heard he was hurt. You looked good out there working with the girls."

"Thanks. I enjoyed it."

They talked in the hallway until Sheila saw her dad's car pull up along the curb. They walked out the door together and she waved to him as she got into the car.

"Who's that, honey?" her father asked.

"That's my history teacher for this semester. I think I'm gonna like his class a lot." She smiled as she again waved to him as her father drove away.

Chad climbed into his car, feeling very satisfied that the day had gone well. He grabbed his cell phone and called Belinda. "I know it's a bit late, but would you mind if I stopped over for a few minutes? I miss you."

"Please do. I'll make us some fresh coffee and whip up a little snack. See ya soon."

Chad's expression turned into a huge smile. "YEAH!" was the only word that came from his lips.

Chapter 4

Feeling good with the way the girls had responded, Chad was eager to tell Belinda all about his first coaching experience.

Belinda greeted him with a warm hug and kiss and led him inside. "Hi honey. Come on in and give me your coat. Why don't you go relax on the sofa and I'll get you something to drink. I baked brownies earlier. Want some?"

"Mmmmm, I could get used to this treatment. The brownies sounds great, but first, maybe a bit more of this," he said and wrapped her in his arms, kissing her.

When they finally came up for air, Belinda took his coat and nudged him in the direction of the couch. She hung his coat in the closet and went to the kitchen, returning almost immediately with a cup of coffee and a plate of brownies. "How did your first practice go? I want to hear all about it." Belinda set the cup and plate down on the end table next to where Chad sat and held the plate of brownies out to him.

"Thanks," he said as he took the plate from her, devouring one brownie before taking another. When he finished the second one, he put the plate down on the table and picked up the cup of coffee. After taking a careful sip of the hot drink, he continued. "It went much better than I could have hoped. The girls were very cooperative."

"Great! I knew they would be. You might be demanding, but you're popular with the kids. Matt'll be able to rest easy knowing they're in good hands." Belinda made a motion to pat herself on the back and said, "Sometimes I have really good ideas!"

Belinda moved behind the couch and put her hands on his shoulders and started to massage his back.

"Mmmmm, talk about being in good hands. That feels great!" Chad moaned and then he finished the coffee and polished off another brownie. "They're small and I'm starved," he said defensively when he saw Belinda's look at the plate of brownies. "Besides, after all the calories I burned tonight, I can finish the whole plate and still be ahead!"

Belinda smiled and quickly reached over him and grabbed a brownie for herself before he did just that. "So, tell me how it went."

"I actually enjoyed it. It was different from being with the kids in a classroom. These kids are there because they want to be, and it's obvious in their enthusiasm. I noticed a couple of girls who have enough talent to play in college if they keep up with the game. I've got to give Matt a lot of credit because, despite all the individual talent I saw tonight, they showed a great team spirit as well."

"So you're confident that you'll be able to handle them," Belinda said, more as a statement than a question.

"I can't say I'd like to do this on a permanent basis, because it's so time consuming, but for a short while I think it'll be fun. They won their first two matches under Matt's guidance. Tomorrow's their third match. They have twelve more matches to play this season, including tomorrow's game."

"What about the playoffs?"

"The twelve games don't include the playoffs, though after seeing how good they are up close, I bet these kids can make it all the way to the title."

"What did you do with them at the practice?"

"I called Matt yesterday for some advice about that. He gave me some suggestions how to run the session. I followed his instructions with a few minor changes. Fortunately, none of the girls compared what I had them do with Matt's routine. Practice ran a bit longer than normal, but I think that was due to my getting acquainted with the girls and none of them seemed to mind." Changing the subject momentarily, he reached for another brownie and said, "Mmmm. Did I mention that these brownies are delicious?"

"Good, I'm glad you like them. So, what time's the match tomorrow? I'll have to brush off my pom-poms."

"Will you wear that short skirt too? And jump up and down? Hehehe, my own personal cheerleader." Chad looked at Belinda with a lecherous wink, delighted with the idea. "The junior varsity match begins at four. The varsity girls play right after that, but not before five. It depends on whether the JV needs two or three games to decide the outcome."

"I'll be there! When you win, I'll bring you back here for a victory celebration," she offered seductively, as she pulled him back, leaned around him and kissed him passionately.

Coming up for air, he whispered, "Now that's a real incentive to win!" He kissed her again.

"Did you have them play a game?" Belinda asked as she moved to sit next to him.

"I sure did. Not only that, but I played with them." Chad snickered as he recalled how the girls had fought to have him on their team. "And after I played on one team, we had to play again so I could give the other team equal time."

"Poor baby, you must be exhausted after all that exercise," Belinda said sympathetically and, maneuvering him to turn around with his back to her, continued with the massage.

"Yeah, I'm exhausted, but ohhhhhhh, that feels wonderful." Chad, enjoying her touch, moaned encouragement when she rubbed a particularly good spot. After a few more minutes, he pulled her around to sit next to him and drew her head to his chest. As she cuddled with him, he stroked her hair with one hand and held her hand with his other hand.

They relaxed together that way for a while until, with her free hand, Belinda reached for the TV remote and turned on a program that they both enjoyed.

It was well after eleven when Belinda noticed Chad try unsuccessfully to stifle a yawn. She could see the exhaustion on his face. "Honey, I could easily cuddle with you all night, but you need some rest before tomorrow. I'd invite you to stay overnight, but we wouldn't get much sleep if you did. Maybe you should go home and get some sleep."

"Yeah, I know you're right." Chad stood and pulled her to her feet so he could take her into his arms. "I love you."

Belinda returned Chad's embrace , and after handing him his coat, said, "I'll see you in the morning. I love you too."

* * *

Classes on Tuesday went smoothly for Chad despite the nervous anxiety in anticipation of that night's games. He was thankful that none of that tension seemed to have spilled over onto the kids, but he realized that he needed some time alone. Instead of eating lunch in the faculty room with his colleagues as he normally did, Chad ate in his classroom and reviewed the list of players on the opposing team for the match. Deeply involved in concentration, he was startled when the phone rang in his room.

"Chad?"

"Yes."

"It's Matt. I hoped I might catch you now. I just wanted to wish you luck. Be wary of Taylor High's Tanya Nicholson. She's tall and a helluva spiker. You'll need two girls at the net to try blocking her shots."

"Thanks, Matt. I appreciate the advice. I'm sure the girls will do their best. Tell me, do you get nervous on the days that you have a match?"

"Are you talking about that pain in your gut? The one that feels like someone's twisting 'em over and over?" Matt was describing Chad's symptoms exactly.

"Yeah, that's it. So it's normal, huh? I've gotta tell you that I am not enjoying this part," Chad said, though he was truly relieved that the feelings he was having seemed to be normal.

"Better you than me today; I've got enough other pains just now, but don't worry. I heard that you were in control, and I know the girls will do well under your guidance. I wish I could be there to watch."

"Hey, I have an idea. I'll make sure that you get a video tape of the game. Maybe you can watch it and give me some tips on what needs work. It'll help you pass the time, and I'd appreciate any advice you can offer."

"That'd be terrific. I admit that I miss the action. I'll still feel a part of the team that way. Thanks for thinking of it. It looks very much like these girls are yours for the rest of the season, my friend. I doubt from the doctor's latest report that I'll be back before the end of the season, except maybe to watch the matches from the stands. Besides, once you take the girls that far, it would be unfair to switch coaches again."

"I'm sorry to hear that, Matt. I'm warning you now that you'd better get yourself together. I didn't take this on as a long-term deal, and these girls are definitely gonna go to the finals. If you aren't back by the end of the season, you'd better be back for the post-season games. While I appreciate your confidence, Matt, this is your gig, not mine. I hope I can get them to be as successful as I'm sure they would've been with your coaching."

"Just give it your best shot and things'll work out fine. Again, good luck tonight. Give me a call when you can on the results."

"You got it," Chad promised. "I'll talk to you later then. Bye."

Although Matt might not have realized it, his call rejuvenated Chad's enthusiasm. By the time school ended, he practically raced to the gym. While two hours still lay ahead before the game, his mind constantly worked and reworked details of the match. Several girls saw him sitting in the bleacher area and joined him.

"Hi, Coach. Nervous?" asked Kara, his most efficient setter.

"Who, me? Why should I be nervous?" Chad chuckled. "Just because it's my first game as a coach and you girls are undefeated, do you think I'm feeling the pressure?" Then he admitted, "I'm nervous as hell."

"Don't worry, Coach. I'll set the ball perfectly for Keri. It'll be high and just a foot from the net."

"And I'll put it away for the kill, Coach," spoke Keri. "Point, set, match!"

"I'm worried a bit about their best player, Tanya. Do you girls know her?"

"Yeah, we played against her last year. She's very good, but we have a plan."

"Oh yeah, and what's that?" asked Chad.

Kara laughed and said, "Sandra's gonna trip, fall under the net, roll and hold onto her ankle so she can't jump up and spike the ball." All of the girls laughed at that, wishing they had some foolproof way to neutralize Tanya.

"I'll be happy if you just keep the ball away from her. She can't beat us if she doesn't touch the ball too often." They sat together offering each other a pep talk for a while, until thirty minutes later when Chad told them it was time to head for the locker room to change. They had to be on the floor for warm-up activities and then sit near the bench to root for the JV girls during their game.

While he waited for the girls to dress, Chad spotted Belinda walking into the gym. He made his way to her and greeted her with a big smile. "This is the cheerleader outfit I've been dreaming about all day?" he asked, looking disappointed at Belinda's choice of outfit. These pants don't look like that short cheerleader skirt I was hoping for," he said with a frown.

"I'm saving the outfit for later, Chad," Belinda whispered. "I was afraid if I wore it now, you wouldn't be able to concentrate on the games. I came now to wish you and the kids good luck. I'll be cheering for you from the bleachers."

"I'll be looking forward to later." Chad and Belinda had agreed to be discreet about their relationship at school, so instead of sharing the kind of kiss they both wanted just then, they settled for a quick squeeze of hands before Belinda went to sit with some of the teachers and parents who had come to watch the game.

As she walked away, Belinda called over her shoulder. "Don't take prisoners. Whomp that other team good."

When if finally came time for the match, Chad stood on the gym floor with the girls circled around him, giving them last minute instructions. Then he sent the six starters to the court, with Sherry Williams, the best server, to start the match. The girls jumped to a quick 5-0 lead and never trailed in the first game, winning 15-6. Making frequent substitutions throughout the second game to give more girls playing time, Chad watched as the girls squandered a six-point lead. Tied at 15, they exchanged serve back and forth several times before Sherry closed out the match. First she scored with a service ace and followed that with a low serve that proved unreturnable, winning the match.

The girls on the court celebrated jubilantly, cheering, and hugging each other. They ran over to Chad, who had lifted his hands to offer "hi-fives" to the girls. Although a few of the girls lifted their hands and slapped his, most of them ignored his raised hands and hugged him too. He gave them a couple of minutes to rejoice, before telling them to line up and offer congratulations to their opponents for a good match.

Only their agreed upon discretion prevented Belinda from running down to the gym floor to give Chad a hug and kiss. Instead, as the bleachers slowly emptied of fans, she sat and waited for him to finish talking with the players, dreaming of the way she'd congratulate him later.

As the girls entered the locker room to change, Chad turned and looked for Belinda. He started climbing up the rows of the bleachers towards her when suddenly, seemingly out of nowhere, Sheila McMasters grabbed his arm and planted a big kiss on his cheek. Startled, Chad shrank back. He glanced around to see if anyone noticed her behavior.

"I just wanted to congratulate you on your first victory as coach, Mr. Peterson."

"Uh, thanks Sheila, but I think a verbal congratulations or handshake would be more appropriate."

"I didn't mean to embarrass you. I'm sorry," she said, walking away towards the exit of the gym, but her tone didn't seem to reveal regret. If anything, Chad would swear that she seemed quite pleased with herself.

"Well, it seems you have an admirer," said Belinda as Chad approached her. "Well, maybe two admirers. I'd offer you a similar congratulations, but I'll be more dignified and wait until we have some privacy."

"There's only one admirer I care about, sweetheart, and it's not that young flirt." Chad shook his head in dismay, hoping that this kid wouldn't become a problem. "Listen, sweetheart, I need to hang around to make sure all the girls leave safely and then we can go to your place. I'm looking forward to that celebration you promised me."

"Do you know how long you'll need now, Chad? Do you want me to wait for you? You seem to be on a high right now. Do you need me to hang on and keep you on the ground?"

"I don't know, maybe half an hour or so? I admit I'm flying high now. It was great to be part of the excitement. Maybe I wasn't playing, but I was on the sidelines, offering encouragement and watching the girls play according to my instructions. I made a few mistakes that almost cost us the second game, but I'm learning."

"How about if I leave for home now, set up some nice relaxing music, fluff up a few pillows by the fireplace, and change into something much more comfortable? When you're finished here, come straight over. I'll be the one lying on the floor with a couple glasses of wine and we'll celebrate your victory properly."

"It sounds perfect. I'll be there as soon as I can. Don't start anything without me," he chuckled.

"Honey, it's no party without you. I love you. I'll see you soon."

While he waited for the girls to come out of the locker room, Chad used his cell phone to make a short but promised call. "Hey, Matt, we did it. Took them down in two straight sets. The girls played together so very well. I'm proud of them."

"Terrific job, Chad. I appreciate the call. Keep the momentum going. I love those girls, and I want to see them win a championship. You loved it too; I can tell from your voice."

"It was exciting. You were missed, though. Get well fast so you can come back."

"I'll do my best. I appreciate your taking the time to call me, Chad. Thanks and have a good night."

"It was my pleasure. Say hi to Maggie for me. Bye."

After making sure that all of the girls hooked up with their parents or had a means of getting home, Chad said goodnight and reminded them that practice started at 6 p.m. Wednesday. "Get a good night's sleep. Tonight's win took a lot of energy and the match on Friday against Hillsdale will be even tougher." He waved to the maintenance staff on his way out of the gym.

When he arrived at Belinda's, she was indeed lying on the floor, wearing a sexy white satin nightie! She lay on a blanket spread before a glowing fireplace and Chad heard the mellow tones of some instrumental music playing. Removing his jacket and tie, he sauntered to her. She held up her hand and, taking his, guided him to the floor beside her.

As he knelt beside her, she said in a very sultry voice, "Gimme a C, gimme an H, gimme an A, gimme a D. Yay Chad! Now you can be bad!"

They both giggled as she ended her cheer and their lips grew nearer. Their first kiss ignited their passion and, taking time to enjoy each other, Belinda made good on her promise to reward him.

A couple of hours later, and quite reluctantly, Chad picked up his clothes and was getting ready to go home when Belinda moved behind him and began pressing kisses to his neck as he tied his shoes. "I wish you didn't have to go," Belinda complained. "But you must be exhausted, so I won't whine about it now."

"How about if you bring an overnight bag to Friday night's match, and afterwards we can go out for a late dinner and then go back to my place? There's no practice scheduled for Saturday, so you can stay overnight and we can sleep in late and spend the entire day together." Chad's enthusiasm for his idea was evident.

"I'd love that, Chad, but I can't guarantee how much sleep we'll actually get," Belinda whispered as she nibbled on his ear.

"You won't hear me complain. I promise you that, Belinda."

Chad climbed into his own bed exactly at midnight. He took a moment to offer his gratitude to God for all the wonderful things in his life. He had a good job, an exciting coaching position and, more importantly, a beautiful woman to love.

Chapter 5

One of the perks (and there weren't many, according to the staff) for the personnel at Emerson Central High was the privilege to use the sports facilities of the school during off-hours. Chad appreciated that it was a lot cheaper than joining a club and was rarely crowded. He regularly took advantage of the pool and tennis courts. At least three times a week, Chad went to school in the early hours of the morning to swim in the pool. When enough of his colleagues showed up, they'd often organize impromptu games of water polo or volleyball. Occasionally he'd meet Jim Morris, the high school swim coach, and they'd swim laps together. No matter what the activity, Chad discovered that it provided a good morning wake-up and the exercise invigorated him for the day ahead. It also established a camaraderie among the staff members, who seldom had time to meet and chat during the day.

Chad woke up on Friday at 5 a.m., looking forward to a morning swim. He dressed in a comfortable pair of old jeans and a sweatshirt, gathered the clothes he'd wear during school, grabbed his swimsuit, goggles, and a towel. He remembered to grab a few pieces of fruit before he left for school. Although there weren't many cars in the parking lot when he got there, he hoped that some of his colleagues would show up soon. He looked forward to any opportunity for some social interaction with adults after all the time he'd been spending with the kids lately. Using his teacher's identification card to open the electronic door, he entered the building and walked down to the locker room. There he met one of the new teachers, Bill Thorndike.

"Morning, Thorny," Chad said, using Bill's nickname. When he had been selected as liason between the teachers and the administrators, a job that experienced staff members shirked, it was Chad who had joked that Bill would become a "thorn" in the side of the administration. Almost immediately, Bill became known as Thorny, and the nickname stuck.

"Mornin', Chad. How's it goin'?"

"Fantastic! I'm ready to kick a little butt. Do we have enough guys this morning to play some volleyball?"

As he walked around the corner of one of the locker areas, Jim Morris chimed in with, "Three are in the pool already, and Leroy and Tony should be here soon. That'll make eight of us."

"Hey, Jim. That's great. Eight's perfect. If everyone's willing, we should be able to get a good workout. I'll meet you in the pool as soon as I change and shove this stuff into my locker."

"Great, I'll set up the net," Bill offered as he left the locker room for the pool area.

Jim was searching for something in his locker and he said to Chad, "Big game tonight, huh? How's it feel to be a successful coach?"

"One win hardly qualifies me as successful," Chad said modestly, "but I'm enjoying it so far. It does take a lot of my free time. And yeah, if we get past Hillsdale's Eagles tonight, we'll be in good position to take the league title. They're not only our school rivals, but they're very good. It's going to prove to be a tough task, but they're good girls, very talented; I'm confident they can do it."

"Hey, Chad," Jim asked, offhandedly changing the subject, "Did Belinda see you kissing that little pixie in the gym the other night? You'd better be very careful there. You can get into a lot of trouble hitting on one of the kids."

"Oh yeah, that's just what I need, some seventeen-year-old booty," barked Chad. "I don't know what got into that girl. She got overly enthusiastic, I guess," he added, hoping that it wasn't becoming an issue.

"Hahaha. I'll tell you, Chad, it sure looked like a lot more than enthusiasm; she seemed to be on the make…and, my friend, you didn't look like you had a problem with it."

"I didn't even realize what was happening until she was all over me. I certainly didn't kiss her!" Chad was becoming agitated, and he tried to explain what had happened. "I was excited about winning the match, and I'd just caught Belinda's eye in the bleachers. I have no interest in…awww, let's just drop it, ok?"

"What's that saying about protesting too much?" Jim teased as he walked out of the locker room toward the pool. When he saw the scowl on Chad's face, he backed off. "Ok, sorry, I didn't mean to touch a nerve."

Chad shrugged his shoulders before jumping into the pool. The others jumped in after him, and they split up into two teams. It was a vigorous match. The guys played to win and held nothing back. After the game, they showered and prepared to face the day. The mood had lightened following the fiercely competitive match and laughter abounded as the joking going on there could definitely be classified as "locker room humor." All in all, it was a good way to start the day. Or so Chad thought until, as they were walking out of the locker room together, the group suddenly halted. Chad grimaced when he noticed Sheila McMasters sitting on the bench.

"Hi, Mr. Peterson," she said brazenly.

Chad's first instinct was to just walk past her without saying a word, but it was getting irritating the way she almost seemed to be stalking him lately. He decided it was time to put an end to it. He stopped to tell her so. The other men just chuckled under their breaths as they continued to walk. "See ya later, Mr. Peterson," several mocked in unison. Jim winked to him and then said, "Good luck tonight."

Chad gave a halfhearted wave goodbye and then turned toward Sheila. "What are you doing here so early and how did you get in? School doesn't start for another hour," he said, obviously annoyed.

"They unlock the doors at seven. I'm waiting for a friend," she lied. The truth was that she knew about Chad's swimming habits and had hoped to catch him alone. When she peeked into the pool area and saw all of the men there, she decided to wait outside in the lobby, hoping for a chance to talk with him. "She and I have work to do in the library. I guess she's not going to show. I'll have to work on it alone."

Chad wasn't buying any of it. He spoke harshly. "This area isn't anywhere near the library. You better go there now before you get into trouble for being here without authorization." He was frustrated to see that she didn't seem to notice his angry tone, or if she did, she chose to ignore it.

"Is it ok if I walk along with you? Nobody will question my being here then."

Unable to think of a good reason to object, Chad nodded and set a quick pace for his room.

"I'd like you to know that I really enjoy your class, Mr. Peterson. You're interesting and funny." She knew that most guys liked flattery, but Mr. Peterson didn't seem to appreciate her efforts.

"That's nice, Sheila, but you've only been in my class for a few days. Having fun is not my primary goal though. I expect all students to participate in class and keep up with the assignments."

"Oh, I intend to do my best for you, Mr. Peterson. But I've been hearing for years that you're a lot of fun. I'm looking forward to having fun with you too."

Wondering if she realized how her comment sounded, Chad quickly corrected her. "If you do fun things in my class, Sheila, it'll be with the other students."

"Oh, yeah. Sure. That's what I meant," she stammered. "He's gonna be one tough nut to crack," she told herself.

Arriving at his room, Chad said, "I'll see you later today in class. Hurry now and get to the library before someone wonders why you're roaming the halls this early." He unlocked his door, turned on the room lights, and walked over to his closet to deposit his gym bag and coat. No sooner had he turned around than he spied Sheila standing in his doorway.

"I've been meaning to ask you, Mr. Peterson. Do you let students do extra credit for your class?"

"Possibly, if they've finished their regularly assigned work and want to earn some extra credit, or sometimes I offer struggling students an opportunity to do some extra work to help improve their grade. Why do you ask?"

"Oh, no special reason. I was just wondering."

It was the manner in which she flipped her long blonde hair to one side when she said it that alarmed Chad. He knew he had to get her out of his room promptly. "Sheila, I have a lot of work to do before class begins. You said you have an assignment to do too, I believe."

Not taking the hint, she said, "I do, but it's not due today."

Chad was trying desperately to find an excuse to rid himself of this pest. Just then, to his relief, Jim Morris walked into his room. Sheila beat a hasty retreat when he entered.

"See ya later, Mr. Peterson."

"Fine," he answered brusquely, relieved that she was finally leaving. Turning then to Jim, Chad said, "Thanks, buddy. I appreciate it. I couldn't get rid of her. She just wouldn't take a hint."

"I noticed as I walked by that she seemed to have you cornered. Is she becoming a problem for you, Chad?"

"It's not a big deal. She's really becoming a pest, but I can handle it. It seems to be a bad case of puppy love. Remember your first crush on a teacher?"

Jim thought for a moment and then sighed longingly,"Oh, yeah, I remember.

It was fourth grade. Miss Hapgood. She was incredible! I just knew I was gonna marry her when I grew up. But this is different, Chad. This girl is a junior and very good looking, and from what I hear, she knows her way around. You better be careful."

"She seems to keep popping up in the most unusual places and situations. I'm being very cool and professional about it. I certainly don't want to encourage her."

"Good luck then. Maybe if you and Belinda were a bit more open about your relationship, this girl would lose interest," Jim suggested.

Trying to end the discussion, Chad said, "I'm sure it'll be ok. I'll be careful not to be alone with her."

Jim laughed. "You were alone with her now when I walked by the room. She outmaneuvered you."

"Thanks again for rescuing me." Chad looked at his watch, picked up some papers, and motioned toward the door of his classroom. "I need to get to the copy machine to run off copies of my research project. I'll talk to you later, ok?"

As he left the room, Jim waved a hand before parting. "Sure. Have a good day."

Chad laughed to himself as he noted that unlike Sheila, Jim was able to take a hint. He began to walk towards the library to make his copies when he realized that he was headed directly to the place Sheila was supposedly working. "I can do this later," he mumbled to himself. Turning in the opposite direction, he headed instead to the faculty room. He had a sudden bright thought. "I wonder if Belinda is here yet."

Chad walked into the faculty room and looked around. Belinda wasn't there but neither was anyone else. The smell of coffee percolating appealed to him, and he decided he'd wait there for a bit. He took one of the Styrofoam cups from the table and helped himself to a cup of coffee. He took a seat on the sofa opposite the door so he'd see Belinda in case she walked past the room rather than coming in, and propped his feet onto one of the nearby chairs. He sipped the hot coffee and mentally reviewed his lesson plans for the day.

It was almost ten minutes later when Belinda entered. "Hi, honey," she said as she spotted him deep in thought. She leaned over and kissed him. "Mmmmm, the coffee smells so good." She walked over to the cupboard, took out her mug, and poured some coffee, leaving room for the milk and sugar he knew she'd add. "You look so engrossed in thought. Am I interrupting something important?"

"Not at all. I was just sitting here waiting for you to arrive." Taking advantage of the fact that they were alone in the room, he got up and wrapped her in a loving embrace.

They shared a quick kiss, and then Belinda moved with him over to the sofa. "How'd the swimming go today?"

"We played a mean game this morning, but it was fun. It gets us all pumped up for the day ahead."

"Hehehe. Come over to my place some morning. I'll get you pumped." She laughed.

Chad laughed at that and raised and lowered his eyebrows suggestively at her. "Did you pack an overnight bag? We're still on for the weekend, right?"

"Yes, absolutely! My bag's in my car. I'm looking forward to some intimate time with you. I sure hope you win the match tonight. I don't want to spend the weekend with a grump."

"I'll do my very best; I promise you that, sweetheart." Chad would have loved to continue the conversation, but just then some of their colleagues came into the room. One thing Chad liked about the morning time in this room was the upbeat mood. He frequently avoided some of the other faculty rooms where the teachers were always whining and complaining. Chad hated being drawn into that sort of negativity.

There were another ten minutes before it would be time to go to their classrooms when Tony Baker came into the faculty room. Tony had a reputation as a prankster and when he and Chad got together they could always be counted on to do a routine where they did impressions of their colleagues, members of the administration, and even some of the students, which never failed to elicit howls of laughter. Today was no exception. As soon as Chad spotted Tony, he began to imitate Rose, the school's somewhat obsessive-compulsive secretary.

"Mr. Baker," Chad began in a falsetto voice, "You are tardy in returning the form I left in your box. I must have it back immediately in triplicate, with your signature on lines twelve and twenty-six. You must initial line six and nine and don't forget to include a complete set of fingerprints at the bottom of each page."

Chad's impression of Rose was right on the mark, but Tony had his own contribution to make as well, with his impression of Helene, an extremely neurotic teacher's aide, who had a very obvious crush on Tony. "Oh, Rose!" he wailed, in a crying voice. "Mr. Baker, did sign that form, and he gave it to me, but it had his signature on it, and his fingerprints, and ooooooooooh, he's so dreamy, I took it home and I keep it under my pillow..."

It was all in good fun, and everyone was laughing when the morning bell rang. There was a mad dash for the door, wishes for a good day exchanged as everyone headed for their own classroom. There were five minutes until the next bell would ring, and the students were also racing about, banging lockers and moving quickly through the halls.

Chad raced to the library and managed to make the copies of his schedule and get to his homeroom just before the period began. After the morning announcements, he went with his students to attend a morning assembly in the auditorium. A young woman whom Chad guessed to be in her mid-20s stirred the entire audience as she spoke on sexual attitudes, behavior, sexually transmitted diseases, and abstinence. "Normally," Chad thought, "kids would tune out this type of speaker but, when she told them her personal story and revealed that she was a victim of AIDS, she had their full attention."

Her final demonstration, intended to show how easily STDs spread, involved audience participation. Each student, upon entering the auditorium, had been given a 3x5 card. In addition, five students were randomly selected and called up to the center of the stage and privately given a number from one to five and instructions. Then she told those in the audience to go and introduce themselves to one of the five people and ask them to shake hands and sign each other's card. They had ten minutes to get as many signatures from the five as they could. When time was up, she told everyone to sit and called the five selected students back up on stage.

She then asked numbers one, two and three to step forward. She explained that Number One was instructed *not* to shake hands with anyone nor to sign their cards. This person represented abstinence. Numbers two and three only shook hands with each other and signed each other's cards but nobody else's. They represented monogamy. Then she asked those in the audience who had the signature of a number four to stand. "Number Four," she said, "had a rubber glove, representing contact with a person using a condom. Your contact with this person reduced but did not eliminate the chance of an STD."

Finally, she called on those who had the signature of Number Five to stand. A large number of students in the audience stood. "This person is HIV positive, and all of those standing now have been exposed to the HIV virus because you had unprotected sex with that person." Then she asked number five how he felt about infecting so many people. She ended the discussion by asking several of those who remained standing if they felt embarrassed, surprised, or angry by being deceived by number five." When she finished, Chad noticed moments of stunned silence among the audience as she thanked them for being attentive.

Chad was impressed. The presentation, which was not meant to frighten them as much as it was to inform, was quite effective. Apparently the kids agreed, as when she finished they gave her a standing ovation.

After lunch, Chad, as usual, greeted his American history students as they entered his classroom. They were all still enthusiastically discussing the earlier assembly, and it took a few minutes to settle them down and get to the business at hand. After taking roll, he began to explain his latest brainchild.

"Your assignment," he began, "is to split into groups of four to five students who will work together. Each group will choose a decade in American history. Then, collectively, your group will research and present the highlights of that decade to this class."

"What kind of stuff do we have to include in this?" asked Travis Fuller.

"That's a good question, and I'll give you some ideas and guidance, but it's up to each group to decide together what's really important and how to present it. I'll sit with each group once you begin. You'll need my approval for the areas you've chosen."

"Do you mean this is a group research paper?" asked Nicki Thompson.

"No, this is not a paper at all. Let me explain. Someone in the group might decide to investigate the fashions of the period. You might even ask your parents and grandparents if they have any samples which you can wear to class or display—with explanations. I'm sure someone in each group will choose the music of the decade; find examples to bring in and play for us. Then there are possible areas such as foods, news events, politics, and sports."

Chad was pleased with their excitement, and while he didn't want to curb their enthusiasm, he had to be sure that the teamwork aspect of this project was clear. "The ability to work together is an important part of this exercise. I want to make it clear, though, that while you may choose the people you want to work with, everyone in the class must be included and no group can have more than five students." He knew that while group efforts often challenged their problem-solving skills and taught them to work as a team, there was the danger that the less popular kids might not be included. Chad hoped that this particular group of kids would see to it that noone was excluded.

"Which decades can we choose from, Mr. Peterson?" asked Tim O'Reilly. "Are we talking modern times or periods like the Great Depression?"

"That's another good question, Tim. Let's start from the 1920s. That gives a choice of eight decades. I suggest that you choose the decade you prefer and try to form a group for that decade."

Chad gave his students a few minutes to process the options he'd just offered among themselves. The discussion was lively, but remained under control, until suddenly Sheila burst out with a declaration decibels above the others, "I'm doing the 60s!"

Before anyone could react, she began to sing, "It was an itsy bitsy teeny weenie, yellow polka dot bikini."

The boys broke out in a chorus of wolf whistles.

"Mr. Peterson," Sheila asked flirtatiously, "You did say we could model outfits of that decade, right?"

"Everything is subject to my approval, Sheila," he quickly qualified, realizing the mayhem it would cause if he allowed her to model a bikini in class.

"Oh, believe me, Mr. P., if Sheila wears an itsy bitsy bikini, you'll approve," joked Travis, adding an exaggerated wink for emphasis.

Sheila stood and took a bow. It was obvious that she thrived on being the center of attention.

Trying to regain control, Chad said, "As soon as you've chosen your decades and organized the groups, the first thing you'll need to do is to divide up the research areas of each decade. You might want to organize a scavenger hunt to find things you might need or want for the presentation. You can include records, videos, or any kind of visual aids that accurately reflect the time. Remember, though, that you must do much more than just put up posters or displays. You must *teach* the decade to others."

"Excuse me, Mr. P.," asked Alison, "what kind of records do you mean?"

Chad laughed when he realized what he'd inadvertently said. "I meant CDs, not records. Although if you're looking for music from before the 1980s you'll most likely find it on records. In order to play those, you'll need a turntable."

When his explanation met a series of "huh's?" Chad tried to clarify. "A record player—ask your parents if they have one."

Eager to get to work on what sounded like a fun assignment, Travis asked, "Can more than one group do the same decade, Mr. Peterson? And what else do we need to do?"

"I'm going to limit one group to a decade. That way everyone will learn more about the recent history of our country. As you progress, I'll add more details. I don't want to overwhelm you right now. I'll tell you now that each group must make up ten questions, which will be passed out to each of your classmates before each presentation. The presentations should lead them to accurate answers to all of the questions. They must be more than just "yes" or "no" type questions, but we'll get into the specifics of that later."

For the rest of the period, Chad let the kids work on choosing their groups and decades. He was pleased to see that everyone was included. He then asked each group to outline what they knew about their chosen time period and list what areas they preferred to investigate. Finally, he explained that the next couple of classes would be devoted to using both Internet and library resources to further their research.

At the end of the school day, Chad had a couple of hours before the volleyball match. He went to the faculty lounge looking for Belinda.

"Hi, honey," she said as she greeted him with a hug. "I thought you'd be secluded someplace brooding about the match. Anything wrong?"

"No, I'm as prepared as I can be and the girls are psyched. There's nothing more I have to do for the next couple of hours. Even though we made plans for a late night dinner, I thought I could persuade you to go for a cup of coffee." In case she needed some convincing, he added, "if you agree, maybe I can be convinced to spring for some pie too."

"Sure, I'd love to do that. I'll even drive. Let me grab my purse. Do you want to go to Stranahan's?"

"That's fine with me." As they walked to the car, he confessed, "I have a knot in my stomach from the anxiety. I'm glad this is only a temporary job. The stress is too much." They got into the car. Chad squeezed Belinda's hand and told her, "I could really use this time to relax before the match—with you."

Belinda took her hand back to maneuver the car out of the parking lot. Once she turned onto the street, she reached for his hand, squeezed it back and said, "I'm glad if I can be of some help, Chad. So sit back and relax; we'll be there in a couple of minutes."

They went into the restaurant and sat in a booth, waiting for the waitress, Marla, to take their orders. Marla had grown up in the house next to Chad's family, and they'd been good friends since their childhood. Whenever Chad came into the restaurant, Marla made sure she'd be the one to wait on him.

She greeted Chad and Belinda warmly. "Hey there! How ya doin' today? You have a good day?"

Belinda answered, "It's been a good day so far, Marla. How are you? How are your boys doing?"

"I'm good, thanks. As for the boys, they're typical two-year-olds. Having twins is double trouble, but I love 'em beyond words. What'll you have today?"

Chad tilted his head in Belinda's direction, to let her answer first. "Mmmm," she said, smiling in anticipation. "I know exactly what I want." She turned to Marla and said, "Apple pie á la mode, please," and before Marla could ask, she added, "Chocolate ice cream and a cup of hot tea."

Marla scribbled the order on her pad and then turned to Chad questioningly, "And for you, sir?"

"I'd like a piece of lemon meringue pie and a cup of coffee."

"Coming right up. Be right back."

Belinda didn't know if Chad wanted to talk about the upcoming match or pretend it wasn't happening, so she let him lead the conversation.

"I had a really good day today. I gave a new assignment, a group project, to the kids and they really responded positively. That always makes me feel good. How was your day, sweetheart?" he asked.

"I'm glad it went well for you. I want to hear all about it, but I have to tell you something that happened today first, ok?"

"Sure, tell me," Chad encouraged.

"You know Robbie Simpson, right?"

"Isn't he the kid you're always bragging about? Didn't he make the backdrops for the school play?"

"Yeah, that's the one. Robbie's my most promising artist. A few months ago, I helped him assemble a portfolio for his application to Pratt." At Chad's questioning look, she explained. "Pratt is the leading art school in New York City."

"Okay." Chad acknowledged the explanation. "Right, I knew that."

Belinda continued. "Well, today Robbie came into class bursting with excitement. When I asked him what had happened, he showed me the letter of acceptance he received yesterday from Pratt. And then, get this, he hugged me! All during class he kept thanking me for my help and encouragement. It's so rewarding when one of the kids not only succeeds, but actually thanks you for your efforts."

"That's great, sweetheart. Congratulations." Chad reached for her hand and squeezed it. "I'm sure you deserve a lot of credit for his success. Even with his talent, you were the one who helped him recognize his potential." Chad could see that she was bursting with excitement and pride. "You have a positive effect on a lot of kids, Belinda. Look how many of our graduates attend art schools or major in photography or graphics. You've created a very successful program."

Belinda was touched by Chad's testimonial and his obvious sincerity. "Thank you. It means a lot to me to hear you say that." She returned the squeeze before continuing. "I joked with him that, when he's famous someday, he'll owe me one of his works as payment. Chad, he's so talented. I'm so happy for him."

"I agree that it's a very special feeling as a teacher to see a student succeed. It's also a big ego boost when they're appreciative of our efforts."

Marla brought their desserts. "I made sure you got extra big pieces," she said. "Gotta fatten you up a bit, Chad. You're still as skinny as you were when we were kids and we used to take baths together," she teased.

Belinda laughed and Chad's face flushed. "If you're trying to embarrass me, Marla, it's working." Then he tried to return the zing with, "We were what, fourteen or fifteen years old at the time?"

"In your dreams," Marla howled. "Enjoy the pie. Much as I'd like to sit and join you, I've got to bus those tables before the boss gets on my case." She walked away with a wave.

"Thanks, Marla," they said in unison while she was still near enough to hear.

When they'd finished their pie and drinks, Chad caught Marla's attention by making a scribbling motion in the air, indicating that they were ready for the bill. Marla came over right away and tore the bill off the pad in her pocket. Chad and Belinda thanked her again before he dropped a couple of bills on the table to cover the tab and his usually generous tip for Marla.

On the way to the car, Chad wrapped his arm around Belinda's shoulders as he directed their conversation toward their plans for the weekend. "We're on for tonight after the game, right?"

Her arm instinctively wrapped around Chad's waist. She looked up at him with a smile, "Count on it, babe. The whole weekend too. I've been looking forward to this all week."

"Me too. What do you say before I have to be back at school, we stop and pick up a movie for later?"

"Mmmm! Something nice and romantic sounds great."

Still in a playful mood, Chad said, "I was thinking more of a horror movie. You know, something with lots of blood and guts. Maybe a vampire movie!" When he saw Belinda cringe at that, he added, "There's a method to my madness. If we get a really scary movie, you get all squeamish and then that makes you cling to me…hehehe!"

"We can compromise," Belinda said with a wicked smile. "We'll pick a romantic movie, and I'll pretend to be a vampire. I can suck your neck…mmm, maybe I'll leave a hickey!" Belinda giggled and Chad pulled her closer to him and tickled her. She retaliated by pinching him at his waist and threatened playfully, "That'll be fun to explain to the girls on the team next week."

Chad let out a sidesplitting yelp, as if he were a helpless victim. A couple of nearby pedestrians looked at him as if he were deranged. Belinda's laughter was intense and she tried to escape from the tickling that was quickly getting out of hand. Chad stopped tickling and managed to grab her hand before she escaped. He pressed a kiss to her palm.

They reached the car and, before getting in, Chad turned serious for a minute. He took her face in his hands and pressed a tender kiss to her lips and said, "Sweetheart, thanks for distracting me. You're so much fun. I love you."

They drove to the video store and miraculously found a place to park right in front. They went in and, since time was so limited, they settled quickly on a romantic video. Belinda gloated as they walked out of the store. "I'm glad you're learning early in our relationship that I'm always right," she joked.

"I've learned something more important than that, sweetheart. I've learned that when I give in, I win." Chad smiled and gave her a lustful look.

* * *

The volleyball match proved as difficult as Chad had anticipated. Neither team ever led by more than two points throughout the first game. The score was 11-13 in their opponent's favor. During a timeout he called the girls over for some direction. Chad reminded them of their strengths and tried to point out some of the weak spots he'd observed. Specifically, he drew their attention to the fact that the girls from Hillsdale seemed to be favoring one side of the court in their attempts to neutralize Keri's cross-court spikes.

Chad tried to set up a plan to take advantage of this tendency. "Kara, I want you to set the ball toward Keri just like you normally do. Keri, you jump high as if you're going to spike it, but instead I want you to set the ball over to Leah. Turning to Leah, he said, "They're favoring the right side of the court. There's an opening on the other side. After Keri sets the ball for you, either spike or dink it over the net to the open side. Alternate this maneuver with what you've been doing until now. That should confuse them and give you a chance to pull ahead."

The girls slapped hands and charged back onto the court just as the timeout period ended. The strategy worked perfectly. From that point on through the rest of the match, Hillsdale's girls were confused. They couldn't concentrate only on Keri's spikes anymore, which made them more devastating. Leah's opposite side attacks proved just as awesome.

The match remained close, but after three long games, the girls from Emerson High, under Chad's coaching, remained undefeated and took over sole possession of first place in the league.

Chad's reaction was as enthusiastic as the girls', and he was right in the midst of them as they all exchanged high fives and hugs. He hadn't even noticed until after he had hugged her that Sheila, in her cheerleader's outfit, had run onto the court too. At that moment, the local video station interviewed the team's co-captains, Keri and Kara, who were quick to give credit to their coach for spotting a weakness in their adversary's play. Nobody noticed at the time that the cameraman had caught Chad in the background joyfully celebrating the victory.

As if the victory didn't provide enough of a high, Chad saw Belinda climbing down from the bleachers. He watched her as she crossed the court to where he stood with the team and quickly extricated himself from the girls so he could meet her.

When she reached Chad's side, she exclaimed, "You did it! That was so exciting. I'm surprised I didn't lose my voice from cheering so much and my hands hurt from clapping."

Chad took her hands into his. "I'll have to find some way to soothe the hurt then, won't I? Maybe a massage with some oil would do the trick. I bet there are other parts that ache too," he whispered suggestively. Chad was totally focused on Belinda now and he didn't see Sheila standing at the side watching them.

Belinda giggled. "Oh God, my own private masseur. Let's get out of here."

"Wait, I'm hungry. What about dinner? We have to go out and celebrate."

"Go out? You offer me a massage—with oil—and then say you want to go out?" Belinda asked incredulously. Then her tone turned seductive, "The thought of having oil massaged all over my body sounds soooo tempting I could skip dinner and go straight for the dessert."

Just then Chad's stomach grumbled, and Belinda got the message. "Okay, okay, I'll be good. This is your night, honey. I'll try to be patient. Where would you like to go for dinner? Have you ever heard of fast food? I think they call it that because you can get it fast—and eat it fast—and go home fast."

Chad leaned his head toward hers and laughed. "I'm sensing a pattern here. Are you trying to rush me? I thought we'd go some place with atmosphere and class. What do you think about driving to Middleton and eating at Rosario's? Are you in the mood for something Italian?"

Belinda groaned with impatience, but she put on her best smile and reminded herself that Chad deserved a celebration of his victory. She squeezed his hand before saying, "Sure, I love their lasagna. That sounds perfect to me."

When they arrived thirty minutes later, they were seated almost immediately in a secluded corner where they could talk without distractions. Belinda let the atmosphere wash over her. "This place is so romantic, Chad." She looked around, admiring the ambience of the room. "Wow, checkered table cloths, linen napkins, the candles in the little red jars gives everything a pinkish kind of glow...and the violin music is really a nice touch."

Chad held her hand while they waited to place their order. When he ordered a bottle of wine, Belinda could feel her body heat rise. Looking directly into his brown eyes, she murmured, "You know I love you, Chad."

Chad squeezed her hand in his and, looking into her eyes, he responded, "And I love everything about you, Belinda."

The wine was poured and they both tasted it and smiled approvingly to the waiter. After they'd finished their appetizer, Chad excused himself under the pretense of visiting the men's room. His real motivation became apparent a few minutes after his return when the violin player moved over to their table and played a special request just for them. After a few notes, Belinda could feel a twinge in the region of her heart as she recognized the song as "My Love" by Paul McCartney.

After dinner, as they made their way back to the car, Belinda thanked Chad for one of the most romantic and enjoyable evenings she'd ever had. He responded with a line from an old Carpenter's song. "We've only just begun," he crooned as he got behind the wheel of his car heading for home with the woman he loved.

Belinda was soon to discover that the romantic evening had indeed only just begun. Once inside Chad's apartment, he invited her to have a seat on the couch for a few minutes while he made some preparations in the other room. She had some preparations of her own to make, as she picked up her bag, which Chad had retrieved from the trunk of his car, and went into the bathroom and changed into something more comfortable.

She stepped out of the bathroom and almost bumped into Chad, who was coming back into the room. Chad stared at her open-mouthed for a long moment, before telling her how beautiful she looked. His comment, muttered almost under his breath, "I sure hope you're comfortable, cause all of a sudden I'm not!" broke the tension that had been created when he saw her in the filmy gown, or robe, or whatever it was—Chad wasn't sure, he just knew he liked it. They both began to laugh.

Chad took her into his arms. She turned her face up to his and their lips met in what began as a tender kiss and started to build into a lot more. Chad had made a promise he intended to keep and he stopped the embrace before it went any further. Belinda had a puzzled look on her face as he pulled back and all but pushed her onto the couch and then excused himself and went to the bathroom.

Understanding dawned on her face when he returned with a bottle of baby oil in one hand and a towel in the other. "I didn't forget, sweetheart. I'm gonna start with your feet and work my way up. How does that sound?"

"Heavenly! Mmmmmmmmm, I knew being patient would pay off."

From the expression on Belinda's face, Chad knew he'd scored some major points for remembering his promise of a massage. They had a whole weekend before them, and he wanted to show Belinda how much he cherished her.

Before beginning the massage, Chad dimmed the lights in the room and lit a few candles. He put the DVD they'd picked up earlier into the player and moved to sit at the opposite end of the sofa from where Belinda sat. He spread the towel over his lap and invited her to, "Put your feet on my lap, sweetheart. We'll cuddle later but for now I want to pamper you. You've been my most supportive fan these past few days and I want to show my appreciation."

"Mmmm! You're the best," she moaned as he applied the first touches of oil to her feet. He continued to massage her feet, occasionally making forays a bit higher, as they watched the movie.

After a while, she moved beside him so that he could hold her in his arms as they watched the end of the movie. They exchanged frequent kisses and, when the movie ended, they talked of how their relationship had blossomed since they first realized that they were meant to be together.

Chad waved his still greasy hands and said, "I think I'll take a shower."

Belinda wiggled her still greasy feet in the air laughing and said, "Want some company?"

Chad didn't hesitate to accept her offer; in fact, he scooped her up off the couch and gallantly carried her towards the bathroom. Belinda wrapped her arms around his neck and kissed his cheek. She began to express her admiration for his "manly gesture" and that sent them both into a fit of giggles.

They hit a little snag when Chad found he couldn't maneuver through the bathroom door with Belinda in his arms. He tried to turn every which way and was unable to get through the doorway without banging Belinda into the wall. When she realized what was happening, she started to giggle harder. Chad's oh-so-suave move was spoiled when he started to drop her.

Belinda stopped giggling as her feet touched the floor. She looked directly into Chad's eyes as she pushed the straps of her negligee off her shoulders and let the wispy material fall to the floor. She heard Chad's quick intake of breath as he watched her, and feeling very sexy and powerful, she reached to pull off his shirt.

Chad stood there and let Belinda take the lead, which she did willingly. Kisses followed the path her hands took as they undid the buttons on his shirt and pushed it off his shoulders. While she worked on opening his belt and pants, Chad reached inside the shower and turned on the water, so it would have a chance to adjust before they got in.

The bathroom quickly steamed up, but neither could say if it was a result of the steaming water or from the passion between them.

They were still joined in an embrace as they carefully stepped into the shower. Time seemed to move very slowly as they moved under the hot rush of water. Chad reached for the soap first and, after lathering up his hands, began to spread the latter on Belinda's shoulders, slowly moving lower. Chad offered the soap to Belinda, suggesting she might want to return the favor.

There was a distinct twinkle in her eye when she took the soap and put it back in the soap dish. Chad had a puzzled look which very quickly disappeared when she pulled him close and began to lather him up with her body. Their bodies were slick as they rubbed together, and both were breathing heavily as their lips met. The spray of the shower was surprisingly erotic. They continued moving against each other, their hands caressing, sliding, and gliding across their slippery skin. Belinda felt Chad's hardness press against her and he could feel the heat of her body. Chad moved his hands to cup her face, being careful to block the water from spraying her in the face and he kissed her again. But this kiss was different than the others. This kiss was full of urgency. They both felt the change and, in an unspoken, yet coordinated move, they pulled apart far enough to let the water rinse off the leftover lather. They stepped out of the shower and Chad handed Belinda a towel, and then he took one for himself.

They toweled each other off and then, dropping the towels to the floor, Chad led Belinda into the bedroom.

Belinda loved it that they could walk around naked, so unselfconsciously, and she voiced the sentiment. "I love it that we can be together this way." She reached out a hand and stroked his chest. "I love you."

Chad took her hand in his and raised it to his mouth and pressed a kiss into her palm. He watched her eyes glaze over in excitement. He sensed her desire but wanted to prolong their enjoyment. "I know we just cleaned off, sweetheart, but I promised you a full body massage and I'm gonna make good on that promise. So roll over now and I'll go get the oil and finish where I left off."

This was one of those offers that was too good to pass up and Belinda happily obliged. The oil felt wonderful, but Chad's touch was heavenly. She wasn't sure if she was becoming more relaxed or more aroused by his attention to her body, but it definitely made her want him even more.

When she finally rolled over onto her back, he leaned forward and kissed her gently, first on the tip of her nose, then on each eyelid before moving to her lips. The urgency that had begun earlier was back, and he didn't want to hold back any longer. His hands and mouth brought her to a peak of excitement. Her hands did the same for him. They loved each other vigorously, changing positions often to access different places from various angles. Except for repeated murmurs of their love, they moved silently and instinctively, each knowing the best ways to please the other. Belinda reached for Chad and, pulling him on top of her, she urged him to come inside. He moved over her slowly and felt himself glide easily inside her as their bodies created a rhythm of their own. When they were spent, they lay together, legs entwined, face-to-face, frequently exchanging kisses and whispering endearments and promises of forever.

"I love you so very much, Chad."

"You're wonderful; I love you too," he responded. "You make me so happy."

Happy and sated, they drifted off to sleep in each other's arms.

The next morning, they awoke together and automatically moved again into each other's arms. Belinda moved astride his hips and lowered herself onto him. Chad's response was immediate and very obvious.

Leaning forward, Belinda pressed her breasts to his chest and placed kisses all over his face and lips. She rode him until they climaxed simultaneously.

Trying to catch their breath, they lay side by side. Chad looked into Belinda's eyes and said, "I love you, but if we keep this up, I have to wonder if I'll survive the entire weekend."

"I can promise to try to keep it up, darling," Belinda laughed, "pun intended. What can I say? When it comes to you, I'm insatiable," she retorted with no hint of an apology. "We'll just see if you can keep up with me." She laughed at her pun.

"I'll do the best I can, sweetheart." He laughed. "You inspire me."

When they finally managed to get out of bed, they worked together in the kitchen to prepare a hearty breakfast. After all the strenuous exercise, they needed sustenance.

After breakfast, they discussed a few options and decided to go cross-country skiing. Both loved the outdoors in winter. The crisp, clean air and the quiet solitude of the woods offered a strong appeal. Chad collected his skis and a few other things he'd need and brought them out to the car. "Wilderness Lodge will be the perfect place to spend the day, Belinda. We'll ski a few miles along some of the trails, and then sit by the warm fireplace with some hot chocolate."

Belinda was enthusiastic about the plans, and when they stopped at her apartment for her to get some warmer clothes and her skis, she hurried to get her things together. Eager to get going, she asked, "Chad, can you please wax my skis while I get organized? The skis are in the closet in the hall, and the wax is in the kitchen drawer next to the sink."

"I'm glad to help, my love. It'll take me a few minutes and then as soon as you're ready we'll be on our way. We should be at the lodge in about an hour." He walked over to the window. "The sun is shining brilliantly; it's making the snow glisten. It should be beautiful on the trails. We should be able to get in a few hours of good skiing."

When they arrived, Chad paid the entrance fee and followed as Belinda led the way along one of the trails marked "moderately difficult." Even though there were a lot of cars in the parking lot, once they moved into the woods, they seldom saw other skiers. The sun shone through the barren trees and the only sound was the whoosh of the skis on the snow.

"Chad, this was a terrific idea. I love it out here," Belinda said as they came to the top of a small hill. "You ready to shuss down this grade, or are you a chicken?" she teased, making a clucking noise.

He accepted her challenge and, without hesitating, skied past her and shouted, "I think I can handle it without too much trouble." He patted her butt as he passed, calling, "See you at the bottom. And what a bottom you have."

"Oooh, now you're gonna get it. I'm gonna get you!" She took off after him.

Chad just laughed as he traversed the hill, and he could hear Belinda yell, "Wheeeee!"

Almost three hours later they found their way back to the lodge. While they weren't cold, the inside of the lodge with its roaring fire felt good. They lingered there for another hour before packing their skis onto his car and heading back to Chad's apartment.

On the way home, Belinda said, "Honey, this has been the most wonderful weekend so far. I look forward to having you to myself for the rest."

"I love you, sweetheart. You know it's been fun for me too. Tonight for dinner we'll grill some steaks on my George Foreman grill, steam some veggies, and make a couple of baked potatoes. How does that sound?"

"Mmmm! Positively marvelous."

"And tonight we'll indulge in a banana split."

"You're gonna take me to the Dairy Queen?" she asked.

"Well, not exactly. I was thinking of putting whipped cream all over your body. And maybe a couple of marachino cherries on two strategic spots."

"I thought you said a banana split!" she began and then realized his intent. "And you'll provide the banana too, I suppose," she giggled.

Giving her a lustful wink, Chad smirked, "Of course, my dear. And then we'll slowly lick it off each other."

They made dinner working side by side in Chad's small kitchen, something which gave them excuses to "bump" into each other often. They took advantage of the closeness to touch frequently, exchanging kisses and squeezes. They talked about many things, never seeming to run out of things to discuss.

Satisfied from their meal and exhausted from the day's and night's exotic activity, they fell asleep quickly in each other's arms and they both slept late the next morning. They had a leisurely breakfast and read the Sunday paper together. Belinda noticed some sales at the mall, so they spent Sunday afternoon shopping.

They both had some work to do before Monday's classes and agreed that if they stayed together, they'd never get it done, so Chad dropped Belinda off at her place on the way home from the mall. He came in for a little while. They took their time saying goodbye and thanking each other for a wonderful weekend. They promised each other that they'd share many more such times together and, despite their good intentions, it was hard to tear himself away.

Chapter 6

Sheila met Cindy in the lunchroom. They hadn't talked for several days since Cindy had been absent from school with the flu and was still forbidden to use the phone.

"Hey Cin, snu? You feelin' better?" Sheila dropped her books onto the table where Cindy was sitting and plopped herself down on the chair opposite her friend.

"Hi, Sheila. Not much. I was goin' nuts being cooped up at home. My mom nags at me 24/7. If I have to go straight home after school every day for a month, I'm gonna die. Just these few days home sick was bad enough."

"Your dad getting on your case too?" Sheila asked, uncharacteristically sympathetic.

"Yeah. He keeps harping on how disappointed he is in me for what I did. I can handle his anger. I just don't want to hear how much I let him down."

"It's too bad, Cin. I know the party was my idea, but I hope you're not blaming me for this. You didn't have to agree to have the party."

Cindy groaned inwardly. This was the Sheila she knew, and despite herself, loved. She said to herself, "Why did I even think for a minute that Sheila would show some real compassion for my predicament. Sheila only cares about Sheila, but she's still my best friend." Keeping that last thought in mind, Cindy tried to play down her situation. "Things'll calm down. My dad always spazzes out when something goes wrong. I'll let a few more days pass before I begin whining and pleading. If he follows his usual pattern, he'll first let me use the phone to talk with friends. Then he'll eventually let me go to some school events where there are large crowds. As long as I let him drop me off and pick me up, I can maybe go to some of the school games or events, even though he'll give me some ridiculous curfew."

"Hey, maybe you can meet me at one of the volleyball games when he gives you permission. As a cheerleader, I've been enjoying them even more now that Mr. Peterson is coach."

"How's it going in his class?" Cindy asked, hoping to catch up on the latest.

Sheila didn't disappoint. "Terrific! It didn't take me long to get his attention. I keep finding all kinds of excuses to get up close to him. I make him think I'm helpless, and he's always so sweet; when the class is working independently, he'll come over and see if he can help me. The other day I kept going up to him for advice on a project we're doing and bent over to make sure he got a good view. He pretended not to notice, playing it really cool."

"Geez, Sheila. You've got it really bad for him, huh?"

"I've been trying to find some way to be alone with him. I almost managed it the other morning but Mr. Morris interrupted," Sheila whined.

"God, what were you gonna do?" Although Cindy thought nothing Sheila could do would surprise her, this seemed to be serious stuff. Chad Peterson was really hot and if Sheila was determined, Cindy had no doubt that she would try to get him.

"Nothing yet, of course. I have to take it slowly. I was just flirting. Oh, and I asked him if I could do some extra credit."

"Hahaha! I know what kind of extra credit you'd like to do. Did he know what you had in mind?" Cindy could only imagine the scenario Sheila was painting.

"No, I doubt it. Like I said, we were interrupted. But next time, watch out!"

"You know he'd get into so much trouble if he fooled around with you, Sheila. He'd be risking his career."

"I don't want him to risk anything, but he's sooooo hot. If I get the chance, you gotta know I'm gonna go for it. Don't worry, I'll be very discreet. The first thing is to get him to notice me." Sheila had a dreamy look in her eyes, then suddenly remembered something. "Hey, on Friday night I ran out onto the court after the girls won the volleyball match and he *hugged* me! The hug lasted just a second more than it had to—that tells me he's interested. Anyway, it was a start."

"I think you're imagining things." Cindy found it a bit hard to believe that Chad would have hugged her like that in front of people.

"Oh, no. If you'd been there you'd have seen how he hugged me. In any case, you know me when I set my mind on something. I've definitely set my sights on Chad."

"Ooooh. So he's Chad now, huh?" Cindy teased.

Sheila winked at her friend and suddenly jumped up from her seat and said, "Watch this."

Chad had just entered the cafeteria. He got into line with some of the kids and stood there chatting amiably with them as they waited to buy their lunch. He wasn't like a lot of teachers who cut in front of the line and he enjoyed the opportunity to talk informally with the kids. He was listening to one of the kids talk about a problem he was having in one of his classes when he felt a nudge at his arm and turned to see Sheila standing there.

"Hi, Mr. Peterson," she said with her usual flirtatious tone.

"Hello, Sheila," he answered, trying to keep the exasperation out of his voice. "Excuse me, but I was in the middle of a conversation with Andy." He turned to find that Andy had moved on.

"I guess Andy figured you'd finished." Sheila shrugged her shoulders, dismissing anything that didn't involve her. "So, Mr. Peterson, I have a little problem. I was hoping maybe you could help me out."

"I'm always a sucker for a kid in need," Chad muttered to himself, and despite his growing impatience with Sheila, he responded caringly, "What's the matter? I'll try to help if I can."

She reached out and put her hand on his arm. "Thank you so much. I knew I could count on you."

"So what seems to be your problem?" he prodded, letting her hand drop as he moved back to break the contact.

"I forgot my lunch at home," she whined, "and I'm really hungry. Could you lend me some money to buy something to eat? Fifty cents is all I need. I promise. I'll pay you back tomorrow."

Torn between amusement and annoyance, Chad chose to find her whole act funny. "Sure, Sheila, we can't have you starving all afternoon." He reached into his pocket and pulled out some change. He picked out two quarters and dropped them into her outstretched hand. As she closed her hand around the money, he said in his usual joking manner, "I hope you're aware that I charge interest. The interest is compounded every fifteen minutes." Looking at his watch he pretended to do some quick calculations, and then he told her, "By this time tomorrow, I figure you should owe me about twenty-two dollars."

Sheila laughed and reached for his arm again. He carefully side-stepped her, and she missed her target. "Oh, Mr. Peterson, you have such a wonderful sense of humor." She pretended that she was waving her hand in amusement. "But don't you worry, I'll make it worth your while." Her voice dripped with innuendo as she noticed that the other kids in the line near them were hanging on her every word.

The kids who heard her hooted. One of the boys spoke up and teased, "You'll have to find some way to work off that debt, Sheila."

Sheila was quick to take advantage of that remark. "Maybe I can do some odd jobs to repay you," she said flirtatiously, still laying it on for the audience. Before Chad realized her intent, she patted his shoulder and said, "Thanks again. I'll see that you get your money's worth."

Chad didn't much like the direction the conversation had taken. He was about to put a stop to it when, apparently, Sheila realized that she'd pushed this as far as she could and quickly made herself scarce, running across the room to her friend.

"Did you see how happy he was to see me?" Sheila said when she reached Cindy. "Look what he gave me." She showed the two quarters in the palm of her hand. "I'm gonna go buy some ice cream or something…Chad's treat!" She walked over to the snack bar and bought a slush.

When Sheila returned to the table, Tim was sitting with Cindy. "Hey there, Tim. Sup? You makin' a move on my friend, Cindy?"

"I sure hope so," he said as he wrapped his arm around Cindy. "And what've you been up to lately?"

"Nothin' much. I've just been working hard on school stuff."

"Yeah, I noticed your school stuff. Is Mr. Peterson your project? Or are you just workin' on being a teacher's pet?"

"Oh, Tim, mind your own business. You just worry about keeping Cindy happy."

"You better be careful, girl. Play with fire and you'll get burned," Tim warned, pulling Cindy closer to him, showing Sheila that he was taking care of Cindy just fine.

"I don't have to be careful; I have to be good," Sheila retorted with a devilish smile." She got up and, nodding her head towards Cindy, uttered an old cliché. "So, you both be good too and remember, don't do anything I wouldn't do, and if you do, name it after me." Then she sauntered out of the cafeteria and into the student lounge.

"That leaves us a lot of leeway, huh?" Tim joked to Cindy when Sheila had gone.

In the lounge Sheila joined a group of girls who were sitting around a table talking about boys, mostly about who was having sex. When one of her friends, Becky Finch, noticed Rod Lawson standing near the juice and soft drink machines, she said to Sheila, "I hear you got lucky at Cindy's place during the party. Or should I say all the kids there heard the moans and groans," she laughed. "Is it true what they say about Rod?"

"He was good for a one-time fling, I guess. He's like most boys, though. 'Wham, bam, thank you ma'am', but yeah," Sheila snickered, "his nickname 'Mr. Big' suits him."

"I wouldn't mind a good 'wham' with him," Becky said. "but I thought you had your hooks on him."

"Nah. I need someone more mature. I want someone who knows how to take his time and treat a woman right. Rod was okay, but if you want leftovers, help yourself. He's all yours. Go for it, Becky."

"Hehehe, I'm on it." Becky didn't hesitate, and all of the girls giggled as she walked over to talk with him. The laughter increased when, a few minutes later, Becky strutted by them with a big grin on her face and holding onto Rod's arm. She winked at Sheila as they passed.

Sheila looked at her watch and shot up from the table. "I almost lost track of the time. I have to get to history class, and there's barely time for me to get to the bathroom. I gotta fix myself up a bit. See you later, girls." She bolted from the lounge.

Chad was closing the door when Sheila squeezed her way through. "Thanks for waiting for me, Mr. P.," she said breathlessly as she took her seat.

Chad moved in front of his desk and began to explain the day's activity. "For the first forty minutes or so, I want you to break up into your groups and discuss what you've accomplished on the project so far. I'll visit briefly with each group to listen and ask questions, and maybe offer some suggestions. In addition to the worksheets I'll pass out in a minute, I'd like each group to prepare, on a separate page, the following details which I'll collect when I sit with you. I want the name of the group leader. If you haven't chosen one yet, please do so first. I also want you to list the area each group member will contribute and what that person plans to do."

Several students raised their hands to ask questions before he dismissed them to their groups. Following that, he passed out the worksheet that he wanted completed and then let them work.

The first group that he sat with planned to cover the 1920s. He was impressed with some of the ideas that he heard. Cassie Thompson intended to have her mother help her create a dress from the period. Susan Trent's grandmother had offered to teach her the Charleston, after which Susan would demonstrate it and teach the rest of the class. Kyle Simmons had researched the criminals of the decade and planned to create a PowerPoint presentation of such things as bootlegging and the government's attempts to control crime. Ron Wolf wanted to know if they could convert the room into a speakeasy.

Chad approached the group doing the 1960s, when he overheard bits of an argument. As he got closer, he noticed that the kids in that group all seemed to be arguing with Sheila. Chad broke up the argument and, although he asked what the problem was, none of the kids was forthcoming.

Sensing the tension, Chad insisted. Finally one of the kids blurted out, "Sheila hasn't done a thing yet, Mr. Peterson. She's gonna bring down our group's grade."

Chad turned to her. "Is that right, Sheila? You haven't begun to do your part of the assignment?"

Sheila batted her eyes at Chad. "I told him to chill out, Mr. P. I simply forgot my stuff in my locker today. I know what I'm doing."

"Why don't I give you a hall pass, so you can go to your locker and get whatever you need," Chad suggested.

Sheila had been caught in her lie. "Well, maybe it's at home. I'm not sure. But they don't need to worry. I'll be ready by the time our project is due."

"Let me see the paper from your group." Chad took the paper and perused it. "So, Sheila, your part is to cover the historical events of that decade. That should be easy enough."

"But it's so *boring*! I wanted to do the fashions of the time or maybe the music, but Alyssa and Sarah took those areas. I'd already done some work on the fashions when we were in the library. Don't you remember?" Sheila was back to whining again and Chad's patience was being stretched to the limit.

"I recall your telling me that you were very excited about the things you found, but at that time all of you were just doing some preliminary research. You hadn't decided yet on specific areas for each group member," Chad reminded her.

"But I don't want to do *events*! It's just too boring," she whimpered.

"I'm not going to make decisions for your group. You have to solve the problem together. Besides, Sheila, I'm sure you have a way of making anything you present interesting." Chad hoped that a bit of flattery would persuade her to give it a whirl.

At the end of the group time, Chad had reviewed each group's list and announced that they would begin to present their projects in two weeks time. He assured them, when he heard them groan, that two weeks should give them more than enough time to gather and create materials for their presentation.

After class he glanced at the papers, looking specifically to see what Sheila had designated as her role within her group. He chuckled when he observed that it said "historical events" and beside it she had written the words "under protest." *I'm not sorry to see that, for a change, she didn't get her way*, he thought.

When school ended for the day, Chad headed, as had become his habit, to find Belinda. He was surprised to see Sheila waiting for him in the hallway. "Mr. Peterson," she moaned. "Can't you do something? The kids in my group are being so stubborn. I can do a *much* better job on the fashions than Alyssa." Tears began to well up in her eyes.

Chad's opinion that Sheila was just a spoiled girl who was used to getting her own way was reinforced and he remained firm. "I'm sorry, Sheila. I told you that being a team player is an important part of this exercise. Sometimes you have to give in gracefully." He sensed she was about to start whining again and he tried to inject some humor. "You remember that show called *Survivor*? It seems that the tribe has spoken!"

Sheila suddenly became defiant. "I won't do it then. They can all just flunk, for all I care." She started to storm her way down the hallway.

"The group won't fail, Sheila, but if you refuse to do your part, you will." Trying again to win her over with flattery, he said, "I think you're too good a person to disappoint your friends."

The last words he heard were, "It's just unfair!" as she ran crying down the hallway and out of the building.

Chad decided that he'd give her some time to cool off and he hoped she'd work it out with her friends. He was about to turn and continue on his way to find Belinda when she appeared behind him and tapped him on his shoulder. Obviously she had witnessed at least some of his encounter with Sheila. "Troubles, honey?" she asked, sympathetically.

Chad shrugged it off. "Just a minor one with Sheila McMasters. It'll be ok. How was your day?"

"Hectic, as usual, but good," said Belinda. "You can make it even better if you come over after practice tonight."

"I'd love to, sweetheart, but I'd better not. I have some essays to grade from my sociology class. I was hoping that maybe we could grab a cup of coffee now." Checking his watch, he said, "I have just under an hour until I have to be at practice. I'd love to spend that time with you, if you can spare it."

"Sounds good to me," she said with a grin. She checked the hall to see if anyone was there, and when she saw the hall was clear, she gave him a hug. "It's a shame about tonight though. I hope you aren't planning to make a habit of this. All work and no play, you know…" she said with a smirk.

"Don't worry, I have every intention of playing…next chance I get." Chad returned the hug and then extended his arm for her to grab hold. "Let's get out of here now, ok?"

Belinda put her arm through Chad's as they headed out of the building towards the Starbuck's coffee shop that had recently opened nearby. She kept her arm there as they decided that rather than sit in the shop, they'd order it to go and take a walk until it was time for Chad to get back to the gym.

Back at the school's parking lot, Chad walked Belinda to her car when it was time for him to get to practice. "Have a good night, honey," Chad said as they stood by her car before he went back into the school building. "Remember, tomorrow night you're mine," he reminded her.

"Then make sure you get some rest tonight," Belinda advised him. "I can't promise you'll get any tomorrow night."

Chad bent and kissed her once she got into her car and carefully closed the door for her. "G'night, sweetheart."

"G'night. I hope the practice goes well. Have a good time."

He watched her drive out of the parking lot before going into the gym.

Volleyball practice and grading essays put it well past midnight when Chad finally crawled into bed. He was asleep almost as soon as his head touched the pillow.

Chapter 7

It had been almost two weeks since Chad and Belinda had managed to spend any private time together. Between Chad's schoolwork, the volleyball practices, and the matches, there was always something that interfered. Torn between the euphoria of coaching a still undefeated volleyball team and the frustration of not having time with his girl, Chad planned to make the most of their time together for the upcoming weekend. He arranged a special surprise for Belinda. He hadn't told Belinda much more than to plan on being available for the whole weekend. He didn't have to twist her arm, and once she assured him that she'd be at his disposal, he secured use of a cabin at nearby Lake Witonka.

Belinda's curiosity was overwhelming and she wheedled and cajoled—unsuccessfully—to find out what plans Chad had made. Despite her pleas, Chad refused to reveal anything. The only thing he would tell her was to pack warm clothing and boots. He assured her that he'd provide everything else.

The suspense both tortured and intrigued Belinda. "Can't you give me a little hint, honey?"

Chad uttered a villianous laugh and twirled his imaginary mustache as he continued tormenting her. "It'll spoil the surprise, sweetheart. I just want to get away from everything here for awhile. No schoolwork, no volleyball, just you and me."

Belinda sat in the bleachers during the game on Friday night, cheering as Chad led them to yet another victory. As soon as the match ended, Chad quickly congratulated the girls and made his excuses to leave right away. Matt Stairs, who was now able to watch the volleyball matches from the stands, had agreed to wait until the girls left. Chad followed Belinda to her apartment and went in to help her get her luggage and put it into the trunk of his car. He gallantly helped her into the passenger seat. When he leaned in and reached across her to close her seat belt, she teased him about being overly solicitous. He chuckled wickedly as he pulled out a scarf and proceeded to blindfold her. "No peeking," he instructed. "I want this to be a surprise."

"I love the mystery, honey, but don't you think you're overdoing it?" she asked, but he could hear the laughter in her voice.

"I promise you won't be disappointed." He gave her a warm, tender kiss before starting the car and pulling out of the parking spot, promising her an adventure.

The drive would take a bit more than a half hour. Until they got out of town, Chad kept up a steady chatter, distracting her. Once they had left the local streets, he challenged Belinda to listen and see if she recognized anything along the way. When they crossed the railroad tracks, Belinda correctly guessed that they were headed north as they were the only tracks out of town. Later she could hear the sound of the car traveling over a gravel type road and suspected that they were in the country, but with the blindfold on, she had lost all sense of direction and really had no definite idea where they were. When Chad finally stopped the car and told her that she could remove the blindfold, the headlights revealed the front of the log cabin.

"Oh God, Chad," she squealed with delight. "We have this cabin for the whole weekend?" She leaned over the center console and wrapped her arms around his neck. "This is incredible! Have I mentioned that I love you?"

"I told you I wanted you all to myself. Do you remember my mentioning an old family friend, Mr. Delaney? I hadn't seen him in years, and then last week I ran into him at the bank. We were just talking, catching up, and I remembered he had this cabin. I figured a way to work into the conversation that I wished I had a romantic getaway where I could take you."

"You told him about me?" Belinda asked, touched at how naturally he mentioned telling his old friends about their relationship.

"Of course I told him. You're a major part of my life, sweetheart." Chad seemed surprised she had to ask. "Anyway, I asked him if he still had the cabin. He was sorry to tell me that, in fact he did, but it was booked for months in advance. Then, out of the blue, on Tuesday, he called and told me that he had a cancellation for this weekend and asked if I were still interested. I figured I'd kidnap you if it became necessary, but I wasn't gonna let this opportunity pass.

So, here we are!" He dangled the keys in front of her and offered, "Wanna go in?"

Belinda's delight was evident. She jumped out of the car and ran to the cabin and up onto the front porch. Trailing behind her, Chad grinned at her enthusiasm. He asked her to pause long enough for him to snap a picture of her with the point-and-shoot camera he'd brought along. When Chad opened the door, Belinda walked into the cabin and, after taking a quick look around, she threw her arms around his neck and exclaimed, "Chad, it's perfect!"

The living room had a cathedral ceiling. Spacious windows loomed on the upper level. A second-floor balcony overlooked the living room and the workmanship of the all-wood interior added class. The fireplace and the stack of logs that were outside the front door suggested that the evenings would be very cozy.

"My parents used to bring my brother and me here in the summers," Chad said. "There's a lake about a quarter of a mile from here where we did a lot of fishing. It's frozen now. There are two bedrooms upstairs; if we make it all the way upstairs we can check them out," he chuckled, reaching for her. "If you're a good girl, maybe we can 'check' them both out," he promised before taking her into his arms and meeting her lips with his.

Belinda melted in his arms. They were locked in a firm embrace when suddenly Chad's stomach made some grumbling sounds. They ignored it at first, but his belly became more persistent. They pulled apart a bit, and looking into each other's eyes, began to laugh. "Chad, I bet you didn't even have anything to eat tonight. She looked towards the kitchen and asked, "Do we have any supplies? Can I fix you something to eat? I have a feeling you're gonna be needing your strength this weekend."

"I admit I'm hungry, but honestly, I'm hungrier for you. I've missed having you in my arms. I admit that I'm really enjoying the volleyball coaching, but I miss you so much, sweetheart." He kissed her again, and his stomach started to rumble. "OK, I put enough food and snacks into the trunk of the car to last for the entire weekend. I didn't want you to see it until we arrived, but I guess we better unload things before they freeze. Then we'll bring in a few logs from the porch and start a fire."

They went back out to the car where Chad grabbed the suitcases and took them to the bedroom. Belinda made a few trips to bring in the food stuffs and finally they brought in towels, bedding, and other things that Chad had thought to bring. There were a few heaters around the cabin that were powered by a generator, but they decided that they'd like a fire. Chad went out and brought in some kindling and half a dozen logs. Soon he had a crackling fire going.

A short while later, after organizing their supplies, preparing, and eating dinner together, Chad turned off the lights and they snuggled on a pile of pillows on the rug in front of the fireplace. Belinda admired Chad's handiwork as the fire, which earlier had blazed high, settled into a steady, warm flame.

Chad talked about some of his childhood memories of family visits to the cabin. "It's very remote here. No television to watch, sweetheart. We'll have to create our own amusement."

Belinda smiled at him. "I'm happy just to be here with you, honey. Cuddling by the fire is a wonderful activity…to start." Belinda turned in his arms so she was able to wrap her arms around him and lay her head on his chest."

"Mmmm, yeah. You have good ideas!" Chad made himself comfortable with Belinda in his arms, and gently stroked her hair. As they stared into the crackling fire, Chad described some of the possibilities for outdoor activities in the area. "So, if we manage to get out of the bedroom, what would you like to do this weekend?"

Belinda considered the choices and chuckled as she asked, "If we do manage to get out of the bedroom, do you think you'll be able to walk? I'd love for you to be my tour guide and show me around the area. Maybe we can go on a hike tomorrow."

"I'm not making any promises, honey, but if I am able to walk, I'd love to show you around. That's the advantage about my having been here before; we won't get lost. I can show you some of my favorite places."

They talked, catching up on the past couple of weeks. Their conversation was punctuated with frequent touches and kisses. Belinda snuggled close to Chad, resting her head on his shoulder and it wasn't long before both fell asleep. A few hours later, Chad awoke and felt a chill in the air. He checked and saw that the fire had totally extinguished and, rather than relight it, he carried Belinda to the bedroom. She didn't stir as he placed her, fully clothed, onto the bed. Then he stripped to his boxers and t-shirt and climbed next to her. She let out a little moan as he kissed her cheek. Pulling the covers over them, Chad wrapped one arm over her and went back to sleep.

It was sometime in the middle of the night when Chad awoke to feel Belinda's hands moving under his t-shirt. She whispered in his ear, "I'm sorry, honey. You got me so relaxed, I must have fallen asleep. I'm awake now…are you up?"

Chad took her hand and moved it lower to show her just how "up" he was. "I am now, baby," he snickered devilishly and then he pulled her on top of him and began caressing her. Their lovemaking was passionate, filled with frequent declarations of love and moans of pleasure. Afterwards they fell asleep again in each other's arms.

Chad was the first to wake up the next morning and a little while later the sounds and smells of bacon sizzling on the stove and coffee percolating aroused Belinda from a sound sleep. Before she got out of bed, Chad appeared at the bedroom door with a fully laden tray of something that smelled really good.

"Mmmm! Something smells positively tantalizing. I could get very used to this treatment," Belinda cooed. She sat up and stretched, the blanket falling away to reveal her nakedness.

Chad put the tray down on the dresser and said, "Morning, Belinda. I thought you might like some breakfast in bed," and when he looked up at her and saw her stretching, he left the tray where it was and moved right to the side of the bed. "But with a sight like this," he said, reaching for her breast, "food is the last thing on my mind," He bent down and placed a kiss on the taut nipple.

She moaned and he asked, "Did you sleep well?"

"I can't remember the last time I slept so well, honey. I love sleeping in your arms."

"So, what did you want for breakfast, this morning, ma'am?" he asked, continuing to kiss her body; her quickening breath and moans of pleasure encouraging him in his explorations. They forgot about the breakfast he had prepared and set about satisfying other appetites.

Later, they showered together and, shivering in the cold air, dressed quickly. As they dressed, Chad told her what he'd been up to before she awoke. "Earlier, I went out onto the porch to get some more firewood. It's a beautiful day today. The sun is shining and the air is brisk—great weather for a hike. D'ya think you're up for a hike? There are over twenty miles of awesome trails."

"Sounds great. I hope you'll be able to keep up with me," Belinda teased as she finished tying her shoe.

"I'm starved." Chad was picking through the tray he'd prepared earlier looking to see if anything was still edible. "You wore me out and I need to eat something before we go out. How about you?"

"Awww, is all that delicious food you made before ruined?" Belinda asked as she moved up and saw him frowning at the now-congealed pile of food on the tray.

Unable to salvage the lovely meal that had chilled on the tray, they went down to the kitchen together to see what was left. "Breakfast will be kind of skimpy now, but I'm not sorry." Chad winked lecherously as he reached for the bread while Belinda put the kettle back on the stove to make some more coffee.

Once the fire was lit under the kettle, Belinda turned and put her arms around Chad's waist as he put slices of bread into the toaster. "I'm not sorry either; I got what I needed and wanted this morning." Chad turned into her embrace and they stood holding each other.

Chad challenged her to a race. "I'll bet the toast pops up before your kettle boils."

Belinda chuckled at his silliness, willing the kettle to boil quickly. She felt him reaching over to the toaster and, seeing what he was doing, tickled him to make him stop. "No fair! You've moved the controls over for light toast." She tried to reach the toaster to slide the controls back. "I like my toast almost burnt," she declared.

Chad tried to distract her with a kiss, and just as the kettle began to whistle, the toast popped up. Declaring a tie, they set about making coffee and putting out the butter and jam for the toast.

After breakfast, Belinda dressed in a pair of old Levi jeans, a sweater, and put on the boots Chad had insisted she pack. Chad helped her into her parka and took her hand as they stepped out onto the front porch.

"Ok, lead the way," she said, putting her hand in his and letting him set the pace.

"Let's head to the lake first. I want to show you the natural beauty of the area," he suggested. She indicated her agreement by squeezing his hand.

Two inches of new fallen snow lay on the ground as they hiked along a marked trail. When they reached the lake, Belinda exclaimed, "It's like a scene from a Hallmark card, Chad. I can picture it now, two lovers embrace in the foreground with the lake and mountains behind them. Or…" she paused for a moment for effect and then bent quickly, "one of them gets hit with a snowball, SPLAT!" Chad ducked too late and the snowball hit its mark.

Doing his best imitation of Yosemite Sam, Chad yelled, "You'll *pay* for that, varmint!"

Belinda squealed and sprinted along the lake's edge, with Chad in hot pursuit. A hundred yards later, he caught and tackled her. He grabbed a handful of snow and rubbed it gently over her face. Then, as he pulled her again to her feet, he said, "Be careful, my love, or next time you'll get some of that snow down your pants."

"Then I'll need something to warm me up down my pants," she shot back, "and I know just the warming tool to use."

"Again?" he asked, amazed at her stamina. "My, my, you're insatiable. But I guess if I must, I must," he declared, making it clear that he was a willing participant. They both laughed heartily, and she grabbed his gloved hand, exchanging a quick kiss before they continued their walk.

Chad took Belinda to the top of a peak that overlooked the frozen lake. He pointed to an area about a mile in the distance. "If you like, sweetheart, we can hike over there and rent some ice skates. Mr. Delaney said that they keep a large section of the lake clear of snow for skaters."

"I haven't skated for years, Chad. I'll likely spend most of the time on my butt, but if you promise not to laugh at me and to help me up when I fall, I'm game."

"I can promise to help you up, but as for the laughing—no promises. Let's take the long way around, though, and we'll end up at the lake."

"Lead on."

As they walked the trail, they spotted a white-tailed deer grazing on the foliage. They paused for several minutes, and Chad pulled the camera from his pocket and took a picture. When the deer finally moved off the trail, they continued hiking, stopping occasionally to take more pictures and admire the beauty of the scenery.

When she spotted the office area where they rented the ice skates, Belinda could barely contain her excitement. They were both fitted for skates, and then moved carefully out onto the ice. As it was still relatively early, there were only a handful of skaters out. Belinda held tightly to Chad as they made their first circuit. Eventually her confidence grew and she skated off by herself, attempting some fancy moves she thought she remembered from childhood. Some were more successful than others. Chad took lots of photos, especially one of Belinda on her butt after a fall, and later asked a stranger to take one of them both. They skated for an hour, taking frequent breaks to sit on one of the nearby benches.

After returning the skates, they discussed plans for the rest of the day. "I know a nice restaurant where we can go for dinner tonight. It's about a ten-minute drive from the cabin. I remember they had the best steaks."

Belinda put her arms on Chad's shoulders and pressed a very suggestive kiss to his lips, "Mmmm! I think we can work up quite an appetite by then. Sounds great. Can we go back to the cabin now?"

Chad didn't need to have his arm twisted, "I'll race ya!" he challenged.

"Chad, thank you for planning this getaway. It's been so romantic. The place is so beautiful, but most of all I love having you to myself."

"I'm glad you're enjoying this too. I love you and I want to show you that...always. I also know that with playoffs looming in the not too distant future, we won't have many opportunities to be alone together."

Belinda put a finger to his lips. "Shhh! Don't think of anything related to school right now. Let's just enjoy this time while we can."

They had barely gotten back inside the cabin before they were all over each other. They didn't even take time to start a fire since the touching and kissing generated enough heat between them to melt any remaining vestiges of the outside cold. They left a trail of their clothes as they made their way to the bedroom.

Chad moved slowly lower, pressing kisses from her face and lips to her breasts. Cupping her breasts with his hands, he used his tongue to fully arouse her nipples. Belinda's moans of excitement spurred him on and when he moved still lower, she gave herself to him completely.

Belinda gently nudged Chad until he rolled onto his back so she could give him similar pleasures. She nipped lightly at his nipples as her hand stroked below. Her fingers found his most sensitive areas and, when she saw he couldn't take much more, she lowered herself onto him. He arched his hips upward as he tried to bury himself inside her. They moved in a rhythmic dance that increased in tempo with each thrust. She squeezed as he exploded in a torrent of pleasure and she collapsed onto Chad as the tremors overtook her as well. Her breathing was still erratic and hard, but she managed to moan, "I love you, Chad," and then clung tightly to him.

Afterwards, while they were showering together again, Chad murmured, "This is getting to be a habit. A very erotic habit. I love feeling our bodies all slick and slippery against each other. I'm glad there's plenty of hot water," he joked, "because I could stay here for hours."

"Mmmmmmm," Belinda snuggled up closer if that were humanly possible. "Yeah, this is heavenly."

When they finally shut the water, the rush of cold air had them scampering to dress quickly. Since they still had a few hours before they planned to go out to dinner, they dressed casually, more for warmth, deciding that they'd dress up later, just before the time they would leave. Chad suggested that they spend the time until then playing one of the board games that Belinda had discovered earlier in one of the closets.

"That sounds like a great idea," Belinda agreed and went over to the closet to review the choices. Looking at the shelf with the games, she asked, "Which do you prefer, Chad? There's Monopoly, Scrabble, Chinese Checkers, Backgammon, or Chess."

"I like Backgammon and Scrabble best. Maybe we can save Monopoly for later, after dinner. That takes longer to finish and we'll need some time to change for dinner."

"So for now, how about Scrabble?"

"Ok. Why don't we move the coffee table next to the fireplace. Then, if you'll set up the game on the table, I'll get a few more logs and start up the fire."

"Sounds perfect!" Belinda moved to lift one end of the coffee table as Chad grabbed the other end.

They both played to win as their competitive instincts took over. It was a close game until the end when Belinda made the word zoology, placing the Z over a triple letter space.

"Eat my dust!" She laughed, getting up and doing a little victory dance. Then she tried to soothe his bruised ego with a kiss. "I was just lucky," she said.

"You can buy your own meal tonight," he pouted teasingly as they put the game pieces back into the box."

"I'm sorry, baby," she mewled in her most seductive tone. "If you buy dinner, I promise I'll make it up to you later tonight."

"And how do you plan to do that?" he asked straight faced. "You're wearing me out."

"Oh my God! What an old man you are!" Belinda teased. Grabbing the pillow off the couch, she conked Chad over the head with it, before tossing the pillow back onto the couch and running upstairs with Chad in hot pursuit.

Chad loved this playful side of their relationship. Belinda got to the bedroom before him, but he was close behind. Just outside the door he hesitated, hoping to enter the room quietly, and catch Belinda unaware. He waited a few moments in the hall before tiptoing into the room. He looked about for her and didn't immediately see where she'd gone.

Belinda was using a similar strategy and she lay in wait behind the half opened door. When he came all the way into the room she jumped out from behind the door and caught him flush in the face with a pillow. "Gotcha!" she shrieked, wondering how he'd retaliate.

Unhurt, he played the game to the hilt, pretending to stagger and then fall onto the bed unconscious.

"Oh, no…my poor baby!" Belinda came close, carefully, expecting him to move suddenly. "Are you injured? Nurse Belinda will kiss and make you better. Do you need me to make CPR?"

Chad forgot he was supposed to be unconscious and laughed. "You don't *make* CPR! What kind of nurse are you? CPR is cardiopulmonary resuscitation—maybe you *do* it," he explained.

"Hey, baby! You do it your way and I do it mine. I know you don't need cardiopulmonary resuscitation. I'm gonna *make* C P R—Chad's Penis Rise!" At that Belinda burst into giggles and rolled over the bed. She was laughing so hard that, had Chad not grabbed onto her, she'd have fallen off the bed.

Chad joined in the laughter. "That's a good one, sweetheart. You got me. But I gotta tell you, if you can 'make CPR' again now, you must be one hell of a nurse. I need a nap first," Chad groaned.

Belinda lowered herself on top of his body, and said, "Ohhh, Chad, do you need to sleeeeeeeeeeeeeeeeep?" She started kissing his neck and her hands began to roam all over him.

Chad wrapped one arm around her waist and with the other began to tickle her side. "Yes, pleeeeeeeeease! Let me sleeeeeeeeeep!" he begged. "Just for a little bit. I can't keep up with you."

"Gee, that's too bad." Belinda was squirming, trying to get away from the tickling. Finally they called a truce. They cuddled together, exchanging light kisses and stroking each other's face. They both must have dozed off for a bit, because the next thing they knew, it was dark out and they agreed to get up and dress for dinner.

Chad drove to the Inn at the Pines. It seemed to be a slow night. They had their choice of tables and the service was efficient and quick. Chad ordered a twelve oz. strip steak and a baked potato. Likewise, Belinda chose a petite steak but with fries.

While they waited for their meal, Belinda surveyed the restaurant. "That's quite an impressive moose head hanging on the wall. Those antlers must spread over four feet."

"My parents told me that the first owner shot that moose on an expedition to Colorado, but I'm not sure if they were fibbing or not."

Belinda continued to examine the décor. The open flame on the wood fired grill created an atmosphere that suited the outdoors type environment. When their salads arrived, both realized how hungry they were. "This house dressing is marvelous," said Belinda. "It has a tangy flavor, but there's something unique about it." She offered Chad a forkful of her salad, and he leaned over the table as she fed it to him.

"Mmmmm, yeah, that's good. I ordered the ranch dressing; do you want to taste mine?" When she declined, he commented, "I hope the steaks are as delicious as I remember them. They flame broil them right over there. You can sit here and watch the chef prepare them. I haven't ever been to any other place like this."

"This is a perfect ending to a perfect day, Chad. You couldn't have chosen better." She reached across the table and took his hand in hers. "Thank you again for all of this."

"I hope we can share a lot of times like this. I'm so glad we were able to get out here this weekend. I wish we didn't have to leave tomorrow."

Belinda again hushed him. "We have a lot of time before we have to worry about tomorrow. I know it's a cliché, but let's live in the moment."

After dinner they drove straight back to the cabin. The snow had begun to fall and Chad took extra care on the slippery roads.

"So, do you want to play Monopoly now?" Chad inquired.

"If it's ok with you, I'd rather just sit and talk and cuddle. I'd enjoy that much more."

"I'd like that too, sweetheart. I'm stuffed after that delicious meal, but if we get hungry again later, I brought the fixings for S'mores. We can keep the fire going and make some later."

"I could use a snack right now, but save the S'mores for later," Belinda said as she threw her arms around his neck and kissed him.

They spent the next few hours talking and cuddling. They had made an unspoken pact to hoard this special time to tide them over once Chad had to return to the volleyball team. Chad confessed that, although he was glad that he could help out a friend and even though he was enjoying the challenge and experience of coaching, once Matt was able, he'd be glad to step aside and let Matt resume his job as coach. Belinda promised her support for whatever decision Chad made.

By ten, Chad was ready for a snack. He reached over, took the long stick he'd picked up during their hike, and stuck two marshmallows on the end. He extended them into the fireplace and in seconds the marshmallows had caught on fire. He pulled them out and watched as they turned black on the outside. "I love them this way. Crispy on the outside and inside it's all gooey and soft." He pulled the first one off the stick. "Here, taste this but be careful. It's hot."

Belinda sampled the marshmallow. "Mmmm. It's good. We were always careful *not* to burn them as kids. We would take a long time to just get them a golden brown, but I must admit, this is tasty too."

Chad toasted a few more, some his way and some the way Belinda described. Then they were ready to try making S'mores. Belinda took the mini sandwich maker, put a graham cracker on one side, then added a piece of Hershey's chocolate bar, a couple of sliced in half marshmallows, and finally another graham cracker. Holding the long handle of the device, she placed it over the fire long enough to melt the ingredients inside the graham cracker.

"It's scrumptious," Chad said when he tasted it. "How 'bout S'more?"

"I've had enough. I'm stuffed, but I'll make another one for you. It's almost as much fun making them as eating them."

She made another one, which Chad happily scarfed down, after which he reached for her hand and licked the chocolate off her fingers. He made it into a very erotic act, which led to more kissing and touching.

They stayed cuddled by the fire until it died down and the last log was little more than glowing embers. Chad made sure that it was safely extinguished before they went upstairs. In a matter of minutes they lay beside each other. Without saying a word, but knowing that this might be their last time for intimacy any time soon, they made love.

The next morning they arose early to make breakfast, clean the cabin, and gather their belongings. Chad shut down the generator while Belinda took one last look around to make sure they hadn't forgotten anything. Chad locked the door and they stood on the porch for just a moment before leaving. "Chad, promise me we'll come back here again."

"I promise. Maybe we can reserve an entire week this summer. There are all kinds of great summer activities here too. We can try canoeing, horseback riding, and do a lot more hiking. Do you like to fish?"

"Me put a worm on a hook? Ewwww!"

"Then I'll do the fishing and you can clean them," Chad said.

"I'll make you a deal. You catch 'em, you clean 'em, and you cook 'em, and I'll eat 'em!"

Chad let out a loud laugh. "It's a deal." They got into the car and he started the engine, slowly pulling away from the cabin. The weekend with Belinda was just the tonic he needed to carry on as coach and teacher. He felt Belinda put her hand on his thigh as he drove away. Concentrating on the snow-covered road, he reached down momentarily with one hand and gave hers a gentle squeeze. He didn't dare take his eyes off the narrow roadway, but he felt the love.

Chapter 8

Working on the history projects was taking longer than the kids had anticipated. Chad was thrilled to see how motivated the kids were. When several kids from most of the groups approached him to say that their projects couldn't be done in a single class period, Chad pretended to reluctantly agree to let each group take up to three class periods, if needed. Inwardly, he chuckled. He had known from the beginning that a good job on such a project would take multiple periods, but letting his students discover that fact for themselves proved to be more exciting.

Wanting some chronological sequencing for the projects, Chad insisted that the decades be covered in order. "You have to see how history unfolded," he argued when the group doing the roaring twenties realized that they'd have to go first. "It won't make much sense to jump back and forth."

Finally, when it appeared that most of the groups were well-prepared, he announced that the presentations would begin the next day. Chad sat back and watched as the first group arrived early in the morning and began to decorate the room with posters and paraphernalia from the 1920s. The actual class presentation took two days and included a nicely covered explanation of prohibition, the music of Louis Armstrong, and a demonstration of the Charleston where everyone, including Chad, had to get up and follow the instructions. On the second day, each member assumed the identity of a famous figure and, with the help of video clips that they had found on the Internet, covered famous people such as Johnny Weismuller, Babe Ruth, Bobby Jones, Sonja Henie, Walt Disney, and the actor, Rudolf Valentino.

Since no group had chosen the 1930s, Chad assumed the responsibility for presenting highlights from that decade. The kids listened attentively, but he could tell that they were more anxious to hear and see each other's efforts. He limited his presentation to just one day's class.

The group focusing on the 1940s, while also covering other segments, focused mainly on World War II. Heather Joles and Paul Stone took an entire day's session to talk about the Holocaust. They hung posters around the room with pictures from concentration camps and maps of Germany, Poland, and Czechoslovakia. Randy Thomas and Seth Beckman used the next day to cover famous battles of the war. Chad was impressed when they brought out a map tracking the Allied Forces as they moved into Europe. He thought he'd burst with pride when he saw that they didn't stop there, but had also prepared a presentation on the battles on the other side of the world too—touching on Pearl Harbor, Hiroshima, and Nagasaki. They even prepared a very informative presentation about the detention camps for the Orientals. The third and last day presented information about life in the United States after the war.

Clearly the first two groups had divided the work so that everyone had a part and their joint efforts were very impressive. Chad was delighted by a suggestion made by Laura Thompson, one of the kids who had worked on the 1940s.

Laura approached him somewhat hesitantly. "Mr. Peterson," she started, "you know that we've worked real hard on these projects and…it's been a lot of fun." When Chad smiled at that, her confidence grew and she continued. "Some of us were talking, and we thought it might be cool to make our presentations to the other classes too. So we were thinking that maybe we could use all this stuff and make it into a presentation for a school assembly."

Chad loved it when students offered their input and actually volunteered to do work and he didn't hesitate. "That's a terrific idea, Laura." He then turned to the rest of the class. "So, how do the rest of you feel about this? Does everyone want to participate? Raise your hand if you're willing to give it a whirl."

Immediately most of the students' hands went up. There were a few shy students who seemed reluctant to perform in front of such a large group, but when Chad offered that they could work in the background if they were too nervous, they were quick to agree.

"I can just see old Mrs. Fogerty doing the Charleston," chimed in Samantha Woodley. "I'll be rolling on the floor laughing my…" she paused for a second, "you-know-what off."

Chad too laughed at the thought. "Maybe she'll surprise us," he added. "I'll talk with Ms. Hargrove and see if I can get permission to use the auditorium and set up an assembly."

* * *

That night after school, Chad went to Belinda's apartment for dinner. Belinda had been planning a very special evening for a few days to celebrate Chad's birthday. She had created a very romantic atmosphere with candles placed around the room and a selection of his favorite CDs playing on the stereo. Belinda had also made Chad's favorite food: baked chicken. She set the table with her good dishes and wine glasses. The atmosphere was happy and festive.

Chad was touched by her efforts. They ate and talked and even danced. Chad's enthusiasm was twofold as he told Belinda about the success of his class project so far. "It's absolutely amazing, sweetheart. I'd hoped that the kids would be inspired to work on the project, but I never expected the quality of the work or the competitiveness they're exhibiting. Now they even want to extend this to an assembly for the entire high school."

"You really bring out the best in your kids. I'm so proud of you, Chad."

Chad was beaming at the way she took pride in his accomplishments. "When I was in high school, history was little more than lectures and note taking and an occasional filmstrip or movie. Kids are so turned off by that kind of class. I'm sure they're really learning. You should hear the kinds of questions that are being fired at those who are presenting the material. What's really amazing is that if they don't know the answer, they don't turn to me. They tell the kids they'll look first to see if they can find it."

"Having classes like that really makes teaching fun. You're really good at motivating them."

Leaning over to Belinda, he kissed her on the cheek. "You're *my* inspiration."

It was the best birthday he could ever remember and after helping her clean up, he led her to her bedroom and proceeded to thank her.

The bubble burst the next afternoon.

* * *

Sheila McMasters was absent on the first scheduled day of her group's presentation. The following day she came unprepared. If looks could indeed kill, Chad knew from the glares of her partners that they would have murdered her. Finally, on the third day, she gave a short five minute oral report on three events from the entire decade. She offered no visuals and showed little enthusiasm.

At the end of class, Chad called her aside and admonished her. "Sheila, more important than the information from these projects is learning to work as a team. You let your friends down today by putting so little effort into your presentation."

Sheila tried making excuses and manipulating Chad as she often did with men and boys, but nothing she said assuaged Chad's disappointment.

"I'm not going to penalize the others for your irresponsibility, Sheila," he said, "but I'm afraid that I can't justify giving you a passing grade for your participation."

Again Sheila tried playing the victim but Chad dismissed her. "You can go, Sheila. Hopefully, you'll learn a valuable lesson from this."

She stormed from the room and slammed the door behind her. The next day when she saw her failing grade, she fumed. A plan hatched in her mind to get even.

"What are you going to do?" Cindy asked when they talked over the phone later that night.

Sheila's anger consumed her. "It's *his* fault for not letting me do the part of the project that I wanted. Listen, Cindy, I have an idea that'll force him to change my grade." She revealed the details of what she hoped to do.

Sheila bided her time as she waited for a chance to put her plan into action. She found reasons to hang around after regular school hours, hoping for an opportunity to find Chad alone so she could talk to him. A few days passed with no luck, and Sheila was becoming impatient.

Many of the kids in her class, especially those who had been in her group and felt that she had let them down, were treating her like a pariah; the anger and resentment was building up in Sheila.

Still unable to find Chad alone, Sheila decided that it might be better to confront him outside of school. One afternoon after school, she followed Chad out of the building. She was about to approach him when he raised his hand to wave to Belinda who was standing near his car in the parking lot. When Sheila saw them get into his car together, she muttered some obscenities under her breath and turned to go home.

The next evening was a regular volleyball practice session and Sheila convinced Cindy to hang out with her to watch, hoping that she'd catch him alone afterwards. When she saw Chad heading for his classroom, she told Cindy to give her a few minutes and ran off behind him.

Chad, psyched up after a very spirited practice session, decided he'd finish grading some papers in his classroom so that he wouldn't have to take work home. He wanted to get as much work done before the weekend so he'd be free to spend his time with Belinda. He was concentrating on his paperwork when Sheila knocked on the door.

She came into the room without waiting for an invitation to do so and walked right up to his desk. In a pleading tone, she asked, "Mr. Peterson, could I talk to you?"

"Come in," Chad answered somewhat sarcastically, since she was already in. "What are you doing here, Sheila, and what do you want?"

"Mr. Peterson. You know I like your class and you. I'm sorry that I didn't live up to your expectations. My parents are gonna kill me if I get a bad grade in history. I'll do *anything* to improve my grade." She sat at a desk directly in front of him.

"Sheila, I hate to say 'I told you so,' but I did warn you. You could have saved us all a lot of effort if you had just done your assignment in the first place. You deliberately let down your friends, and I was very disappointed in you."

"Mr. Peterson, I know you're right, and I'm really sorry." She was really laying it on. Sheila surreptitiously glanced at Chad to see if her attempt at contrition was hitting its mark. "There must be something I can do for you to make up for it."

Chad wasn't making it easy for her, but he felt he had to give her a chance. He was sure that, more than her parents' anger, she'd have a hard time dealing with the other kids in the class who were really angry at her for what they saw as a sabotage of their hard work. "If you're really sincere, Sheila, I might be able to come up with something that you can do for extra credit. I'll expect you to 'put your money where your mouth is'."

She thought, *I'll put my mouth anywhere you want, honey*! But she said, "I'll do whatever you want, Mr. Peterson." Sheila thought they were on the same wavelength. It never occurred to her that he was talking about schoolwork now. "He wants me!" she deluded herself. "If he really means that I can make it up to him, I might just find it in my heart to forgive him." She wondered if he'd want to do "it" right here in the classroom, or maybe he'd ask her to meet him outside of school.

"You know that the class wants to put on a show for the entire senior high student body. If you take an active part in organizing and participating in that endeavor, I'll see what I can come up with."

"Huh?" Sheila was imagining that Chad was about to touch her, and it was a shock when he started talking about schoolwork again.

"Sheila, I said that you'd have to take an active part in the assembly. Can you do that?" Chad was getting impatient. He just wanted to end this conversation, finish the papers, and get over to Belinda's place.

Suddenly, she understood. Of course Chad couldn't just come right out and proposition her; he'd have to be very subtle about it. Sheila, certain that she knew what he wanted, didn't want to waste any more time and offered suggestively, "I was thinking of something more personal that I could do to please you."

"Please me? Just do what I say and you'll please me and your friends."

Sheila suddenly opened her blouse, exposing her breasts to him.

"I'll do whatever you want, Mr. Peterson."

Chad was stunned. "What are you doing?"

"See anything you want?" she said as she moved closer, offering herself.

"My God, Sheila, I want you out of here, NOW!"

Sheila just smiled and kept moving toward him. Chad backed up against the wall as she threw herself against him. He placed his hands on her shoulders to push her away.

At that precise moment (later, in retrospect, it seemed to Chad that it was as if by plan) Cindy Bennett walked into the room. "Omigod!" she shouted. "What's going on here, Mr. Peterson?" she asked, incredulous at what she was witnessing. "Holy shit! Sheila was right. He's making a move on her," she said to herself as she backed out of the room and got out of there quickly.

Sheila didn't seem at all surprised that Cindy had come in. In fact, she seemed very pleased at having been caught in such a compromising position. She leaned in to Chad and whispered, "Last chance, Mr. Peterson."

"Get out! Do it now!" Chad was shaken. In his wildest imagination he never thought Sheila would pull a stunt like this. He just wanted her out of there and he wanted to get out as well.

"See ya later," she said with a smirk on her face and began to close her blouse slowly. Her scheme had worked. She'd show him. If he'd taken advantage of her offer, she'd have been pleased and happy. She'd gladly have given him anything he wanted. An improved grade would have been an added bonus. She had to admit to herself that she was surprised at how this went down. She'd really thought she had him. "Just you wait, Chad my dear," she said to herself. "You're gonna be sorry you didn't take advantage of what I offered." Now she had proof of an indiscretion that she could use against him. She caught up to Cindy outside the school building and, reaching into her purse, she turned off the tape recorder she had hidden there. "I've got him!" was all she said with a smug laugh.

Chad waited a few minutes after Sheila had gone. He wanted to make sure that he wasn't seen anywhere near her as he exited the building. He sat in a state of semi-shock with his head in his hands. Finally, he pulled his cellphone from his pocket and called Belinda. "Hi. I need to talk with you. Can I come over now?"

"Of course, Chad." She detected the worried sound of his voice. "Is something wrong?"

"I'll tell you all about it when I see you. I don't want to discuss it over the phone. I'll be right over."

"I'll be here. Just come in when you arrive."

Chad quickly gathered a few personal belongings. He didn't even consider taking any work with him, and he left the pile of papers he'd been grading on his desk. Looking around as he left his room to make certain that Sheila wasn't lingering nearby, he made a hasty retreat to the safety of his car.

Belinda greeted him with a big hug when he came in the door. "Your voice sounded so distressed, honey. I was worried about you. What's wrong?"

"You remember the cheerleader who kissed me in the gym after one of my volleyball games?"

"Yeah, I seem to remember that I teased you about that at the time."

"Tonight she came to my room while I was grading some papers. She asked to talk with me. She was the only one of the kids who didn't participate in the assignment I've been telling you about and I had to give her a failing grade for her efforts—or lack thereof. I expected her to whine and cry about it."

"And did she?"

"Oooh, the little bitch!" Chad was so upset he could hardly talk.

Belinda was getting scared. He was totally losing it. "Calm down, Chad. Tell me what happened."

Chad took a deep breath and began pacing as he told her. She walked up to me, acting innocently enough. Then she asked if she could do something to improve her grade. I presumed that she meant extra credit and, after giving her a short lecture, I suggested some work she might do."

"And?" Belinda prodded.

"It seems that she wasn't interested in extra credit. She wanted to engage in some extra curricular activity." Chad shook his head in disbelief. "She sat right in front of me and opened her shirt. She wasn't wearing anything underneath. She said she'd 'do anything' for a good grade."

Belinda was stunned. "Oh my God!"

"I know. My reaction was total disbelief."

"Oh my God!" Belinda kept repeating. "So, what did you do?"

Chad stopped his pacing for a minute and looked at Belinda. "Less than politely, I told her to leave immediately."

Belinda was trying to piece all the facts together. "Was anyone around at the time to see or hear what happened?"

"The whole encounter lasted less than ten minutes but just at the end some other girl—I think it was one of the kids I've seen hanging around with Sheila—walked into the room when I was pushing Sheila away. I can't imagine what she thought was going on." Chad resumed his pacing.

Belinda put herself right in his path and stopped him. When he looked at her, she said, "Chad, this girl is gonna cause you trouble. You need to report it."

"I don't know if that's wise. If I report it, I'll be opening a can of worms. She'll say I harassed her and it'll be her word against mine. I can't prove that I'm innocent. These days, in situations like this, I'll be considered guilty till proven innocent. Maybe she just wanted to embarrass me."

"Maybe you should consult someone. I'm scared, honey." Belinda put her arms around Chad.

Chad returned the embrace, hugging her, seeking the comfort she was offering. "I'm scared too. Who could I contact? I don't know what to do, and I'm afraid of what will happen if this gets out. Maybe we should just wait and see."

"I hope you're right, but she sounds like trouble to me."

Despite Belinda's protests that he stay the night, Chad insisted that he needed some time alone to think and he insisted on going home alone. Belinda made him promise that he'd call her if he needed her—at any hour—and then, despite her reluctance to let him leave in this state, she let him go.

* * *

Sheila knew that she had to move fast. She went straight home, prepared to put on a show. Her father was sitting on the couch watching TV, and she, uncharacteristically, went and sat down with him. He seemed somewhat surprised, but he was engrossed in his program, so he patted her hand and absentmindedly said hello, before returning his complete attention to the screen.

Sheila fidgeted next to him, trying to distract him. When she finally caught his attention, she let her tears flow freely.

"What's wrong, honey?" her dad asked, torn between the show he was watching and talking to Sheila.

"I don't want to talk about it," she pretended at first. "I'm embarrassed."

That caught his attention. "Something happened at school today?"

After some feigned reluctance, she finally began explaining. "Daddy, I went into Mr. Peterson's class after school to ask about extra credit for his class. I'm not doing as well as I should. He…" she stopped briefly at this point for effect and whimpered, "made me do something bad. He made it sound like it was my only choice."

"Oh my God!" screamed Sheila's mom who had just walked into the room and heard the end of the conversation.

"What did he make you do?" her father asked, fury evident in his tone.

"First, he made me open my shirt and come up to him. I think he also wanted me to perform oral sex on him," she cried, but Cindy walked in just then and he pushed me away."

Steven McMasters flew into a rage. "I'm gonna kill that child molester," he shouted. "That son of a bitch is gonna pay for this!" He grabbed his car keys and moved toward the door.

It took all of her willpower for Laura McMasters to restrain her husband. "No! You can't do that; attacking him won't solve anything," she said. "I'm calling the police right now to file a complaint. We won't let him get away with this."

* * *

After a sleepless night, Chad made a decision to try to maintain his normal routine and see what happened. He left early, headed for school and met his friends in the locker room for their usual morning workout. As he changed into his swimsuit, Chad talked with Jim Morris and Thorny.

"How're things with you and Belinda, Chad?" Thorny asked. "You gettin' any?" he teased.

Chad ignored his latter question. "I've barely had time to spend with her. Volleyball is taking up most of my evening time. We do manage to spend some time together on weekends, though." Chad smiled and merely said, "Things are going well."

"And what's new with Miss Hot to Trot?" asked Jim.

Chad was taken aback by the question. "Excuse me?"

"Yesterday, I was here late for a meeting and on my way out, I walked by your room and saw what's her name in the room with you. That girl who's been shadowing you."

Chad was not sure what Jim had seen so he just avoided the subject. "Sheila McMasters. That's a touchy subject right now, Jim."

"Yeah, she's the one. Every time I turn around she seems to be near you. In the gym, outside the locker room, in your classroom after hours..."

Chad got testy. "Damn! She's been...nevermind, just drop it!" He slammed his locker shut and headed for the pool.

Jim and Thorny followed with a puzzled look on their faces but they were perceptive enough to let it go."

The volleyball game in the pool was competitive as usual, but everyone was noticing that Chad seemed to be hitting the ball with more than his usual exuberance. He wasn't himself and when one of his spikes gave Thorny a bloody nose, Chad swam over to apologize. Realizing he was out of control, Chad apologized to the others as well before leaving the pool. "I'm sorry, guys, go on without me, I'm not really up for this just now."

Puzzled by Chad's strange behavior, they discussed it for a few minutes and decided to call it quits for the day. They headed back to the locker room and found Chad already dressed for class. He quickly left the locker room without even saying goodbye to his friends. He tried his best to keep the classes moving smoothly, but he was clearly distracted. Even the kids noticed.

* * *

The chief of police assigned Officer David Howell to investigate the complaint. Dave Howell was a member of the community, familiar with the people involved, and he was determined to get to the bottom of this. It was standard procedure, in cases involving a teacher's inappropriate behavior, to begin the investigation by interviewing the complainant.

After calling to make an appointment, Officer Howell showed up early in the morning at Sheila's home. In the presence of her parents, he questioned her.

Steve McMasters welcomed Dave into his home. "I'm glad you could come, Dave. We're counting on you to see that this bastard is punished."

Dave shook hands with Steve and reassured him, "I'll do the best I can to see that the truth comes out."

Declining the coffee that Laura McMasters offered, Dave asked if they could all sit down to discuss the incident.

Steve led them to the dining room table, where they all sat. Turning to Sheila, Dave said, "Sheila, I'd like to hear, in your own words, exactly what happened."

"Tell him what happened, honey, and don't leave out any details," Sheila's father insisted.

Sheila recounted her version of the events of that night in school. Officer Howell made some notes in a little pad he carried and asked Steve and Laura if the details Sheila had just related were the same as she had told them earlier.

Confirming that they were, Steve declared, "I won't rest until that SOB is fired and put away in jail. Sheila's never been anything but nice to him."

"What do you mean by that? When has she been nice to him?" asked Dave. "Was there something between Sheila and Mr. Peterson before this?"

Sheila shook her head. "When he became the volleyball coach, I was there cheerleading for the matches and saw him during practice a few times. I told him I liked his class and him. I didn't do anything else."

When the interview ended, Officer Howell said that he would file a report. It would be several days before the McMasters heard anything definite.

"You mean that bastard can still be around kids like my daughter? I'll tell you this. I will not allow my daughter to be in his class again."

"My job is to gather the facts, Steve. Before I can make any recommendations, I'll need to talk with Mr. Peterson's co-workers and other students, including Cindy Bennett. We can't press charges and alert the defendant until we've done some digging around, but in a case of this nature we usually notify the school administration that there is an investigation."

* * *

Two days later, Chad was in his first block class when Darren Porter, the school's physics teacher, showed up at his door. "Mrs. Hargrove wants to see you in her office immediately, Chad. I'll cover for you."

Chad quickly gave the students the day's assignment and left the room. He sensed trouble and he was positive of the source. Mrs. Jones, the school secretary, led him into the office.

"You wanted to see me, Helen?"

"Chad, I have some disturbing news to tell you. One of your students has made an accusation against you."

"Sheila McMasters."

"She claims you made sexual demands on her when she asked you about doing some extra credit. She says fear of her family's wrath for a low grade made her susceptible and she gave in to you."

"You know it's a lie!"

"Nevertheless, I'm bound by law to investigate the matter. Until this matter is cleared up, you're suspended with pay. You'll have to leave right away. I'm sorry."

Without another word spoken, Chad rose from his chair, went to his classroom, grabbed his coat, and headed for the nearest door.

Coming down the hall at that moment, Belinda saw Chad with his coat and ran up to him. "Chad, what's the matter?"

"I have to go," he said curtly.

She tried to take his arm and pry some information from him, but he just uttered the words, "Sheila McMasters." He broke free and stormed out, leaving her in total dismay. She learned from Helen Hargrove that Chad had been accused of coercing sex from a student and had to be suspended pending the outcome.

Chad left the parking in reckless haste, oblivious to the wintry road conditions. He had no place he wanted to go and drove aimlessly all morning. If anyone had asked him later where he'd been, he couldn't have told them much. Eventually he stopped at a bar and spent the afternoon drinking beer.

The events of the past few weeks just kept playing over and over in his mind. "Could he have done things differently? Should he have been more careful in dealing with Sheila? What had he done to deserve this?"

Several hours later, realizing that he was too drunk to drive, he used his cell phone to call Belinda. "I don't even know where I am," he stammered. "Some place called Joe's Bar and Grill."

"Give the phone to the bartender, Chad, and I'll ask him for directions. Stay there. I'll ask Maggie to come with me so she can drive one car back and I'll bring you home."

Belinda asked the bartender for directions and found that the drive would take more than ninety minutes. "Please don't give him anymore to drink," she pleaded.

The bartender looked down at Chad, whose head lay on the table top. "Don't worry, lady. He's had more than enough. You two must have had one helluva fight."

Belinda didn't respond to that comment but quickly hung up and called Maggie, who instantly agreed to help. Almost two hours later they found Chad, passed out, and still resting where the bartender had described him hours earlier. With the help of two friendly patrons, she put Chad into the passenger seat of his car, strapped his seatbelt in, and drove him home.

By the time they arrived, he was conscious enough to stumble his way along the path and through the entrance. He flopped into bed and without attempting to undress him, Belinda pulled the covers over him. She wasn't about to leave him. She got herself ready for bed and got in next to him, stroking his forehead. He moaned once or twice but did not stir through the night.

The next morning, Belinda arose and saw that Chad was sleeping soundly. Since she had to be at work, she dressed quietly and left a note on the nightstand beside Chad's bed. Then she drove to her apartment, showered and changed, and arrived at school a few minutes late.

Helen Hargrove stopped Belinda to inquire about how Chad was dealing with the trauma of the situation. "How's he doing, Belinda?"

"How do you think he's taking it? He's given all he has to his students and this school for the past eight years and he's facing charges for assaulting a student. You know he didn't do this!"

"Belinda, I had no choice. It's the law. I want you and Chad to know that I fully support him in this. I'm really sorry."

"I do know that, Helen. I'm sure that deep inside Chad does too, but how does a teacher, male or female, refute charges like this?"

"Believe me when I tell you that we'll investigate this thoroughly. If there's any discrepancy at all, we'll find it, and Chad will be exonerated. Meanwhile, look after him and tell him that we care."

"I have a short break at eleven. I'll try calling him then. I suspect he'll sleep for awhile yet. I didn't want to leave him this morning, but I knew there wasn't much I could do until he awoke."

"Be sure to tell him that we'll deal with this issue as promptly as possible. Do you know of any reason why this girl would want to accuse Chad?"

Not certain how much to reveal, Belinda said, "I know that Chad was concerned about her. He's mentioned her a few times to me. Apparently she's been following him around, but nothing has happened that would explain why she's doing this to him."

Belinda had a few things to gather before her first class, so she excused herself and told Helen that she'd keep her abreast of Chad's condition.

It proved very difficult for Belinda to concentrate in class. She was worried about Chad's being home alone and though her students didn't know the reason, they could tell something was wrong.

During her break, she tried to call Chad, but didn't get an answer. She left a message on his answering machine that she would try again after school. She ended with, "I love you, Chad."

Chad had crawled out of bed around 9:30. His head pounded as he tried to recall what had happened. He went into the bathroom and opened the medicine cabinet looking for some aspirin. He shook a couple into his hand and popped them into his mouth as he filled a cup with some water. Looking into the mirror above the sink, he was shocked at the way he looked. "I look like crap," he said aloud. "I don't even remember how I got home last night." Suddenly he remembered his conversation with Helen. "But I remember that little bitch's role in getting me into this predicament." He stripped, tossing his wrinkled clothes into the hamper, and turned on the water in the shower. He stepped under the spray and let it pound on his body. While it helped his physical condition somewhat, it did little to temper his mood. Several times over he just shouted, "Fuck" as loud as he could.

Afterwards, he paced back and forth around his bedroom. He tried to think of some way to deal with the problem. He knew that the lawyers for the union would defend him, but unless he came up with a clear way to prove his innocence, he was doomed. When the phone rang, he ignored it. Even when he heard the message and realized it was Belinda, he didn't answer. "I don't feel like talking to anyone right now, not even Belinda."

Belinda called again after school. This time Chad answered.

"Hi, honey. I tried calling you earlier, but you must have been still asleep. I want to come over and spend some time with you."

"I don't think that's a good idea, Belinda. I'm not very good company right now. I don't want you dragged into this mess."

"Chad, I love you. I'm involved and I'm not going away. We'll see this through together—to the end."

He argued a bit but realized she wasn't about to change her mind. "But if I tell you I want you to leave me alone, you'll listen to me," he said, trying to set some ground rules before agreeing.

When she arrived, Belinda was a bit shocked. Always neat and well kempt, Chad hadn't shaved, his hair was gnarled and uncombed, and he wore ratty looking clothes.

"Good God, Chad, you look like hell." She moved closer to him and put her arms around him. "You went beserk yesterday. C'mon, honey, you can't give in and let this girl win." Again she hugged him tightly.

"I feel so lost, Belinda. I don't know what to do. Everything's gone—my job, the coaching. I've lost the respect of the kids and people in this town."

She tried desperately to rally his spirits. "You've only lost if you give up."

They moved to the sofa to discuss details of what happened. Belinda cradled him in her arms as they talked. "Why is this girl out to get you?" she asked. "You've been nice to her from what I've heard you say these past weeks."

"She's been manipulating things from the start. I admit that I didn't see it, though I was alert enough to rebuff her a couple of times. This attack on my character, it seems, stems from my refusal to accept her efforts in class."

"Did you do or say anything to her that she could have misconstrued?" Belinda prodded Chad to consider every conversation he'd ever had with the girl.

"No! I was careful with her that way. Whenever she did something inappropriate, like that kiss in the gym after our victory, I admonished her. And when she made that sexual overture the other night, I pushed her away and told her to leave." Chad wracked his brains to think of something he might have done differently.

Belinda gave him a kiss. "Honey, it'll be ok. It's her word against yours, and the people of this school and this community will believe you."

"I wish I had your faith, Belinda, but you know that we're very vulnerable to this type of accusation."

They talked until dinner. Belinda made some soup and sandwiches and they watched some television until about 8 p.m. "I'd like to stay with you tonight, Chad. I can run home and pick up some clothes for tomorrow and be right back."

"Thanks for being so supportive, sweetheart, but I really feel like being alone tonight. Please don't be upset about that. I just need some time to think."

"I understand. Just promise you'll call if you need to talk tonight, okay?"

"I'll do that. I promise."

He helped Belinda with her coat and then they said goodnight. Throughout the rest of the evening, Chad replayed all of the times that he'd encountered Sheila in the past few weeks. He wrote down conversations as he remembered them. He recorded every occasion where he recalled coming into contact with her.

Chad spent the next week developing a routine to keep occupied during his suspension. Although he had notified the union and requested a legal consultation, the lawyer had only made a brief phone contact with him. It also disturbed him that nobody besides Belinda and Matt Stairs had called. Had his other friends and colleagues abandoned him?

The following Wednesday afternoon, Chad heard a knock at the door. Officer David Howell stood solemnly there. "Chad, I'm sorry to have to tell you this. The district justice has issued a warrant for your arrest. You're being charged with indecent assault. You'll have to come with me to the station."

Chapter 9

Chad moved to his closet to get his coat. He had known David Howell since they were kids, and the embarrassment he felt at having his friend see him like this was overwhelming.

Dave was uncomfortable as well. He'd always had a fondness as well as a lot of respect for Chad and was sure that something was not right with the McMasters girl's story, but he had to do his job. That didn't mean he couldn't try to make it easier on Chad. In a compassionate voice, Dave offered, "Do you want to call anyone before we go?"

Chad found it difficult to look David in the eyes. His head held down, Chad said, "I need to contact my lawyer, okay?"

Dave agreed and apologized. "Go ahead and call. And if there's anyone else, I'll give you the time. I'm sorry that I have to do this, Chad."

"Thanks, Dave, I appreciate it. Is it okay if I also call Belinda? I need to let her know what's happening."

"Sure, Chad. I'll wait over here." Dave moved to the other side of the room to give Chad a little privacy.

Several minutes later, Chad hung up the phone. The union's lawyer would meet him at the police station and in the meantime he'd been instructed not to say anything to the police. He could hear the distress in Belinda's voice despite her efforts to remain calm. She too would meet him at the police station as soon as she called in to request a sub.

"I'm ready now," Chad said to Dave nervously. They stepped outside and once Chad had locked the door, Dave followed behind him as he walked slowly to the police cruiser. Although Dave had graciously refrained from handcuffing him, Chad could feel the stare of a few of his neighbors as he moved down the path to the car. When Chad glanced helplessly at them, they turned their eyes away as if embarrassed to be spying on what was happening. Dave opened the rear door of the cruiser as Chad climbed into the back seat. He sat back and watched impotently as the door was closed behind him.

The ride to the station took fewer than five minutes, but it seemed like a lifetime to Chad. Nothing in his experience had ever felt as suffocating. He thought for a moment about the worst case scenario. "Could he, if convicted of a crime, survive being locked in a cell? How could the happiest days of his life have turned so quickly into this nightmare?"

At the station, Chad was seated inside a small room and offered some coffee, which he accepted. "Nothing will be said or done," said the sergeant who manned the desk, "until your lawyer arrives."

Since the lawyer for the union did not live in town, Chad realized that he would be confined there for at least an hour, maybe more. All he could do was wait.

Chad was mostly left alone, although different officers came in and out of the room intermittently for one reason or another. Each time the door opened Chad's attention focused on the person coming into the room, disappointment rising each time he saw that he still had to wait. The anticipation was taking a toll on him, and he was fidgeting nervously, losing patience.

At one point he thought he'd heard Belinda's voice outside the door, and he was surprised that she didn't come into the room to join him. He asked the next person who came into the room if indeed she was out there. The policeman confirmed that she was waiting for him, but until he'd been interviewed, he wouldn't be allowed to see anyone aside from his lawyer.

Finally, the union lawyer arrived. Dave brought him in. The lawyer greeted Chad with a handshake, introducing himself as Sam Ludwig.

Chad stood and took the outstretched hand. "Thanks for coming, Mr. Ludwig."

"Please, Chad, if I may, call me Sam," the lawyer insisted. "I got here as soon as I could. I'm sorry it took me so long to get in here; I'm sure you've been anxious. I just spoke with Officer Howell, who's handling your case. He filled me in on what's going on, but I'd like to hear your version of what happened."

Dave interrupted only to tell them that they could have some time to confer privately. Then he left them alone in the room.

Sam sat at the table across from Chad, took out a legal pad and a pen and began asking Chad a series of questions. Chad answered quickly and honestly, occasionally repeating something when he saw that Sam was writing it all down. After getting a general idea of Chad's version of the events, Sam put his pen down and spoke to Chad, explaining the technicalities of what was going to happen.

"Apparently, the police and the district attorney feel that they have enough evidence to charge you with indecent assault and corruption of a minor. A warrant was issued and on that basis you were arrested," Sam explained.

Chad interjected, "How can they have evidence? It *never* happened!" Chad shouted, losing his temper. Sam reached over and grabbed Chad's arm to get his attention and shushed him.

"Shhhhhhh. Please. Calm down. I'm on your side. I'm just trying to explain to you what's happened so far."

Chad tried to gain control. He lowered his voice but continued speaking through clenched teeth. He spoke slowly and deliberately and Sam could feel the restrained anger in his words. Sam understood Chad's need to vent, so he let him continue. "They're taking the word of that little tramp. She's a spoiled rotten little princess who's never heard the word *no* and the first time something doesn't go her way, she's out for blood—my blood!"

Sam didn't interrupt and Chad continued to rant for a few minutes.

Eventually, Chad ran out of steam, realizing that his outburst wasn't accomplishing anything. He sat back, defeated, and quietly asked one last question, "How can they take her word for this?"

Sam was sympathetic to the frustration felt by his client. "I understand, Chad. I'll do my best to help you, but now we need to discuss what happened. Are you ready to talk about it?"

"Yeah, sorry for my outburst," Chad apologized and composed himself. "So please explain to me what's going on."

Sam was grateful for Chad's regaining control; this was going to be an uphill battle. "A complaint was filed against you."

"Yeah, I know that much," Chad said, and in a tone full of disdain almost spit out her name, "Sheila McMasters."

Sam checked the notes he'd made during his meeting with the police officer before he spoke to Chad and nodded, "Yes, McMasters. Anyway, this has become an official investigation by the police. Have you told them anything yet?"

Chad assured his lawyer that he'd followed instructions and maintained his silence.

"Good. So let's get down to business now." Sam looked to Chad for his agreement and, when Chad nodded, he continued. "The police are waiting now to question you. Before you answer any questions, I want you to follow my lead. If it's ok, I'll let you know and if I feel it's inappropriate, I'll tell them that you're not to answer that now. If there's anything they ask with which you're uncomfortable, just say that you'd rather not comment on it until you've discussed it with me. Do you understand?"

"Yes, I understand and I admit that I'm nervous as hell. I can't believe this is happening." Although Chad's despair was evident, he had another immediate concern, for which he hoped Sam could help. "Sam, my girlfriend is outside. Do you think they'll let me see her for a few minutes before we go on. She's been out there for over an hour and she must be going through hell."

Sam tried to reassure him. "It's understandable that you're nervous. Just tell the truth. It'll be ok. I'll go ask about your girlfriend. What's her name?"

"Belinda Landis."

"Okay, let me check." Sam went to open the door and found it locked. He knocked and the door was opened immediately. Sam spoke briefly to the officer standing there and then he turned back into the room and informed Chad, "I'm sorry, but they won't let Belinda in here until they've finished the processing. They're waiting to question you and they'd like to get to it now."

"Sam, do you think you can go out there for a minute and at least let her know what's going on? She must be frantic," Chad pleaded. "Please, just tell her I'm okay."

"Well, I'd be lying if I told her that, but I'll go see if I can speak to her for a few minutes and tell her what's happening."

Chad nodded. "Thanks."

Sam left the room and had no trouble finding Belinda. She waited outside the room, pacing the floor frenetically. As soon as Sam stepped out of the room, she came right up to him and asked eagerly, "Are you Chad's lawyer?"

"Yes, you must be Belinda." He extended his hand and introduced himself. "I'm Sam Ludwig. Chad asked me to come out here to look for you. Since the police won't let you see him yet, he wanted me to let you know what's happening and tell you that he's okay."

"Is he? Is he really okay? I don't know how he can be!" Belinda was borderline hysterical and her voice cracked as she spoke. She stopped for a moment trying to regain her composure. She took a deep breath and tried to speak again, hoping this time to make a better impression on the man who would help Chad.

"Losing it won't help anyone now," she reprimanded herself. She accepted the hand he'd extended and, shaking it firmly, trying to stay calm, she said, "Mr. Ludwig, thank you. Yes, I'm Belinda." Suddenly, the tears that she'd been keeping in check as she paced, waiting to see Chad, began to spill over and run down her cheeks. "Is he really okay? What's going on? Why is this happening? You've gotta know that Chad would never have done this. That girl's been a pain in his butt since the first day of the semester."

Sam, fearing that Belinda was about to become hysterical, led her over to the water cooler in the corner. He pulled a paper cup from the holder and filled it with water, handing it to her, encouraging her to drink. Once she had taken a sip, he motioned her to the bench against the wall where he sat down and filled her in on what had happened so far and what was about to happen. "I'm sorry, but I don't think that they'll let you see him until the processing has been completed. They're waiting now to question Chad, so I need to get back in there now. If you want to go home, give me a number where I can reach you, and I'll call and let you know as soon as you can see Chad."

"Thanks, Sam. I'm not going anywhere." Belinda wiped her tears, put on a brave face, and assured Sam she'd be fine. "I'll wait here for as long as it takes." She stood and gently nudged Sam in the direction of the room where Chad waited. "You go and do whatever you can to help Chad end this nightmare. Please tell him that I love him and I'll be here."

Sam nodded and told her, "I'll do my best, Belinda," and then he turned and went back to Chad.

Chad jumped up as soon as Sam came back in the room. "Did you see her?"

"Yes. She sends her love and asked me to tell you she'll be here. Chad, are you ready now for them to question you?"

"Yes, as ready as I'll ever be," Chad mumbled. Sam knocked on the door again, and told the officer at the door that they were ready.

The chief of police came into the room with Dave Howell. Having grown up in this small town, Chad knew the chief casually. Just as he'd felt when Dave showed up to arrest him, Chad was mortified to be in this situation, especially in front of a man he respected.

The chief had been surprised and skeptical when he'd heard about the charges being brought against Chad, but once the warrant had been issued, he had no choice but to follow procedure. Although he normally wouldn't be present during the questioning of a suspect, under the circumstances, he wanted to make this as easy as possible. When he came into the room though, he sensed Chad's embarrassment, and almost regretted his impulse to become directly involved.

"Chad, I'd like to help figure out what's really happening here. Unfortunately, though, we have to adhere to protocol," the chief began in an apologetic tone.

Sam, sensing that Chad was overwhelmed and unable to respond, answered on Chad's behalf, "Thanks, chief. We appreciate your involvement and hope you can help us prove that these charges are bogus."

"First, I have to 'Mirandize' you," the chief said and proceeded to inform Chad of his rights. After receiving confirmation from Chad that he understood, the interrogation proceeded.

"A complaint has been filed by the parents of one of your students stating that you sexually harassed their daughter. Such a charge is classified as indecent assault. Based on some preliminary investigation, mostly from the girl's side, the district attorney requested that a warrant be issued against you. We'd like to hear your version of the events now."

Chad looked at Sam and nodded. Then he looked at Dave and said, "Go ahead."

Dave put a tape recorder on the table and asked, "Does anyone object to having this conversation taped? If at any time you want me to turn it off, you can let me know and I will stop it." Neither Chad nor Sam voiced an objection, so Dave turned on the recorder and spoke into the machine, "Today is March 19, 2004..." Then he listed those present in the room, and referring to the notes in front of him, read the case number, and stated that this investigation was to determine whether Chad Peterson was involved in an instance of indecent assault, clarifying that the charge involved a minor.

Once Dave had finished with the formalities, he deferred to the chief, who had indicated earlier that he'd like to conduct the questioning.

The chief began, "Can we assume that you are aware who it is that brought these charges?"

Chad looked to Sam again, who indicated with a nod that Chad could respond. Chad took a deep breath, hoping to gain control, before responding, "Yes, we're talking about Sheila McMasters."

The chief looked at Dave who, in addition to the tape recorder, was taking notes, and then back again at Chad before he continued. "Under what circumstances did you first meet her?"

"I teach at Emerson Central High, here in town. She's a student in one of my history classes this term."

"Have you had any private contact with her prior to the incident in question?" asked the Chief.

When Sam didn't object, Chad thought for a minute before responding. "I've talked with her on several occasions, mostly in the presence of others. There was only one other private contact, as you put it. One morning, a couple of weeks ago, she came to school early and talked with me in my classroom. A fellow teacher, Jim Morris, came to my rescue, and she left the room."

"What do you mean by rescue?" pursued the chief.

"I couldn't seem to get her to leave and I had work to do that morning. I was trying to be polite and despite a number of subtle attempts on my part suggesting she leave, she didn't seem to get the hint. She bolted from the room as soon as Jim came in."

"And that's the only other time you've been alone with her?"

"Yes, I think so, until the other evening when she came into my room."

"You never met her outside of school alone?"

Sam Ludwig interrupted at that point. "I think we've covered that, Chief. Chad said that he hadn't met the girl alone."

The Chief started a different tack. "Tell us about the other night. What happened?"

Chad hesitated a moment and nodded toward the tape recorder. Dave immediately turned it off and then Chad asked to speak privately with Sam before answering the question. Dave and the chief left the room for a few minutes while they consulted.

"Exactly what should I tell him?" asked Chad. "Should I be answering that?"

"Tell them exactly what you told me before. You have nothing to hide." Sam knocked on the door and the policemen returned.

"Can we put the tape recorder back on?" the chief asked as they sat down again.

Sam and Chad agreed and the chief started the recorder again. "Why don't you tell us, in your own words, the events leading up to the other night," the chief suggested.

"Okay," Chad agreed. "I'm not really sure where to start."

"Take your time, and tell us whatever you remember," recommended Dave.

"I've been coaching volleyball this semester. Sheila's not on the team, but she and some of her friends are cheerleaders and frequently practice at the same time as our sessions. The other night, after volleyball practice, I went to my classroom to finish grading some essays. Sheila followed me into my room and asked if she could speak with me. I was a bit short with her and asked her what she was doing there at that hour. She said something about doing some extra credit work, so I told her to come in."

Dave asked, somewhat surprised, "Did Sheila McMasters make a habit of doing extra work?"

Chad laughed bitterly. "Are you kidding? She barely does the regular work I assign."

"So why would she approach you about doing some extra work?" the chief asked.

"She'd recently gotten a bad grade on a project for which she'd made no effort. She said that her parents were…to quote her, 'gonna kill her' and she wanted to find a way to make up the grade. I offered her an idea that I thought would work."

The chief interrupted. "What did you suggest?"

"My class is preparing for a school assembly where they will be presenting some material we've been working on in class. I suggested she actively participate in the assembly and if she did, then I'd see about adjusting her grade."

Again the chief spoke. "This somewhat differs from the girl's version. Go on."

"Yeah, I'm sure it does, but I swear that's all I offered or suggested." Chad was becoming agitated.

Dave tried to get the conversation back on track, "So, Chad, what happened next?" he prompted.

"I was generously suggesting a way she could earn a better grade and make up for screwing up, and all of a sudden she started saying something about pleasing me. I told her that she would please me and her friends if she didn't let them down again. Next thing I knew, she opened up her sweater or blouse. I don't remember what she had on, but she exposed her breasts. She got up from her seat and moved toward me, saying she'd do anything I asked to get a better grade. I was in shock! I remember telling her to get out. Oh, and I remember that just then her friend came into the room."

"Did you touch her?" the Chief asked.

Chad thought about it for a moment. "She walked right up to me with her top open. I think I might have put my hands on her shoulders to push her away. But I *never* touched her the way she's saying. What the hell is wrong with that girl?" Chad shook his head helplessly.

"Is there anything else you want to add?" the Chief asked.

Chad hesitated a bit and, then remembering, he added, "Yeah, I remember that when Sheila threw herself at me and I pushed her away, I never touched her anywhere except her shoulders!" And when I told her to get out, that was the exact moment that her friend walked into the room. Actually, now that I'm thinking about it, her friend's timing was very convenient. I wonder if she planned this all along."

"What happened next?" the Chief asked.

"Her friend ran out, and Sheila followed. I called my girlfriend and asked if I could come over to her place. I waited a few minutes to be sure they'd left the building, and then I headed straight to Belinda's apartment."

The tough question immediately followed. "Why didn't you report this to the principal?"

Chad answered truthfully. "Honestly, I was afraid to stir up trouble. I felt vulnerable, and I still do. I didn't know if Sheila would make an issue of it; after all, she was the instigator. I was afraid that just what is happening now would happen. I know in these cases, it's her word against mine, and with no way to prove what had really happened, my reputation could be ruined."

The chief reached over at that point and turned off the recorder. "Ok, thanks for being cooperative. I think we've heard enough."

Chad looked at Sam who nodded, showing that he'd done well.

"What happens now?" Chad inquired.

"We need to finish processing your arrest now. You'll be fingerprinted and photographed," explained the chief. "Sometime before noon you'll be brought before the district justice for an arraignment. He'll read the charges against you, set a hearing date, and set bail."

Chad lowered his head in disbelief. His shoulders slumped as he remained motionless in his chair. "So just what I feared would happen is happening. How can I prove my innocence?" he asked somewhat rhetorically.

The chief, unable to answer Chad's question, continued explaining the procedures, "If you make bail, you'll be allowed to go home, and you'll be instructed to stay in town."

Dave showed compassion as he escorted Chad for the fingerprinting and pictures, apologizing often for having to do it.

"Not as sorry as I am, Dave. I understand you're just doing your job, but this is just ridiculous. I never did what this girl is accusing me of." Chad was mortified by what was happening to him, struggling to maintain control when Dave handed him a wet towelette to wipe the ink off his fingers when the fingerprinting was done.

Dave permitted Chad to sit in the meeting room with Sam while they waited to go to the courthouse. Chad thanked him for not making him wait in a cell.

Although Belinda hadn't been allowed to join them during the questioning, once the processing was over, Dave told her she could join Chad and Sam in the meeting room. Chad told Belinda what had happened so far. Sam explained to them both what awaited them at the courthouse, mostly repeating what the chief had already explained to Chad. When Belinda offered to go to Chad's place to bring him a suit and tie to wear when he was brought before the judge, Chad gave her the keys to his apartment and told her where to find what he'd need. They checked the timing with Dave and determined that she'd have enough time to find Chad's things and bring them back to the police station. She'd then follow them to the courthouse in her car.

It was only a couple hours later when Chad stood before the judge. The arraignment was handled quickly and it seemed to Chad, almost by rote. The judge read the charges from a page he'd been handed by the clerk. Although he formally asked Chad for his plea, he didn't really wait for an answer before he turned the pages in his calendar and announced, "A preliminary hearing will be held on April 8."

The judge looked questioningly at the district attorney and Sam, and merely asked, "Bail, gentlemen?"

Sam jumped to his feet and began telling the judge of Chad's clean record, his ties to the community, when the district attorney interrupted saying, "We have no objection to a reasonable bail, Your Honor."

Chad was amazed at how this was being handled so coldly and impersonally while his whole world was falling apart at his feet, but he was relieved when the judge declared, "Bail is set at five thousand dollars." Then he banged his gavel, dismissing them. Sam turned to Chad and told him that he'd take care of the bail immediately.

Until the bail was dealt with, Chad was officially in police custody, but since the bail clerk's office was in the courthouse building, Dave offered to wait with Chad on a bench in the hallway, right outside the courtroom, while Sam made the arrangements.

Belinda walked out of the courtroom with Chad and Dave and tried her best to be optimistic, although her heart was breaking for Chad. Dave led them to the bench and Chad sat down, dejectedly, unable to fight off the depression that had been gnawing at him since all this began.

Belinda sat next to him, holding his hand in hers, murmuring words of love and support, though it seemed that she wasn't getting through to Chad. He seemed to be retreating more and more into a depression.

It took fewer than ten minutes before Sam returned and handed Dave the paperwork which allowed him to release Chad from custody. Chad seemed oblivious to what was going on. He seemed to snap out of it for a minute, long enough to thank Dave for his consideration under the difficult circumstances, before retreating again into himself. Sam tried to make an appointment to meet with Chad the next day, but when Chad remained unresponsive, Belinda said she'd have Chad call him in the morning. Dave sincerely wished Chad good luck and stood with Sam as they watched Chad and Belinda walk out of the courthouse hand in hand.

Despite Belinda's attempts to get Chad to talk to her, he stayed quiet, lost in his own thoughts. Belinda still had Chad's keys and when she opened the door, he followed her inside, in some kind of trance. Belinda made another attempt to reach him, but his only response was to insist that she leave.

"Please, Chad. Don't ask me to leave you alone. We need to stick together; let me be here with you," Belinda begged.

Chad remained stoic. "Belinda, I know you're here for me, but I need to be alone now. Please don't make this any harder than it has to be."

Belinda was torn. She needed Chad's support just as much as she knew he needed hers, but she couldn't make him see that. Finally, she relented, but not before he promised to call if he needed her.

"I promise. I'll call you if I need you. I'm sorry, Belinda. You don't deserve this heartache." He gave her a quick hug and led her to the door despite her protests.

Belinda made one last attempt to reach Chad. "Neither of us deserves this heartache, but we can get through it together. I can't bear to see you go through this alone."

"If you leave now, you won't have to see me go through this," Chad said brutally, immediately regretting his harshness when he saw Belinda flinch. He held himself back before he took her into his arms to comfort her and apologize for his cruelty. She really didn't deserve this, but if he weakened she wouldn't leave, and he wanted her to go. "In the long run it will be better for her if she leaves," he told himself.

In tears, Belinda turned to go. "I know you don't mean that, Chad," she said, and despite the pain she felt at his rejection, she reminded him, "I love you and I'll be here if you want me—just call."

Chad softened long enough to thank her, but not enough to touch her again, because he didn't think he could bear to touch her and then let her go. And for her sake, he had to let her go.

The next week passed for Chad in a cloud of depression. Belinda called often and he started letting the machine pick up the calls. When he did speak to her, he kept it short and found a limitless number of excuses to avoid seeing her.

When she became insistent, he would tell her that he had to meet with Sam about the hearing—an excuse he knew she'd have to accept. He ignored her pleas and remained secluded as much as possible from contacts with anyone, which was a lot less of a problem than he thought, since these days, not many people were seeking him out. His only outings in town were, in fact, to meet with Sam, to discuss the case. When he needed groceries, he called a local store that delivered. If there was anything else he wanted or needed, he did without.

Chad wallowed in self-pity and continued to regress. He'd begun drinking heavily (the liquor store also delivered), and he left both his person and his place unkempt. Belinda continued to call frequently, and he continued to refuse to see her. A couple of times she came to the door without calling first. The first time he ignored her, pretending he wasn't there. The next time she came, he callously shouted through the door, "I don't want anyone around me right now and that includes you. There's nothing you can do for me! My life is fucked up and you don't need to be around a loser like me. Just leave me alone!"

Although the sound of Belinda crying broke his heart, he forced himself not to give in, for her sake. But despite the harsh way he was treating her, Belinda didn't give up on him. When he let the machine answer, she left loving, supportive messages. On the occasions he answered the phone, Belinda tried to reason with him. She could tell he'd been drinking and tried to make him see how it was only making things worse. In response, he slammed the phone down and took another drink. The alcohol contributed to his depression, but he couldn't see it.

Sam Ludwig was unaware of the severity of Chad's situation until, out of desperation, Belinda called him.

"Sam, this is Belinda. I need your help with Chad," she pleaded.

"Belinda, how are you?" Sam greeted her pleasantly. "What can I do for you?" he asked but before she had a chance to respond, he continued, "I'm surprised that you haven't come to any of the meetings I've had with Chad. I'd like to speak with you before we go to court."

"Thanks, Sam. Actually, I'm not doing very well." Belinda got to the point. "I haven't seen Chad since the arraignment. He won't talk to me and when I go over to his place, he won't open the door for me."

"I had no idea. Did you two have an argument? He really needs you now," Sam asked, concerned. Unpleasantly surprised at this development, he silently calculated the effectiveness of using Belinda as a character witness if she and Chad were at odds.

"No, Sam, you don't understand." Belinda explained. "Chad has shut me out. I know he thinks he's protecting me, but he doesn't need to do that. I want to help him. I know he's going through hell, but he won't let me near him. I need you to help him."

Sam had been unaware of the situation between Chad and Belinda. He was sorry to hear that Chad was being so stubborn, because he knew that Chad could really use her support now. "I'm doing my best to help Chad, Belinda. What more do you think I can do?" He had been so intent on everything that needed to be discussed before the hearing, he hadn't focused much on Chad's relationship with Belinda, assuming that they were together.

"Sam, Chad's been drinking. The few times that I've spoken to him on the phone, I could tell he'd been drinking. His speech was slurred and he wasn't acting himself. I'm so worried about him. He doesn't usually drink, and he's not handling it well." Belinda appealed to Sam, "Please, he needs help; he won't let me and there's nobody else I can turn to. You're the only one who can get through to him now. He doesn't see anyone else."

Sam thought back to the few meetings he'd had with Chad since the arraignment. He hadn't particularly noticed any signs of drinking, but then he wasn't looking for any. Trying to recall if he'd noticed anything out of the ordinary, he suddenly remembered a conversation with Chad. Sam had been trying to make some small talk, to put Chad at ease, and he mentioned something about Chad's breath. He recalled that it wasn't liquor he'd noticed, but rather a strong scent of mouthwash. Sam smiled when he remembered that he'd told Chad that since he had no plans to kiss Chad, it would be okay if he went a bit easier on the mouthwash. Chad had mumbled something about having had a lot of onions on his burger before their meeting, but after what Belinda had said, it made more sense that Chad was probably trying to mask the scent of alcohol.

Alarmed at what it could do to their case if Chad were to be seen in an intoxicated state, Sam thanked Belinda for calling it to his attention, promised to do what he could to help. He then hightailed it over to Chad's apartment.

Chad wasn't expecting Sam, but he couldn't very well refuse to open the door. Sam was shocked at what he saw. The apartment was a mess. Clothes and food wrappers were strewn all over. There was a collection of empty beer cans on the end table; there were even a few on the couch. There were dirty plates and crumpled paper towels on the chairs, on the floor near the couch, and on top of the television. Chad was a mess too. He hadn't shaved in a couple of days, his clothes were rumpled, and as Sam wrinkled his nose at a sour stench, it became apparent that it had been a while since Chad had showered.

Sam confronted Chad, unwilling to accept any excuses for Chad's loss of control. "You have to pull yourself out of this, Chad. You can't appear in court like this. Appearance and demeanor count for a lot. I'm doing all I can to help you, but you have to do your part."

Chad was full of self-pity. "My reputation is ruined here forever. There will always be that cloud of doubt hanging over my head, regardless of what happens."

Sam refused to enable Chad's self-inflicted punishment to continue. "Don't be so sure of that. First, we have to see what the DA has against you. If it's just a matter of hearsay by the student, there's always the possibility that the judge will summarily dismiss the charges."

Chad perked up for a minute, "Is that really a possibility, Sam?" He was afraid to hope that it could be that easy.

Sam didn't want to raise any false hopes. If Sheila had let things go this far, she'd likely have cooked up enough of a story that the judge wouldn't be able to dismiss it so easily. "It's not likely, but it's definitely an option. I have to tell you, Chad, if you show up in court looking the way you do right now, not only will you raise doubts about your innocence, but the judge may be inclined to revoke your bail."

"Can he do that?" Sam had definitely gotten Chad's attention now.

"Yes, he can and I can almost guarantee he will if he sees you like this." Sam took a firm stand. He believed in Chad's innocence, but would need Chad's full cooperation to get through this. "It's obvious that you've been drinking. If I were that girl's father, and I found out you've been drinking, I'd make sure that the judge knew you were a danger to my daughter's safety and demand you be locked up. Frankly, Chad, if the judge sees you in this condition, I'd be hard pressed to talk him out of revoking your bail."

Chad nodded, realizing the truth of what Sam was saying. "Okay, Sam. I hear you."

Sam, taking charge, declared how it was going to be. "I'm going to plow my way into your kitchen," he said, already collecting some of the plates and cups littering the path to the kitchen. "If I can find what I need, I'll make some coffee. Meanwhile, you get in there," Sam added, pointing towards the bathroom, "and shave and shower, now!" Before he went into the kitchen, he was glad to see that Chad was following his orders. He watched Chad bend over and pick up some of the clothes from the floor on his way to the bathroom. As soon as Chad closed the bathroom door behind him, Sam went into the kitchen. He put the dishes into the sink and looked around for the coffee pot.

He actually found everything he needed and he filled the water, measured some coffee into the filter, and turned on the machine. Then he straightened up a bit in the kitchen, and when he didn't see a dishwasher, he rolled up his sleeves and started doing the dishes. "My mother would have a cow if she saw me putting my law degree to use this way." He laughed to himself.

The plates had obviously been sitting around for a few days, since some of them were encrusted with old food that resisted the sponge Sam was using. He filled the sink with hot, soapy water and put the plates in to soak, hoping that would make them easier to wash later. The coffeemaker was gurgling away when he went back into the living room. He could hear the water running in the shower, so he started straightening up the room while he waited for Chad to finish in there.

Sam tossed the empty beer cans into the trash. He also found a couple others in the fridge that weren't empty and took matters into his own hands, pouring their contents down the drain.

Chad came into the living room, barefoot, wearing a clean t-shirt and a pair of jeans, rubbing his hair with a towel to dry it just as Sam brought the coffee pot into the living room. "Thanks, Sam. I'll get the cups," he offered, dropping the towel around his shoulders and going into the kitchen.

He returned a moment later with two mugs, the milk and sugar. Once Sam had poured two cups of coffee, they sat down and Chad thanked him again. "Sam, you really didn't have to begin cleaning my apartment, but I appreciate that you did." Trying to lighten the mood a bit he added, with a wink, "But I think you missed a spot over there."

Sam smiled and said, "You're welcome…this time, but you should know that I don't do windows."

They drank their coffee in silence and when Chad finished his cup, Sam immediately refilled it. Chad looked at him questioningly, and Sam stared and suggested strongly, "Drink it."

Chad, not wanting to try Sam's patience, picked up the mug. "Yes, sir!" he said and took a sip.

"Okay, we have to get down to business. There will be no more drinking. No arguments. We have to be in court in two days. Do you have any clean clothes to wear? If not, you'd better get moving with your laundry. You have to make a good impression; your future can depend on it."

"I'll do a load of laundry when you leave, Sam. I'll be okay," Chad promised. Suddenly curious why Sam had come over in the first place, Chad asked, "By the way, you never said why you came over. Is there something we need to discuss?"

"I came over because Belinda called me. She's worried sick about you, Chad. Why are you shutting her out?"

Chad glared at him, "Sam, stay out of it, okay?"

Sam didn't back down. "Hey, I figure doing your dishes and cleaning up your crap gives me the right to stick my nose in your business."

"Really, leave it alone," Chad insisted.

Sam wouldn't let go. "I can't leave it alone. You need someone and it's obvious that Belinda loves you. The impression I had from you back at the police station was that you love her too. Why would you shut her out?"

"I'm trying to protect her. Why would she want to be involved in something like this?"

"Chad, she loves you. Tell me honestly, don't you love her too?" Sam wasn't just asking to be polite; he was trying to make a point.

"Of course I love her. Pushing her away is killing me, but I don't want her to go through this hell," Chad explained.

"Listen to me. You're putting her through a much worse hell. She loves you, and you're breaking her heart by pushing her away." When Chad started to interrupt, Sam held up his hand and continued, "Now there's something else you need to consider as well. Think about the impression you want to make. Don't you want people to see that you're involved in a healthy relationship? I interviewed a few of your friends and colleagues, looking for character witnesses for you and every one of them commented on how ridiculous these charges are, because they all know how committed you are to Belinda. In my opinion, that works in your favor."

"I'm not going to expose Belinda to all this shit just so it can help me! I can't do that to her," Chad shouted.

Sam kept his voice low, trying to avoid letting this get out of hand. "But you need each other." Sam tried to get Chad to listen to reason. "Do you hear me? You need each other. You're not exposing her to anything she doesn't want to be involved in—she loves you. She wants to help you and whether you want to admit it or not, you need her help."

Chad felt like he was being torn into pieces. "Yes," he admitted, "I need Belinda, now more than ever. But how can I do this to her? I love her. Why would she want to be involved in this mess?" Chad had been living in a cloud of embarrassment since the incident. Did he want to see Belinda suffer through it too? Suddenly Chad remembered the sound of Belinda crying outside his door when he wouldn't open it for her, and it hit him just how much his shutting her out was hurting her. If something had happened to Belinda, he knew he'd want to be there. Why did he think that she wouldn't feel the same?

Finally, he admitted, "Oh, God, Sam, you're right. I've been so caught up in self-pity, I didn't even think about what I was doing to her. Do you think she can forgive me? I don't even know how to start making this up to her." Chad looked to Sam for advice on how to begin.

Sam was glad to see that he was finally getting through and smiled as he offered a suggestion. "You can start by calling her, telling her you're sorry, and begging her forgiveness. See if that works. Tell her how much you need her; grovel if you must. I'll leave now and let you do it privately."

"Thanks for bringing me to my senses."

"One more thing before I go. You do remember that we have to be in court day after tomorrow, right?"

Chad looked at Sam with a wry expression, "Duuuh, could I forget?"

They both laughed at that. "So, do you want a ride?" Sam offered, glad that he was able to get a smile out of Chad.

"I'll have to let you know," Chad said with a wink. "I'm gonna call Belinda and if she doesn't hang up on me, maybe I'll be able to convince her to pick me up. I hope so. Anyway, I'll let you know either way."

"Okay," Sam agreed. "I hope everything works out for the two of you on all fronts. I'd like to have a least half an hour to talk to you before we go into the courtroom, so if you're coming with Belinda, plan to be there by one-thirty. If she can't get out of work that early, I'll be happy to pick you up."

"You do know that I know how to drive. I'm capable of driving myself," Chad reminded him.

"I know, Chad, but it's going to be a very emotionally trying day for you. It's really not a problem for me to pick you up. I'd rather you weren't alone, okay?"

"If you're worried that I'll start drinking again, don't. I'll be okay." Chad extended his hand. "I really do appreciate everything you're doing for me."

Sam took the hand and, with a firm grip, solidly shook it. "I'll do my best. I hope that my efforts will be good enough."

"Me too," Chad said, wishing he felt more confident. He walked Sam to the door and said, "I'll see you day after tomorrow. Thanks."

"Bye. Remember, if you need me before then, just call, and good luck with Belinda," Sam said and lifted his hand in a casual wave as he walked away.

Belinda answered the phone on the second ring and burst into tears as soon as she heard Chad's voice. She barely gave him a chance to say anything, much less apologize. In between her sniffles and hiccups, she repeated how much she loved him, how she only wanted to help, and how happy she was that he'd called.

Finally, Chad managed to break through and get her attention. "Belinda, I'm sorry for shutting you out. I hope you can forgive me. I love you too," to which her response was to start crying all over again.

They talked for a few minutes more, when Chad told her, "Belinda, I'd really like to see you."

Belinda didn't need to hear anything else. "I'll be right over," she said and hung up. It took her fewer than five minutes before she was out the door heading over to Chad's place.

* * *

Sam was delighted to see Chad and Belinda walking toward the courthouse hand in hand. He greeted them warmly as they reached the courthouse steps together, about half an hour before the hearing was to begin. There were a few newspapermen with cameras, standing on the steps. When they saw Chad arrive, they moved to approach him.

"It doesn't take long for news to travel in a small town, Sam. They smell blood." Chad was apprehensive.

Sam whispered, "Don't make eye contact, just come with me and don't say a thing." He grabbed Chad's arm and with Belinda on Chad's other side, they moved quickly past the reporters without stopping.

It was a media frenzy. "Do you have anything to say, Mr. Peterson?" one reporter shouted and then it seemed as if they were all shouting at once.

Chad just looked at the floor and continued walking.

"No comment," Sam shouted over the din and that's all he said.

Sam led Chad and Belinda to the meeting room where they'd met after the arraignment. It was empty, and Sam deliberately closed the door before the reporters could intrude. Chad breathed a sigh of relief at having escaped the melee, for now. "Did you know it would be like this, Sam? What a zoo!"

"I wasn't sure, but I feared there might be a circus. I didn't want to take a chance that they'd corner you and have you unintentionally say anything that could damage our case." When he saw that Chad had calmed down, Sam once again reviewed the procedures of the hearing and reminded Chad to maintain his composure, regardless of any provocation from the district attorney or the McMasters, who would certainly be there.

"Chad, I can't stress this enough. Under no circumstances should you speak unless the judge asks you a question directly. You must keep your temper under control."

"I'll do my best, Sam," Chad promised, "but it's not easy. There's something intrinsically wrong with the system. I understand and agree that children must be protected from things like this. It's a horrifying thought that there really are teachers out there who take advantage of kids, but that's not the case here. This girl is a vindictive bitch, who was pissed at me because I gave her a bad grade. And when she made a pass at me, thinking I'd give her a good grade in exchange for sex, I turned her down. She can't take being turned down! She's taking advantage of a law that's meant to protect her. How can I fight against that? I bet she's gonna sit in court gloating while I'm impotent against her lies. How can I prove my innocence when it's her word against mine?"

"Don't worry about her gloating. It's not likely that she'll even be in court. She's a minor and will be allowed to testify behind closed doors," Sam explained. "They can just present her statement in court."

"What? Are you kidding? She can accuse me of this and not even face me in court?" Chad was flabbergasted. He slumped down at the table, putting his head in his hands in defeat.

"In some cases the defendant isn't even told the name of the accuser when a minor is involved. In this instance, you knew who it was, so protecting her identity wasn't an issue."

"I don't understand. How can this be called justice? This little bitch doesn't need protection, I do!" Chad railed against the injustice.

"Chad, it's almost time to go into court, pull yourself together. We'll call your friends and colleagues as character witnesses. I've met with a number of your friends and they're all supporting you. They know you couldn't have done this."

"I wish that made me feel optimistic. This is all just so unreal. How can this be happening?" Chad was distraught and Belinda moved to wrap her arms around him.

Sam gave them a moment and then he stood up, "Come on, let's go." Sam picked up his briefcase and moved to the door. He peered out to see if the reporters were waiting, and when he saw that the hallway was clear, he opened the door for Chad and Belinda, gesturing for them to lead the way to the courtroom.

Officer Dave Howell was already seated, and he nodded at Belinda, Chad, and Sam as they approached their seats. Sam led Chad to the table in front and indicated that Belinda should sit directly behind them.

The district attorney was seated at the table next to them. Sam had never met Jack Montgomery, personally, but he knew of him through a number of mutual acquaintances. Sam was aware that the DA was well-respected and had a reputation for being very good at his job.

Chad looked around the courtroom and was surprised to see Sheila there. She was sitting with a couple he assumed were her parents. "I thought you said she wouldn't be here," he said to Sam, who turned to look at the girl Chad had indicated.

Sam shook his head noncommitally. "I admit, I'm surprised she showed up. But then we've learned that the girl has a lot of *chutzpa*."

"Will I be allowed to question her?" Chad asked.

"If there's a trial and they call her to testify, I'll be able to cross-examine her, but you won't be able to question her," Sam explained.

Chad glared at Sheila and her parents, and he said to no one in particular, "I bet if I could question her, I could get her to admit that she made all this up…"

There was something different about her, but Chad couldn't quite put his finger on what it was. He continued to stare at her for another moment before it hit him. He leaned back a bit so that Belinda could hear his next comment. "Look what she's wearing. She looks like a fucking girl scout! Have you ever seen her in clothes like that?"

Belinda looked and immediately understood what Chad was talking about. She called Sam's attention to the girl's attire. "Sam, I swear that Sheila only owns transparent tops and four inch skirts. She never even wears pants and she doesn't own anything remotely modest. Her wardrobe is one of the standing jokes in the teachers' room. You wouldn't believe how each outfit she wears is more outrageous than the one before. It looks like she borrowed these clothes from a parochial school!"

They were now all staring at Sheila, who seemed oblivious to the attention she was receiving.

Chad asked, "Who's she trying to kid?"

Sam was scribbling something on his legal pad when the court clerk instructed, "All rise." Everyone got to their feet.

The judge came in and sat down, saying, "Be seated."

Everyone did so. The clerk continued, "Case number 33047, the State vs. Chad Peterson, Judge William Longfellow presiding." He handed the judge a folder and stepped back to a desk next to the judge's bench where he sat down.

The judge perused the contents of the folder before turning and asking both attorneys if they were ready to proceed. Jack Montgomery and Sam both stood, asserting that they were ready, and then the judge turned to the DA and requested that he begin.

"Your Honor," he started, "we contend that the defendant, Chad Peterson, did willfully and knowingly violate the sanctity of his position as a teacher by engaging in improper sexual conduct with one of his students. We will call on several witnesses who will testify that Mr. Peterson has acted inappropriately with this student on more than one occasion." As the prosecutor spoke, he approached the bench and handed the judge his witness list. He then returned to his table, handing Sam a copy of the list before he continued.

"We will also present an audio tape that will clearly show that Mr. Peterson asked for sexual favors from this student."

Sam, forgetting the paper in his hand for the moment, turned in shock to Chad who sat there dumbfounded. He leaned over and whispered in Chad's ear. "What's this about a tape?"

"I have no clue what he's talking about. I'm telling you. I never said anything or did anything to this girl of a sexual nature. *She* propositioned *me*, and I turned her down. It's a damned lie."

Mr. Montgomery continued. "Your Honor, I believe that our evidence will prove that Mr. Peterson is guilty of violating this student's rights by making inappropriate, sexually motivated demands. The official charge for this crime is indecent assault, but in my opinion that is a mild description of the betrayal of trust of which he is guilty. By allowing Mr. Peterson to teach our children, we place their safety and well-being in his hands, and he has willfully violated this trust and should be punished severely. His actions have severely traumatized a young girl, and she will suffer the results of his actions for a long time. Thank you, Your Honor," he said before sitting down, indicating he'd finished.

Sam perused the list of witnesses quickly while the prosecutor was speaking, but none of the names on the list were familiar to him. Unable to discuss the list with Chad at this time, he set it down and gave his full attention to Mr. Montgomery.

Once he'd finished, the judge turned to Sam, ready to hear from the defense. "Mr. Ludwig?" he said simply. It seemed obvious that this judge did not waste any time or words and got right down to business.

Unable at this point to relate to the DA's list of witnesses or the prospect of a possible tape, Sam's opening remarks related to Chad's character and innocence.

Sam stood, stepped away from his table and faced the judge. "Your Honor, Chad Peterson has been a valued member of this community throughout his life. Born and raised here, he returned after college to teach at Emerson Central High, the school which he'd personally attended as a student.

"Chad Peterson has been a well-respected and very popular teacher for the past eight years. We, too, have a list of character witnesses who will attest to these facts. As a matter of fact, since the news of these ridiculous accusations became known, I have been inundated with calls from his colleagues, neighbors, local clergy, and merchants, as well as current and former students, who have all volunteered to testify on behalf of Mr. Peterson. Any so-called evidence the prosecutor claims to have is either fabricated or circumstantial. We also plan to call witnesses to show that the student in question has a reputation for being spoiled and selfish. She has attempted to cover the fact that she received a failing grade in Mr. Peterson's class in a most malicious manner—one which has already put the reputation of Mr. Peterson in question. His only mistake was in trying to help an ungrateful student earn a passing grade. Thank you, Your Honor," Sam said and then he returned to his seat.

Although Sam's speech had been interrupted several times by Sheila's obviously intentional coughing, as well as by some audible muttering from her father, Belinda was pleased with Sam's presentation. She let herself hope for a moment that the judge might be influenced enough to drop this whole farce. With crossed fingers, she looked up at the judge to see his reaction.

The judge took a few moments to review the papers in front of him before addressing those in the courtroom. Apparently unmoved by Sam's appeal, he declared, "I find that there is enough evidence to bind the defendant for trial." He then opened his calendar and flipped a few pages before declaring, "Trial date is set for one month from today, at 9 a.m. Is that agreeable to both parties?"

Both lawyers, after consulting their calendars, assented and marked the date down.

The judge banged his gavel, called the hearing to an end, and when the clerk announced, "All rise," everyone stood up and watched the judge leave the room.

Steve McMasters shouted, "Yes!"

Sheila sat there with a satisfied smile on her face.

Chad hung his head in defeat, wondering how someone could prove his innocence when all he could offer in his defense was his word.

Belinda burst into tears.

Sam went over to the prosecutor and spoke to him quietly, shaking hands with him before returning to the table where Chad still sat. Meanwhile, Belinda, who tried to come around the divider but was stopped, reached over with her hand and placed it on Chad's shoulder, trying to offer her support. Chad was too bound up in his own pain to appreciate her gesture.

When he returned, Sam tried to reassure Chad. "I'll get all of the evidence that the prosecution plans to present, including a copy of that tape. Then we'll plan our strategy for your defense. We'll find the flaw and you'll walk away from this."

"I wish I had your confidence, Sam. The world seems to be crashing down around me. I just feel so betrayed by the entire system."

Belinda followed Sam and Chad out of the courtroom. "Let me drive you home," she offered.

"Thanks. I've got nothing to do and there's no place I need to be. He took her into his arms for a moment before they all turned to walk out of the courthouse.

Belinda tried to compose herself.

"The reporters will be waiting like vultures. Be ready. Just hold onto each other and ignore them. Actually it'll be a good print image if they photograph you clutching onto one another. I'll handle them if anything needs to be said. You just quickly get into Belinda's car and leave."

As they departed, Chad observed Sheila and her parents talking with the press. "I'd like to wipe that little smirk from her face," Chad screeched.

* * *

The days were agonizing for Chad. The hours dragged on and each day seemed endless. With nothing to do to occupy his time, he grew increasingly restless.

Belinda's faith in him remained steadfast. Every day she called him at lunchtime and visited in the evenings. She often tried to reassure him that his friends hadn't deserted him. "Everyone is worried about you, Chad," she voiced during one phone call. "They want you to know they believe in your innocence."

"Yeah, right. That's why so many have called me since this all began," he said sarcastically."

Another time she said, "Your students miss you too. They often come into my room to ask how you're doing. They want you back."

"Tell them to buy a lottery ticket," he responded. "They'll have a better chance of getting lucky on that."

It hurt Belinda to hear his negativity, but she persisted. The following day she said, "I have some news for you. Matt Stairs is going to resume coaching the volleyball team. He's determined to make sure that these girls don't lose an opportunity to become state champions, even if he's not one hundred percent back to himself physically yet. He wants you to know that when you're vindicated, he's gonna insist on having you work with him."

A week passed. Belinda could sense that Chad was gradually sinking into a depression again. Aside from Sam, Belinda, and Matt, who had often called, he hadn't spoken to anyone. Most nights, they talked for hours about his feelings, the upcoming trial, and what had been happening in school. When she mentioned school, Chad once more grew angry.

"Nobody has called to talk with me except you and Matt. I thought that I had friends there."

"You do have friends, Chad. Everyone knows that you didn't do this. Several have called Sam and offered to testify for you. I'm not defending their actions, but I'm guessing that most of them just don't know what to say and don't want to say the wrong thing, so they just don't call. It's human nature to avoid unpleasantness." Belinda didn't mention how she'd pleaded with some of their colleagues to call, to offer their support, and let Chad know that they believed in him. But it was an awkward situation. She was embarrassed for them and hurt for Chad, but she hadn't had much influence over anyone.

"At least I have you, Belinda. Thank you for sticking by me."

"You're the most important person in my life. I was afraid for awhile that you'd forgotten that fact and how much I love you."

Chad leaned toward her, pressed his lips to hers and as he pulled away, murmured, "I love you too. I realize now that you're my strength to hang on."

"I don't care what people think or say anymore, honey. I want to move in with you. Whether you realize it or not, this hurts me too. Let's face it together."

Chad agreed that Belinda should stay with him, and she went home just long enough to pack some things. On the way back to Chad's place, she stopped at the market and picked up some staples and the makings for dinner.

Having her there with him helped Chad get through the waiting. Except for when she had to go to work, or run some errands for Chad, she never left his side. However, despite her pleas, Chad remained a recluse. He wouldn't venture into town and used Belinda as his 'go-fer.' Although she constantly encouraged him to go out, she enabled him to avoid doing just that. She shopped for him and ran any other errands that needed doing.

At times she tried desperately to reason with him. "Don't you think hiding out like this makes you look guilty? I think you should get out more and show that you're unafraid."

"I just can't, Belinda. I don't want to hear the gossip and see the stares of those who've already decided I'm guilty. Even when I walk out to get the mail, my neighbors avoid me like I'm some sort of pariah."

"You can't give in, honey. You have to hold your head up and show them that you have nothing to be afraid of. You did nothing wrong!"

"It's not that simple, Belinda. We have to be realistic."

"Chad, you sound as if you're expecting to be convicted." Belinda didn't want to give up, but he seemed resigned to a bad ending.

"You've read the papers and heard the stories. You have to face the facts. Teachers are vulnerable now. Kids have all the power to destroy our careers and our lives, and they're starting to realize it and take advantage."

"I'm aware of it, but we're *not* gonna let it destroy you." She recognized the signs of his depression and tried to change the subject. "Would you like to do anything together this weekend. We could go someplace away from here."

"I'm not allowed to leave the county. It's a nice suggestion, though. We'd better just stay here. Just be careful that someone doesn't accuse you of acting immorally or we'll both be hung out to dry."

Together they waited. Belinda spent every moment she could with Chad and they spent much of the remaining time before the trial just holding each other.

Chapter 10

Chad met with Sam Ludwig in preparation for the trial. They reviewed the list of those who would give testimony, and Chad was surprised to see the names of so many of his colleagues on the list. They were especially concerned about the tape that appeared on the list of evidence to be presented by the defense. They had just received a copy of the tape and Sam had brought it straight to Chad's house so they could hear what was on it.

Sam shook his head as he clicked the cassette into the tape recorder. "How in the world did this girl manage to tape your conversations?"

Suddenly a thought occurred to Chad. "Obviously she was planning to set me up. Shouldn't that prove it?"

Sam considered Chad's comment and made a note of it. "Good point. But still, how did she do it?" He looked questioningly at Chad.

Frustrated, Chad muttered under his breath, "Damn!" before he responded, "How the hell should I know? I can only imagine that she had it hidden somewhere, 'cause I never saw a tape recorder. I know I didn't say anything of a sexual nature to her."

"So let's see what all the fuss is about," Sam suggested, placing the tape recorder he'd brought on the table.

Chad reached out and pressed the play button and said, "Yeah, let's get this over with."

The tape began, and Chad instantly recognized Sheila's voice. "Mr. Peterson, my parents are going to kill me if I get a bad grade in history."

"Yes, that's what she said to me," Chad nodded, remembering the conversation.

"Sheila, I might be able to come up with something that you can do for extra credit. But you'll have to be more enthusiastic and willing."

Chad also recognized his own voice and nodded at Sam, who was waiting for confirmation that it was, indeed, Chad.

"Whatever you say, Mr. Peterson."

"Just do what I say and you'll please me."

Chad was spluttering with fury. He reached out and punched the stop button. "Wait a minute! There are parts of this conversation that are missing. Where's the part where I told her she'd have to work on the assembly?"

"I'm glad to hear you say that; it's what I suspected. Obviously, the tape was edited. Let's hear the rest and figure out what's missing, and then we'll decide how to proceed," Sam said calmly before reaching out to press the play button again.

"If I have to do it to get a better grade, I'll do whatever you want, Mr. Peterson."

Chad and Sam heard what appeared to be the moving of a desk or some object and then footsteps.

"My God, Sheila. I want you."

There was a moment of silence and then Chad said, "Do it, now!"

An undistinguishable sound could be heard and then came a distant voice. "What are you doing, Mr. Peterson?"

At that point the tape ended. Chad sat in stunned silence. Finally he said, "It's incredible. That's not how it happened at all. Is there a way to prove that this tape has been doctored?"

"Yes, there is." Sam said pensively. "But, I've gotta say, this sounds very damaging, Chad. Just having the jury hear this will be very hurtful to our defense." And then he said, more to himself, "I wonder how they thought they could get away with this." Sam was scribbling some notes on his ever-present legal pad while Chad could actually feel his blood pressure rising.

"I swear. This girl is setting me up. I've never been anything but professional with her. What could I have done to make her hate me so much? What did she want from me?"

"There's another possible angle that we'll have to explore." Sam leafed through his notes before continuing. "You said, more than once, that Sheila had a crush on you. A crush on a teacher isn't the same these days as it was when you and I were in school. These kids aren't content with daydreams anymore. What if she was hoping for a real relationship with you?"

Sam paused for a few moments. "You said she came on to you, so she decided to go for it. She went so far as to expose her breasts to you, but she had that tape recorder going, just in case. When you rejected her advances, she must have been humiliated. She must have realized that she'd blown her chance to get a good grade, so she made up this story to distract her parents from her failure. Once she made the accusation to her parents, she had backed herself into a corner and couldn't take back what she'd already said, and it snowballed into this."

Chad had a lot of questions. "So, how can we prove that? I still don't understand how she made this tape."

"These days, even with simple equipment it's not hard to edit a tape. It's not like in the old days where you had to cut the tape and splice it together. We'll get an expert to examine its authenticity. And we'll certainly ask during the trial why she carried and recorded the conversation in the first place. It smells of a set up to me. I hope to convince the jury of that too."

When they finished talking, Sam paused for a moment and then broached a subject that hadn't come up to this point. "I know you feel you're being railroaded by this false accusation, Chad, but as your lawyer I need to bring this up. We have to consider the option of a plea bargain."

"What exactly would that involve?"

"In return for what would likely be a lighter sentence, you plead guilty to inappropriate behavior. You don't have to admit to the charges per se, but that you acted in an unprofessional manner."

"But I'm *not* guilty, Sam."

"I know that. It's just a possibility that as your counselor, I have to present to you."

"And what would be the consequences if I did cop a plea?"

"Most likely, since you have no previous scrapes with the law, we argue that you be granted probation along with some kind of community service."

"And the community sees me as guilty!"

"It would appear that way, yes. And there's a more serious consequence. You'd lose your teaching certificate."

"Then I have nothing to gain with a plea bargain."

"You could go to jail if we go to trial and you're found guilty. Understand that I'm just providing you with an alternative. The choice must be yours."

"I'm not going to let that little liar ruin my life without a fight."

"I thought you'd feel that way, but I had to discuss the option. I'll do my best to bring out the truth."

The trial began on May 8 with the jury selection. Many of the prospective jurors were from Emerson and knew either Chad or the McMasters personally. Assuming that it would be difficult for them to be impartial, they were automatically disqualified. Because of this, the process of selecting the jury took up most of the first two days. Sam and the prosecutor took turns asking the prospective jurors questions, either accepting or rejecting a number of them. In general, they agreed, but a couple of times one or the other objected to a specific choice the other had approved.

There had been very few spectators in the courtroom for the jury selection. Apparently this wasn't a popular part of a trial. Although his fate would lie in the jurors' hands, even Chad found the process boring. He had insisted that Belinda not waste her precious personal days by being there for the tedious procedure. Chad was getting impatient and wanted to get on with things.

Once the jury had been selected, the judge dismissed them for the day and told the relevant parties to be back in court first thing the next morning to start hearing testimony.

The next morning, Chad dressed conservatively in a suit and tie and was waiting for Sam on the courthouse steps at 8:30, for a last minute conference. Sam arrived moments later, and they headed for a conference room down the hall from the courtroom.

Almost half an hour later, Chad sat straight faced beside Sam Ludwig in the courtroom, when Sheila McMasters came in, followed by her parents. She carefully avoided looking at him as they took a seat right behind the district attorney.

After the preliminaries were dispensed with, the prosecutor, Jack Montgomery, began by calling Steve McMasters to the witness stand. The prosecutor stood at his table, reviewing his notes as Sheila's father walked up to the witness box and was sworn in. Once the witness was seated, he approached him and began his questions. "Mr. McMasters, your daughter is the student making this accusation, is that correct?"

"Yes, my daughter, Sheila."

"Would you please relate to the court how you were informed of the sexual nature of this case?"

"My daughter came home from school rather late one night in a state of emotional distress. My wife and I tried to calm her and we asked her what had happened. At first she didn't want to talk with us, but finally explained that Mr. Peterson had sexually harassed her. He tried to get her to…"

"Objection, Your Honor. That's hearsay," Sam said and stood up when

Sheila's father began to recount his version of what he had called sexual harassment.

"Sustained," agreed the judge, and he reminded both Mr. McMasters and the prosecutor that the testimony can only relate to what was personally witnessed.

Mr. McMasters' temper rose and he shouted, "Judge, my little girl was hysterical. I personally witnessed that! When I asked her what had happened, I personally witnessed her telling me that, that man," he rose and pointed to Chad, "had made sexual overtures toward her."

"Sit down, sir," the judge interrupted and then facing the prosecutor, he admonished, "Mr. Montgomery, kindly instruct your witness on the proper decorum in this courtroom. Hysterics will not be tolerated."

Both men replied, "Yes, Your Honor."

"Before this time had you any indication of some interest that Mr. Peterson had in her?"

"One night when I picked her up late after cheerleading practice, he came out of the building with Sheila. He seemed very familiar when he waved to her."

"Did your daughter say anything at that time about Mr. Peterson?"

"Only that she liked him."

Sam whispered to Chad, "I can object to that too, because it's also hearsay, but the judge is getting impatient, and it really isn't worth making a fuss about."

"Has there been any physical contact between Mr. Peterson and your daughter?" The DA must have noticed that Sam was about to object to his question, because he added quickly, "that you personally witnessed?"

"There was a video on the local news after a volleyball match and I saw him giving my daughter a hug. Everybody saw that!" Mr. McMasters declared smugly.

Mr. Montgomery stepped over to his table and picked up a videotape. He brought it over to the judge and stated for the record, "I'd like to present this videotape as evidence, Your Honor."

The judge handed the tape to the clerk, who marked the tape with an evidence number. The clerk then put the tape into the VCR which had been set up on the side of the courtroom and pushed the play button.

Everyone's attention moved to the TV screen where the local reporter was interviewing one of the players from the volleyball team. In the background, Sheila could be seen embracing Chad. The DA, who had taken the remote control from the clerk, froze the frame so that everyone could be sure to see the embrace.

Chad was visibly upset at the way an innocent encounter—at least on his part—was being made to look vulgar and dirty.

Sam grabbed Chad's shoulder to calm him, when suddenly, pointing at the screen, he whispered, "Chad, wait! This doesn't mean anything. Look at the angle of the camera. It doesn't show you returning the embrace; it just shows that Sheila has her arms around you. We're claiming that she's the one who made the advances, so this fits into our take on things. How long did this encounter last?"

Chad sat up and looked where Sam was pointing. "Sam, that whole incident took a fraction of a second; he's pausing it and making it look like we were hugging for a long time. Let him keep running the tape and you'll see that I pushed her away." Chad was cautiously hopeful that if the judge and jury could see him push her away, he'd see what had really happened.

Sam scribbled some more notes on his legal pad and bided his time.

Montgomery stopped the tape then, and obviously feeling that he'd managed to leave an impression with the jury, told the judge that he'd finished with this witness.

The judge turned to Sam and said, "Mr. Ludwig, you may cross examine now."

Sam knew he'd have to make the jury understand that they'd received the wrong impression of the events. He approached the witness box and addressed Sheila's father, "Mr. McMasters, would you say it's unusual to have a teacher wave goodbye to a student?"

"No."

"At the time, did you interpret the wave as some kind of sexual interest?"

"No, I didn't."

Sam continued. "In the video we just watched, Mr. Peterson was in the midst of congratulating his girls' victory at that moment, was he not?"

"I couldn't say. I only saw him with his arms around my daughter."

"Isn't it possible that a lot of the girls on the team, including your daughter, ran to him to hug the coach?"

"My daughter is *not* on the team!" Mr. McMasters declared indignantly.

"That may be, but I understand that she was a cheerleader. She was nearby at every practice session and present at every game. If you'd like, I can call a number of witnesses who will testify to this."

Mr. McMasters was starting to lose his composure. "What's your point?"

"My point is, sir, that she sought out Coach Peterson in that clip. It doesn't appear that he went looking for your daughter!" Sam hoped that the jury understood his point.

Mr. McMasters felt that they were getting off the track here. He wanted the jury to focus on the wrong done to his daughter. He brought their attention back to the tape. Pointing to the screen where the tape had been screened, he shouted, "But you saw the tape, he had his hands on *my* daughter."

"Again, I'll ask you, isn't it possible that, in the excitement of the victory, several girls came up to thank him for coaching them to victory, some possibly even hugged him. Is it possible that your daughter did likewise?"

"I guess so, but we just saw that tape and it was *my* daughter he was touching!" McMasters repeated, hoping to drive that point home.

Following McMasters' outburst, Sam addressed the judge. "Your Honor, it's true that we just witnessed Sheila McMasters embracing Mr. Peterson, but by pausing the tape and holding it on that frame, the prosecutor deliberately gave a false impression of the incident. In fact, Mr. Peterson's immediate reaction to her impetuous and inappropriate embrace was to forcibly remove the girl's hands from him."

The judge considered this and requested that the clerk play the tape again without pausing. This time, knowing what they were looking for, everyone focused on what was happening behind the interview—in the background of the picture.

Chad leaned forward, hoping that the tape would clearly show that he had pushed her away. Unfortunately, although it was clear that Sheila had approached Chad and threw her arms around him, at the very instant after the prosecutor had paused the tape, the camera had turned to capture the interview from a different angle and Chad and Sheila were no longer in the shot. Chad could feel his heart sink, the disappointment overwhelming.

Sam had hoped for more from the tape. Although seeing Chad reject Sheila on tape would have been much more effective, he did have a few witnesses that he could call who would testify that they saw Chad push her away. Meanwhile, he had to do what he could to neutralize McMasters' testimony now. "Mr. McMasters, although the footage we just saw didn't show Mr. Peterson's rejection of your daughter's impulsive reaction to the volleyball team's win, it also did not show Mr. Peterson's hands on your daughter, as you claimed."

Mr. McMasters spluttered, "I tell you, he manhandled her! That bastard," and he shook his fist in Chad's direction. "He should be locked up for what he's done to her."

The judge quickly interrupted and castigated the witness, "Sir, you have been asked to control yourself. One more outburst and you will be removed from this court."

Sam made a final comment before telling the judge that he'd finished with the witness. "In fact, he didn't manhandle her, and nothing in your testimony has indicated otherwise. I'm through with this witness, Your Honor."

The judge nodded and spoke to the DA. "Mr. Montgomery, call your next witness."

The prosecutor next called Jim Morris. As he approached the stand, Jim shrugged his shoulders at Chad to indicate that he was sorry. In fact, after he'd received the subpoena, Jim had asked Belinda to tell Chad that he was being called against his will. After being sworn in, the questioning began.

"Mr. Morris. You are a colleague of the defendant, is that right?"

"Yes."

"How well do you know the defendant?"

"Besides working together, we often get together socially and in the mornings for some swimming."

"On any particular occasion, have you observed Mr. Peterson to be alone with Sheila McMasters?"

Jim hesitated. The judge ordered him to answer the question.

"I saw them together a few times but…"

The DA cut him off before Jim could elaborate. "Please just answer my questions," he instructed and continued his questioning. "Would you please describe these times you mentioned?"

"There was one time that we were coming out of the locker room after a morning swim. Sheila was sitting in the hallway. The other guys and I went to our classrooms and Chad remained behind to talk with her."

"Was there any physical contact between them or did you overhear anything that might make you suspicious of improper behavior on Mr. Peterson's part?"

"No, of course not!" Jim answered with conviction and nodded at Chad in a show of support.

"Tell us about the second encounter," the DA continued.

Jim thought a minute and then responded. "It was that same morning, a few minutes later. I walked by Chad's room and noticed that Sheila was in there with him. I stepped into the room to make sure that everything was ok."

"What made you suspect that something might not be right?"

"Nothing in particular. We teachers have been warned, whenever possible, to avoid situations where we're alone with students. I was just helping a friend."

"What happened then?"

"Nothing. As soon as I came in, Sheila McMasters bolted from the room as if she were embarrassed."

Sam Ludwig objected to the use of the word embarrassed. "Speculation, your honor," he argued. His objection was sustained.

"I understand that you were present on the night in question?" Mr. Montgomery placed an inflection at the end of his statement turning it into a question, implicitly asking for a description of the circumstances on that night.

"I walked by Chad's classroom on the way out of school and glanced into Chad's room. I saw Sheila McMasters sitting in a desk and Chad appeared to be talking with her," and Jim quickly pointed out, "from behind his desk."

"Did you overhear anything that was said?"

"No, I didn't stop, nor did I hear anything. I just thought it was unusual for her to be there so late."

"Why didn't you go into the room as you did on an earlier occasion?"

"I was late and in a hurry to meet my wife for dinner."

"And you observed no activity of a sexual nature?"

"Absolutely not!"

When it was Sam's turn to question Jim, he tried to rebut some parts of the testimony. "Mr. Morris, it's not unusual for a teacher to talk with a student in a public place, is it?

"No."

"And a hallway certainly is a public place, is it not?"

"Yes, it is."

"You testified that on two different occasions you saw Sheila in a classroom alone with Mr. Peterson. Was the door closed either time?"

"No, it wasn't.

"Don't you think that if Mr. Peterson wanted to do something of a sexual nature, he'd close the door for privacy?"

"Objection, your honor!" yelled Mr. Montgomery. "Calls for speculation!"

"I withdraw the question, your honor." Sam knew he didn't need an answer to the question. He'd scored points with the jury just by asking it.

At this point Judge Walters called for a recess for the rest of the day. "Court will resume at nine o'clock tomorrow morning. The jury is dismissed," he said.

All those in attendance rose as the jury filed out and Judge Walters left the courtroom.

Sam took Chad into an empty conference room. "I think we scored a few points today, Chad. I'm hopeful that you'll be vindicated, but the trial isn't over yet. None of the testimony was too damaging. A lot of it is circumstantial evidence pointing to the fact that you used bad judgment to be alone with the girl. Nothing so far proved that you made any sexual advances toward her."

"I've never felt so physically and emotionally drained," said Chad. "This is so hard to deal with."

Belinda, who was using her personal days from school, had been sitting faithfully behind Chad in the courtroom during the trial. She followed them into the conference room and moved over next to Chad, putting her hand on Chad's shoulder.

They sat at the table and Sam went over a number of points he'd written down during the proceedings. Together they discussed different approaches in dealing with them. When they finished, Sam suggested, "Go home and try to get a good night's sleep. It'll be another long day tomorrow, and the most hurtful evidence is yet to come."

Belinda agreed. "That's a good idea. Let's go home and I'll make you a good dinner."

Chad took Belinda by the hand. There was no intent to hide their relationship as they walked from the courthouse and past the waiting reporters. When they walked into the apartment, Chad collapsed into a chair and Belinda moved behind him and massaged his shoulders.

"You're going to come out of this ok, Chad," she reassured him. "Somehow that girl's lies will crumble around her."

"I was just thinking of the consequences if Sheila testifies to all this crap and we can't prove she's lying. I mean it's her word against mine. I still don't see how we can prove that she's lying if she doesn't back down. I could spend time in jail. I'll be branded a criminal, and everywhere I go to live, I'll have to register as a convicted child molester. I won't be allowed to live near a school and parents will fear my being near their kids. I don't know if I can handle living like that."

Belinda leaned forward and embraced him. He leaned back and tried to feel some sense of comfort from her.

"And then there's our relationship, Belinda. I know you don't want to hear this, but I can't let this follow you for the rest of your life. You deserve much better. If I'm convicted, I want you to walk away."

Tears welled in Belinda's eyes. Not wanting to break down in front of him, she managed to say, "I'll make some dinner," and she walked out of the room. In the kitchen, she let the tears flow, going through half a box of Kleenex as she worked.

The next morning, back in court, the first witness to be called was Cindy Bennett who testified about what she saw when she walked into the classroom. "Sheila's breasts were exposed," she said, "and Mr. Peterson had his hands on her shoulders. It appeared as if he was pushing her to her knees. Then I heard him say something like 'Do it, now!'"

Sam Ludwig immediately raised an objection. "Your honor, the witness is offering speculation about my client's intention to 'push her to her knees'." The judge sustained the objection and ordered it stricken from the record.

Sam didn't have much to ask Cindy beyond reiterating his point and having her admit that, in fact, she really couldn't tell what Chad was doing with his hands—whether he was pushing her to her knees or pushing her away. He was returning to his seat, but just before he reached the table, he turned to ask, "One more thing, Ms. Bennett. I'd like to clarify something you said earlier. I'm referring to what you said." Sam referred to his notes, reading back what she'd said. "You testified that you heard Mr. Peterson say '*something like…*' etc. My question is, did you hear him say, 'Do it now!' or was it just 'something like' that?"

Cindy looked puzzled for a moment. She wasn't sure what to say. Sam reminded her gently that she was still under oath, and she became nervous and scared.

Sam took advantage of the moment to discredit her previous testimony. "Ms. Bennett? Did you hear what Mr. Peterson said or didn't you?"

Cindy sheepishly replied, "I guess I didn't." And trying to explain what she'd said earlier, she added, "Maybe that's what Sheila told me he said."

"In that case, it would be considered hearsay and not admissible," Sam pointed out for the benefit of the jury.

Bill Thorndike was questioned next and the DA managed to draw him out to reveal that Chad was very testy in the locker room one morning when the subject of Sheila McMasters was brought up in some good natured teasing. Under further questioning he admitted that Chad had slammed a locker door and stormed out of the room.

Sam's cross examination was short and to the point. "Mr. Thorndike, did you have any reason to believe that there was substance to a relationship between my client and the defendant?"

"No, in fact the joke was that she seemed infatuated with Chad and that was the reason for the teasing," Bill explained.

"Objection, Your Honor!" Mr. Montgomery jumped up. "The witness has no way to determine if Ms. McMasters was infatuated or not."

Before the judge could rule on the objection, Bill interjected, "Sure I can, Your Honor, sir. That girl was practically stalking Chad. She was turning up everywhere, looking at him with those puppy dog eyes. Everybody knew she had a thing for him—everybody except for Chad."

Sam was delighted with the way Montgomery's witness had helped confirm the impression that Sheila was the instigator. He hoped that the jury understood the implications of what Bill had said. He decided that he wouldn't push his luck though, and he told the judge, "Thank you. I have nothing further for this witness."

"Redirect?" the judge asked the prosecutor.

To which he replied, "No, sir, nothing further at this time."

"Alright then," said the judge as he banged his gavel and declared a recess until after lunch.

Chad and Belinda followed Sam into a conference room. "How about I order some sandwiches and coffee?" Sam asked, and when they nodded, he took out his cellphone to place an order. While he waited for the deli to answer, he asked them what they wanted.

"Whatever you're having will be fine, thanks," Chad answered and Belinda agreed.

While they waited for the food, they discussed the testimonies of the morning. "I think you scored some points this morning. Thanks, Sam." Belinda smiled encouragingly.

"Yeah, it went okay, don't you agree?" Chad asked Sam, looking for his take on things.

"I think I managed to salvage something from the testimonies, but that videotape was hard to deal with. Sheila's been in court the whole time. I'm certain they're gonna call her to testify. In fact, I'll bet that they call her after this Thomas Stenson whose name is on the list. Her appearance is gonna be hard, Chad. Be prepared and don't lose control in the courtroom," Sam warned.

"I'd like to wring that girl's neck and force her to tell the truth. She's wasted weeks of my time and possibly ruined my career and my life. I don't think I've ever really hated anyone before in my life, but I could make an exception for that manipulative little bitch."

Remaining upbeat, Sam responded. "She's the one who'll suffer the disgrace once we win the case."

"So who's this Stenson guy?"

"I imagine he's going to verify that the audio tape is authentic."

The trial resumed at one o'clock. As Sam expected, Montgomery began by calling the last name on the list of witnesses. After the swearing in, Jack began the questioning. "Mr. Stenson, would you please tell the court what you do for a living?"

"I work as a sound man in a recording studio. My job is to work with music and dub audio recordings to clarify such things as sound, volume, special effects etc."

"How long have you been doing this type of work?"

"Fifteen years now. I'm the head technician at CRV studios."

"And you previously listened to the tape presented in this trial. Is that correct?"

"Yes, I did."

"And would you tell us, sir, what conclusions you reached about it?"

"The voices were a bit muffled as if the recording were made under some kind of covering but the audio was clear enough to hear the words being said."

"Would you say that the voices were clear enough to be identified?"

"Yes. I did a voice analysis compared to those of the defendant and that of the young girl. They matched perfectly."

"Your job often requires you to do editing of the material you're given, is that correct?"

"Yes."

"And to do that editing requires careful reproduction so that no trace of its being edited is apparent?"

"That's right. We use sophisticated equipment."

"To the best of your knowledge, has any editing been done on this tape?"

"If it was edited, it was done professionally. I doubt that an amateur could manage it."

"Let me repeat the question. Do you think the tape was altered in any way."

"No. I found no evidence of that. There were a few minor clicks on the tape but that could have occurred as the recorder was bumped or even if something else in the room was moved."

"Thank you. No further questions, Your Honor."

"Mr. Ludwig, do you have any questions for this witness?"

Sam rose from his chair. "Yes, Your Honor. I do."

"Mr. Stenson, your job as I understand it deals mostly with music then. Is that right?"

"Yes, that's correct."

"So you're not an expert on voice tonality. You mainly try to mix the performer's voice to blend with the music for the best sound."

"I guess that's true."

"Thank you. No more questions, Your Honor."

Jack Montgomery then asked Sheila McMasters to take the stand. As she had been since the trial began, Sheila was dressed in her "parochial school" outfit. She had little, if any, makeup, and her hair was brushed demurely into some kind of schoolgirl style. Once she'd been sworn in, Sheila spoke softly and politely, rather than in her usual brash manner.

"May I call you Sheila?" the DA began gently.

"Yes, sir," she whispered.

She spoke so quietly that the judge instructed, "Miss McMasters, kindly speak up."

Again, looking contrite, she said, "Yes, sir. Sorry, sir."

Chad almost laughed out loud at her manner. "Who is she trying to kid?" he asked Sam.

Montgomery continued, "Sheila, you have accused Mr. Peterson of a very serious violation. You're claiming that he made sexual advances toward you, are you not?"

"Yes, sir." Chad could see the members of the jury straining to hear her response.

"Please tell us, in your own words, exactly what happened on the night in question."

Sheila repeated verbatim the same sequence of events as reported to her parents and then to the police.

Chad was furious. "What a pack of lies! This little bitch is a real actress; I've gotta give her that," he whispered to Sam.

Sam tried to calm him, but he, too, was a bit shaken by Sheila's performance. "Shhhh, Chad, we have to pay attention, so we can find where to poke holes in her story."

That got through to Chad, and he returned his attention to the prosecutor and the witness.

As if her testimony hadn't been bad enough, Mr. Montgomery tried to drive his points home. He wanted to draw her out and he asked, "Did Mr. Peterson make any clear and direct statement that he wanted sex in exchange for a better grade?"

Sheila pretended to consider the question. It was obvious to Sam that she'd been coached, and he had to admit that Montgomery had done a good job of it. She appeared uncomfortable with the details. "He never came right out and said the word sex, but it was clear to me that he expected something sexual."

"And you agreed?"

She sniffled as if she were trying not to cry. "I was scared. I didn't want a bad grade in his class to ruin my academic record. Yes, I agreed."

"What did he do *then*?" the DA said with a sneer, making it seem really dirty.

Sheila took a tissue and dabbed at her eyes and then made an effort to blow her nose.

Belinda leaned forward and whispered to Sam and Chad. "I gotta hand it to her, she's really making a show out of this."

Chad was seething. "I can't believe this. Look at the people in the jury; they're eating this up!"

Sheila continued, "He motioned with his hands that I should open my top. I hoped that was all he wanted, but after I did that he indicated that I should come up closer to him."

"What did he say, exactly?"

"I don't remember what he said exactly, but he motioned with his finger, you know, curling it in a 'come here' motion." She demonstrated it to the courtroom. "I looked around to see if anyone was there and then got up from my chair and walked towards him." She wiped her nose again, sniffling.

Chad watched her and he was amazed to see that, as she hid part of her face behind the tissue, she surreptitiously glanced around to see if everyone was paying attention. From the angle where he was sitting, he could see her smile. "Oh my God! Sam, look at her! She's enjoying being the center of everyone's attention!" he whispered.

Sam shushed him again.

The DA, who had also missed Sheila's smile, tried to be solicitous of her. "I know this is hard, but we need you to tell us what happened next."

Sheila looked at her father. It was obvious that his blood pressure was rising. He was red in the face and unable to control himself any longer. He called out to her, "Tell them, baby. Nail that bastard!"

The judge banged his gavel and reprimanded Mr. McMasters. "Believe me when I tell you that if there is one more outburst, you will be removed from my courtroom." Then he added, somewhat compassionately, "I do understand that this is difficult for you, but that doesn't mean I will let my courtroom turn into a free for all."

McMasters mumbled under his breath, "I'm sorry, Your Honor."

The judge turned to Sheila. "Young lady, please answer the question. What happened next?"

Sheila was thrown for a moment. She forgot that she'd been trying to cry and tried, unsuccessfully, not to smile, but it was such a novel experience to see her father reprimanded, and even stranger to see him meekly apologize; she couldn't suppress a grin.

The judge, surprised at her demeanor in the midst of her previously tearful account of what was supposed to be a traumatic experience, was becoming impatient. "Ms. McMasters, we're waiting…"

Reprimanded, she apologized and tried once again to turn on the waterworks, but she wasn't as good an actress as she thought. "Yes, Your Honor."

Chad whispered to Sam, "What the hell is she smiling about? She's lying through her teeth and she's enjoying every minute of this!"

Sheila coughed then, hiding her eyes and mouth behind her hands until she had composed herself, and then she continued. "I was very close to Mr. Peterson when he put his hands on my shoulders and started to push me down. I knew he wanted me to…" she hesitated, embarrassed, and sniffled, "to perform oral sex on him."

"Objection, Your Honor!" Sam declared. "The witness is testifying to her interpretation of the incident. Mr. Peterson never indicated that he wanted any such thing."

"I'd like to hear the rest of her testimony before ruling on your objection." The judge turned to Sheila. "Young lady, I will give you a little latitude here, but just tell us what happened, not your interpretation."

"Yes, sir," Sheila answered. Turning haughtily towards Sam, she continued, "I knew what he wanted. He said to me, 'Do it now!' and I thought I had no choice. Just then, my friend, Cindy Bennett came into the room and he panicked. I took advantage of the interruption, covered myself, and raced out of the room with Cindy. I wasn't going to tell anyone, but when I got home, my parents could tell that something was wrong."

The district attorney nodded, indicating that she could stop at that point. He turned to the judge and said, "Your Honor, I'd like to play an audio tape now of the incident that my client managed to record that night."

Mr. Montgomery picked up a cassette from his table and as he brought it up to the judge, he asked Sheila, "Did you record the conversation you had with Mr. Peterson?"

"Yes, sir," she answered meekly.

The judge took the tape, handed it to the clerk and instructed him, "Mark this as the people's Exhibit B."

The clerk returned to his desk, registered the information and placed a tape recorder on his table next to a microphone.

Mr. Montgomery gave a short explanation to the jury. "Ladies and gentlemen, this tape was made on the night in question. Miss McMasters had a tape recorder concealed in her schoolbag."

The clerk inserted the tape and when the judge nodded, he pressed the play button.

Chad cringed. He knew the jury would likely believe the tape more than any of the testimony given thus far. As it played, his eyes surveyed each juror. At least he was prepared for the lies. Had he not heard the tape before, he'd have had a lot more trouble controlling himself. As is, it was all he could do not to walk over and strangle Sheila for her treachery. Sam had warned him that any severe reaction on his part would not work in his favor and that was the only thing keeping Chad in his seat.

Though it lasted only a minute or so, the tape clearly created doubt on Chad's credibility. Ever the actress, Sheila wept as the tape played. When it finished, Mr. Montgomery turned to the judge and said, "I have no further questions for this witness, Your Honor."

Sam took over. "Sheila, how is it that you happened to have a recorder in the room at that time?"

"I always have it in my bag. I often use it to tape classroom lectures and for my notes," she answered confidently.

"And you don't expect us to think it's strange that it was *on* when this incident supposedly occurred with your teacher?" Sam asked skeptically.

"I thought it would be a good idea to record whatever Mr. Peterson wanted me to do for extra credit, if he agreed to let me do some, so I'd be able to do what he wanted," she explained.

Sam tried to show that this wasn't normal procedure. "And you hid the recorder in your purse? Wouldn't it have been more clearly taped if you had it, say...on the desk?"

"I didn't think of that," Sheila admitted.

"The fact is that you came into the room to set up Mr. Peterson to blackmail him into giving you a good grade. Isn't that true?" Sam persisted.

"NO!" Sheila shouted angrily.

"And if you couldn't blackmail him, then you would punish him by claiming he did something bad to you."

"NO!"

"Let's talk about the tape, Sheila," Sam continued. "Is this a word for word original copy of the tape?"

"Yes, it is. It's what he said."

"Oh, I have no doubt that's what he said, Sheila. An expert would verify that it's Mr. Peterson's voice. What I want to know is if you edited the tape to make it sound like your teacher tried to seduce you."

"I didn't do that," she contended.

"So, Mr. Peterson didn't say things like, 'Do it, now. Get out!'"

Sheila lost her composure and shouted at Sam. "He wanted to take advantage of me. From the very first day of class, he was trying to be extra special nice to me. Then he gave me this bad grade to get me to do things."

"I guess Cindy Bennett's arrival into the classroom at that particular moment was purely coincidental, huh?" Sam asked, sarcastically.

"If she hadn't come in then, he'd have made me give him a blowjob. That's what he wanted." All pretense of being embarrassed had disappeared.

"And under oath you're testifying that you didn't arrange to have Cindy show up then?" Sam asked, trying to put the lucky coincidence into question.

Sheila thought a minute. "I think I told her that I was going to see Mr. Peterson about some extra credit and to meet me. I didn't tell her to come in and catch him, if that's what you mean."

Sam had no further questions for Sheila. She wiped a tear from her eye as she walked back to the table where her lawyer sat. She was convinced that she had nailed Chad.

Judge Walters recessed for the day when Mr. Montgomery rested the case for the prosecution. Sam would begin the defense the next day.

Belinda spent the night at Chad's place, but neither of them got much rest. The anxieties of the trial wore heavily on Chad. He hadn't slept well for weeks and he had dark circles under his eyes. His entire face appeared haggard and worn, as if he had aged overnight. His demeanor, too, gave evidence of defeat. Despite trying to find something else to talk about, they were unable to focus on anything else, so they discussed the trial.

"We really have only a few character witnesses. Sam had the tape analyzed by an expert who will testify that it's been edited. I'm counting on that to put some doubt in the jury's mind, to show them that Sheila's lying. After that, it'll be up to me to convince the jury that I'm the one telling the truth. I'm afraid that even with the evidence that the tape has been tampered with, the jury will believe a young girl's testimony over a male teacher's.

Belinda held him. "I have faith in you and in the system of justice, Chad. It's gonna be ok."

Chad wasn't as confident. He remained in Belinda's arms, returning the embrace and said to her sadly, "More than one innocent person sits behind bars because the jury found him guilty. I know Sam's a good lawyer, but it's going to come down to my word against hers."

The following morning, clouds darkened the sky. Chad sat motionless as the jury filed into the room and stood with slumped shoulders when Judge Walters entered from his chambers. Sam admonished him to stand straight and not give the jury reason to think he's guilty.

Sam called Helen Hargrove to the stand first. After she was sworn in, Sam began the questioning.

"Mrs. Hargrove, you are the principal of Emerson High School, is that right?

"Yes, I am."

"How long have you been principal there?"

"Eleven years."

"So you have known Chad Peterson for the entire time he has been employed at Emerson?"

"Yes."

"Has Chad ever given any reason in that time to make you concerned about his behavior as a teacher?"

"None whatsoever. He's a very popular teacher at the school and is an excellent teacher."

"I understand that up until the time of this incident, Chad has been filling in for an injured teacher as girls volleyball coach. Did you approve of that decision?"

"Yes, I recommended it."

"You had no qualms about his being involved with a group of girls in that capacity?"

"I had none."

"In the time that he acted as coach, did any parents express any concerns about his getting too personal with the girls? He was described earlier in the trial as hugging several girls."

Mr. Montgomery objected at that point. "Your Honor, testimony described the defendant as hugging only my client."

"I'll withdraw the question." Sam shrugged his shoulders. His point had been made and arguing about the objection was counter-productive, so he let it go.

"Mrs. Hargrove, did any parent, at any time, express a concern about the safety or well being of their daughter on the team?"

"No. In fact most seemed happy that the team continued to play well under his guidance."

"Were you at the game the night that Mr. Peterson allegedly hugged Ms. McMasters?"

"Yes, I was there; it was an important win, and everyone from Emerson was very excited about it. In fact, the general feeling was that it was Mr. Peterson's coaching that was responsible for the win, and most everyone went over to congratulate him. I was talking to several people after the match, though. I didn't see the incident in question."

"Let me conclude then, Mrs. Hargrove, by asking if you have any doubts about the character and behavior of Mr. Peterson as a member of your staff."

"None whatsoever! Chad has acted reputably throughout the duration of his teaching career at Emerson. It has been my pleasure and my privilege to work with someone so committed to his students. If only all the teachers had his dedication." Helen smiled at Chad, sincere in her assessment of his character and reputation.

Mr. Montgomery had no questions for Helen and the judge thanked her for her cooperation and told her she could step down. Chad offered a weak smile and mouthed a thank you in her direction as she walked past him.

Although Helen had given Chad an excellent character reference, Sam had a list of Chad's colleagues and friends who had agreed to testify on his behalf, and he spent the rest of the morning calling on them to confirm Helen's assessment. When the judge called a recess for lunch, Chad turned sarcastically to Sam, "Pinch me. I need to be sure that I'm still alive. It just sounded like they were all eulogizing me and everyone knows it's not good to speak ill of the dead."

Sam felt he'd made his point about Chad's sterling character, so after lunch he began by calling Belinda to the stand. Chad admired the confident way that she walked up and took her oath.

"Ms. Landis, how long have you known the defendant, Chad Peterson?"

"We were both hired to teach at Emerson at the same time, just over eight years ago."

"Please describe your relationship with him?"

"Until a few months ago we were just good friends. Although we have a lot in common, we didn't want to jeopardize our friendship and working relationship by becoming romantically involved."

"But the truth is you *are* romantically involved now, is that correct?" Sam wanted to make it clear to everyone that Chad was involved with this lovely young woman.

"Yes. Our friends kept acting as matchmakers and eventually we began dating."

"How long have you been dating?"

"For several months now."

"Is it public knowledge that you're seeing each other?"

"We agreed to be discreet in school, though we usually spend our breaks together and frequently, when our schedules coincide, we leave together. Our friends and most of our colleagues are aware that we're seeing each other. Even many of the students are aware that we're dating."

Sam asked, "How would you describe your relationship now?"

Belinda answered proudly, "I love Chad very much, and I know that he feels the same about me."

"Have you two made any long-term plans?" Sam had prepared Belinda that he would find some way to intimate that she and Chad were involved in a healthy, sexual relationship to show the jury that there would be no reason for him to solicit a little tramp like Sheila.

Although generally modest and not one used to broadcasting her business to others, Belinda understood how this information could help show that Chad was involved in a stable, healthy relationship and had no need to fool around with a child.

"We haven't made a formal commitment yet, but we both know that it's in our future to do so." Belinda looked at Chad as she said this and the love radiating from her eyes was evident to everyone. "We spend a lot of our time together. Although we both still have our own apartments, I often stay over at Chad's place. Sometimes he stays over at mine." Belinda paused, she wasn't sure the jury understood. She told herself, "In for a penny…" and decided she might as well make sure they got the point. She smiled and added, trying not to let a hint of caustic humor show, "Most times, though, I stay at his place—he's got a bigger bed." Belinda spoke proudly, unashamed of her relationship with Chad.

Sam paused for a moment to let that image sink in for the jurors and then he continued his questions, "Has Mr. Peterson ever made any mention of Ms. McMasters?"

"He talked about her a couple of times. Chad thought she had a case of puppy love for him. You know, every kid at one time or another is attracted to a teacher," Belinda stated very matter-of-factly.

Sam pointed out, "But this girl is no kid! Was Mr. Peterson concerned about this?"

"Chad's very professional. He'd never let it get out of hand. He'd never have done anything to hurt a child's feelings nor would he do anything to take advantage of her."

"Were you aware that something had happened between Ms. McMasters and Mr. Peterson before the charges were filed?"

"Chad called me later that night and asked to come over to my place. When he arrived, I could tell he was emotionally distressed. He revealed to me that Sheila McMasters made advances to him and it frightened him."

"Objection, Your Honor; hearsay!" interrupted the prosecutor.

"Stick to what you personally know, Ms. Landis," the judge instructed.

"What was your reaction to Mr. Peterson's distress?"

"I trust Chad implicitly. I had no doubts that what he told me had happened. I told him to report it," Belinda said with assurance.

Sam asked, "Did he do that?"

"No, he said he didn't want any trouble and hoped that when he turned her down, it would be the end of it," Belinda added.

"Objection, hearsay!" the prosecutor jumped up again.

"Sustained," the judge ruled.

"Let me clarify one more time, if I may. At the time of this alleged incident, your relationship with Mr. Peterson was intact. You hadn't had a fight or misunderstanding of any kind."

"Our relationship was and remains solid. We love each other very much."

There wasn't much more that Belinda could add at this point, so Sam turned to the judge and said, "Nothing further for this witness, Your Honor."

The judge called upon the prosecutor to cross examine the witness.

Mr. Montgomery's questioning was clearly in an attack mode. "Ms. Landis, you say you love Mr. Peterson. Do you love him enough to protect him?"

"I would do anything I could to help him; he's innocent!" Belinda declared.

"Would you lie to protect him now?"

Sam stood immediately and declared his objection to Mr. Montgomery's question. Obviously knowing he was out of line, Montgomery didn't even wait for the judge to rule on the objection and withdrew his question.

"Ms. Landis, was your relationship with Mr. Peterson intimate?" Apparently, Belinda hadn't totally satisfied his curiosity.

At that point Chad stood up and yelled, "That's none of your business! Don't answer that, Belinda!"

The judge quickly demanded order.

Sam apologized and pulled Chad back into his seat.

Once order was restored to the judge's satisfaction, Sam raised an objection. "Your Honor, Ms. Landis is not on trial here. She's already testified to her relationship with Mr. Peterson. Is it necessary to try to turn their relationship into something sordid? Surely Mr. Montgomery has crossed a line here with his question."

The judge turned to the prosecutor. "Mr. Montogmery, would you like to respond to the objection before I rule?"

"Thank you, Your Honor," Montgomery responded. He checked his notes before continuing. "The witness testified that she hasn't given up her apartment although she is living at Mr. Peterson's place for some time now. I think that we need to clarify exactly what their relationship is. If the witness' relationship with

Mr. Peterson lacks a sexual intimacy, it could well explain why he used his power as a teacher to seduce my client."

Chad wanted to jump over the table and put his hands around Montgomery's throat. Anger rippled through his entire frame. Almost out of control, he was restrained by Sam, who held him by the shoulders. "Calm down, Chad. You're not doing yourself any favors by letting him get to you."

"How much of this shit does Belinda have to take?" Chad whispered through clenched teeth. "Let them do what they want to me, but why must she discuss our personal relationship with everyone? It's none of their fucking business."

"I know, Chad. I do understand, but I'm afraid there's nothing you can do about it now, and if you have another outburst, it will just make things worse. I told you, you have to control yourself no matter what." Sam kept his voice low so that only Chad could hear him, but there was no mistaking the seriousness of his tone.

Chad looked helplessly at Belinda and mouthed an apology to her.

Belinda, for her part, had remained calm. She merely smiled at Chad and with a slight shrug of her shoulders tried to send him a telepathic message that she was fine and had no problem with the line of questions.

The judge had taken a moment to consider the objection before ruling. "Mr. Montgomery, the witness has already testified to the closeness of her relationship with the defendant. She's established by her testimony that they were romantically involved. I believe that goes far enough. Objection sustained."

"Thank you, Your Honor," Sam said.

"Ms. Landis," Montgomery continued,. "if you were aware, as you testified earlier, about an incident involving my client, why didn't *you* report it? You must, by law, report any suspected case of child abuse."

Again, Sam objected. "My client is not on trial here, Your Honor."

This time the judge allowed the question.

Belinda stated adamantly, "This was not a case of child abuse. Chad told me that she came on to him. If Chad and I are guilty of anything, it's a misjudgment that Sheila would actually realize that she was out of line and this would simply go away."

It was too late for Montgomery to object to her last statement, so he just let it go. He had nothing more to add and Belinda was excused. As she returned to her seat in the courtroom, she squeezed Chad's shoulder in a show of support.

The judge checked the clock to see if they had more time before continuing. "Mr. Ludwig, call your next witness."

Harold Burns, an audio expert, was questioned next about the tape. "Mr. Burns, would you please explain your background in the field of audio technology?" Sam asked.

"Yes, sir. Currently I work for the Federal Bureau of Investigation. It's my job to verify the validity of wiretaps and other recorded evidence."

"And how long have you worked for the government?"

"Thirty-two years."

"Have you ever been asked to analyze audio tapes for a criminal investigation?"

"All the time. That's mainly what I do."

"You were asked to analyze the tape that we heard yesterday in this courtroom. What did you find?"

"There was a series of almost inaudible clicks at several points on the tape, as well as a number of other technical peculiarities indicating that the tape may have been edited."

"Edited? How?" Sam asked.

"Parts may have been cut out or moved to different places. You see, every time a recorder is paused or stopped, it creates an almost indistinguishable sound. It takes a trained ear and some special electronic devices to recognize them."

"So, your conclusion is that we shouldn't accept what we heard on the tape as an accurate recording of the conversation?"

"That's what I believe."

"Thank you. That's all." Sam returned to his seat.

Mr. Montgomery stood up at his table and asked somewhat cynically, "Mr. Burns, is it possible that these clicks, as you put it, *could* have come from another source, maybe the movement of an object in the room or some other source?"

"It's not likely but it's possible," Harold admitted.

"No further questions, Your Honor," and he sat down.

Sam stood and asked for permission to address the witness again. "Redirect, Your Honor?"

"Go ahead, Mr. Ludwig," the judge instructed.

"Mr. Burns, you said that aside from the clicks there were other technical…you called them 'peculiarities,' I believe." He referred to his notes. "Can these also be explained by an object in the room moving?"

"Definitely not," Mr. Burns attested. "The tape was definitely edited."

"Can you explain why you are so certain of this?" Sam asked.

"For example, if you listen carefully, especially if you use some of my equipment, you will hear the variations in the voice levels and inflections within the spoken sentences."

"Meaning?" Sam prodded.

"This is an indication that the tape was spliced together from different sentences."

"How do you reach that conclusion? Can you explain it in a way that we can understand?" Sam could see that some of the jurors were puzzled. Discrediting the tape was very important to their case and Sam needed Mr. Burns to make certain that the jurors understood that it was not a true indication of what had happened between Chad and Sheila.

"Without getting too technical, I can explain that when you speak, the words spoken take on different inflections depending upon where in the sentence they fall. Whether it's emphasized as the object of a sentence, or the tone goes up as in a question," Mr. Burns made a point of emphasizing different words as he spoke, demonstrating what he was explaining. "Now, say I take a word that has been emphasized in one sentence and splice it into another, taking it out of context, the tone, or inflection, slight though it might be, wouldn't quite fit into the other sentence."

Mr. Burns reached into his pocket and took out a tape. "If you like, I brought a tape that more clearly demonstrates what I mean. The tape is of a short conversation, followed by the same words spliced together to form a different conversation. Although both sound like regular conversations, if you listen carefully, the second sounds just a bit off, stilted…"

Sam looked to the judge for permission to demonstrate what Mr. Burns was explaining. The judge nodded to the clerk to take the tape and put it in the machine.

Everyone in the courtroom listened to the tape. Sam, Chad, and Belinda watched the faces of the jurors searching for looks of comprehension on their faces.

After the tape played, Mr. Burns added a few more comments explaining what they'd just heard, pointing out how the inflection of a question on a specific word in the first conversation sounded out of place in the second. He pointed out how in one of the sentences it seemed that more than just the object of the sentence was being emphasized. Sam was gratified to note that some of the jury members were nodding, indicating that they understood.

Sam thanked Mr. Burns, and as he returned to his seat, he gave Chad a discreet thumbs-up sign.

The judge turned to Mr. Montgomery. "Anything further?"

Standing, he said, "Nothing, Your Honor," and sat down.

The judge excused the witness and called a brief recess for lunch. "We'll resume in an hour."

The clerk called "All rise," and when everyone did, the judge rose and left the room.

Chad and Belinda followed Sam to the conference room, where they discussed what had happened, and what Sam had planned for after lunch. They ordered some sandwiches and ate while they talked.

Sam tried to be optimistic. "Discrediting the tape was an important accomplishment. It doesn't prove our case, but I think we managed to cast some doubt on Sheila's story." Being realistic though, Sam admitted that this was far from over.

When court reconvened, Chad was called to testify. After being sworn in, he sat in the witness box.

"Chad, you've heard the testimony of the witnesses in this courtroom. Is any of it valid?"

Chad and Sam had discussed his testimony at length. They'd decided that Sam would ask general questions which would allow Chad to speak freely. Chad spoke clearly and confidently, glad to finally have an opportunity to speak his piece. "I suspect that's how things went with Sheila's parents. I believe they think I did something wrong. I did talk with Sheila a couple of times in the hallway and after school. An incident did occur that night, but not as it was described here. That's about the extent of the truth that we've heard so far."

"Before you tell us what really happened that night, can you provide any reason why this girl would want to ruin your reputation and career?"

"Only she knows that for sure. I've never been anything but professional with her. I have *never* given her the slightest impression that I was interested in *any* kind of personal relationship with her."

Sam directed Chad to explain some of the specific points that had been raised in previous testimonies.

"A couple of times Sheila approached me in an aggressive manner. Once she kissed me after I had coached the girls' volleyball team to a victory. I immediately admonished her that it was inappropriate behavior for a student to kiss a teacher. Another time she came into my classroom when I was there alone, and I tried nicely to get her to leave.

"In retrospect, I suspect that she may have seen these incidents as rejections which hurt her ego. I think the final straw was when I gave her a failing grade for refusing to prepare adequately on a group project. It's clear to me that she's out for revenge."

Sam Ludwig fully expected Mr. Montgomery to object to Chad's testimony but when he failed to do so, Sam proceeded.

"Now, tell us what happened that night in school."

"Well, I *was* grading papers. After volleyball practice the school is often deserted and I wanted the quiet to concentrate and finish them. I don't recall the exact time but Sheila showed up and asked to talk with me."

"Aren't there clear instructions from the administration *not* to get into situations where you are alone with a student?" Sam asked.

"Yes, but I didn't foresee a problem and didn't think she'd stay long. I thought maybe she had come to ask about making up for her failing grade, and I did have a suggestion for her, so it seemed alright to inform her."

"What was that suggestion?"

"I told her that she could work on a school assembly that my class wanted to do and if she worked hard, I'd improve her grade by giving her that extra credit."

"So, you didn't initiate a sexual demand?"

"No, I didn't."

"Then what happened?"

"Sheila suggested an alternative, something personal, I think she put it, and then opened her shirt, exposing her breasts."

"There's something on the tape, I believe, where we heard you say, 'Do what I say and you'll please me.' Could you please explain that?"

"I was referring to her work on the assembly. It was said before she made her suggestion, when I was telling her that she could earn extra credit by making up the work she'd blown off earlier."

"And the part on the tape where you say, 'Do it, now.' How do you explain that?"

"When she came up and cornered me against the wall, I grabbed her shoulders and told her to get out of my room. I said, 'Do it, now!'"

"Mr. Peterson, you had no sexual interest in Sheila McMasters, did you?"

"No! Of course not! I'm in love with Belinda, I mean, Ms. Landis. Sheila McMasters is a kid, a spoiled, immature and totally selfish one, at that."

Mr. Montgomery had just two questions for Chad. "Mr. Peterson," he asked, "why didn't you call for help or run out of the room when, as you say, Sheila initiated the sexual encounter?"

"Frankly, I was too stunned to move. I just wanted her out of there," Chad admitted.

"And why didn't you report the incident to your principal?"

"I didn't want trouble. I've heard what happens when a teacher is accused of assaulting a student. The first thing that happens is that the teacher is suspended, his reputation is put into question. I had hoped that Sheila would realize what she'd done and that would be the end of it. It could have hurt her as well."

"Oh, and you didn't want to hurt Sheila," Mr. Montgomery said sarcastically. "How ironic! No more questions," he said as he returned to his seat.

Chad looked at the judge and tried to explain. "I was in a no-win situation. I had *never* been anything but kind to Sheila, just as I am to all of my students. I *never* treated her differently from any of the other kids in my classes. She's ruined my life with her stupid prank and for what? Revenge?" He directed his next words to Sheila, "Are you happy now? What did you get out of all this?"

Although the DA objected to Chad's speech, the judge ignored his objection and let Chad have his say.

Both attorneys had finished their presentations. The judge called for another short recess, informing them that closing arguments would begin in half an hour.

After the recess, each lawyer gave his closing summation. The prosecutor explained that sufficient evidence had been presented during the trial which warranted a conviction. He spoke confidently and the discrediting of the tape didn't seem to affect his arguments that Chad deserved to be punished for the crime he had committed against his student.

Sam pointed out that the evidence was entirely circumstantial. Though he conceded that it basically boiled down to Sheila's word against Chad's, he reminded the jury that the evidence she'd provided had proved to be a fabrication, which should be an indication that Sheila had lied. He spoke eloquently, and it was clear that he believed in his client, but he knew that it might not be enough.

Despite the judge's instructions to the jury that they judge the facts and make a decision based upon the evidence and the testimony they'd heard, Sam knew that in such cases, often the jury would give the benefit of the doubt to the child, preferring to err on the side of caution, just in case. It wasn't fair, but that was the way things were.

Once the jury had been dismissed for deliberations, the judge closed the proceedings, instructing the key people that they'd be notified as soon as the jury reached a verdict with a message when the court would reconvene.

Once again, Sam led the way to the conference room down the hall from the courtroom. Chad and Belinda both expressed their gratitude for all of Sam's efforts, all three voicing the hope that it had been enough.

Chad and Belinda moved to the middle of the conference room and stood there just holding each other, trying to be hopeful, each trying to comfort the other. Sam went down to the cafeteria to get some coffee for the three of them, giving Chad and Belinda a few minutes alone. They were still in the same position when Sam returned.

They took the coffee gratefully. Chad sat nervously in the conference room as the jury deliberated. Belinda paced back and forth, and Sam kept vigil with them. "I hope the jury deliberates for a long time. The longer the better. It suggests doubt, and that's good in this type of case. Three hours later, the clerk entered and notified them that the jury had reached a verdict.

They made their way nervously back into the courtroom. Mr. Montgomery came in a few minutes later, Sheila and her parents following close behind him.

Chad noticed that there were also a few reporters present, waiting to call in the verdict.

Inside the courtroom, the judge called everyone to order. He instructed Chad to stand and face the jury as they read the verdict and then he turned to the foreman, asking, "Mr. Foreman, have you reached a verdict?"

An older gentleman, Chad recalled that he was a retired businessman from the jury selection process, stood up and announced, "We have, Your Honor."

"What say you?" the judge asked.

He read from the slip of paper he held in his hand. "We find the defendant, Chad Peterson…guilty as charged."

Upon hearing the verdict, Chad slumped into his chair, a broken man. Sam, unable to console him, assured Chad that he would file immediately to appeal the verdict. Belinda cried openly, unable to believe that this was truly happening.

Judge Walters thanked and excused the jury.

Sam addressed the judge, "Your Honor, we'll be filing an immediate appeal. I'd like to ask for an extension of the bail arrangement pending the appeal."

The judge consulted his calendar and responded, "That is your right, gentlemen. Meanwhile, we will schedule sentencing for three weeks from today at nine o'clock." He turned to the bailiff and instructed, "Bailiff, the defendant can remain here until his attorney returns with the appeal papers. Terms of the bail remain in effect." He banged his gavel, dismissing the court.

Steve McMasters jumped out of his seat in a rage. "What the hell is going on here? This son of a bitch has just been found guilty of sexually harassing my little girl, and you're letting him walk out of here as if nothing has happened? You call this justice?"

The judge, who had not yet left his bench, again banged his gavel. "Mr. McMasters, you're out of order. I warned you, and now it'll cost you one hundred dollars."

McMasters couldn't believe what was happening. "That son of a bitch molested my little girl and nothing seems to be happening to him! Am I supposed to be afraid of being out of order?" He stood there spluttering, "They found him guilty! How can you let him just walk out of here? He should be behind bars!"

"I can assure you, Mr. McMasters, that justice will be served." The judge decided to be lenient, taking into account that this man's daughter was the victim, and he responded patiently. "There is a system. Most of the time it works. Sometimes it takes time to reach the end of the process. The defendant has a right to appeal the decision reached here in this court and based on the court's discretion he is entitled to a reasonable bail until such time as the appeal can be heard. While you might wish the system to work just a bit faster, this is what we have."

McMasters, still shaking with rage, tried to control himself. He questioned the judge's decision again, "Your Honor, what if he does it again? To my daughter or to some other unsuspecting child? Who will protect them?"

Again, the judge answered patiently yet powerfully, unwilling to continue debating this issue further. "The terms of his bail are quite clear. Mr. Peterson is not allowed to be in the presence of minors—unsupervised. If these terms are not met, bail can be revoked and he'll sit in jail until the end of the appeal."

"Yes, sir," McMasters answered, finally realizing that he wasn't going to make the judge change his mind.

The judge, who had not sat down during this exchange, turned to leave, and the bailiff called, "All rise." Everyone in the courtroom stood and the judge left. Over the shuffling sounds of people leaving the courtroom were the sounds of Belinda's sobs and Steve McMasters' angry shouts at Chad.

Chapter 11

Chad cuddled with Belinda on his sofa. Lost in their own thoughts, they didn't speak often and both were oblivious to what was playing on the TV. Chad stared straight ahead, wondering what lay ahead for his life. He suspected that a jail sentence awaited him, despite his innocence. "Even if I'm given probation, after that, what?" he thought. "I'm twenty-nine years old with no future. I'll never teach again. I have no other training." He felt despair as he had never known it. He imagined himself sitting in a jail cell with nothing but a solitary bunk, a toilet and a sink. "What a great environment to stifle the hopes and life of a person."

Belinda Landis, absolutely devastated by the verdict, sobbed endlessly and constantly used Kleenex to wipe her tears. "I still can't believe this," she kept repeating to herself as she sat next to Chad. She thought about the aftermath of the trial. Belinda remembered the smug look on Sheila's face as the guilty verdict was announced. Also, Matt and Maggie Stairs both hugged Chad as he was led from the courtroom and had tried to offer some hope that Chad could win an appeal. But it was the look of despair on Chad's face that haunted her thoughts. Finally around 11 p.m., Belinda urged Chad, "Honey, let's go to bed and try to get some sleep."

"I guess you're right. He kissed her cheek and led her to his bedroom. Belinda was not aware of when she finally fell asleep in Chad's arms but being close to him offered her some comfort.

The next morning, Belinda dressed for school. She had little desire left within her to function in the classroom. Jim Morris approached her in the hallway. "I'm really sorry, Belinda. I never wanted anything that I said at the trial to hurt Chad. I received a subpoena. I had no advance knowledge of what I would be asked. I tried under cross examination to be helpful."

"I know that, Jim. I'm certain Chad understands that too and harbors no resentment toward you."

Several other teachers hugged Belinda and offered supporting comments. Their sympathy provided some consolation, but knowing that she wouldn't see Chad in the faculty room as usually was the case caused her to avoid spending time there in the morning.

She seemed more robotic than personal in classes all day. Students who liked her and also liked Chad often came up during breaks in their artwork to chat. "It's really a rotten deal," said Tim O'Reilly, who also had Chad for history. "Mr. P. isn't the kind of teacher who would do that. The jury doesn't know him like we do."

Just before lunch, Robbie Simpson, her best student, approached her and gave Belinda a sympathetic hug. "It's teachers like you and Mr. Peterson who really care about us students, Ms. Landis. I wish we could do something."

"Thanks for your concern, Robbie. I don't know what can be done now. I feel so helpless. I'm afraid I'm not such a good teacher today. I can't concentrate on schoolwork. I think I'm going to ask Mrs. Hargrove if I can leave at lunch. She can get someone to cover my last class."

"The kids are all talking about Sheila McMasters. They're very angry. She better watch what she does and where she goes."

"Robbie, I don't want anyone getting into trouble over this. She mustn't be threatened or hurt in any way."

"I promise that I won't do anything to her, Ms. Landis. But I've already heard rumors that some kids in Mr. Peterson's American history class, who were pissed at Sheila for screwing up their project, plan to retaliate."

"I have to report that to Mrs. Hargrove. Exactly what've you heard?"

"No details. It's just the beginning of a rumor that I heard as I stood at my locker this morning. She came in gloating about the outcome of the trial and several kids made some nasty comments to her. The one thing I did hear was someone shout, 'We'll get you for this.' She just gave him the finger. If she had any popularity before the trial, she blew it with this charge against Mr. Peterson."

Skipping her lunch, Belinda walked into the high school office. She waited for a couple of minutes and then Helen invited her into her office. "Helen, I'm an emotional basket case. I'd like you to get someone to cover my afternoon class. There are plans on my desk, but the kids know what to do. It's just too difficult to stay here for the rest of the day. I'll use half a personal day."

"You've been through a trying time, Belinda. I understand that. I'll excuse you as leaving ill. It's not a problem. I think Teri Fogerty has that period free. I'll ask her to cover for you. I'm sure she'll be glad to do it."

"Thanks. One more thing. I've heard rumors that some of the kids may be plotting some kind of revenge against Sheila McMasters. I don't know what, but I thought you should be alerted to it."

"We've already heard the rumors and we're keeping a watch on things. Thanks though for telling me." Belinda turned to leave when Helen added, "Tell Chad I said hello, and that I'm sorry." She smiled at Belinda.

"I'm worried about him. Thanks for understanding. I'll see you tomorrow."

* * *

Sheila McMasters made sure to stick to her closest friends any time that she left the security of a classroom. Cindy Bennett and Tim met her in the hallway and walked with her to the lunchroom. There they were joined by some of the others who attended the wild party several weeks ago, including Tara Litz, Rod Lawson, Becky Finch, Jimmy Clark, and Andy Stewart. Sheila underestimated the hostile feelings she generated by accusing Chad Peterson. "I got quite a few stares and under the breath comments as I waited in line to get my lunch."

"It'll blow over in a couple days," voiced Cindy. "Teachers come and go. We don't need scum like that pervert in our school." Cindy was aware of what really happened but lied to make the others rally around Sheila. Her loyalty to Sheila was unquestioned. Sheila had done many things to help her, including winning Tim, and this was payback.

"What I can't understand is why you turned him down," said Tara with a smirk. "I would have gone to my knees in a flash for a chance to take him on. He's gorgeous."

"I did have an infatuation with him at the beginning of the semester," Sheila responded, "but he treated me like shit. He was rude to me, insulted me, and then deliberately lowered my grade to get sex from me. I don't take that from any guy, including a teacher." Her acting was meritorious and those in the group unaware of what really happened nodded their approval.

When Tim O'Reilly walked by and "accidentally" dropped his tray and spilled milk on Sheila, Rod jumped up and grabbed him. A quick punch to the stomach dropped Tim to the floor. "You do anything like that again, you son of a bitch, and I'll lay you out permanently," Rod shouted as he stood over a gasping Tim.

Tony Baker and Helen Hargrove immediately charged into the melee. "Go straight to my office, Rod. I'll deal with you in a few minutes." Rod just continued to glare at Tim as he moved away. Tony escorted him out of the cafeteria and to the office.

"Are you alright, Tim?" Helen asked. "I think you should go see the nurse."

"I'm ok, Mrs. Hargrove. I don't need to see the nurse."

"I insist that you go there first, just to be safe. Then I want you in my office as soon as she declares you're uninjured."

Then Helen turned to Sheila. "Go to the restroom and clean yourself up. Cindy, you go with her. I don't want more trouble today." She turned to some of the other staff members assigned to cafeteria duty. "Nobody else is excused to the restroom until Sheila returns."

Order was eventually restored. Several kids sitting at nearby tables who witnessed the incident turned their backs to Sheila as she passed by on the way to the restroom. Included among the group were some of the school's cheerleaders.

"I don't know about you girls, but I don't want to be associated with that girl anymore. She casts a bad image of us cheerleaders,"said Nicki Thompson. "Mr. Peterson has been nothing but kind to us as both a coach and a teacher."

"Maybe if we give her the silent treatment during practice, she'll get the hint and quit," offered Heather Joles. "No way am I gonna have anything more to do with her. I didn't mind when she partied and manipulated her way with some of the boys, but what she did to Mr. Peterson was wrong."

"Is it possible that she's right and Mr. Peterson *did* try to have sex with her?" asked Paul Stone. "She is very pretty and I could see a man trying something with her."

Nicki jumped immediately to Chad's defense. "He tried to be cool about it but most of us knew he had a thing for Ms. Landis. Why would he ruin that for someone like Sheila?"

"What about the tape. From what I heard about it, he did make some suggestive comments to her," continued Paul.

"I can't explain the tape. I just have a gut feeling from what I know about Sheila that she somehow got him to say things. Things that were misinterpreted."

Heather interrupted. "I wish we could do something to get the truth out of her."

"Maybe there is," said Nicki. Keep your eyes and ears open. In class, eavesdrop when you can as they talk. Make some comments about Mr. Peterson that makes them think you doubt his innocence. Maybe they'll make a slip-up."

"I doubt that they'll trust us, but it's worth a try," said Heather.

The others nodded. Nicki added, "Pass the word among some other friends to do the same. We have to find a way to get Sheila or one of her cronies to confess."

Rod Lawson was seething with anger when Helen Hargrove arrived at her office. Tony Baker returned to the lunchroom after being reassured that everything was under control. Before he even sat down in her office, Rod began ranting. "That bastard deliberately spilled milk on Sheila. It was no accident."

"That doesn't give you the right to attack him and don't use that language in here with me. Do you understand? You know that any fight on school property necessitates my calling the police and notifying them."

"I don't care what you do! He deserved it. I'll argue self defense."

"He didn't spill the milk on you, Rod."

"Ok, so I'll argue that I helped a friend who was attacked."

After a few more minutes of discussion, Helen could see that she was getting nowhere. "You're suspended from school for ten days."

"Fine! Nobody assaults my friends and gets away with it! After today, they'll realize that! Why are they in sympathy for that sex fiend anyway? He got what he deserved!"

"That's enough. Wait in the area outside the office. I'm also calling your parents and you're to stay in the office until they and the police arrive."

The nurse, for protective measures, kept Tim O'Reilly under her watchful care for an hour. She called Helen Hargrove to explain that Tim seemed ok, but for his protection she wanted to observe him to make sure no delayed complications occurred. Helen gladly accepted that information, hoping that Rod would be gone by the time Tim arrived for his disciplinary punishment.

Meanwhile, Belinda went home, showered, and changed into more comfortable clothes. Then she phoned Chad. "Hi, honey, how're you doin'?" she began.

"About as well as can be expected, given the circumstances."

Belinda's concern immediately raised a notch.

"What've you been doing all day, Chad?"

"Sittin' here watching television. Not much else to do, really."

"Chad, I took the rest of the afternoon off to keep you company. Helen is generously calling it sick time. I'll be over in about ten minutes."

"I look forward to that," Chad offered. "I love you."

"Love you too." Belinda was heartened by Chad's reaction. Hearing him voice his love encouraged her. Jumping into her car, she hurriedly made her way to his place. When she first spied Chad as he opened the door, she noticed a faint smile on his face and put her arms around him and squeezed.

When he finally broke free of her, Chad asked, "You want something to drink? I have iced tea or Coke? I'm not drinking beer anymore, even though I'll never get any in jail."

"I'll have a glass of Coke. Thanks. I came here to be with you. You're the most important person in my life and school today seemed kind of meaningless. I don't want you to think you're in this alone."

"Yeah, right! I'm still upset that none of my so-called friends showed up or called," he said forcefully.

"Don't blame them, Chad. They don't know what to say or how to handle this either. It's uncomfortable for everyone." Then she added, "A lot of students send you their best wishes and love, Chad. Tim O'Reilly and Robbie Simpson came up to me today and voiced their anger over what happened. I'm afraid I didn't hide my grief too well today."

Chad was skeptical. "Kids only care about themselves. Don't be fooled. If they miss me, it's 'cause I give them good grades."

Belinda looked around the room. "How would you like to spend the afternoon? We could go for a walk." She spotted a Monopoly game on a table in the corner. "I could beat you at Monopoly," she laughed. "Or we could go to your room and make mad passionate love."

"As tempting as that last offer is, sweetheart, I'm afraid I wouldn't be a good lover today. I'll take a rain check on that, ok?"

Belinda leaned over and gave him a peck on the lips. You're a terrific lover any time, but that's ok. However, you want to pass the time is fine as long as we're together."

They settled on Monopoly and for two hours the game proved a distraction. Chad actually let out a loud laugh when Belinda landed on Boardwalk, one of Chad's properties with a hotel. "Oh, yeah!" he squealed. "You'll pay big time for that one. Let me check the card to see how much you'll have to pay."

Belinda scanned the money she had left. "I'm afraid I don't have enough. Maybe we can work out some kind of arrangement," she said suggestively.

"No way, baby! It's money or I win!"

"Either way, you win, my dear. I'm just offering to pay off my debt."

Even though earlier Chad had refused her offer to make love, this time there was no hesitation. He crawled across the board on the floor and pushed her onto her back and lay on her, crushing her with his weight as he planted a long deep kiss on her lips.

"I love you, Chad, and nothing will ever change that," Belinda moaned when their kiss ended.

Chad's hands began to explore her body. He stroked her fingers and the palm of her hand. His touch slowly moved up her arm and as he kissed her again, he curled her hair in one hand and stroked her face with the other.

Slowly, as if taking time would make them forget their troubles, they continued to make love. Pieces of clothing were removed until their naked bodies, urgent to express their needs, took control. When Chad delicately touched her breast, Belinda felt the fire of desire explode within her. Each of them longed for and devoured the pleasure derived from the other's touch. Finally, Belinda raised her legs to wrap around him and arched her back as he moved inside her. Their slow rhythmic movements gradually became more passionate and both satisfied the need within them. They clung to each other as if breaking away would somehow hurt them both.

It was hours later when they jumped into the shower. "That wonderful sex made me hungry," Chad blurted out as he washed Belinda's back. "I was thinking maybe we could call and have a pizza delivered."

Belinda turned to face him. She pressed her body to his and kissed him. "I'm shocked that you're hungry," she joked. "I thought you got your fill of me."

"I can never get enough of you, sweetheart, but you know that they say the way to a man's heart is through his stomach and my stomach is saying 'I need food'."

A half hour later, Chad and Belinda feasted upon a pizza with all the trimmings. It was during this time that their discussion once again turned more serious. "Belinda, I know there'll be an appeal of my conviction," Chad stammered. "How long that'll take I don't know. I do know that I'll probably be sentenced and likely spend some time in jail." Chad looked into her eyes and with a serious expression added, "You know that I love you. I love you so much, and I'm afraid that this incident may ruin your life too. I know I mentioned this before, but if I'm sent away, as hard as it is, you have to consider forgetting about me and moving on. I'll be marked forever as a child molester. I'll have to move away from Emerson. I can't live here with that stigma. I don't want to drag you down with me."

"I still can't believe this has happened to us, but, honey, can't you see that what happens to you affects me too? I can't turn off my love like a faucet, Chad.

I refuse to desert you in your time of need. This whole affair is an unending nightmare.

"I can't escape this nightmare but it doesn't have to follow you." He took his can of Coke and took a long drink. "You'll just have to go and not look back."

Trying to avoid an argument, Belinda responded. "Chad, honey, we'll cross that bridge when we come to it. This isn't over yet. I don't even want to think of life beyond our being together."

Belinda stayed with Chad and late at night he fell asleep with his head on her lap. With one hand she often wiped tears from her eyes and with the other she lightly stroked his head as he slept.

The next morning, Helen Hargrove grabbed Belinda as she entered the hallway and dragged her into the faculty room. She looked around the room and spotted eight faculty members gathered there. Among them were Don Klingensmith, the guidance counselor, Matt Stairs, Jim Morris, Bill Thorndike, and Tony Baker. They all greeted Belinda cordially.

Helen spoke first. "This is an informal meeting, Belinda. We're here to brainstorm some ideas that might help Chad. We firmly believe in his innocence."

Belinda was touched by their compassion. "Thank you," she said. Helen handed her a cup of coffee as Belinda took a seat on the couch. "Does anyone have an idea?"

Thorny jumped right in with a suggestion. "We'll never get Sheila to change her story. Somehow we need to get to Cindy Bennett. She's Sheila's closest friend and if we can somehow get her to admit that she knew Sheila's story is a lie, we can win the appeal."

Helen replied. "That won't be easy. Cindy blindly follows Sheila's directions. I don't know what hold Sheila has on her that would make her turn against a respected teacher like Chad. She's extremely loyal, though, to Sheila."

"Maybe if we threaten to make her life miserable in this school, she'll change her tune," said Thorny.

"I can't be a party to that," Helen said. "We can't intimidate any student. That would be unprofessional. Besides, that would just make her change of testimony less believable."

Everyone nodded. For several minutes, nobody offered anything constructive. Finally, Belinda chipped in with a suggestion. "Maybe we can't find a solution right now to get Chad out of this mess, but one thing you all can do is go see him. He believes that you've all turned your back on him. He needs to know that you care about him, and not just hear it from me."

"You're right, Belinda. We need to be more obvious in our support of Chad. I'll go over there after school and apologize. We won't desert him," said Jim.

The others voiced agreement. Although they didn't succeed in coming up with a plan, Belinda went to class feeling much better after the impromptu meeting with her colleagues. Their concern warmed her heart, and she had left the faculty room with a positive feeling again. Somehow, this would turn out right in the end.

Chapter 12

Sheila McMasters sat at the breakfast table eating a bowl of Cheerios. Her dad, hiding behind the morning paper as he ate, seemed oblivious to Sheila's presence. Laura McMasters stood at the stove preparing scrambled eggs. She turned to Sheila.

"Your dad and I have to leave tonight for the funeral of Aunt June. I know you didn't know her very well, Sheila, and that's why I'm not making you go with us." Then her voice became commanding. "I'm telling you right now. You're not to have any parties over here while we're gone."

"Awww, mom. Ease up on me, will ya? Every time you go away, you think I'm gonna have some kind of orgy here. Is it at least alright if I invite Cindy to come over and spend the night with me so I won't be alone?"

"I'm not too happy about that. She got you into trouble at her place. NO BOYS!" Laura demanded.

"Yeah, mom. I hear you," Sheila whined.

Steve McMasters put down his paper and picked up a glass of orange juice. "Oh, good morning, sweetie. Ready for another day of school?" Obviously he hadn't heard a word spoken between Sheila and her mother.

"Yeah, I'm meeting Tara at the corner in about ten minutes. We'll walk together."

"How have things been at school lately? What's the talk about that bastard Peterson? I hope he gets ten years for trying to corrupt my little girl."

"Some of the kids feel sorry for him, but most are on my side," Sheila lied.

Steve got up, walked over to Sheila, and pressed a kiss to her cheek. "Don't worry. That man'll never bother you again. I promise you that."

Sheila practically gulped her breakfast and a few minutes later made a hasty move to the door. "Bye daddy. Bye mom! I'll skip cheerleading practice so I can see you before you leave."

Tara was right on time when Sheila arrived at the corner. "My parents have to leave town. My mom's aunt died. I'm gonna ask a few friends to come over after they leave. Of course, you're invited."

"Count me in," Tara said. "Frank's been looking for a place where we could shack up. Do you think we could stay?"

"Sure, you can use my brother Mike's room. He's away at college, but I'll want all the details the next day."

"I'm gonna give him a night he'll never forget," Tara said with a wicked grin. "You won't need the details. You'll probably hear everything."

When they arrived at school, they met Cindy, who was searching through her locker. Sheila said, "Hey, Cindy, sup?"

Cindy looked aggravated. "I'm looking for a locket that Tim gave me. I couldn't find it at home, and it's not here either. He's gonna be so pissed."

"I'm sure it'll turn up. Meanwhile, if your parents will allow you out of the house, you can soothe his hurt feelings by bringing him over to my place tonight around eight. Mom and Dad are leaving for Detroit. They'll be gone all weekend."

"Cool! I'm sure he'll come," she replied and then added, "Hahaha, pun intended!" All three girls broke into laughter. "Things have cooled at home since I served most of my punishment. I'll tell dad I'm going on a date. He'll be fine with that. but I'm still not allowed out overnight." Just then Cindy spotted Tim coming down the hall. "You both better go. I've got some explaining to do."

Tara and Sheila walked past Tim as they departed. Sheila, with her usual smart ass remarks, greeted him. "Hey there, Tim. Got something in your pocket or are you just happy to see me!" she teased. Sheila continued walking without waiting for a reply but her sly grin said it all.

At lunch, Sheila sat with her usual pals. "I was going to invite some of the cheerleaders over tonight, but they've been avoiding me. Screw 'em! I don't need 'em."

Cindy was first to attempt to calm Sheila. "We're still with you. We won't abandon you." Even though Sheila pretended not to care, Cindy could see that it hurt to have some of her former friends, especially the cheerleaders, turn against her.

Trying to change the tone of the conversation, Tara said, "So, what's planned for tonight, Sheila? Besides Frank boinkin' me, that is!" she added with a snicker.

"And Tim and I doing the horizontal mambo," chipped in Cindy.

"Guess we'll just call it Hawaiian night then, huh? Everyone gets leid!" Sheila snapped back with a giggle. "I better get a date. Don't wanna end up watching you all night."

Cindy interjected. "Hey guys, you heard the latest gossip? Mr. Peterson's falling apart. Rumor is he's been hitting the bottle pretty hard for the past few weeks, and his relationship with Ms. Landis is shaky."

Sheila didn't respond verbally but her fantasy immediately kicked into high gear. *Hmmm, I'd still like to rock and roll with him*, she thought. *Maybe now that he's not so high and mighty, he'd give me a tumble.*

Tara interrupted her musing. "We both have dates. Who're you gonna ask, Sheila?"

"Hmmm. Andy Stewart broke up with his girlfriend a couple weeks ago. He's cute and I bet horny as hell. Maybe I'll see if he's up for some fun. And if he won't come, I can ask Rod Lawson. He was good at your place, Cindy."

"Rod's attached to Becky Finch now," Tara said. "I don't think he'd come as your date."

Sheila just laughed. "If he finds out I'm interested, he'll come. In more ways than one. Remember, I'm pretty good at getting my way."

Both girls winked in agreement.

"Let's keep this small and intimate," Sheila added. "Nobody comes stag. I don't want guys crashing the party thinking they can join in the fun. I'm not into doing threesomes…yet!"

The girls broke into a loud fit of laughter and nearby students looked at them. A few glared in their direction, and Sheila gave them an uplifted middle finger. "I better look for Andy. I'll see you girls after school at our lockers."

Sheila's history class was now taught by a substitute named Mrs. Longden. She was strict and a by-the-book teacher. Most of the class resented losing the fun-filled activities that Chad Peterson often presented. Sheila became an outcast in class, sitting in a seat in the back of the room.

After class, Sheila spotted Andy walking down the hallway and ran up to him. Grabbing his shoulder, she turned him to her. "Hey, big guy. Where ya headin?"

"Gym class. What's up?"

"I'm havin' a small party tonight. Just a few specially invited friends. I was hopin' you'd come and hook up with me."

"Hook up?"

Not one to beat around the bush, Sheila traced her fingers alongside his face and said, "It's gonna be really hot." She looked for and wasn't surprised at Andy's reaction. The bulge in his pants indicated that he understood. She smiled a knowing smile at him.

"What time?" Andy stuttered.

"No earlier than 8 p.m. My parents are leaving town for the weekend. You can come over soon after that. Just look to make sure their car is gone from the driveway."

"Who else is gonna be there?" Andy asked as he neared the locker room door.

"Six for sure. You, me, Cindy, Tim, Tara, and Frank. There might be a few others but only if they come with a date."

Excited, Andy said, "We'll have some privacy though, right?"

Sheila just smirked. "It'll be wild. Don't be too late!" She stood on her toes and gave Andy a kiss on the cheek. She whispered in his ear. "Don't forget to bring some condoms."

Later, Sheila met her two girlfriends after school. "I talked with Becky Finch and she wants to bring Rod tonight," Cindy informed her.

"That's ok. I got Andy to agree, so everything is set. We need someone to get us some beer. Any inhibitions we might have will disappear after a couple drinks."

"You set up everything else. I'll take care of getting the beer. Jimmy Clark got it for us before with a little persuasion on my part. He'll do it again."

"Tara, you're such a slut!" Sheila chuckled. "Ok, I'll make sure we have some snacks and my dad has lots of movies to get us started." Turning again to Cindy, she said, "You've got some great CDs. Bring a few, ok?" Then she quickly added, "I gotta go home to say g'bye to my parents. See you tonight."

A few hours later, Steve and Laura McMasters hugged their daughter before climbing into their PT Cruiser. Her father said, "You have our cell phone number if you need us for anything, honey. We'll be home mid-afternoon on Sunday."

"Ok daddy, I'll be fine. Say hello and offer my sympathy," Sheila spoke sweetly. "Cindy's coming over later. We're gonna make some popcorn and watch a couple movies."

"I'm still not certain I like her coming over to spend the night. She's a bad influence on you," Laura said.

"Oh, Mom. One mistake. Let it go! I'll keep things under control." She kissed her mom on the cheek and politely closed the car door after her mom climbed inside. She waved across to her dad and watched as they drove away.

Finally, she thought. *I thought they'd never leave.* Sheila looked at her watch. It was 7:20. She drew a deep sigh, then ran into the house to make preparations for the party. She arranged pillows around the living room floor, selected a few possible movies to set the mood, and set some potato chips and pretzels on the coffee table.

The doorbell rang at 8:10. "Hey, Sheila," Jimmy Clark said. "I got something for you. Where do you want it?"

"You better pull your car up into the garage, Jimmy. I don't want the neighbors seeing us carrying in beer. How much did ya get?"

"Two cases ought to be enough, doncha think?"

"More than enough. You joinin' the fun?"

"Nah. No way I could get a girl to come for what you're planning tonight. Tara told me about it."

"How much for the beer, then?"

"Thirty-five'll cover it."

Sheila went to her purse and pulled out three tens and a five. "Thanks," she said, "but don't tell anyone about what's going on tonight. Promise?"

"I won't breathe a word. Boy, I'd sure like to be here. Guess I can't stay, huh?"

"Sorry, Jimmy. No peeping Toms allowed." She laughed.

The others began arriving between 8:30 and 9:00. "I didn't miss anything good, did I?" Andy asked when he was the last to arrive.

Sheila walked up to him, wrapped her arms around him, and grabbed his buns. "Things are just heating up but now that you're here, I imagine it'll get hot!" She winked at him. "Come in and grab a beer."

The couples positioned themselves on the floor around the room. Sheila spoke first. "Listen, everybody. We all know why we're here. Before we lose our clothes and get involved, just be really careful not to spill any beer on the carpet. I don't want to explain how it got there."

A bit nervous, Becky Finch spoke hesitantly. "Could we put on a movie first and turn down the lights?"

Tara laughed. "Nervous Becky? You can watch Frank and me. We'll give you a few pointers." She turned to Frank. "Won't we, Frankie?"

Frank didn't answer but leaned in close and kissed Tara hard on the lips. His hand went to her breast and squeezed. Together they lowered themselves to a lying position and wrapped themselves in an embrace."

"OOOOOH! Someone doesn't need a movie for motivation," Sheila squealed. She put a DVD into the player and settled back on the floor in Andy's arms. "Mmmmm, this is comfy," she crooned. She took the can of beer from Andy's hand and chugged what remained.

When he had a good buzz from the beers, Andy began groping Sheila. Also feeling the effects of the alcohol, she turned and kissed him. Aggressively taking control, she moved her body to lie on top of him. Her hips ground into his pelvis and she delighted in the effect she had on him.

As Andy nibbled on her ear, Sheila glanced over at Tara who was half naked. *She always was a fast worker*, Sheila thought.

Eventually, the others moved to an area of the house where they could be alone. Sheila grabbed Andy's hand and led him to her bedroom. They lay on the bed making out passionately. As they kissed, Andy rolled Sheila onto her side and began to unbutton her blouse. His hand moved to touch her breasts and he was pleased to feel that she wore no bra. She helped him remove the blouse from her shoulders.

Losing control, they abandoned themselves to the pleasures of touch, exploring each other's bodies. When Andy's hand snaked inside her panties, Sheila arched her back and willingly let him remove them. With her eyes closed and feeling the effects of the alcohol, Sheila, without warning, fantasized that it was Chad Peterson making love to her. Physically she took Andy inside her but she imagined it was Chad that she felt. With each thrust, she arched up to take him deep inside her. When Andy exploded, Sheila was wrapped up in her fantasy and made an egregious error. "Oh God, Chad," she moaned.

Andy instantly pulled out and knelt between her legs. He angrily ripped off the condom. "CHAD?" he screeched at her at the top of his voice. "You were imagining fucking that teacher?"

"I'm sorry, Andy. I didn't mean it."

Andy quickly dressed.

Moments later, the others appeared in the living room to see Andy standing there arguing with Sheila.

"You have a thing for Mr. Peterson, don't you? You set him up, probably after he rejected you."

Sheila pulled him closer to her and whispered into his ear. "No, it's not! I don't know why I said that, Andy, but I want you to stay. Let me show you."

"It *is* true. I don't want to be with someone who is using me for her fantasies. I'm leaving. Thanks for nothing." He stormed out of the house, slamming the door behind him.

The others gathered around Sheila. "What happened?" Cindy wanted to know. "Why did he accuse you of that?"

"I lost control for a moment. He heard me use Chad's name."

Rod asked, "Tell the truth. Mr. Peterson was innocent and you sent him to jail?"

Sheila tried desperately to lie her way out of it. She screamed, "I'm telling you that man tried to force me to have sex with him." Her twisted mind actually made Sheila believe that Chad Peterson was guilty. With no remorse, she added, "He deserved what he got!"

The others looked at Sheila with doubt. "Don't look at me like that," she screamed as she again lost control. "If you don't believe me, get out of here! GO!"

Cindy Bennett, Sheila's best friend, and the only other person who actually knew the whole truth about the incident involving Chad, remained with Sheila. The others hastily retreated. As Rod Lawson moved through the door, he turned to Sheila and just shook his head in disbelief.

Sheila cried uncontrollably. "They'll all hate me now."

Having somewhat of a change of heart, Cindy said, "They're not gonna hate you, but it's not too late to change your story, Sheila. Mr. Peterson hasn't been sentenced yet."

"Great! Like that'll fix everything. He'll go back to being Mr. Popularity and I'll be scorned as some kind of tramp and liar."

"Look at what this has done to you. You're an emotional wreck. Many of the kids who were your close friends have turned against you. You've always been a master at manipulating your way out of things. You can manage this too."

Sheila screamed at her. "NO! It's all that man's fault. I want him punished for what he did to me."

"Or what he *didn't* do to you."

Suddenly belligerent, Sheila said, "Are you turning against me too? You can leave too if you want."

"Don't be that way! I'm trying to help you."

Sheila remained silent for a few minutes while Cindy sat holding her hands. "At least I'm not lying to my mom and dad now. Nobody's gonna spend the night. But Cindy, I can't face my mom and dad and tell them the truth about Mr. Peterson. You have to stick by me on this."

Cindy reached over and hugged her friend. "It'll all be ok," was all she said.

Chapter 13

Chad sat on his bed reading *The Rebel's Pledge* by Rita Gerlach, an author whom he'd met at a local book signing. He liked reading, especially novels with a historical theme. Uninterrupted for hours, he found that even though this was historical fiction he couldn't put it down. Then a thought occurred to him. "I'm gonna have a lot of time to read if I'm sent to prison. At the very least, it'll keep me occupied and help pass the time."

That evening when he saw Belinda, his mood was once more downbeat. "It's only gonna get worse, and you know it, Belinda. My scheduled sentencing is going to come fast. After that, I could be put into a state prison, and I won't be as close to you as I am now. It's gonna be tough. To be honest, I'm a bit afraid I'll end up becoming some guy's playmate."

"It's not certain that you'll go to jail. I want you to stop thinking that way," she admonished him. Quickly changing the subject so that his mood wouldn't worsen, Belinda asked, "So what did you do today?"

"I finished that novel I bought at the mall. You remember. The author autographed it for me."

"Was it good?"

"Yeah, I really enjoyed it. One advantage of not having lesson plans to do is that I have more time to read."

"Have any of the staff been here to see you? Several said they'd come."

"Jim and Thorny stopped by this afternoon for about forty-five minutes. Jim apologized over and over about giving testimony that hurt my case. I kept reminding him that he only told the truth, but I couldn't assuage his guilt."

"I know. He feels as if he betrayed your trust."

"Oh, Marla also stopped by around lunch time to see me. You remember her, the waitress?

"Yeah, sure."

"She was practically in tears. She, like the others, said that she wished she could do something to help me. She called my conviction 'a crock of shit' and hoped Judge Walters is lenient. She's convinced that I'll get probation instead of jail time."

"You've no past criminal record."

"Teachers hold the trust of the community and the students. If I read his face and tone of voice correctly, he seemed surprised by the verdict. However, he's bound by law to pass judgment and may fear the wrath of the community if he grants me probation. I suspect he'll feel compelled to make an example of me. I can only hope for leniency."

"Any others come to see you?"

"Yeah, right after school Matt came hobbling in to visit and Maggie was with him. That was nice. I'm sorry I let him down. He thinks some of this is his fault for asking me to take over the girls' volleyball team. Of course, that's ridiculous. Sam came over at lunchtime to discuss my appeal."

"We had a meeting in the faculty room to brainstorm some ways to help you. Short of blackmailing someone, we came up empty. I'm sorry, Chad."

"I know you're trying, sweetheart. I do appreciate your standing by me, especially after that damn lawyer embarrassed you and tried to suck you in about our sexual relationship."

"I'm a big girl. I can take care of myself. More important is discovering a way out of this mess."

"Even if I do get probation, I'll have to find another job. My teaching days are done. That's for sure. I guess you heard that the school board plans to pass a resolution firing me."

"Yeah, we've all heard the news. I'm sorry. What would you do?"

"I haven't thought much about it. All of my education and training is for teaching. I don't really know what I could do. Maybe I can work as a guard in a museum or look for a job with a newspaper. Or get a job as a freak in a circus," he joked.

Chad fixed a snack and then turned on some music. "Would you like to dance, sweetheart? I have this strong need just to hold you."

"I'd love that," she quickly responded as she moved in close to him.

Even after the song ended, he continued to hold her and they swayed in unison for several more minutes. "You've steadfastly stood by me, Belinda," he whispered to her. "I was such a fool to avoid you. If it hadn't been for you, I'd have lost my sanity." He looked straight into her eyes. "I love you so much."

"I've always known in my heart that you'd never betray that love. This isn't over yet. I'm here to help you remain strong, for as long as it takes."

She wanted to hold him all night, but finally admitted that she had school work to do. She fought hard to hold back the tears as she worked, but Chad saw her occasionally dab at her eyes with a Kleenex as he occupied his time reading a book.

Belinda spent several hours grading art projects. They formed a temporary distraction and for that, at least, she was grateful. She was thankful that the next day was Friday and looked forward to spending the entire weekend with Chad.

At 11 p.m. she heard her stomach growl. "No wonder my clothes are beginning to get a bit loose," she thought. "This whole matter has changed my eating habits." She walked into the bathroom and stepped on the scale. It surprised her to see that she'd dropped eight pounds in this short time. She toasted a bagel and after undressing, she crawled into bed next to an already sleeping Chad.

On Friday morning Belinda arrived at school later than usual. Her mental exhaustion finally caught up with her and she had overslept; both she and Chad were oblivious to the alarm clock providing the normal morning music wake up call.

She hadn't even made it to her room when two students accosted her. "We have to talk with you, Ms. Landis. It's urgent."

Belinda unlocked her room, turned on the lights, and walked over to her desk to drop the student projects she was carrying. "What's the matter?" she asked.

Becky Finch blurted, "We weren't sure how to handle this, but we think we have proof that Mr. Peterson is innocent."

"You kids are close friends with Sheila McMasters, aren't you? Why suddenly have you changed your mind?" Belinda wondered.

"It's like this," Becky continued. "We were at a party last night. Sheila didn't come right out and confess to us, but we're now skeptical." She turned to Andy Stewart. "Go ahead, Andy. Tell her."

Andy hesitated. "It's kind of embarrassing."

Becky gave him a shove. "You have to tell her. Sheila is railroading Mr. P. Please, Andy!" she begged.

Andy sat in a student desk and without looking at Belinda directly, began speaking. "Ummm," he dragged out. "I was Sheila's date at a party at her place,

Ms. Landis. "I, ummmmm, was, you know, doin' it with her when she said Mr. Peterson's name. It really upset me. I accused her of lying about him."

"Did she admit to lying?"

"Not exactly, no, but I'm convinced now that she used everyone, including us, to get revenge on Mr. P."

Belinda contemplated for a moment what Andy had said. "I'm grateful that both of you came to me about this. However, it really doesn't change things. Even if Sheila had openly confessed to you, it still would be only your word against hers. There's no conclusive proof..."

"We talked about that too, Ms. Landis," Becky interrupted, "and we know that our opinions won't clear Mr. P., but we're convinced that Cindy Bennett knows the truth."

"Cindy testified at the trial. Even if she knows what really happened, she won't cooperate."

Becky said, "She might—if some of us pressure her. Cindy's very vulnerable and insecure. That's why she's so close to Sheila. Sheila kind of watches out for her and helps her. If she thinks we kids will turn against her the way they've done to Sheila, it might scare her."

"We'll still need something more definite than her changing her story. A good lawyer will argue that she was coerced."

Becky continued. "It's worth a try."

The bell rang and students began heading toward their homerooms. "There were some others at the party too, Ms. Landis. We'll try to get their help."

"I really do appreciate your coming to me." She looked at Andy. "I know this was really difficult for you. I promise I won't mention the circumstances of what you revealed to anyone, Andy. Thank you."

"Sheila fooled all of us, Ms. Landis. She used me to indulge in her fantasy of Mr. Peterson."

"You both better hurry now before you're tardy for homeroom. Thanks again."

After school on Friday, she stopped at her place to pick up some personal things and headed over to Chad's place. She debated whether to tell him about her meeting with Becky and Andy. Afraid that such inconclusive evidence might send him into another fit of despair, she chose to avoid the subject. She was delightfully surprised to see that he had planned dinner for them.

"If it's ok, we'll eat later, sweetheart," he said after showing her the preparations he'd made. "I need something more than dinner right now. He led her to the sofa and they kissed and talked and then kissed again. Belinda put her head on his shoulder and snuggled in close as he held her and stroked her hair. It was the first time since the trial that it seemed he was comforting her instead of the other way around. Belinda felt secure in his arms.

At six, Chad forced himself to pull away from her. "I'm hungry. I think everything's ready now, so you light some candles and I'll bring in the food. There's a bottle of wine and some glasses on the table too. Why don't you pour us a glass as I get the salads."

Belinda was impressed that Chad, given all the stress of the past weeks, had gone to so much trouble to create such a romantic atmosphere. She admitted to herself that it puzzled her how his mood swings were so frequent, but she was grateful for the times he was upbeat. She watched as he brought in the salads first.

"I know this isn't the same as eating at a fine dining restaurant, but it'll be nice."

"It's perfect, Chad. Thank you."

After the salads, Chad went back into the kitchen. He brought out a tray holding lasagna.

"Yum! That looks scrumptious. You must have worked a long time to prepare for this."

"It keeps me busy during the long afternoons. I've always loved creating little surprises for you."

They sat at dinner discussing plans for the weekend. Belinda was hopeful of getting him to leave the house and quit his hermit-like existence. "Chad, how about if we go out somewhere tomorrow. Maybe we could catch a movie. I know you wouldn't like to go to one of the sporting events in school, but you *need* to get out of the house."

"I'm sorry, but I really don't want to go to any place so public. I have a suggestion if you're up for it. Why don't we go for a hike along some of the trails in the woods nearby. It'll be less stressful for me."

"That's a terrific suggestion. The exercise will do us both good, and some fresh air will improve our mental spirits too. I'll have to run home in the morning to get some hiking shoes and some suitable clothes, but yes, let's do that."

"When they crawled under the comforter in Chad's bed later that night, they made love. It was a fulfilling experience for both, and neither managed to get much sleep as they talked and cuddled through the night.

The hike the next afternoon proved to be just the right thing for Chad. He seemed to forget his troubles, at least momentarily, and enjoyed teasing and taunting Belinda as they climbed hills and descended into gullies.

"Not one to admit being outdone, Belinda accepted the challenge. I don't spend as much time in the woods as you do, but anything you can do I can do better," she chortled. She pointed to a boulder high above them. "I'll bet I can beat you to that rock up there," she added as she grabbed the back of his pants and yanked him backward. Then she started climbing.

Chad took off after her. "What do I get when I win the bet?" he yelled at her.

Still ten yards ahead of him, she screamed, "You can name your prize *if* you win!"

The climb was arduous and both were huffing and puffing as they navigated their way to the top. Despite carrying the weight of his backpack, Chad scrambled past her in a final sprint to reach the boulder. Perched on top, he glanced down and laughed when she stumbled on the path. Hearing him laugh proved better than victory to Belinda, even though she didn't admit it.

"Let's rest here for a bit. That was quite a challenge. I packed a couple of sandwiches, some soda, and two Milky Way bars."

Out of breath, Belinda readily agreed. "I guess you win," she admitted. "What would you like as your prize?"

"I have my prize already," he said as he leaned over and kissed her tenderly.

The rest of the weekend passed too quickly. When Belinda moved beside Chad in bed late on Sunday night, she thanked him for acting like the old Chad that she knew and loved. "I had a wonderful time. I don't want these times to ever end."

Chad wanted to say that they wouldn't, but he couldn't muster the words. How could he make such a guarantee, knowing what lay ahead? Instead, he just muttered, "I love you, sweetheart."

* * *

On Monday morning, with little to do and a desire to again escape the confines of his apartment, Chad risked the wrath of the community and went for a walk into town. He wasn't wrong. Those who only knew him from the publicity of the trial scorned him, some verbally and some only with their stares. When he saw Maggie Stairs standing on a street corner, he invited her into the café for some coffee. "If you don't mind being seen with me in public, Maggie, I sure could use some company."

"Don't be silly, Chad. I don't care what those jerks think. They don't know you as I do. Matt and I won't turn our backs on you."

Over coffee and some Danish, they talked. Maggie could see some positive changes that had overcome Chad. "You look better, Chad. Your eyes aren't as glassy and your face isn't pale."

"I can thank Belinda for that. We had a very good weekend together."

"I'm glad to hear that. We've all known for a long time that you two belong together. It was painful to hear that you shut her out of your life for awhile."

"I was a fool to act that way. We're on the right track now, though I admit I'm still worried about the effect this will have on her if she stays with me throughout this ordeal."

"She loves you. She's a very strong-willed person. You needn't worry about her."

Their conversation left Chad hopeful. He realized that he'd been wrong to criticize his friends. They did believe in him and care about him and for that he was grateful. Chad carried her bags to her car and waved as she drove away.

Chad had nowhere in particular to go so, after saying goodbye to Maggie, he decided to go for another hike. There were several good hiking trails on the outskirts of Emerson and the chances of meeting others on a weekday were slim. Satisfied that his hiking boots and other clothes would keep him comfortable, he walked north to another of his favorite trails. "When this is all over, maybe I'll become a hermit and live in a cabin in the woods," he joked aloud to himself. "I'll live like the philosopher and writer Henry David Thoreau. Simplify my life. I'll hunt and fish for my food. Stay away from civilization as much as possible."

He hiked for hours through the woods. Climbing huge boulders and traversing streams again made him forget his troubles. At times his breath became labored as the strenuous climb up steep hills took its toll on his body. Despite how physically tiring it was, it proved good therapy for his mood. Chad felt free. As he continued walking, his mind moved to the good times he and Belinda had shared at the cabin several weeks ago and the fun they'd had the past weekend. He craved more of those good times.

When finally he returned to Emerson, it was like a shadow had again descended over Chad. He walked into Jake's Bar and Grill and took a seat at the counter. "Gimme a burger with everything on it, Jake."

"You want a beer with that, Chad?"

"No, not this time. I'll have a coke and add an order of onion rings too."

"One house special comin' right up."

While he waited, Chad surveyed the scene around the bar. It was still too early in the afternoon for the place to be occupied with a lot of customers. Two elderly men sat at one table, laughing and obviously enjoying themselves.

Chad sipped his coke. He watched the overhead TV behind the bar and occasionally chatted with Jake, the owner and bartender. Like everyone else in town, Jake knew of Chad's conviction. He had no intention of aggravating Chad by discussing the matter, so when they talked, it was about the weather, sports, or other town gossip. Before long, it was time for school to end and Chad headed back to his place to wait for Belinda.

* * *

After school, Becky Finch, Andy Stewart, Rod Lawson, and Tara Litz cornered Cindy Bennett. "Meet us at B.J's tonight at six," Becky said. "And come alone."

Recognizing B.J.'s as the local teen hangout ice cream place, Cindy insisted, "What's goin' on?" noting the almost threatening tone of Becky's voice.

"We have something personal to discuss and we need you there. If you don't want to lose our friendship, you'll be there."

"Why're you being so mysterious? Can't you tell me now?"

Rod Lawson interjected, "School isn't the place to talk. Too many kids around here."

Cindy acquiesced. "You want Sheila there too?"

"NO!" Becky said. "This is just between the five of us."

"I wish you'd at least give me a hint."

"You'll find everything out tonight. Look for us at a booth in the back and be on time."

Becky Finch arrived at B.J's ten minutes before six. Rod Lawson accompanied her. Andy and Tara walked in a few minutes later. "No sign of Cindy yet, huh?" Rod asked.

"Do you think she'll come?" Andy wanted to know.

Becky reassured them. "She'll be here. She's too afraid of losing what few friends she has now. Besides us, who's close to her besides Tim and Sheila?"

Exactly at six Cindy entered, looked around the place, and spotted Becky and the others at a booth. She joined them and began firing questions at them. "So what's the big deal? Why the secret meeting? And what're you getting me involved in?"

Becky assumed control. "Listen Cindy, this is about Sheila and Mr. Peterson. We suspect that she lied and that *you* know the truth."

Cindy panicked and began to get up from the booth but Rod blocked her path. "I don't know what you're talking about. I told what I saw and I don't know anything more."

"You're lying," Andy interjected. "I knew she set up Mr. P. the instant she moaned his name at her place, and you stayed behind when the rest of us left. You must know more. She tried to seduce *him*, didn't she? Sheila's the type of girl who can't stand rejection, and I bet he shot her down! Tell us the truth," he demanded.

Cindy sat without speaking, looking first at one and then the others. "Sheila's my best friend," she insisted.

Becky tried to be consoling. "We know that, Cindy. We don't want her to get hurt, but sending a man to jail for a crime he didn't commit is wrong. We wanted to believe Sheila's story, and when you corroborated it, we stuck by both of you. But now we don't believe her. She's changed. You've seen that change too."

Cindy nodded. "Yeah, I'm worried about her. She's always gotten her way with boys, but this thing with Mr. Peterson has made her crazy. She really had a crush on him. It was almost like she was stalking him."

"She tried to seduce him for a good grade, didn't she?" asked Andy.

Finally, Cindy admitted the truth. "She was determined to make it with him. She was willing to give him anything he wanted, and she figured he'd improve her grade too."

"Why did you go along with it?" complained Becky.

"I owed her for helping me get Tim. I didn't think Mr. Peterson would be convicted. Things got out of hand. By the time of the trial, I got scared and stuck to my story. Sheila practically begged me to help her. I couldn't back out."

"You can back out now before he spends time in jail. We have to go to Ms. Landis. She'll know what to do."

"I can't do that. Sheila's my best friend."

"Think about how the kids will treat you if *we* turn on you and tell them you lied," threatened Andy.

"The other night when you all left the party, Sheila broke down and cried and cried. I thought she was gonna have a breakdown. She's deluding herself into thinking Mr. Peterson really did sexually attack her."

To this point in the conversation, Tara had been quiet but now she joined in. "You'll be helping her and Mr. Peterson, Cindy. You gotta tell."

Fearful, Cindy said, "NO! I won't betray Sheila, no matter what you say or do. You don't turn on your best friend, and I won't do it!"

Frustrated, the group left Cindy sitting in the booth and charged out of B.J's. All five piled into Rod's car and headed for Belinda's apartment. When she opened the door, Belinda looked questioningly at them. Becky began. "We didn't have much luck, Ms. Landis. Cindy won't budge."

Belinda listened intently to every detail of their meeting as Becky continued. "Cindy admitted that Sheila lied, and she recognizes how this is affecting her, but when it came right down to helping Mr. Peterson, she refused."

"I'm not surprised," Belinda said.

"We won't give up, Ms. Landis, but I'm not too hopeful."

Belinda hugged each of them as they left her apartment. She uttered a thank you for their help. When she closed the door, she leaned against it and prayed. "Dear God, help us find a way."

When Chad arrived home, he noticed the answering machine blinking and checked the messages. The calls came from Belinda. She expressed delight that he had gone out. "Maggie told me that she saw you this morning. Please call me when you get in."

A second apologetic message informed him that she'd be late coming to his place. She'd explain when she saw him.

Chad picked up the phone and called her.

"Do you want me to come over now? There was an unexpected parent conference after school. Helen invited me to stay, and since it involved one of my students being caught using drugs in his car at the school parking lot, I couldn't refuse. Then a couple of kids stopped by for a few minutes." Again she decided not to reprise the details of the kids' meeting with Cindy Bennett.

"That's ok, sweetheart. I understand. Actually, I'm rather tired from the physical day I had. I'll take a raincheck, ok?"

"Chad, is everything ok?"

"I'm fine. I'm sure you had a long day at school. I'd just like some time to relax tonight. I think I'll go to bed early."

Belinda immediately backed off. "Ok, I'll see you tomorrow then. I love you. G'night, Chad."

"Belinda?" He hesitated a moment and then said, "You're the best!"

A smile filled her face as she again repeated her love for him. "If you need me at any time, just call."

"Ok, I will. G'night."

The next morning as soon as she was dressed for school, Belinda phoned Chad. "Hi, sweetie. How're you this morning? Did you manage to sleep without me next to you?" she chuckled.

"Good morning, sweetheart. I must admit it's a lot more comfortable sleeping with you nearby. I was very tired from the long hike I took yesterday. It felt good to get out again, but after our weekend hike and the one yesterday, my body aches."

"What you need is a tender loving massage. I can come over after school today and soothe what ails you."

"I'll look forward to that. You have a busy day at school today?"

"Just the usual. If it stays nice, I might take my photography kids outside for some outdoor shots. The drawing classes will work to finish up their sketches. My graphics kids are working on designing logos for a business competition, so it should be an easy day for me."

"Good. Enjoy the day."

"Do you have any plans, Chad?"

"Well, I can guarantee you that I'm not going to do another hike. I don't think my body would handle that. If I knew I wasn't going to jail soon, I'd stop at the sports store and get a fishing license, but until I know for sure, that's pointless."

"Think positive, Chad. Get the license. It's only a few bucks. You can make me a fresh fish dinner tonight with what you catch. Go up to the lake and enjoy yourself."

"It would be great to spend the day outside again. Ok, I'll do it."

"I have to finish getting ready for school. I'll talk to you later, sweetie." Feeling positive that she'd persuaded him to go fishing, she added, "I'll call you when I get home to make sure you're back from fishing. I'll come over when you're ready."

"Sounds like a plan. See ya soon. Bye, Belinda. Love ya."

"Love you too. Mmmmwaaaaa. Bye."

* * *

Later, Belinda left for school, encouraged that the day would go well for them both.

Although Chad hadn't been fishing since the previous summer, the idea appealed to him. He went into his storage closet and found his rod and tackle box. He cleaned and checked everything to make sure it was in good working order, even replacing the line on his reel with new line from a spool that he had in the tackle box. He grabbed a small folding chair and put everything into his car.

I'll make myself a sandwich for lunch, take a few cans of soda and I'm set, he thought. *I'll make a quick stop at the sports store to get my license, and then head for the lake. It's still considered within my boundaries, so I won't get into trouble for leaving the area.*

Chad paid the seventeen dollar fee, put the license into the holder on his hat, got some bait, and drove to the lake. Glancing around the perimeter, he saw two elderly men about 250 yards away. He opted to fish alone and found a spot near a tree that had fallen into the lake. Again he reveled in the freedom provided for him there. "I never got to fish on a weekday while I taught school," he thought. "It's nice and peaceful here."

After baiting his hook, he tossed his line into the water and waited. It wasn't long before he reeled in the first of twelve nice sized bluegills and crappies. He put each on the stringer to keep them alive in the water while he continued to fish. Meanwhile, the warmth of the sunshine relaxed him. He wasn't able to totally escape his thoughts about what lay ahead, but every time he seemed to get bogged down with thoughts of despair, another fish nibbled at his bait and distracted him.

* * *

In school, things changed also. The usual crowd that sat with Sheila and Cindy at a table in the lunchroom now sat at a different table. Sheila was more defensive than ever. "I don't need those creeps," she argued. They're just a bunch of phonies, pretending to like me because I set up great parties. Well, now they can find someone else who shows them a good time."

"They don't trust you, Sheila. They're convinced that you're willfully destroying Mr. Peterson and they don't like that. He was very popular."

"So, fuck 'em. You're my only loyal friend."

Cindy recognized that everything Sheila said about not caring about her friends was pretense. She liked being popular and this affair had changed things. She was hurting.

After lunch, she grabbed Sheila by the shoulder as they walked alone down the hallway to class. "I heard my dad talking with my mom about Mr. Peterson this morning. He said Mr. Peterson will be fired, and he's certain he'll get jail time."

"Awwww! Pity! Pity!" Sheila retorted sarcastically, making it sound as if she were glad to hear that news.

Cindy added, "His relationship with Ms. Landis must be gettin' rocky too. A lot of the kids say she's close to tears half the time in class."

"My dad said he saw Chad walking in town the other day. He was talking with Mrs. Stairs. Dad wanted to punch Chad out but figured his rotting in jail would serve the SOB much better."

Cindy suddenly blurted, "I'll see you after school. I gotta run or I'll be late."

"See ya," Sheila said. Then she slowly strolled toward history class. During class, Sheila's mind wandered as usual from the daily lecturing of Mrs. Longden. *I bet Mr. High and Mighty ain't too proud to look at me now*, she thought. *If he's willing to beg, I might negotiate with him.*

Sheila only halfheartedly overheard the students in the class turn the day's history lesson to a discussion of an assembly.

"Please, Mrs. Longden," Heather Joles pleaded as the period came near the end. "Mr. Peterson was gonna let us do a variation of our history projects for the entire school as part of an assembly. Mrs. Hargrove gave us permission to do it just before Mr. P. got into trouble. We'd still like to do it, as kind of a tribute to him."

Several others added support for the idea. It was then that Sheila awoke from her daydreaming and became fully aware of the discussion. "Why would you want to honor that bastard?" she interrupted.

"Shut up, Sheila! Nobody's asking you to do anything," Heather yelled. "We'd already be doing this if it weren't for you." She then turned again to Mrs. Langdon. "PLEASE, Mrs. Langdon. We really want to do this."

Mrs. Langdon was hesitant. "I don't know. I've never organized an assembly before. It's a lot of work, and I'm just a substitute teacher."

"We'll do everything, Mrs. L.," Paul Stone begged. "You just need to give us some class time to plan everything. We already have the material. Each group just needs to decide what to include. You can help us with that. You know a lot about history," he added, hoping the flattery would persuade her.

"I'll tell you what I'll do," she responded. "I'll give you tomorrow's class period to discuss and show me what you want to do. If it'll work well *and* will be interesting to the whole school, I'll agree."

The entire class, except for Sheila, applauded her decision. "We won't disappoint you, Mrs. Langdon," Heather said as the dismissal bell rang.

They filed out of the room exuberantly slapping hands. Sheila trailed behind, wondering what role she'd be forced to play in this unfolding drama.

* * *

Chad glanced at his watch and saw that it was 3 p.m. "Time to head back to the apartment and wait for Belinda. I'll tell her I caught 'em; she has to clean and cook 'em. She'll just *love* to hear that."

Belinda called a half hour after he'd arrived home. "Hi, sweetheart. Hurry over. I'm busy cleaning fish for dinner. If you get here quickly, you can cut off a few heads and gut those still left."

"Hahahaha. Thanks for the offer. Now I'm sure I'll be delayed for no special reason except to miss out on that experience."

"Awww, shucks. You're such a city girl. C'mon over now. I'll be done by the time you get here. We're gonna have a tasty meal tonight. Oh, by the way, could you stop at the grocery store and buy some bread crumbs. I'll need some to fry up the fish."

"Sure thing. Anything else you need?"

"Ummmm…let me think. Oh, look for some seafood sauce, and maybe a loaf of their fresh made bread."

"Ok. I'll see you in a little bit then. Love ya."

"Me too. Bye." Chad pressed the button to end the cell phone call and resumed cleaning the fish. "I should have told her to pick up a bottle of wine too. I guess it's better if we just settle for some iced tea. I'll make that when I'm finished here."

Chad and Belinda spent a pleasant evening together. After dinner they opted to play some cards. Later, Chad removed his shirt and plopped onto the floor while Belinda grabbed the bottle of massage oil that he'd placed on the end table and kept her promise to rub away his aches and pains.

Later, they crawled into bed and Belinda placed her body against Chad's. Both seemed content to just feel the closeness and neither suggested making love. Suddenly, Belinda pulled away from him briefly and said, "I almost forgot. Your history class may do the assembly. I talked after school with Rhoda Langdon and she mentioned that she'd just spoken with Helen about the possibility and had gotten permission to do the assembly."

"Great! I love those kids. I'm glad to hear that they're cooperating with Rhoda. I wish I could be there to see it, but I'm not allowed near them."

"Rhoda also told me that the kids suggested that they do it as a tribute to you. Everyone except Sheila, of course, agreed."

"That's really nice of them. They're a special bunch of kids. You make sure to tell me all about it when they do it."

Belinda snuggled back in close to him. "I'll do that." Then she said, "Mmmmm. Your body is so warm and comforting. I love being here next to you." A few moments later she fell asleep in his arms.

* * *

The next morning, Sheila sat at breakfast as usual. In between spoonfuls of some hot cereal, she spoke to her mom and dad. "I probably won't be home for dinner tonight. Some of the kids wanna hang out at B.J.'s. We're havin' a surprise birthday party for one of the kids, so I'll eat there."

"Just don't be home too late," Laura McMasters said in her usual protective and threatening manner.

"I won't be, Mom. I'm sure I'll be home by nine. That ok?"

"I guess so. B.J. keeps tight control there."

"Everything still ok at school, honey?" her dad inquired.

"Sure, Daddy. My grades are doing better. It looks like there's gonna be a history assembly. I'll probably take part and do something that'll impress Mrs. Langdon. That'll help my grade in that class too. Don't worry." She gulped the last of her orange juice and took her bowl and glass to the sink. Then she grabbed her coat and hat from the chair where she had placed it earlier and kissed her dad's cheek.

"Have a good day, honey," he said.

"I will. Bye, Mom," she said and waved as she left.

The afternoon's history class proved to be exciting for most of the students. The enthusiasm that the class showed toward the assembly idea impressed her. And, without hinting as much, the kids found it a great break from her boring lectures. Halfway through the period, Heather Joles pulled Mrs. Langdon aside and explained the entire outline for their plan.

Convinced that this was a valid learning experience for the entire school, Mrs. Langdon announced, "Alright, I'm satisfied. I'll talk with Mrs. Hargrove and we'll set a date for the assembly. Meanwhile, you may have enough class time this week to prepare and rehearse."

A loud cheer ensued from everyone except Sheila, who remained aloof to the idea and really hadn't been included, even with her own group, despite sitting with them all afternoon.

Mrs. Langdon called her to the front of the room. "Sheila, I'm aware of the situation with you and the other students in your group. I have an idea that might work to include you."

"What's that?" Sheila wanted to know.

"Well, we're gonna need an emcee to introduce each of the historical groups." Trying to impress her with a little flattery, she added, "You seem to be a very outgoing girl, one who's not afraid to speak in public. What would you say to assuming that role?"

Sheila thought about it for a minute. "I wouldn't have to work with my group then?"

"No, your job would be to come up with an introduction explaining what each group is going to present. In a sense, you'll have to deal with all of them, but if you do a good, enthusiastic job, maybe that way you can win back their respect."

Sheila didn't much care if she won back their respect, but her ego at being the center of attention for an assembly won her over. "I guess I can do that, Mrs. Langdon. Thanks."

The idea not only won Sheila's support, but when Mrs. Langdon explained the idea to Sheila's group, they breathed a thankful sigh and agreed.

When the period ended, Mrs. Langdon told everyone that she'd get a definite date for the assembly from the principal and let them know when to be ready. Then she told each one to have a nice day as they exited the room. Sheila had a smile on her face and mouthed a silent thank you to Mrs. Langdon as she walked by her.

After school, Sheila met with Cindy Bennett at B.J.'s. "I told my folks I was coming here for a birthday celebration. I just didn't want to go home to my mother's endless questions. God, she has to know every little thing I do. It drives me nuts."

"Most moms are like that, Sheila. Don't let it freak you out."

"I know. I just wanted to escape. I told them I'd be home around nine. Can I come over to your place for awhile and hang out?"

"Sure. Now that my curfew and grounding is over, I'm sure my parents won't object. We can hide out in my bedroom and watch some TV or just talk."

"Thanks, Cin. You're a good friend. One of the few loyal ones I seem to have anymore."

"Like I said before. Be patient. Things'll die down with time."

"I hope you're right. So, guess what happened in history class today. There's this assembly that they're gonna do. Mrs. Langdon called me up and asked if I'd be the emcee for it. I'll be the star!"

"Cool. What d'ya have to do?"

"Just introduce each of the groups. I'll come up with some witty wisecracks to make the audience laugh about each time period. Maybe I'll come out for the 60s in a micro-miniskirt."

"Sheila, I have a question for you. If Mr. Peterson had suggested that to you, would'ya have still played that routine on him?"

Speaking in a somewhat annoyed tone, Sheila responded, "I don't want to talk about him!"

Just then Tim walked in and joined them in the booth. "Hi guys. What's new?" He leaned over and kissed Cindy's cheek. "Hey there, hot stuff! I missed you today in school, but now that I see you, I'm all excited." He reached over, took her hand and placed it on his lap. "See?"

Cindy quickly pulled her hand away. "You're so bad. I love bad! Hahaha! Sheila and I were just chatting. She's coming over to my place for a few hours."

"Ok, sounds like fun. I have to go to work in an hour. Let me go up to the counter and order a burger and shake and I'll be right back. Don't talk about me now," he chuckled, "unless it's something good."

Sheila joked, "What could we possibly come up with that would be *good*?"

Tim just gave her an evil sneer and then laughed. When he returned a few minutes later, Sheila made an excuse to leave so that they could have a little private talk time and told Cindy she'd come over to her place a little later.

She showed up at Cindy's just before her family sat down for dinner. "Please join us," Cindy's mom said. "We're just having pizza, but it's hot and good."

"Thanks, Mrs. Bennett."

Known as the mistress of gossip, Loretta Bennett was always nosy about the personal matters of people in the community. She wasn't the least reluctant to interrogate Sheila about her controversy concerning Chad Peterson. "How're you doing these days, Sheila? Are you still suffering from that incident with Mr. Peterson?"

"I'm fine. He's gonna be put away where he belongs. I'd have been traumatized a lot worse if Cindy hadn't arrived when she did."

Loretta Bennett glanced over at her daughter and smiled. "You're a heroine, honey."

Cindy just looked at her piece of pizza and said nothing. She didn't much feel like a heroine. Inside she was being torn to pieces. She'd never deliberately betray Sheila's trust and friendship. On the other hand, she had no personal grudge against Mr. Peterson and felt partially responsible for hurting him. Then there was the danger of losing her friendship with some of the other kids that bothered her as well.

Loretta then revealed some of the gossip that she'd overheard. "Judge Walters, from what I hear, is being pressured to punish that man to the fullest extent of the law. If he doesn't, he may be voted out of office in the upcoming election. It's a political thing now."

Sheila said straight faced, "I hope he rots in jail. I think my dad would shoot him if he were set free now. He's still so pissed. Every night he rants about how Mr. Peterson should spend his life behind bars. He says he'll get what he deserves there. I'm sure he means he'll be attacked by some homosexual prisoners."

"I wouldn't be surprised by that," Cindy's mom added.

Cindy grew more and more emotionally upset as the conversation continued. "Can we please talk about something else?" she finally screeched. Then she turned to Sheila. "Are you ready to go up to my room? I've had enough of this."

* * *

Belinda phoned Chad from her apartment. "Hey there, sweetie. How's it going?"

"Not much excitement here today. Matt called earlier to ask if I'd like to come watch the girls play, but I politely declined. I told him I didn't want to be a distraction. He said the girls would love to see me there, but I was adamant. I'm not ready to be anywhere near school-related activities."

"Ok, I can understand that. Listen, Chad. It's a beautiful spring afternoon. I was thinking maybe we could take your portable grill and go to Royce Park and have a picnic. Grill some hot dogs or burgers. We can find a secluded spot, take a blanket, and enjoy the fresh air and sunshine. I'm sure I can add some spice and excitement to your day."

A smile lit Chad's face. "I'd really like that. I'm feeling cooped up here and while I don't want to be in a crowd, getting outside for a few hours would do me good."

"Great. Can you pick me up in thirty minutes?"

"Sure. I'll grab the grill, a bottle of propane, and the blanket. I have some hot dogs and buns if that's ok. And I'll bring the condiments."

"Better bring at least two condom-mints," she laughed, emphasizing the word condom. Then, more seriously, she added, "Sounds good to me. I'll bring something to drink, and I have some chocolate-chip cookies for dessert."

"I was hoping you'd be dessert, my dear," Chad teased.

"Forget the cookies. You can fatten me with kisses."

"See you in thirty. Bye."

The picnic was just the tonic that Chad and Belinda needed to make a nice ending to the day. Finding the park area mostly deserted, they strolled leisurely along the lake's edge. Later, after grilling some dinner, they lay on the blanket until the sun began to disappear behind the horizon. Any discussion of Chad's situation or of things at school never materialized, and both were happy to share the time together.

Chapter 14

As she had promised, Rhoda Langdon provided class time for the students in Chad's American history class to adapt and prepare for the assembly. Sheila remained a pariah among her classmates, but with urging from Mrs. Langdon, they agreed to cooperate and inform Sheila of their plans so that she could introduce each act. When she got enough information, Sheila moved off into a corner of the room to work alone.

Rhoda Langdon observed that Sheila seemed to have the skills and talent to do a good job preparing as emcee and wondered to herself why she'd been so stubborn in refusing to work with her group. "As long as she doesn't give me a hassle," she mused, "I'm glad to get some production from her."

Paul Stone raised his hand to get Rhoda's attention. "Mrs. Langdon, did Mrs. Hargrove tell you how much time we could have for the assembly?"

Rhoda shrugged when she realized that she hadn't mentioned the details of the assembly to the class. She immediately interrupted them, speaking loud enough to be heard over the classroom din. "May I have everyone's attention?" When the noise settled, she stated, "I apologize for not telling you. Mrs. Hargrove said that since this assembly would be an entertaining, as well as an educational experience for the entire high school, you may have the entire afternoon after lunch, which amounts to about two hours. Once you decide upon what you're going to do, you'll have to gauge your time and we'll see how it fits into the time schedule. If it runs too long, we'll have to make adjustments."

"That means we'll need to have a dress rehearsal, Mrs. Langdon," Heather Joles exclaimed.

"Yes, if we want it to look good, we'll have to allow time for that too, so don't waste any of your valuable time now. I've made arrangements for us to use the auditorium when we're ready to run through it."

The students in each group diligently returned to the task at hand. As she circulated around the room, Rhoda smiled when she observed that there wasn't any of the usual digressive talk about dates and weekend activities that usually occurred when she had subbed for other teachers and had them do group work. Having missed some of the initial presentations, she grinned when she overheard the plan to have the entire school practice the Charleston, with several teachers invited to come on stage to perform in front of the audience.

Another group began to adapt their material into a kind of quiz game that would test the knowledge of several members of the senior class and pit them against some of the teachers. Rhoda even wrote a pass for Seth Beckman when he asked if he could run down to the tech shop to see Mr. Fortenski and borrow the system of buttons and lights that he'd created for competitions. Ten minutes later Seth returned with a box of wires and paraphernalia. "I got it," he yelled with great enthusiasm.

A third group, covering the 40s, decided to adapt their presentation and focus on the Holocaust by turning their information into a skit. We'll have to meet together at one of our homes to get this done on time," Paul Stone said. "We already have the visuals that we can use in the background. I'm sure my parents will let us meet at our place if you're willing. And my grandfather has a GI uniform that he wore in the war. I bet we can find some other costumes too that'll make things more effective."

Cassie Thompson interjected, "I can't make it after school tonight. I have softball practice after school, and I can't let Coach Herndon down. We only lost in the state semi-finals last year and we have a good shot to go undefeated this year. I have a big Chem test tomorrow and have to study tonight."

"That's ok, Cassie. That's important too," Paul quickly responded. "How about you, Ron?"

"I'd like to help, but I have to work at McDonald's after school. I won't get home till midnight."

"I can make it, Paul," Heather spoke. She turned to the others and said, "Is it ok with you if Paul and I work on creating the script that'll include parts for all of us?"

"Sure," Cassie and Ron said simultaneously.

Cassie questioned, "Are you sure you don't mind? That's a lot of responsibility for the two of you."

"It'll be fun, and we've already done the research. We'll just work it into a drama that'll really rock the audience." Speaking directly to Paul, she asked, "How about if I come over to your place around six tonight? We'll do as much as we can and bring it here tomorrow for the others to approve."

"Great! I have some good ideas. Let's talk about those now so we'll be ready to write it up tonight."

Class time seemed to pass more quickly than ever and after the bell rang, Rhoda watched as groups continued to discuss their plans even as they exited the room. She stopped Sheila as she walked past the desk. "Sheila, everything's ok now, right?" She obviously wanted some assurance that Sheila, having a very important part of the assembly, wouldn't let the class down again.

"Oh, yes, Mrs. Langdon. I have things outlined in my mind already. I'll have all of my ideas on paper for you tomorrow, ok?"

"Terrific. I'd like to see how you're going to do this."

"I won't let you down. See ya tomorrow," Sheila said as she waved goodbye.

Rhoda Langdon continued to be puzzled by Sheila's attitude. *Maybe she just has trouble with men teachers*, she thought, thankful that whatever troubles she'd caused for Chad hadn't affected her role as teacher.

* * *

Belinda walked into the faculty room at the end of another trying day at school. While her students gave her no behavioral problems, her focus on her job continued to be difficult. She plopped onto the sofa and let out a long drawn sigh. She knew that other faculty members would soon arrive and was thankful for a few moments of solitude to gather her emotions. When she was involved with the students, she forced herself to be strong, but other times she often was on the verge of crying. She dabbed her eyes with a Kleenex as her thoughts turned once more to Chad.

Vicki Bergstrom entered in her usual jolly mood. Vicki worked in the library and though she was an aide and secretary, helped to run the place with an authoritarian demeanor. All of the students, however, knew she was a pussycat and loved her. She always took great pride in listening to what the kids were involved in. "Hi, Belinda." She noticed immediately Belinda's agitated state. "Tough day?"

"Hi, Vicki. They're all tough these days. I love my job, and God knows I love working with the kids. I just can't seem to relax and enjoy them now."

Vicki was sympathetic. "I can see the stress in your face. You and Chad have been put through hell. I'm sorry. I wish I could help."

"Thanks. We seem to have hit a brick wall and can't find a way past it. Chad's certain that he's going to jail. I try to be upbeat, but I'm afraid too."

Vicki, who was deeply religious, said, "God has a way of working things out. I just know Chad's innocent and I have faith that He will show us the way."

"I wish I had your faith, Vicki. For weeks I've prayed for an answer to this tragedy. The whole affair [she apologized immediately for the poor choice of words] has tested me beyond belief. I'm sure other innocent men are in jail now, but I just can't accept God's letting this happen to Chad. He's such a good man."

At that moment, Rhoda Langdon entered the faculty room. Even though she was only a substitute teacher, she had long been accepted by the staff as one of their own. Unaware of their conversation, she greeted them enthusiatically. "Hey guys! You both as worn out as I am?" She sat in a chair and put her feet up on another nearby chair. "Boy, my feet hurt today."

Belinda was first to greet her. "Hi, Rhoda." Wanting to give some news to Chad when she saw him, Belinda inquired, "How're things goin' with Chad's classes?"

Trying to sound humble, Rhoda said, "I'm sure things aren't going as smoothly as if Chad were there. He has a bunch of great kids though."

"Chad remarked that he was glad that they weren't giving you a hard time. We both know it's always difficult for a sub to take over and gain the confidence of students. Everyone's teaching style is different and you came in under trying circumstances."

"Well, I'm managing. Oh…let me tell you about the assembly that his kids are planning. Their enthusiasm is so contagious. I'm so impressed with their work ethic. He'll be proud of them."

"He already is proud. He's thrilled to hear that you're gonna follow up on the plan. He'd love to be there to watch, but he wouldn't risk coming there and becoming a distraction."

"You know that some of the kids proposed making it a tribute to him. In order to create some kind of harmony, I had to ask Sheila McMasters to act as emcee. I'm sure she wouldn't put in anything to give him any credit."

"Yeah, I mentioned that to Chad. I think he was a little embarrassed to hear that the kids wanted to do that for him. He made me promise to tell him all about the assembly."

"I've heard some whispering among a few of the classmates that they're planning to do something at the end of the assembly and leave Sheila out of it. I'm not aware of their plan, but I think it involves Chad."

At this point Vicki interrupted. "I have an idea. You know I'm in charge of the sound and lighting for all assemblies. What would you say if I get the stage crew to hook up a couple of video cameras to record the assembly? That way Chad could see it later in the privacy of his home."

"That's a terrific idea, Vicki. Chad would really appreciate that."

Rhoda added, "I don't think the kids would mind that. In fact, I know they'd love for Chad to see it. Well, all except maybe one student."

Belinda leaned over and gave Vicki a hug. "Thanks." Then she turned to Rhoda. "Maybe you better not create trouble by saying that it's for Chad."

Vicki added, "You can tell the kids that they can get copies for themselves. We'll sell them a copy for the price of the tape or they can provide their own tape and we'll make copies for free."

At that point, several other teachers entered the room and, after inquiring how Chad was faring, the mood eventually became more boisterous. Tony Baker offered a few new jokes to spice up the atmosphere and, as usual, the frivolity helped ease the stresses of the day. When a few suggested meeting at the tavern for a couple beers, Belinda excused herself. "I'd love to go, but I'm heading over to be with Chad."

"Give him a call on your cell, Belinda," Thorny suggested. "Tell him to meet us. He needs the support of his friends now."

"Thanks, but I'm sure he won't come. Now that he's been convicted, he's becoming a hermit. He'll only go out to places where he's sure he won't be in a crowd."

"I'm sorry about that. We really do miss him. Please reassure him of that fact," Thorny said.

"I'll do that. G'night, everyone." She glanced at Vicki and added, "Thanks again."

After stopping at her place for some different clothes, Belinda phoned Chad. "Several of the guys wanted you to join them at the tavern for a couple beers, but I told them I didn't think you'd come."

"I'm sure they mean well, but you're right. I wouldn't have enjoyed it."

"They just want you to know that they care and miss you."

"I appreciate that, but I feel uncomfortable in public places. It's the stares of the others that I can't deal with now."

"I think a lot of that is in your mind, Chad, but I won't push it. I'll be over in a little bit."

"Ok. I'm putting a few things together for dinner later, so just walk in when you get here."

"Will do. Love ya."

"See ya. Bye."

After dinner, Chad and Belinda spent a quiet evening together, cuddling on the sofa, watching some TV and just talking. "Anything new in school today?"

"I'm getting some really great artwork from a few of my kids in painting class. There's some real talent there. I'll have to show you the latest painting from Robbie Simpson. That boy is gonna go far, Chad. He has so much creative talent. I hope college will tap that skill even more. He's by far the best student I've ever had."

"That's great. Maybe we should buy one of his works now, so we can say we knew him before he became another Van Gogh or Matisse."

"That's not as funny as it sounds. I expect his works will sell for a lot someday."

Chad leaned closer and hugged her. "I really miss nurturing that kind of talent."

"I know you do, sweetie. And you're the best. Hey, I have some photos to grade from my photography class. There are some excellent ones there too. I have them in the car. I'll get them now and you can help me evaluate them."

"Sure. You can trust my expert eye to tell you what's good," he joked.

Belinda went to retrieve the portfolio and spread the pictures on the coffee table when she returned. "Their assignment was to demonstrate good composition and contrast."

"I'm not sure I can grade them for that. I'll let you do that job and I'll just see which ones I really like." He picked up one that had a closeup of a cow's face. "This is interesting. I like how the photographer caught the cow's tongue out. The lighting is good too."

"That's Susan Rigby's. She wants to be a professional photographer someday."

"Well, offer her my compliments." Chad surveyed a few others which looked appealing and listened as Belinda commented on each one that she graded.

An hour or so later, she completed her work. "I'm glad I have this done. I'm always hesitant about bringing school stuff here in case it upset you."

"You're silly. Just because I can't do my job anymore doesn't mean that you can't do yours."

Just then Belinda remembered. "I almost forgot. After school today, I talked with Vicki and Rhoda. Vicki is gonna video tape the assembly that your kids are doing. You'll be able to see it all."

A smile lit Chad's face that thrilled Belinda. "That's terrific. I can't wait."

Belinda offered a caveat. "You should know that with Sheila introducing each act, she'll consequently be on the tape a lot."

"That's why they have a fast forward button," Chad teased. "I can live with that as long as I see what the others do. Be sure to thank Vicki and Rhoda for me."

Around eleven, they prepared for bed. "I'd love to stay up later, sweetie, but I better get some rest for another school day tomorrow."

Chad crawled into bed beside her, enveloped her in a loving embrace, and kissed her. " I'm glad to have you here with me."

"I feel very comfortable sleeping here with you. If we were teaching a few years ago, we'd be fired for morally incorrect behavior."

Chad chuckled at her statement. "And today I'm unjustly fired for immoral behavior. There has to be some irony there somewhere, but I'm too tired to figure it out."

* * *

The days moved by quickly. Each group submitted to Mrs. Langdon an estimated time needed to complete their portion of the performance. While they continued to organize and discuss their participation, Rhoda reviewed and calculated the total time allotment. She stopped the discussion to announce, "It appears that if everything goes smoothly, there will be a fifteen to twenty minute window of available time. That's good, because things don't always go as planned. Once we do a full rehearsal, that time likely will be used."

Cassie Thompson raised her hand. "Mrs. Langdon, some of us are ready to practice. It didn't take too long to adapt our projects from the classroom presentations we did for Mr. Peterson. Do you think we could start rehearsing tomorrow?"

"I had to barter with Mr. Brunsworth to get the auditorium. He agreed to have his music class move into the cafeteria for a few days. I don't see how I can get the stage area for more than that. Our class period is only eighty minutes instead of one hundred and twenty. How about if those who are ready do a practice tomorrow without the costumes and scenery unless it's necessary? I'll check with Mrs. Bergstrom to see if I can send a couple of groups who still need to put finishing touches on their act to the library."

Several students voiced approval for the idea. Heather Joles remarked, "I'm sure that the extra time will help our confidence."

"Ok, so let's make that the plan for tomorrow. Which groups are ready to perform tomorrow?" Three groups looked at each other and then raised their hands. Two others didn't feel confident to participate in a rehearsal by then, so

Mrs. Langdon chose them for library work time. "Come to class first, and I'll give you passes once I get approval to send you there. Mrs. Bergstrom is a stickler for passes, even if I get permission."

The students laughed at her comment. They knew how fussy Mrs. Bergstrom was about students having passes, eating food in the library, or reclining their chairs partway back and rocking in them. It was good natured harassment on her part that made the job more enjoyable, but they always adhered to her instructions. "We promise to be *very* good, Mrs. Langdon," Randy Thomas interjected as he took a lollipop from his mouth. "I'll even forego my usual candy treat."

The entire class uttered a loud mocking sigh of shock. Heather chirped, "Are you sure you'll survive, Randy?" He stuck out his tongue at her and the class roared with laughter.

As the bell rang and students filed out of the room, Cassie Thomson stopped briefly at Rhoda Langdon's desk. "I just want to thank you for letting us do this, Mrs. Langdon. To be honest, I wasn't thrilled to have you replace Mr. Peterson, and I still miss him, but this has been a lot of fun so far."

"Thank you for the nice words, Cassie. I know most of you miss Mr. Peterson's unusual antics and I admire your honesty. I'm also glad this is going so well."

While she still maintained her apartment in case the worst case scenario became reality, Chad and Belinda agreed to enjoy as much time together as possible. When she didn't have much school work to do, they'd spend the evening taking walks through secluded areas. Their lovemaking wasn't desperate, but both often felt a strong need to be intimately connected and so frequently took advantage of the opportunity. On Thursday night while wrapping Belinda in his arms, Chad looked into her eyes and said, "I don't want to put a damper on this, our lovemaking was perfect, but my sentencing date is fast approaching. Let's make some plans for the weekend."

"Whatever you'd like to do is fine with me, Chad. What do you have in mind?"

"I know you'll think this is strange after the way I've acted for the past couple weeks, but I want to take you dancing. Let's go to the Starlight Club, where we first realized our mutual attraction, and dance the night away."

"You're not teasing me, are you?"

"Nope. If I'm gonna be shut in for who knows how long, I want to go out with a flurry."

"There'll be a lot of people there on a Friday night. You sure you can you handle that?"

Chad kidded, "If anyone says anything, I'll pop them in the mouth. What're they gonna do? Throw me in jail?"

Belinda recognized his teasing. "Do you want to go alone or would you like some of our friends to join us there?"

"Better not put them in a situation where they might have to defend me…or themselves. Let's just see how it goes. We can leave if it gets too uncomfortable."

Belinda kissed his lips. "You're the most special person in my life. Just keep holding me."

At school, the rehearsal ironed out a few glitches and the kids felt confident that the assembly would be successful. They even had to admit, though not openly, that Sheila's introductory presentations had shown cleverness and wit. Rhoda made arrangements to store the props and costumes backstage for the assembly, which she'd cleared with Helen for Monday afternoon. She then gathered the kids around her to make one last announcement. "I've gotten clearance from Mrs. Hargrove to excuse you from your second block classes so you can get here and set up."

The kids cheered loudly. "Way to go, Mrs. Langdon," yelled Randy Simpson.

"You'll have to bring a lunch or buy something and eat here. We won't have time to take a full lunch break in the cafeteria." As the bell sounded the end of the day, most of the students took time to wish her a good weekend.

Belinda was cleaning after school when Paul Stone and a bunch of others from Chad's history class ran into her room. Their excitement was evident. "The assembly is gonna rock, Ms. Landis. Wait till you see it! I think the kids are gonna love it, especially the way we'll get some of them and the teachers involved."

"Mrs. Langdon is very happy with the effort you've all put into it. She brags about it every day. I'm excited to see what you've created. Mr. Peterson is so proud of you kids. Good luck Monday. And have a good weekend."

"Thanks, you too," they said in unison as they headed out of the room to catch their buses or find the way to their cars.

Chad was waiting for her when she came out to the parking lot after school. "I've left everything in school. I'm not bringing any school work home this weekend," she said as she climbed into the passenger seat of his Mustang. "I'm all yours."

"Just the way I like it," he replied as he leaned over to kiss her.

"I just need to stop at my place to pick up a few things. I don't expect I'll need too many clothes," she said with a seductive voice and with a wicked leer in her eye. "Just something special for tonight if you're still up for dancing."

"I admit I'm nervous about that, but yeah, I still want to try it. It may be our last chance for quite some time."

Trying to be upbeat and not spoil the moment, Belinda slapped him on the shoulder. "Stop that! We're not gonna have any negative thoughts this weekend."

He smiled and promised to do his best. Revving up the engine, he left the parking lot, drawing the attention of a few students as his tires briefly squealed.

Later, at his apartment, they had an early dinner and played some Scrabble before getting ready for their night out. They showered together and that helped to establish a playful mood. When Chad had finished lathering Belinda's body with soap for the second time, she scoffed, "Are we going dancing as prunes?"

"Ok," he replied. "I get the hint." He turned her so that the spray hit her squarely in the chest. "Can I help it if I like my women squeaky clean?"

"Oh yeah? And how many women have you helped to make squeaky clean?" she teased.

"Only you, my dear. Only you!" He pressed his body to hers.

Chad chose a pair of Dockers and a light sweater to wear to the club. He picked a pair of Rockport shoes that he knew would be comfortable for a night's dancing. When he was ready, he waited for Belinda.

Belinda appeared wearing a stunning black chiffon dress accentuated with a beautiful pearl necklace and earrings. Her hair swept over her shoulders, and though Chad always knew she was beautiful, she gave him the impression of a model.

He walked over and took her hand. "You're lovely."

Belinda blushed. "Thank you."

"Now I'm satisfied that nobody will harass me. They won't even notice me. They'll all be staring at you."

"Let's just have a good time."

He put a wrap around her shoulders and escorted her by the arm to the car. After closing her door, he climbed behind the wheel and drove the three miles to the club, constantly glancing over and admiring her beauty.

When they entered the club, the darkened atmosphere helped keep attention away from Chad. He selected a table in a somewhat obscure corner and ordered drinks. When the waiter arrived, Chad said, "I'll have a Michelob draft beer and a wine spritzer for my date."

While they waited, they heard the Righteous Brothers song "Unchained Melody" being played. Since it wasn't yet crowded, Chad felt somewhat secure. "Let's dance."

He pulled Belinda to the floor. As they danced, he mouthed the words "I need your love" and used his hips to guide her around the dance floor. Lost in his arms, Belinda put her head on his shoulder and felt the strength of his love.

They danced, sat, and drank for about an hour when Bill Thorndike and his wife entered and spotted them at the table. "Chad, it's great to see you. You know Lisa, right?"

"Sure. Hi, Lisa. Are you both out celebrating an occasion tonight?"

"Nah," Thorny interjected. "We both love dancing. We come here almost every weekend. Do you want to be alone or would you like some company?"

Belinda looked at Chad, who said, "If you don't mind someone heckling you for associating with a convicted criminal, feel free to join us."

Thorny pulled out a chair for Cindy and said, "Nobody chooses my friends for me, Chad. And if they don't like the company I keep, they can avoid me too. We know you were set up. We've been trying to get Belinda to convince you to come out in public."

"She told me that. It's just hard to deal with all this."

"So what brings you out tonight?"

"I decided to tempt fate. For one thing it isn't fair to Belinda to keep her shut in all the time. And there's not much time left before I'm sentenced. I finally convinced myself that I need to take advantage of every moment of freedom."

Things progressed smoothly until Chad noticed some of the couples on the dance floor staring in his direction and gradually moving away from him and Belinda. One man was close enough for him to overhear only the word "molester" as he steered Belinda back toward their table. A few minutes later he observed the man using his cell phone. Chad became suspicious, but as long as the man kept a distance, he would just be careful to avoid him.

At 10:30 Steve McMasters barged into the Starlight and walked over to the man who had acted suspiciously. Then he and the man charged through the crowd toward Chad and Belinda's table. "Get back to your hole where you belong, you prick," Steve screeched. "We don't want your kind in here." He looked then at Belinda. "I'd think you'd choose your companions more carefully, Ms. Landis. You want a child molester for a mate?"

Belinda was about to speak when Chad stood and put his face within inches of Steve McMasters. "We didn't come here for trouble. Back off!"

"You've got a lot more trouble than you imagine, boy!"

Just as it appeared that a fight would ensue, the owner of the Starlight jumped between them. "This is my place and I'll have you both arrested if you create trouble." Recognizing Steve, he added, "You don't want this. Go home."

"I don't want this scum walking around our town celebrating his freedom when he should be in jail."

Belinda jumped up at this point. "C'mon Chad. Let's just go home."

Angry now, Chad initially refused to back down. "We came here to dance and dance is what we're gonna do. This guy has no right to interfere."

"I've had enough dancing," she persisted. "He's not worth it. *Please*, let's go."

Thorny, who had positioned himself between the other man and Chad, turned toward Chad. "That's probably wise, Chad. I'll walk outside with you and Belinda."

Reluctantly, Chad took Belinda by the arm. She could feel the tension within him. Thorny escorted them safely to their car and watched to make sure they weren't followed as they left.

Chad's anger overwhelmed him and he didn't speak a word all the way back to his apartment. When he got inside, he picked up the nearest object at hand, a glass left on the table earlier, and hurled it against a wall.

Belinda remained strong throughout the ordeal. Taking him by the hand, she said, "I'm sorry things got bad." She led Chad toward the sofa, pushed him gently to the floor, and sat behind him. "Let me massage your shoulders to help you calm down."

"I just wanted us to be left alone tonight. I know that bastard, whoever he was, called McMasters and told him we were there."

"Chad, until McMasters came in, I really enjoyed the time we did have there. Don't chastise yourself for wanting to go out." She leaned forward and kissed the side of his cheek. "I love you."

He turned to face her. "I'm so afraid."

"Baby, I know it seems to be a very frightening outlook for you right now. I'm worried too," she admitted.

Belinda's efforts seemed to have a calming effect on him. He turned back, closed his eyes, and let her continue massaging his shoulders, neck, and temples. After several more minutes, she could feel the tension begin to subside.

Later they crawled into bed. "Just hold me and don't let go," he pleaded.

She tried to soothe his hurt. "You'll always feel me with you. I promise that." With those words she stroked his face until he fell asleep, but she lay awake for hours just touching him gently until she too finally fell asleep.

Since it rained on Saturday and Sunday, they couldn't go to some secluded area and, fearful of public indignation, Chad refused to leave his apartment the rest of the weekend. "I tried, Belinda. I just can't handle it. Even if the people in this town don't say anything, it's the looks I get that hurt. He sent Belinda out to buy some groceries and to rent a few videos. What they had hoped would prove to be a wonderful weekend felt more like the first stages of the imprisonment that Chad feared most.

Chapter 15

Monday morning dawned brightly. Belinda put on a light jacket and gathered her things for school. "The assembly's this afternoon. I'll see if Vicki will let me borrow the original or make a copy for me right after school for you to watch tonight. I might get here a little later than usual. You gonna be ok here today?"

"I've no place to go. I'll be fine. If it's too much bother for Vicki today, I can wait. In any case, please thank her again for me."

He kissed Belinda goodbye and watched from the window as she drove away. At nine, Sam Ludwig called. "I have some hopeful news for you, Chad. I can't delay the judge's sentencing, but I'm still hopeful he'll grant you probation pending your appeal. If he should assign you a jail term, I'm sure you'll be assigned to a minimum security prison. How're you holding up?"

"It's difficult, Sam. If it weren't for Belinda, I don't know if I could deal with it. I owe you a bigger debt than just acting as my attorney. Thanks for making me realize how poorly I treated her."

"Don't give up. We're going to find a way through this."

"I wish I had your confidence, but thanks."

After he hung up the phone, Chad tried to bury his worries and picked up a book. "At least this'll help pass some of the time till Belinda returns."

At school, Vicki was busy setting things up for the afternoon assembly. "Billy, set up a camera at the base of the stage. Josh, you set one up in the booth at the rear of the auditorium. I want to record both up close and from a distance." She directed both boys. "When you're finished, tape a brief segment, then rewind it and look through the viewfinder to make sure everything's working properly. We only get one shot at this."

Using a headset microphone, she spoke to the stage crew manager. "Levi, please give me a center-stage spotlight." When that worked satisfactorily, she proceeded to have all of the other necessary effects tested. "Ok, everyone," she said, finally satisfied, "return to your classes now and use your passes to get back here a half hour before showtime."

Rhoda Langdon was a nervous wreck all morning long. "I've never attempted this kind of program. I'm just a substitute teacher," she said to Principal Hargrove as she entered the high school office.

"Are your kids ready to go?" Helen asked.

"Our rehearsal last Friday went well. Yeah, I think they are."

"Then relax. It'll go fine and the kids will feed off the audience's response. Just take charge and look confident."

"Easier said than done, but I'll do my best. It's times like this that I wish Chad Peterson was here to run the show."

"All of us miss Chad. I'm sure he'll be thrilled with your effort, Rhoda. I'm looking forward to the show too."

"Thanks for your support. This whole thing has been a learning experience for me too. Except for my anxiety today, I've enjoyed all of it."

At ten, Mrs. Kovach knocked on Rhoda's classroom door and entered. "I'm here to cover for you so that you can attend to the assembly matters. Good luck."

"Thanks. I've given the students the last twenty minutes to work on their sociology homework." She gathered a few things and started to leave.

Tim Woodson said, "Good luck today, Mrs. Langdon."

She smiled in the direction of the class. "Thanks. I hope you all enjoy the show." She gave them a thumbs up as she left.

Her students started filtering into the auditorium and Rhoda issued instructions for them to start collecting their props and costumes and to get organized. She was relieved to see that Vicki had returned. "Here's a schedule of the order of presentations. You watched the groups on Friday, so I'm sure you know what they need in the way of lighting etc."

"We've got it covered. Don't worry. I'll use my head mic to direct the crew what to do with each act. I have two cameras taping the show. We'll have two angles and one camera will act as backup in case something happens during the show to one of them."

"Thanks, Vicki." Suddenly Rhoda heard a crash from behind the stage and hastily ran to see what happened. "It's ok, Mrs. Langdon. We just accidentally knocked over a stack of chairs back here. Nothing to worry about."

Finally, when everything seemed to be in place and the groups ready to go, Rhoda called them together. Looking at her watch, she uttered, "You have a little more than thirty minutes before showtime. Get something to eat for lunch and come back here. We'll eat together and discuss any last-minute thoughts."

The group scattered. Some had brought lunches with them; others ran over to the cafeteria to buy a snack and something to drink. When they were together again, Rhoda once more ran through the plan. "There are stage crew members who will help you move the props between each act. Just tell them how you want things set up." Speaking directly to Sheila, she added, "You'll be out front offering your comments about the previous act and introducing the next one. Take your time so that we can set up properly."

When they heard the announcement telling students to report to the auditorium, they hastily tossed the remnants of lunch into the trash. Rhoda screeched, "Here we go, everyone. Break a leg!"

Unknown to Rhoda, Heather Joles' brother, a member of the stage crew, had received permission from Vicki Bergstrom to sneak backstage and use a handheld recorder to tape some of the pre-show antics and preparations. "Just don't get in anyone's way," was the order he'd received, so he stood unobtrusively behind a curtain and was filming some of the hilarious behind the scenes actions.

The first act was already set up and ready to go once the audience had been seated. Sheila stood backstage looking over her prepared script when Cindy Bennett sneaked up behind her. "God, you scared the crap out of me," said Sheila when Cindy tapped her on the shoulder. "What're you doing back here?"

"Just wanted to wish you luck and to warn you of something that I just heard. At the end of the show, the others plan to come out and take a bow in front of the audience. They're gonna carry out a big sign supporting Mr. Peterson."

"And they want to embarrass me by having me stand out there with them. My mom and dad'll be in the audience. Dad will totally freak."

"What're you gonna do?"

"I'd like to come out and throw a middle finger up at the camera when they do it, but it'll just get me into trouble. It's too late to sabotage it. I just won't give them the satisfaction. I won't come out on the stage at the end."

"Some of the kids have been putting a lot of pressure on me."

Sheila momentarily forgot about the show and panicked. She grabbed Cindy's shoulder. "You *promised.* You can't tell. If anyone finds out that I offered sex to Mr. Peterson and he turned me down, I'll be ruined. My parents'll kill me. We've gone too far now to back out."

"I'm your friend, but I'm scared. The kids are turning against me."

Regaining her composure, Sheila said, "We'll talk about this later. I have to go on stage soon. Get back to your seat and just keep your mouth shut."

Cindy turned around and walked out the side entrance to the stage and reentered through the back door to the auditorium. She didn't even give it a second thought when she brushed past Ronnie Joles on the way out.

The assembly went without a hitch. The crowd applauded wildly when some faculty members were called up to demonstrate the Charleston. They were equally enthusiastic when the seniors were questioned during the quiz game, laughing when a senior missed a question, and cheering when they got an answer correct. Every act seemed to elicit a positive response, and Rhoda Langdon stood offstage grinning from ear to ear. The timing worked perfectly, with the show concluding about ten minutes before the end of the school day.

The audience stood to give the performers a standing ovation as they came out for a final bow. They called Rhoda Langdon out with her. Rhoda looked for Sheila but couldn't find her anywhere nearby. Then, Heather Joles walked to the podium and before she spoke, the others unfolded a huge banner that read, "WE LOVE YOU, MR. PETERSON." Simultaneously, Heather yelled into the microphone above the din, "THIS SHOW IS FOR YOU, MR. P."

A huge roar resounded throughout the auditorium. The adult visitors, sitting in the rear, looked puzzled at the show of support for their convicted teacher. Steve McMasters, with his wife trailing behind, stormed from the auditorium. He spotted Sheila standing in the hallway outside the stage area and issued a stern order to her. "Let's go! I'm taking you home right now."

Sheila broke into tears. As they exited the building, Steve wrapped his arms around his daughter.

"I did my best, Daddy."

In a huff, her dad said, "You did just fine. They're not worth the trouble. I'm gonna raise the biggest stink this town has ever heard. How dare that principal allow that to happen! She'll regret it. I promise you that. How they can stand there and applaud for that child molesting bastard, I'll never know."

Belinda, thrilled not only for the quality of the show but also for the overwhelming support from the staff and students, couldn't wait to take a copy of the tape to Chad. "This'll convince him that they still care." Several teachers came up and hugged her after the students had been dismissed. Some had tears in their eyes.

A few minutes later, Vicki Bergstrom, carrying a video tape, approached her. "I can't imagine making Chad wait until I can mix the best parts of each tape, Belinda. Here, take this one with you. Tell Chad I'll give him a copy of the finished product tomorrow, even if I have to work on editing it all day. "That was a fantastic statement these kids made to his effect as a teacher and as a person."

"Yes, it was. But we have to give credit to Rhoda's efforts too. Thanks, Vicki. This'll make Chad's day."

Belinda couldn't wait to get to Chad's place so that they could watch the video together. She quickly collected her things, climbed behind the wheel of her SUV, and drove straight there.

Chad greeted her with a hug even as she waved the video cassette at him. "I missed you," he said.

"I'm glad," she said excitedly. "But I have more important things for you now."

"So how was the show? Did the kids do well?"

"You can judge for yourself, but the audience reception was terrific. They laughed and cheered and gave the entire cast a standing ovation."

Belinda threw her jacket onto the nearby chair. "You set up things and I'll get us something to drink. I'm thirsty."

"There's some iced tea in the fridge or Coke if you prefer."

Chad put the cassette into the recorder and waited for Belinda's return. She came back with two glasses of Coke topped with vanilla ice cream. "I decided that an ice cream soda would be better." She handed Chad a spoon and a glass. "I'm ready. Push the play button."

"I think you're more excited than I am, and you've already seen the assembly."

"It's hilarious. You're gonna swell with pride when you see how well they've adapted your project. It's a very educational presentation too."

Chad pressed the play button on the remote and sampled his float as he settled back on the sofa next to Belinda. He almost spilled the last of his soda onto his lap when he watched some of his fellow staff members, including Belinda, attempting the Charleston. His laughter was loud and uproarious. "Oh God, I think I'm gonna wet my pants. You didn't tell me that *you* were one of the victims. Look at Mrs. Fogerty! She's having a ball. She probably grew up doing the Charleston."

Belinda laughed too. "I wanted to surprise you. I think the kids schemed to include me. How could I say no?"

Chad sat entranced throughout the entire two hour presentation. When it ended, he removed the tape and sighed. "That was terrific. It makes me miss those kids even more."

"I have to return that tape to Vicki, but she said she'd make a dub for you that would include angles from some other cameras."

"I'll treasure it. I'll give her a call tomorrow at school and thank her personally. If you see any of my kids, tell them I really loved the show."

Realizing that it was past dinner time, Belinda asked, "Do you want something to eat for dinner?"

"I'm good for now. How about if we have a pizza delivered later this evening?"

"That's fine with me too. What I'd really like now is to just sit here and be affectionate. Hold me, Chad."

Wrapping his arms around her, Chad closed his eyes and enjoyed the momentary solitude. He felt comforted in her love, and Belinda, likewise, felt warm and secure in his arms.

The next morning Belinda stood in front of her second block class when Jack Dougherty knocked on the door. "Excuse me, Ms. Landis, but Mrs. Hargrove wants to see you immediately in her office. I'll cover for you."

Belinda didn't hesitate. She told the class to continue working and hurried from the room. As she raced down the hallway, a sudden fear raced through her mind. Teachers didn't get called from their classes unless something serious had happened. She imagined the worst. "What's happened?" she practically screamed when she entered Helen's office. She noticed Vicki standing there beside a portable video player.

"I'm sorry if I scared you. I wanted you to see this. You better sit down." Then she spoke directly to Vicki. "Play it now."

For two minutes, Belinda watched the screen. "Oh…my…God!" she squealed.

Chapter 16

Belinda's face was buried in her hands, tears flowing freely as she realized the significance of what she saw. Finally, she looked at Vicki and sobbed, "Miracles do happen."

"I asked Heather Joles' brother, Ronnie, to go backstage and get some candid video of the performers before and after their skits. I'm sure he didn't even realize what he caught on tape. When I was preparing this morning to dub the best parts and angles of the two tapes, I discovered the conversation between Cindy Bennett and Sheila McMasters on Ronnie's version."

Gathering her composure, Belinda turned to Helen. "I have to call Chad. He has to hear and see this."

"I took the liberty to call him, Belinda. I told him to come directly to my office when he arrives. I said that we have something that'll change the outcome of his trial. I'm sorry if I acted too hastily and you wanted to be the one to break it to him."

"No, that's ok. I'm just so happy that this nightmare may now come to an end." Belinda got up and hugged Vicki. "We can never thank you enough for this."

"I never for a minute thought Chad was guilty. We got lucky."

While they waited for Chad, the three of them discussed things that needed to be done. Helen said, "We'll need several copies of this, Vicki. Just to be safe. Mark the original that Ronnie created, and I want at least five other copies."

"Should we bring Sheila in here and confront her?" Belinda asked.

"I don't think that's wise just yet," Helen responded. "I think this needs to get into the hands of the proper authorities first. They'll know how to handle it."

"You're right. I'm just so excited I'm not thinking straight. That girl has put us through hell."

It wasn't long before Chad entered Helen's office. Belinda ran to him and wrapped her arms around him. Her tears flowed again as she gave him the tightest hug she could. "It's gonna be alright, honey."

Chad looked at her, then at Helen and Vicki. "What's happened?"

Vicki answered as Belinda clung tightly to Chad. "Remember that I had two cameras taping the show? I also asked one of my aides to capture some behind the scenes candid footage with a camera. As he stood unobtrusively as possible, he got some really good stuff. The kicker was a conversation between Sheila and her friend Cindy."

"Watch this!" Belinda excitedly added as she led him in front of the monitor. "Play it again, Vicki."

They all watched as Vicki rewound and played the conversation over and over several times. Each time he saw it, Chad responded with a single word. "Amazing, Incredible, Unbelievable!"

"There's no way Sheila can lie her way out of this. It's over, honey," Belinda finally uttered.

"We have to notify Sam and let him tell us what to do next. I'm not sure if he'll want us to turn this over to the police or to him. I'm due for sentencing in just three days."

"I've asked Vicki to make several copies for backup. Then she'll give the original to whomever you want, Chad." Helen walked over to him. "Maybe it's not considered appropriate behavior for a principal, but what the hell." She hugged him. "Sometimes faith is rewarded. Congratulations."

Vicki added her congratulations and then said, "I'm outta here. I'll make those copies right away."

"Is it ok if I make that call to Sam from here, Helen?"

"Of course!"

Chad pulled his cell phone from his pocket and punched in the number. He could barely contain his enthusiasm.

Sam's secretary answered. "Sam's in court on a case at the moment. Can I have him call you back?"

"Yes, please. I need to talk with him as soon as he's available. It's *very* important. Have him call my cell number. I'm not at home at the moment."

"As soon as he returns, I'll have him contact you."

"Thanks. Bye."

He turned to Belinda. "Sam's in court. It might be awhile before I hear from him." Just then the bell rang for the next period. "If you have a class now, sweetheart, you'd better go. You still have a job to do."

Belinda looked at Helen. "I can get another cover for you. I know you want to be here with Chad."

"I do, but he's right. We'll just be sitting here waiting, and I should be with my students. I'll go." Turning to Chad unabashedly, she kissed him and then said with emphasis, "I love you!"

Now more upbeat than he'd been in a long time, Chad said, "And it looks like you're gonna get the chance to love me for a long time." He smiled at her and added, "I love you too."

Belinda practically skipped from the room. As Chad watched from the office, she turned and blew him a kiss. Several students snickered as they walked along the hallway and observed her actions.

"Having a good day, Ms. Landis?" one of them asked.

"The best!" was all she said and offered a broad smile.

After closing the office door, Chad spoke. "Would it be alright if I stayed until I got at least one copy of that tape, Helen? Not that I'm untrusting, but my life hangs in the balance here, and I'll feel much better when I have a copy in hand."

"Be my guest. I have to make my rounds during change of classes. You know I like to keep visible. I'll stop at the library and ask Vicki to personally bring you a copy ASAP. Make yourself comfortable."

Chad stretched out on one of the chairs and breathed a huge sigh of relief. He closed his eyes and offered a silent prayer of thanks.

Less than an hour later, Vicki brought Chad two copies of the tape. "I'm keeping the original for now, Chad, so that I can make a few more. It's also probably a good idea that you don't touch the original. That way nobody can suggest that you fabricated or altered any part of it."

"Good idea, Vicki, and thanks again. After I talk with my lawyer, I'll have him make arrangements to get the original. Be sure to keep it locked in a safe place."

Chad didn't wait for Helen's return. Figuring that she was involved with school business, he left her a short note of thanks. He wanted to go past Belinda's class but decided against it, since his name wasn't yet cleared. He didn't want to create any possible controversy. "I'm sure she'll come straight to my place after school, and I won't be surprised if she calls during her lunch time." He left as unobtrusively as possible, climbed into his Mustang, and drove straight to his apartment.

Around noon, his cell phone rang. "Hi, honey. I just called to see if you've heard from Sam yet and to tell you I love you."

"He hasn't called yet. I'm trying to be patient, but it's difficult. I know that I'm not his only client, but I wish he'd call."

"Then I won't stay on the phone too long. It's just so exciting, Chad. Of course I haven't mentioned anything to the kids, but they've noticed my excited mood. It's pretty hard to keep my feet on the ground."

"You're coming over after school, right? If Sam's in court all day, it's not likely I'll hear from him till later today or this evening."

"I'll be there as soon as I can. We have some celebrating to do."

"Let's not get too celebratory just yet. I haven't been officially cleared. Maybe just some hot passionate sex! Hahaha!"

"Mmmmmm. I can handle that," she cooed. "Pun intended!"

Chad just laughed. "See you then, sweetheart. Keep those feet on the ground, at least till you get here."

They simultaneously expressed their love and said goodbye.

The waiting seemed endless, and Chad tried to find ways to occupy his time. Belinda finally arrived after school, but Chad still hadn't heard back from Sam. "Thank God you're here, sweetheart. I'm going crazy. At least the house got a good cleaning."

Belinda looked around. "Already there's a positive outcome from this news," she chuckled. "And the place needed it."

Chad took her good natured teasing by tickling her until she squealed an apology and surrendered. Then he pushed her back and lay on top of her on the sofa, pressing his body to hers and engaging in a long passionate kiss.

Chad was beginning to give up hope that Sam would return his call when at five his phone rang. "Sorry to return your call so late, Chad, but I've been in court all day and just got your message when I got back to the office. What's up?"

"You're not gonna believe this, Sam. I'm not sure I believe it yet, and I've seen it. We have indisputable evidence of my innocence. Our school librarian caught Sheila confessing the truth behind the stage before a school assembly. And it's all on tape."

"You're kidding. She couldn't be that careless."

"She didn't know she was being taped. In fact, it was all accidentally done by one of the librarian's aides."

"Where's the tape now?"

"I have two copies in my possession right here at the apartment. The librarian is keeping the original locked up. I wanted your advice as to what we do next."

"I need to see the tape. Can I come over later this evening, say around eight? Then we'll discuss our options."

"Belinda's here. We'll wait for you. Thanks. See ya tonight."

"Ok. That's good news, Chad."

After Chad hung up, he grinned at Belinda. It looks better with each passing moment. Sam's coming over at eight to see the tape."

"Terrific. Just think, honey. Instead of passing judgment on you in a few days, the judge will be dismissing the charges against you. We'll be free to move on with our lives. You'll get your job back and things will return to a sense of normalcy."

"I admit that I'm ambivalent about getting my job back. I never felt so vulnerable before, and I'm not sure I can face that again. It's torn me to my very soul. On the other hand, I'm trained as a teacher and it's what I do best."

"Not all kids are like Sheila McMasters, honey. You know that."

"Yeah, but it only takes one. It shattered my trust in teenagers. I'm not sure how long it will take to regain that feeling, if ever. I'm afraid that I'll always be more than cautious in my dealings with any student."

"Hopefully, when you're around the good kids again, time will heal those wounds and you'll be yourself." Belinda hugged him to her. "Obviously, we all have to be very careful not to be in position where we can be accused, but we can't act scared of being around kids either."

They ate a simple meal and Sam arrived promptly at eight. After a cordial greeting, he quickly asked, "So where's this tape?"

"It's all set up to play. Have a seat on the sofa and I'll turn it on. You'll see it very clearly reveals who the real criminal is in this case."

Sam watched intently and focused on every word spoken between Sheila and Cindy Bennett. When it was over a few minutes later, Sam agreed. "This should definitely clear your name, Chad. That little tart is gonna be exposed for the liar she is."

"So what do we do now?"

"You say you have two copies of this?"

"I have two here. Vicki Bergstrom has the original and made a few more copies, which are in school."

"Good. I want one of the copies tonight. Tomorrow morning I'll notify the police department of the situation and ask them to pick up the original and hold it as evidence. I'll also notify Judge Walters of the situation. In light of this new evidence, we'll ask for a review at the time of sentencing. If we can meet in his chambers before then and insist that the McMasters family be present, maybe we can resolve this. If it goes well, the McMasters will be forced to verbally admit that Sheila lied."

"A few hours ago, I thought three days would pass much too quickly. Now it feels like it'll be an eternity to wait."

Sam took a copy of the tape, offered his congratulations, and said goodnight.

"Phew! What a relief! You can't imagine what a weight feels like it's been lifted from my shoulders. For the first time in a long time, I have hope. *NOW*," he said, looking Belinda squarely in the eyes, "you said something about a celebration? Hehehe." He picked Belinda up in his arms and carried her to his bedroom. There they made love with a gusto that even surprised them.

Later, cuddled snugly in his arms, Belinda whispered, "I can't imagine anything more beautiful than spending a lifetime in your arms, Chad."

The next day things progressed as expected. A few hours after Belinda left for school, Sam called Chad to inform him that the police had picked up the original copy of the video and retained it in their custody. They would also notify the McMasters of the situation and request that they appear in court on the scheduled day of Chad's sentencing.

Chad graciously thanked Sam for all of his expertise and help. Now he just had to be patient and wait.

Finally, on May 20, at ten o'clock, Sam Ludwig and Chad, along with the prosecuting attorney, Steve and Laura McMasters, and Sheila met in Judge Walters' chambers. Although it proved a nail biting ordeal for Belinda, she waited in the courtroom since she wasn't directly involved in the case. Several reporters, who had gotten wind of some rumors concerning Chad's case, tried to question Belinda but she refused any comment.

Judge Walters spoke first. "Mr. and Mrs. McMasters, I'm going to present to you a video tape of your daughter admitting to her friend that this entire case against Mr. Peterson was an outright fabrication. She apparently didn't realize that she'd been caught on tape during this discussion. When it's over, I want your reaction."

Having heard from the police about the new evidence, Steve McMasters meekly replied, "Yes, Your Honor."

Following its viewing, the judge asked a one word question. "Well?"

"I think we owe Mr. Peterson an apology, Your Honor. We're embarrassed by the entire situation."

"As well you should be." The judge then spoke to Sheila. "Look at me, young lady!"

Too embarrassed to look up until directed to do so, Sheila, shame faced, glanced at the judge. "What you did to an upstanding member of this community and to the school where he works is reprehensible! You and your family can both be sued for your actions against your teacher. Do you understand?"

"Yes, sir," Sheila mumbled with her head again turned downward.

Judge Walters shouted, "*Look at me and speak up!*"

"Yes, Your Honor!" she repeated, this time louder and with more clarity in her voice.

Turning once more to Steve McMasters, he asked, "So you are now agreeable to the dropping of all charges against Mr. Peterson."

"Yes, Your Honor, we are."

"Now, when we go into the courtroom, I'll ask you, Mr. Montgomery, if you wish that all charges against the defendant be dropped. Since your client has agreed to that here, I'll expect you to answer affirmatively. We'll proceed from there once we're in the courtroom. You're all excused."

Assuming their stations in the courtroom, the group stood when Judge Walters appeared. Without being specific, he briefly announced that new evidence presented to the court had altered the outcome of the trial. After Mr. Montgomery verbally agreed to dismiss all charges, the judge spoke to Sheila McMasters.

"Young lady, after all the trouble that you've caused by this outrage, there's one more thing that you must do. Do you know what that is?"

Sheila shook her head.

"I order you to turn and face Mr. Peterson, and with all the sincerity that you can muster, in front of your parents and those present in this courtroom, apologize to him."

With what appeared to be genuine tears of regret, Sheila McMasters did as ordered. She spoke only two words but they were enough. "I'm sorry!"

"Mr. Peterson, this case is dismissed. The court apologizes for all the hurt and suffering that this incident has caused you and those closest to you."

"Thank you, Your Honor," Chad responded and all stood while the judge left the courtroom. He shook Sam's hand and then leaned over the rail to hug Belinda.

Before he left, Sam said, "The next question is whether or not you want to pursue the matter against Sheila and Cindy Bennett. You can file charges against them for defamation of character and lying under oath."

"I don't want revenge, Sam. I just want this to end."

"I'm sure it won't end until the press asks you for some response. I can deal with them if you prefer."

"No. I'll just tell them what I've told you. I'm happy to be vindicated and I want to move on."

"I'll inform the parents of your decision not to seek damages against them. You're a good man, Chad Peterson. It's been my pleasure to defend you. Good luck to both of you. I hope you can recapture the lifestyle you enjoyed before this all happened."

"Thanks for everything. I know just where to begin."

That evening Matt Stairs came by to offer his congratulations. "We're now the defending state champions, Chad. If you're willing, the girls and I would like you sitting on the bench with us next year."

"I'd be honored, Matt. Thanks."

"And I'll be there watching as they again win the title with the two best coaches in the state," Belinda offered.

A few days later, Chad sat snuggling with Belinda on the sofa of his apartment. Helen called to inform him that he could return to his job at Emerson. The school board, in an unscheduled session, had granted him full back pay for time lost. Since the school year ended in two weeks, they included a paid extension to get his affairs in order. Also, she told him that the McMasters had asked and been granted permission to remove Sheila from Emerson, put their home up for sale, and planned to move to another part of the state.

Things couldn't have worked out better. That would give him time to get himself together. At an opportune moment between kisses, Chad sprung an idea on her. "Let's take advantage after the school year ends. I want to go somewhere where nobody knows us," he suggested.

Belinda looked into Chad's eyes and saw the fire and sparkle that had for so long been hidden. "I'd love that, Chad. Do you want to go back to the cabin again?"

"No, I have something else in mind," he replied, "but it's a secret till I'm sure I can work it out."

"There you go again with those secrets," she squealed as she playfully pinched him in the side.

"You seemed pleased last time, sweetheart."

"Yes, I was, and I'll try to be good this time," she cooed as she moved in to nibble on his ear. "I'll be *very* good, and we'll see how long you can hold out."

Chad gave a hearty laugh, followed by a long moan, as she traced her tongue along the edge of his ear.

Chapter 17

The next morning, while Belinda worked at school, Chad called the local travel agency. "I know this is short notice, Rene, and I understand if we can't work something out, but I'm looking for a cruise for two people, preferably the week after the school year ends. Could you make some calls and search for any available occupancy?" He gave her the possible dates.

"I'll see what I can do, Chad, and get back to you. Are you planning to be home for the next few hours?"

"As of now, yes. If I have to go out, you can call my cell phone number." He gave her the number and thanked her for her assistance.

While he waited, Chad decided to look online. He looked up all of the major cruise lines, investigating any that might fit the length of time and dates he wanted. He wrote down a few possibilities and the phone numbers to call. Royal Caribbean offered a four night cruise from Port Canaveral, Florida, to Nassau. Disney had three and four night cruises. Carnival Cruise line seemed to offer many different short cruises. "I'll wait and see what Rene can find. She probably can get a better deal and has more accurate and up to date access than I can get myself. If all else fails, I'll try these numbers."

During the time he surfed the net, Chad was interrupted by a phone call from Marla. "I'm so happy for you, Chad. Congratulations on your acquittal. I know you too well to believe for a minute that you'd do anything heinous like that. I hope that McMasters girl suffers grief and embarrassment for years to come."

"Thanks, Marla. I appreciate your confidence. As for Shiela, I'm sure she'll never change, no matter where she lives. She'll still find ways to manipulate people so that she gets her way."

"Next time you're in the restaurant, your meal is complimentary. I expect to see you and Belinda here soon."

"I promise. We'll do that. And thanks."

Ninety minutes later, Rene called. "I think I have some good news for you, Chad. I've found a very good deal on a ship that leaves on the Monday of the week you want and travels from Florida to Cozumel, Mexico. It's a four day cruise, and there's an oceanview room available on an upper deck. I need to confirm quickly. Can you come in and we'll talk?"

"I'll be right there. Give me about fifteen minutes. Thanks, Rene."

Chad grabbed his jacket and hastily went to the travel agency. Rene had all of the information ready to show him. "You'd be traveling on Carnival's Fascination. It's a medium-sized ship with a Hollywood style motif." She showed him a diagram of the ship's decks. "The available room is on the Empress deck. Because cruise lines want to sail with a full ship, I can get you an excellent price. Apparently they had a recent cancellation. Do you both have passports?"

"Yes, we've both taken overseas trips in the past couple of years, and they're good for ten years."

"Good. Then we can do this. When she revealed the cost and mentioned that it included airfare, Chad didn't hesitate. "Call them and take it. I'll confirm the reservation with my credit card if it's still available."

"I deal with this cruise line on a regular basis. I asked them to put a twenty-four hour hold on the room, just in case you wanted it. You'll fly out Monday morning, June 7, and arrive in plenty of time to board." She picked up the phone and dialed.

Chad sat back and listened as Rene confirmed all of the reservations. When she was done, she turned to Chad. "Everything's set."

"Great!"

"Take the brochure with you so you can review in more detail where you'll go and you can think about some of the shore activities you might like. I'll call you when the other things arrive."

"Thanks so much for your help, Renee. I really appreciate it."

"Glad I could help. You lucked into a good deal for what should be a fun adventure."

Chad thought about stopping at the school to see Belinda and tell her the news but opted instead to spring the surprise at dinner. He stopped at the market and chose two thick T-bone steaks and the fixings for a good salad. Passing the bakery section, he noticed a scrumptious looking lemon meringue pie and added that to his cart.

On the way home, he stopped and selected a bouquet of fresh cut flowers. "Everything has to be just perfect."

With still several hours before Belinda arrived, Chad set to work creating a romantic atmosphere. He covered the table with one of the linen tablecloths he had inherited from his mother. He carefully arranged the dinnerware according to Emily Post's rules of etiquette. The flowers, arranged in a crystal vase, became the centerpiece. He set out two wine glasses, and also two glasses for water. Chad hoped she'd be impressed.

"Some soft music would add to the mood," he decided. "When she arrives, I'll have the lights low and the music playing. I'll take her in my arms and we'll dance. We'll have dinner and then we'll move over to the sofa and relax. When the timing is right, I'll tell her about the cruise. After she recovers from the shock, we'll just enjoy each other the rest of the evening."

When she arrived at Chad's, he had everything in place. The lights were dimmed and he escorted her into his living room by the hand. "How romantic," she commented as he removed her jacket and then took her into his arms. Classical music played from the stereo system and just as the "Blue Danube" waltz began, he danced her around the floor to the rhythm of the music. As they danced, Belinda noticed the exquisitely set dining room table. She looked into his eyes. "You've really gone all out for this, Chad. It's wonderful. Thank you." She wanted to lay her head on his shoulder, but he kept her at arms length as they continued to waltz around the floor.

When the song finished, Chad pulled her to him. He kissed her gently, stroking her hair with one hand as their lips met. "I wanted tonight to be very special," he said when they ended the kiss, "to make up for the hard times I gave you. Though I may not have always shown it, Belinda, I do love you."

They embraced and just stood together for a full five minutes, not wanting to end the moment. Finally, Chad asked, "Are you hungry?"

"I'm hungry for you!" she teased. "Oh, you mean hungry for dinner?"

Not one to let a comment like that pass, Chad responded with, "I'm the entrée. Everything else will be appetizer or dessert. In this case, though, the entrée comes last."

There was no way that Belinda would let that double entendre pass. "As long as it comes, pun intended, I'll be satisfied." She leaned into him and this time gave Chad a more intense kiss.

He led her over to the dining area and poured her a glass of wine. "Would the madame prefer to sit here and sip on some wine or would she prefer to come into the kitchen and chat with the cook."

"If the cook doesn't mind 'madame' interfering with his preparations with an occasional pinch on the butt or some kisses to add flavor to the meal, she'd prefer to enter the kitchen."

Playing along to the hilt, Chad exclaimed, "*Madame*, I'm shocked! Hanky panky in the kitchen with the hired help! What would the master think?"

"Hehehe! I think he'd be *most* pleased."

"Then by all means, follow me and we'll see what we can cook up."

Chad put the steaks under the broiler while Belinda continued her flirtations. Both were having so much fun that Chad almost forgot to turn the steaks over a few minutes later. They continued the role playing throughout his preparations.

Belinda took a seat and sipped her wine. "You are a very handsome cook. You have a great-looking body. I wouldn't mind a tumble with you in the pantry," she said in a very seductive voice.

"I'm flattered, milady. I'm afraid I must maintain my professional decorum though. The conversation is making me a bit uncomfortable."

"Awwww! I see that," she teased. Taking another sip of her wine, she added, "Perhaps I can find a way to help release your discomfort."

"Everything's ready, madame. Would you like to move into the dining area now?"

"Party pooper." But Belinda followed his suggestion and strutted to the table and let Chad push in her chair as she sat. Then his role changed from cook to lover.

"Everything look ok, my love?"

"Everything's just perfect, Chad. Just perfect!"

He poured some more wine into her glass.

"You aren't trying to get me drunk to take advantage of me, are you?" she cooed.

"I hope I don't need to get you drunk, sweetheart. I want you to be fully conscious of everything that happens tonight. As for taking advantage of you, may I remind you that *I'm* the entrée. Hahaha!"

Belinda picked up a knife and fork. "So let's get to the appetizers. I'm starving for the main course."

When they were ready, Chad brought out the steaks, two baked potatoes, and a large bowl of salad that he'd made earlier. Acting again as if he were the waiter in a fancy restaurant, he served Belinda.

"I hate to eat alone," she chuckled. "Do you think you could join me. It seems my date stood me up."

"It would be my pleasure, madame. That man must be a fool to leave you here alone."

"Well, if he doesn't show soon, I'll spend the night with you."

Chad laughed heartily. "Again, it would be *my* pleasure," he repeated. He sat beside Belinda, took her hand in his, and kissed it. "You are most beautiful."

"Oh, you're going to get the best tip any waiter ever got for being so romantic."

Again Chad laughed. He couldn't resist. "I'm hoping that *you'll* get the tip and a lot more!"

The entire dinner proved to be a humorous series of repartee between them and they loved it. When finally they finished, Chad told Belinda to leave the dishes on the table. He took her by the hand to the sofa. "If I'm to be the main course, let's start with this," he said and gave her a long, deep kiss.

"Wow! You really know how to get my heart fluttering, Chad. That was one powerful kiss."

Wrapping his arms around her, Chad kissed her again. Then, as if struck by an unquenchable desire to blurt out his idea, he looked at her and said, "Do you remember yesterday that we discussed taking a trip together?"

"Sure, you were being very mysterious about it."

He reached under the sofa and brought out the travel brochure. "How would you like to take a four-day cruise to Mexico?"

"OH MY GOD! You're kidding!"

"No, sweetheart, I'm not. I booked it this morning. I've been dying to tell you, but I wanted it to be part of this special evening. Look, here's the ship and here's the cabin I reserved for us."

Belinda was speechless. She looked at the pages Chad had placed in front of her. It was like a dream. "Chad, this is amazing. Of course I'll go with you, honey." She took both of her hands, placed them on his face, and said, "You are absolutely the best!"

They talked for hours about all of the things they'd like to see and do during those four days. Chad wanted to try snorkeling. Belinda said she'd just be happy to get him alone on a ship for four days, but admitted that shopping in Cozumel was tempting. That night they made love, and it was the most satisfying experience of their lives.

In the weeks prior to departure, Chad had one more idea in mind, and since the school board had granted him free time to regroup, he took advantage of it.

He was grateful, actually, that Belinda had to teach during the days. His plan took a few days to complete, but Chad was satisfied with the result.

Weeks later, the cruise proved to be the perfect get-away. Belinda and Chad found the warm rays of the sun to be the remedy they needed to escape the doldrums of a long, cold, and very difficult winter.

The final night's dinner proved to be the *piece de resistance*. Chad put his plan into action. He had arranged for Rolando, their waiter for the entire cruise, to deliver a special gift along with Belinda's dinner. As Rolando set her plate down, he also placed a small package beside it. Belinda looked puzzled, as no other guest had received one. When she opened it, her mouth fell open as she saw a diamond engagement ring. Looking over at Chad, he asked the question.

"Will you marry me, Belinda?"

Tears flowed openly from her eyes as Belinda nodded yes. Rolando gave a prearranged signal, and the maitre d' announced over the loudspeaker to all of the dining room guests that Chad had just asked Belinda to marry him and she had agreed. The room erupted with applause.

The waiters then led the guests in a frolicking Conga line that weaved all through the dining area. Chad and Belinda became the center of attention as they did the Conga to the music. They both knew that their love would last forever and no trial or obstacle could destroy it.